C. M. WENDELBOE

HUNTING
THE
FIVE
POINT
KILLER

A BITTER WIND MYSTERY

MIDNIGHT INK
WOODBURY, MINNESOTA

FIRST EDITION
First Printing, 2017

Book format by Bob Gaul
Cover design by Kevin R. Brown

Midnight Ink, an imprint of Llewellyn Worldwide Ltd.

Library of Congress Cataloging-in-Publication Data
Names: Wendelboe, C. M., author.
Title: Hunting the Five Point Killer / C. M. Wendelboe.
Description: First edition. | Woodbury, Minnesota: Midnight Ink, [2017] |
  Series: A bitter wind mystery; #1
Identifiers: LCCN 2017022250 (print) | LCCN 2017025518 (ebook) | ISBN
  9780738753645 | ISBN 9780738753201 (alk. paper)
Classification: LCC PS3623.E53 (ebook) | LCC PS3623.E53 H86 2017 (print) |
  DDC 813/.6—dc23
LC record available at https://lccn.loc.gov/2017022250

Midnight Ink
Llewellyn Worldwide Ltd.
2143 Wooddale Dr.
Woodbury, MN 55125-2989
www.midnightinkbooks.com

Printed in the United States of America

For Doris Rogers and Charlie Zumo

"There are hunters and there are victims.
By your discipline, cunning, obedience
and alertness, you will decide if you
are the hunter or the victim."

– MARINE GENERAL JAMES "MAD DOG" MATTIS –

One

THE MIDDLE-AGED VICTIM SLUMPED dead in his Barcalounger, one trouser cuff riding up over his snow-white ankle and his zipper splayed open like he expected a happy ending. But there was nothing happy about the small bullet holes in his chest. Or the blood that had seeped down his shirt front, coagulated just short of his Cheyenne Police belt buckle, and pooled atop his polished wingtips.

Beer cans were strewn over the orange shag carpeting in front of the recliner that had been positioned to better catch *America's Most Wanted*. An ashtray made from an engine piston welded to a free-standing pipe overflowed with butts beside one arm of the recliner, and a half-eaten bag of Fritos spilled on the floor beside the other.

Stepping back—and discounting the obvious fresh wounds—it was clear the man would still stop crowds. Even in death his thick black hair remained parted neatly, his pencil-thin mustache like a gentle slash across his upper lip. He could have passed for a modern-day John Dillinger. And like Dillinger in death, the victim's brown eyes, glazed over now, looked with astonishment at the evidence camera's lens.

"Stop and rewind the tape," said Arn Anderson.

Acting Police Chief Johnny White rewound the player until Arn stopped him.

"Can you go half speed?"

"How the hell should I know?" Johnny fumbled with the remote. "Been a while since I worked a VCR," he laughed. But there were no laugh lines around his haggard eyes.

Johnny found the right button, and Arn scooted his chair closer to the television screen. The evidence tech who'd recorded the homicide scene stepped carefully around the chair where Detective Butch Spangler slumped, dead. The camera bounced, zooming in here to get a close-up of the bullet wound, zooming out there to get a better angle on the blood-soaked silk shirt. Two distinct holes off to one side of the monogrammed pocket marred the flawless fabric.

"'An inglorious end to an illustrious career' is how Chief Patterson put it at Butch's funeral." Johnny ejected the tape and slipped it into a protective cardboard sleeve. He paused a long moment before he slid it across his desk. "Here's your damned tape. Good luck finding a player."

"How about—"

"This one?" Johnny grinned and patted the VCR. "No. This little baby is still evidence from a burglary six years ago. You can't have it."

"After six years?"

Johnny shrugged. "Sorry, old friend."

"Like hell you are."

Johnny grabbed a pencil and started chewing the eraser. "What do you want me to say? That I'm happy the community—and especially the city council—has so little faith in our ability to solve cases that they order us to cooperate with some asshole outsider who comes in to find our killers for us?"

"I'm not an asshole."

"Sure you are."

Arn thought a moment. "You're right. I am an asshole. But that's not why you're pissed."

Johnny walked to a coffee tray and picked up a donut. He pinched it between his thumb and finger before he dropped it back onto the serving tray. It landed with a dull thud: it had been there even before the stale coffee. Perhaps before the police station itself moved into the old telephone building in the '80s. "I'm pissed because the city council bought that line of cock and bull the TV station crowed. You know as well as I do, you're not going to learn anything new after ten years." Johnny snapped the pencil and lobbed it into the trash can. "We got more tips back then than a Japanese masseuse with roving hands. We worked every lead imaginable—and we came up blank. And you accuse us of shutting down the investigation prematurely?"

Arn stuffed the tape into his briefcase and walked to the coffee cart. He grabbed the pot and sniffed it before he put it back to scald some more. Screw Juan Valdez and his coffee-hauling ass, he thought. "Nasty cop coffee," he said as he faced Johnny. "Some things never change. Like, a fresh set of eyes looking at the evidence might come up with something new. Remember someone telling you that once?"

"You horse's butt, you're pulling that 'I used to be your training officer' crap on me. Sure, you taught me about fresh eyes." Johnny nodded to Arn's bag that contained the tape. "But this time you're wasting your time." He snapped his fingers. "But then, what do you care if *your* time's wasted? The TV station will still pay you."

"They will. I'm on their payroll. Same as the city will still pay you even if you never solve another case."

Johnny looked around his desk for another pencil before he ripped into Arn. "And just whose ass did you blow smoke up to get this lucrative 'consulting' job?"

Arn nudged a piece of lint embedded in the shit-brown carpeting with the toe of his boot.

Johnny came around his desk and sat on the edge. "It was that TV reporter—that Ana Maria Villarreal—wasn't it? When she came on air two nights ago she seemed to gloat that the station hired an outside consultant."

"She guilt-tripped me into doing her a favor and looking into Butch's death."

"And was it her brilliant idea to lump Gaylord's and Steve's deaths along with Butch's into her TV special?"

Detectives Steve DeBoer and Gaylord Fournier had died a month apart shortly before Butch Spangler was murdered. Arn saw no connection, but Ana Maria's intuition said there was. He'd worked with her enough in years past to trust her intuition.

"All I know is, I'm getting paid to look at Butch's murder and the deaths of the other officers. Whether I'm successful in learning anything new is doubtful. But I intend to work it until I can't anymore. Now, the police reports on Butch ... "

Johnny nodded to the door. "I'll have Gorilla Legs make copies."

"Who's Gorilla Legs?"

"You see that lovely lady out front? With a scowl and a mustache any cowboy would be proud of?"

"Looking like she could ride Steamboat into the ground?"

"The same. I inherited her as secretary when I took over as acting chief. I'll ask her to make copies of Butch's investigation." Johnny grinned. "But you might have to arm wrestle her for it."

"And can she make copies on Gaylord and Steve as well?"

Johnny's smile faded and he leaned across the desk. "Those two deaths were—"

"Suspicious."

"Not connected."

"How did they die?"

Johnny rubbed his temples. "I'm not going to lift a finger to be a part of this charade. Their deaths were accidental. A lot of us still hurt over them. Leave it at that."

"I'll bet I could research the *Wyoming Tribune Eagle* and find out how they died."

"Then hop to it."

Arn set his bag down on the chair and approached Johnny. "We were friends, once upon a time when I worked here. Why are you so hostile to me?"

"I told you: the TV station. The public was outraged—again—this week when Villarreal started airing her special. 'Three officers from the same agency dead in one year is more than coincidental,' she said."

"But you don't think they were murdered?"

Johnny stared at Arn so long that he wasn't sure Johnny had heard the question. Until he finally spoke slowly, deliberately. "Butch Spangler's murder put every swinging dick in the department on edge. Looking over our shoulders. Locking our doors. If someone could get the best of Butch—who was the most paranoid cop in the department—in his own home, no one was safe. But we worked the hell out of Gaylord's and Steve's cases on the off-chance they *were* connected. Nothing linked them to Butch's homicide. Nothing. Those files are not public record. Even I can't release them without authorization."

"Who can?"

"The investigations lieutenant, Ned Oblanski."

"Where can I find him?"

"You don't want to. He's even madder than I am that you're sticking your nose into city business—some outsider from the TV station we're ordered to cooperate with. Like we're a bunch of hicks."

Arn slung his briefcase over his shoulder and headed for the door.

"Watch your ass with Ned," Johnny called after him. "You'd be better off French kissing Gorilla Legs than tangling with him."

Two

ARN POKED HIS HEAD around the corner of the TV station break room. "Your security here stinks."

Ana Maria jerked her head up from her newspaper and knocked an empty coffee cup onto the floor. "Why'd you scare me like that?"

Arn walked around the cubicle and leaned on the short wall. "Just thank God it's not some stalker waltzing in here. Wouldn't be the first time that happened."

Ana Maria bent and picked up the pieces of broken cup. "That was ... about a century ago—"

"Thirteen years ago."

She trembled visibly as she patted the carpet with some paper towels. Then she motioned for Arn to follow her down the hallway. "Is that a purse you've got slung over your shoulder?"

"It's a man bag."

She jabbed Arn with her elbow. "Kind of sissified for a cowboy to carry a purse."

"Man bag."

Ana Maria led him into an empty office and shut the door. "Doc Henry's been paroled for two years now and he hasn't contacted me since, if that's what you're worried about." She wrapped her arms around Arn and hugged him. "Besides, I've got my protector here in Cheyenne now."

Arn held her at arm's length and looked down at her. "Your protector was a spry forty-three back when we were in Denver. Don't count on me riding up on a white horse now."

Ana Maria smiled. "You always were pretty savvy with horseflesh, from what I recall."

"That was a century ago, too. You need to watch yourself."

"Doc Henry's the least of my worries right now."

"What could be more important than protecting yourself?" Arn asked.

"Right now, protecting my job," she said soberly.

"And as I recall, you could always find work turning a wrench if you needed to."

Ana Maria sat behind the desk and propped her feet up on an open drawer. "No one wants to hire a mechanic who can't work on computerized cars." She dropped her feet and leaned across the desk, her frown replaced by a wide grin. Her brown eyes showed the twinkle Arn remembered from when she was a reporter at the Denver television station. The last thing Ana Maria wanted—Arn knew—was to go back to turning a wrench like she did before she got her first reporter gig. "This series on the old murders will help me keep my job. Maybe even get national attention."

"Ah." Arn sat on the edge of the desk. "That's why you conned your station owner into bringing me in. So you could reopen old wounds and propel yourself higher?"

"Yeah," Ana Maria answered. "But I won't admit it to anyone else."

"Bull. Your job might be on the line, but there's another reason you proposed reexamining those three officers' deaths." Arn smiled. "Maybe there's still a sense of justice flowing through those reporter's veins?"

She shrugged. "Just like you have another reason than your consulting fee for agreeing to look into them."

"I needed money to restore Mom's old house."

"Now that's bull. *You* retained a sense of justice from your police days. You'd like nothing more than to see Butch Spangler's homicide solved. Besides, you miss it, don't you? Chasing the bad guys. Outsmarting them."

Arn shrugged.

Ana Maria leaned back. She grabbed an emery board from a center desk drawer and started to scrape grease and dirt from under her nails. Like most mechanics. "Then we might solve a case. Or three."

Arn dropped into a chair beside the desk. "I doubt it. The police investigators and Wyoming DCI turned all three cases upside down. They even called in an FBI profiler. The chance that I find anything new is slim."

"You mean the chance of *us* finding anything is slim."

"No," Arn repeated. "I mean *me*."

Ana Maria dropped the nail file back in the drawer. "I proposed the story. Put my butt on the line selling it to my station manager. I'm going to be actively involved."

Arn started to interrupt, but Ana Maria held up her hand. "I've got to stay connected to this. Last thing I want to do is fall on my butt. Especially on the air."

"Hello," Arn said, "this could get dangerous if I do uncover something new." He stood and paced the room. "Someone murdered Butch Spangler and got away without a trace. I won't have you jeopardized—"

"I need this!" Ana Maria leaned back and crossed her arms defiantly. "The station manager gave me this one story to pull my ratings back up. If I'm not involved, I might as well not be alive, because I'm not going back to fixing cars."

Arn sighed deeply. He wanted to argue. He *needed* to argue. But he also knew that if he were ever to learn anything new about the deaths of the three detectives, he would need community support. And Ana Maria Villarreal, with her engaging smile and dark beauty, just might make the difference in loosening memories of the deaths. It did when she covered a pot convention in Denver all those years ago, exposing the seedy side of that game and earning her enemies. Including one Doc Henry.

"All right," he said finally. "But only because I need the money will we be working together. So to speak. If things get hinky, you pull out."

"I will not—"

"I don't need the money that bad. Either you promise you'll back out if things go south, or I stroll right out of here and go back to Denver."

Even through her dark complexion Ana Maria's face turned red, but she nodded in resignation. "Agreed. But you keep me informed of what you learn."

"Agreed." He sat in a chair again and leaned his elbows on the desk. "Now, what have you found out so far?"

Ana Maria took a thick manila file folder from a drawer and spread papers atop the desk. "Even after I filed a FOIA request, I got very little. Butch Spangler's police investigation is public record—for the most part." She thumbed through the papers and set aside the ones about Butch's homicide. She slid copies of official Cheyenne Police press releases across the desk, including the reports about Steve and

Gaylord's deaths that were so redacted with black marker it must have cost the department a bundle for the Sharpies. "But all I got was press releases about the other officers' deaths."

Arn automatically grabbed for the high-dollar Walmart reading glasses sticking out of his pocket and caught a smirk from Ana Maria. "What?"

"Are those women's glasses?"

"You're being sexist?" he answered. "So what if they're a floral print. They were on sale." He turned the report to the light as he read how Gaylord Fournier had died as a result of a hanging. His wife, Adelle, had found him swinging from their basement rafters when she came home from shopping. "Looks pretty straightforward. No mention that it was anything but suicide." He handed Ana Maria the press release. "Any scuttlebutt that he had work problems? Problems at home? Another woman?"

Ana Maria smiled as she leaned back in her chair. "Remember down in Denver when I covered that group that was into the kinky stuff?"

"I'm still going to therapy over it. Was Gaylord involved in that kinky shit?"

Ana Maria nodded. She glanced out the window for a moment before she answered. "Detective Fournier died an autoerotic death."

"Where'd you get that pearl of information?"

"Rumor. Cost me some lucky bucks to take a junior detective on a dinner date. If you could get Johnny White to open up, he might admit Gaylord was found swinging with a rope wrapped around his tallywacker and butter smeared all over his bare butt."

"That's why Johnny White didn't want to tell me." Arn laid the report aside. "Maybe I'll talk with whoever was Butch's and Gaylord's supervisor at the time, if he's still in the area."

"You'll need a Ouija board for that. The head of investigations then was none other than Steve DeBoer. He went the way of Gaylord, you know."

"You mean he died spanking his monkey, too?"

"No." Ana Maria thumbed through more papers and came away with another press release. "He died from smoke inhalation when he passed out in his recliner in his living room, a Virginia Slim still in his hand."

"You certain it was smoke inhalation?"

"I'm looking for the fire marshal's report to verify it."

Arn glanced at the report and slid it back across the desk. "So how can you make an ongoing investigative series with just this?"

"I can because the public demands it. Look." Ana Maria opened the blinds and pointed down into the parking lot. A circle of people rimmed the front lot, chanting things Arn couldn't make out. Others held homemade signs that read *Justice for the Three*. "That started the morning after I aired the initial setup for the series. People living here still demand the three deaths be investigated as homicides. Connected homicides."

"But why? Steve's and Gaylord's were accidents, if we believe the police investigations."

"The public didn't buy that the deaths of three investigators from the same agency—half the investigative division at the time—weren't related. They *wanted* the three to be connected. They *needed* the three connected. And what better to connect them than airing a television special on the ten-year anniversary of their deaths."

Arn shut the blinds and plopped back into the chair. "There's nothing there. Butch Spangler was murdered by person or persons unknown. Period."

"And you don't think there's a connection with the other two?"

"Like what?"

"They all worked together?" Ana Maria came around the desk. She sat next to Arn, and her cologne wafted over him. He fought to remind himself that he was old enough to be her father and backed his chair away. "Gaylord Fournier was Butch Spangler's partner. And Steve DeBoer was their supervisor."

"So?"

"They were all working on two murders the press had dubbed 'the Five Point Killings' at the time. And the Five Point Killer was never found."

Arn leaned away from Ana Maria to concentrate. "I recall some regional teletypes coming through Denver Metro Homicide during that time. I guess someone figured that being an hour and a half away from Cheyenne, we might have some similar cases. Cheyenne police wanted to know if we had any murders where the suspect dropped one of those goofy plastic police badges at a scene."

"Like the ones the DARE officers used to give out," Ana Maria said. "Some reporter gave the murderer the moniker because of the five points to the badge."

"That's what every killer needs," Arn said. "A catchy name to put on his toe tag. But I'll bet it was the talk of the town, three deaths in a burg this size. Most exciting thing happens here every year is watching who wins the overall cowboy at Frontier Days. What caused you to bring these cases up in the first place?"

"I remember reading the AP articles about the deaths when I worked in Denver," Ana Maria said. "When I moved here and started to interview people, I found folks that still lived in fear. Even now, the old residents shudder when you mention the Five Point Killer."

"Then why didn't Johnny White tell me that all three of them worked on those cases?"

Ana Maria shrugged. "Got to be some compelling reason." She stood and smoothed her skirt. "I've got to tape the next segment of the series for tomorrow. We need to meet up before it airs. Where are you staying?"

"I'm bunked at Little America for now. But I'll be working at my mother's old house tomorrow."

"Then let's plan to go over these police reports there tomorrow afternoon." She was halfway through the door when she stopped and faced Arn. "Thanks for coming aboard on this. Once again, I owe you."

"All you owe me is your safety. After this starts airing nightly, you might draw the attention of someone who doesn't like it."

"Like the alleged killer?" Ana Maria laughed. "Believe me, if I *really* thought all three deaths were connected, I wouldn't have proposed the series," she added over her shoulder as she walked down the hallway toward the recording studio.

"I thought you were ready to walk on coals before you gave up the notion they were all connected?"

"What I was ready to do is walk on coals to get this special. They *may* be connected. But I'm not thoroughly convinced."

Arn headed for the parking lot. As he passed the receptionist seated like a security guard—whom Arn had easily slipped past as he came into the building—the woman stopped him.

"You're that ex-Denver cop Ana Maria goes on about all the time."

Doris was engraved on a brass nameplate on her desk. She sat stoically, pulling her gray hair back behind her ears and over twin hearing aids.

"I met Ana Maria in Denver right after she started for the CBS affiliate there. And yes, we're friends."

Doris took off her glasses and her eyes met Arn's. "Then if you're a friend, you tell that girl to watch her backside."

"Has she had problems lately?"

"She got calls the morning after that first airing of her special." Doris sipped from a Starbucks cup as big as a thermos. "Then two more calls the morning after the next airing."

"What type of calls?"

"Just some man."

"Threats?" Arn asked.

Doris eyed the ceiling fan as if her answer were hidden there. "Not directly. The man just said, 'Kill the story,' and hung up."

"Did Ana Maria recognize the voice?"

"She was out working other stories each time he called. I told her about it, but she waved it away like it was some annoying cigarette smoke that made her uncomfortable." Doris put her glasses on and picked up her copy of *Good Housekeeping*. "But if you want my opinion, the voice I heard on the other end was as threatening as if he came out and said he'd kill Ana Maria if she continued with the special."

Arn opened his man bag and caught Doris's grin as she stared at it. He jotted his number down on a notepad and handed it to her. "You call if that man phones again."

"I will. And check on her now and again, will you, Mr. Anderson? Please."

Three

IN CONTRAST TO JOHNNY'S Gorilla Legs, the investigations secretary—Michelle Gains, according to the nameplate parked at one corner of her orderly desk—smiled warmly as she stood. She took off earphones linked to a transcription machine and smoothed her pleated gray skirt. "Lieutenant Oblanski asked that you have a seat."

Short. Professional. Nothing that indicated to Arn he would be kept waiting for two hours as he read tattered pages of *People* magazine lauding lives he cared little about. Passing investigators eyed him curiously as he thumbed through a last year's edition of *Cosmopolitan* featuring the cover-teasing "Eight Ways to Give Him an Erection All Night." A uniformed sergeant smirked as he walked by Arn reading a story in *Fit Pregnancy*, the closest thing he could come to a men's magazine in the waiting room.

He jumped when Michelle entered the room. "Lieutenant Oblanski will see you now."

The moment Arn started down the investigations hallway, he swore the temperature dropped a dime. Detectives hunched over computers stopped long enough to rubberneck the outsider walking past them, an outsider bulling his way into their agency. An outsider telling them how to conduct a homicide investigation.

He followed Michelle to the office at the end of the hallway. She pointed him to a door marked *Lt. Oblanski* and backed away. She remained in the hall, as if to watch the entertainment.

A man several inches shorter than Arn, and nearly as heavy in the arms and shoulders, motioned him into his office. He stood with a phone cradled in the crick of his neck as he jotted on a notepad on top of his desk cluttered with papers and shift schedules and the *Tribune Eagle* opened to a damning front page article ripping the police for failure to find Butch's killer ten years ago. Arn started to close the door when Oblanski stopped him. "You're not going to be here long enough to get comfortable." His eyes looked past Arn to the audience of investigators craning their necks around their office doors. "Leave it open."

Arn hung his Stetson on an elk antler coatrack and sat with one leg crossed over the other. Ned Oblanski ignored him while he stuffed papers into a thick manila folder marked *Butch Spangler Homicide* in red. He tossed it on his desk and it slid off the edge onto the floor. "There's a copy of Butch's file. Anything else you need?"

Arn picked up the file and slipped it into his bag as he met Oblanski's stare. "There is. I need your help."

He caught Oblanski's faint blink, a micro tic that told him he'd hit a sympathetic nerve. But he'd need much more than that if he were to enlist Oblanski's cooperation. "I'll need your help—and your detectives' help—if I'm going to find Butch's killer."

Light filtering through window blinds reflected off Oblanski's nearly bald head, a short, bristly patch of brown in the middle that gave it the look of a Mohawk. His eyes locked onto Arn's, and he crossed his arms while leaning back. "Someone thinks this agency screwed up the Spangler investigation," he said, loud enough so the other investigators heard. "And some hot dog mercenary the TV station hired is going to waltz in here and set us hicks straight?"

Arn ran his fingers through his wispy blond hair. "I'm not your enemy, Lieutenant ... "

"That's right. We share camaraderie, you an-ex cop and all. You even worked here way back in the day. We're up to our asses in alligators here, mister consultant. I can't spare anyone to help you."

"Don't you want to see Butch's killer brought to justice?"

Oblanski came around his desk and glared down at Arn. "What do you take me for? Of course I want to. But you're not going to learn anything that we didn't."

"I understand you were here in Investigations when Butch was killed."

"Not that it makes any difference," Oblanski said, "but I started the year before. I did the important stuff: grab coffee and donuts, run dead-end leads on the tip line. Important stuff."

"You must have some notion who killed him." The micro tic again tugged at the outer reaches of Oblanski's eye, and Arn pressed the issue. "Someone must have stood out?"

"Frank Dull Knife," Oblanski blurted out. "The Indian who was banging Butch's wife. But we worked that angle to death. In my gut, though, I still feel he was good for it."

"Just because he messed around with a man's wife doesn't make him a killer. You might have even messed around yourself a time or two."

"When I was young and stupid." Oblanski leaned on the edge of his desk. "But Butch had worked up a burglary case on Frank. They were scheduled to go to a preliminary hearing a week after Butch was murdered. A conviction would have made Frank a habitual criminal. Mandatory life. He would have been someone's wife or girlfriend in the joint until he was too old to look pretty. I'd say that's reason enough to murder Butch."

"Is this Frank Dull Knife still in town?"

Oblanski spit tobacco juice in the trash can and wiped his mouth with the back of his hand. "He's breathing air someone else could be breathing. Still at his crappy little mechanic shop over by the refinery. Now if there's nothing else—"

"I want the files on Steve DeBoer and Gaylord Fournier."

"People in hell want ice water. That's what the nuns told me in school." Oblanski grabbed a pouch of Red Man tobacco and stuffed his cheek. He offered it to Arn.

"Never got into the habit myself."

Oblanski chuckled. "And that's what my priest said, too." The smile faded. "But those files are off-limits to you. They weren't suspicious deaths, and I won't taint their memory dragging them into this."

"Even with the mayor's orders? I understand he's on board with this TV series showcasing the deaths of his three detectives. Something about the good publicity it can give him next election."

"Get the hell out before I throw you out."

Arn stood and looked down at Oblanski. The man might get a meal out of a fight, but Arn would definitely get a snack. Oblanski seemed to weigh the possibility of getting his ass beat in front of his officers, and he backed away. "Just get out of my office."

Arn hesitated. He'd too long been the top predator in the police world not to savor Oblanski's defeat. For the moment.

He slung his bag over his shoulder and started for the door, then stopped and faced Oblanski. "One other thing: I want some protection for Ana Maria Villarreal."

"Does she need protection?"

"Some nut called her after she began airing the series."

"Did he threaten her?"

"She didn't talk with him. The receptionist took the calls; the guy made no direct threats. But the timing of the phone calls telling her to stop the TV special is too coincidental. Especially since Butch's killer was never caught."

"Ana Maria Villarreal is no friend of this department." Oblanski raised his voice once again for the benefit of his investigators, who eyed the open office door. "But she can come down and file a report like anyone else. Although I doubt we could do anything with information that sketchy."

"Then how about Doc Henry?"

"I'm healthy. Never went to the man. Whoever he is."

"He's a shithead who stalked—and tried to kill—Ana Maria in Denver thirteen years ago. He got twenty-to-life in the Colorado State Penitentiary. Paroled two years ago."

"Then he's safe and sound and knee-deep into rehabilitation. But I'd worry about yourself, Anderson. With Ana Maria plastering your file photo on air as the one who's going to catch Butch's killer, you'd do well to look over your own shoulder."

Four

ANA MARIA VILLARREAL PUTS on her most serious look as floodlights cast a halo around her darkly beautiful face. Unblinking, she stares into the camera and begins the first broadcast of her special, live from the steps of the Cheyenne Police Department.

"As if I don't have anything else to do but watch her." *Now I'm talking to myself, like a crazy person.*

But I stop short of turning off the television. I wonder just what she hopes to accomplish.

"It was ten years ago," *she explains.* "Three officers dead—all from the same agency, all investigating the Five Point Killer—has to be more than coincidental." *I laugh because it was more than coincidental when I planned those deaths back in the day. It had all seemed so exciting. Selecting my victims like wolves select their prey, based on certain parameters known only to them. Researching the places where I would kill them. Carefully leaving only those clues that I wished law enforcement officers to discover on their own. It was exciting then to get the best of the cops. Back in the day...*

"We need the help of the public," *Ana Maria concludes. She gives a number for a tip line and my head pounds. Why can't she just let it drop? Even though the men I killed deserved it, what I did a decade ago was a mistake. And I've been pure as the driven snow ever since.*

It's said that a murderer never sleeps well after he kills; that his conscience prevents him from ever letting his mind rest. But years ago I came to grips with my crimes. I told myself that what I did, I did because they deserved their deaths. And I've slept quite well since.

But since the TV station began promoting Ana Maria's investigative report, I've begun to sleep fitfully. Not from fear of getting caught—I planned things too well back in the day to ever get caught. And certainly not from anything that retired Denver cop or Ana Maria could uncover. But every few hours I snap awake shuddering, shaking my sweat-drenched hair, reliving those orgiastic feelings that overcame me back then. The newspaper said Butch was killed in cold blood. And possibly the other officers as well. I liked to think of it more like in cool blood. Watching the life ooze out of them. Enjoying their deaths from different angles. Coolly watching.

I reach over to turn the television off, but my hand trembles. I haven't felt this way since then. I fantasize about once again setting the murder scenes up so that every police officer investigating will look in the opposite direction. And I'll stand on the sidelines watching as they stumble by. Just like back in the day.

Ana Maria Villarreal says good night. To me, in her special way, and promises another airing tomorrow night. "And with your help, we will learn who killed these men. Starting with Butch Spangler." *I take deep, calming breaths, and at last I can turn off the television set.*

Will I watch tomorrow? Of course. I cannot not *watch. For every time she goes over the facts in the Five Point Killings, excitement shoots through me like I'm pissing on an electric fence. Excitement that I tossed aside when I—and only because I chose to—stopped killing. Now I am afraid the only way to keep the urges in check is to have knowledge of where the investigation is headed. Ana Maria will give me that knowledge, every night at seven o'clock.*

I hope it works. Because I still tremble with anticipation.

Five

PEOPLE RUBBERNECKED AT ARN as he pulled out of Home Depot like they'd never seen a finely restored classic muscle car pulling a trailer-load of building materials across town. With mud and snow tires that slid his Olds 4-4-2 sideways through the intersection, Arn turned east onto Lincolnway. He thought once again about the folly of restoring his mother's house—now his by decree. His great-grandfather had built the place when he worked the Cheyenne-to-Deadwood stagecoach route as a young man. At the time, the house had every luxury one could hope for in the Magic City: indoor plumbing, electric lighting, even a drive-through carriage port to off-load groceries from the buckboard when the weather turned nasty. That was in the 1870s, and Arn was certain that was also the last time anyone had performed any maintenance on the house.

When his mother was still alive, Arn would drive up from Denver on Mother's Day and Thanksgiving and Christmas. And sometimes she would talk him into visiting on Easter. It had been one of the few times a year that Arn would step foot inside a church. He would help his mother into her best Easter dress, the same one she wore every year. He'd offer to buy her another, but she'd refuse. It was the dress she'd worn the last time she and Arn's father had been to church, the week before he died in 1978. They would mount the steps at Saints Constantine and Helen Greek Orthodox Church, and Arn would stay at his mother's side while she venerated the icons that lined the church vestibule. When he waited in the pew while she joined the others in line for communion, she would look at him and a sadness would cross her face because he hadn't converted to Orthodoxy.

Whenever he'd visit his mother, he'd stay at Little America. He could never bring himself to stay in the house of his youth: too many memories of his drunk father and his thick, stiff, inflexible police belt that was never far out of reach. And as abusive as his father had been, he regretted that his father had passed out on the railroad tracks that night thirty-six years ago. A Union Pacific highballed through and made his father's Ford sedan into a hunk of metal strung out for a mile until the train shut down.

Arn had boarded up his mother's old house twenty-five years ago when she died, and he never went back, paying the taxes by mail. He hadn't seen the old house again until two years ago when passing through on his way to a Yellowstone vacation. He'd stopped at the courthouse to write a check to the treasurer for current taxes. The clerk had looked at him like he'd escaped from the state hospital in Evanston. "So, you're the one who wastes money on taxes. Most places in that part of town are condemned," she said, spitting tobacco juice into an Orange Crush can. "You sure you want to keep this Home-less Hilton?"

Arn had pocketed the receipt and driven by the house. Rain had gotten into the shattered windows, and the front door hung by a single rusty hinge. A hail storm had trashed the roof sometime since he'd buried his mother, the cedar shingles loose and flapping in the stiff Wyoming wind. One of the support spindles his great grandfather had spokeshaved out of a hickory log to support the full-length porch had rotted through, and the overhang drooped on one side like a lazy eye that threatened to close.

He hadn't gone inside that day: he didn't want to spoil his vacation. He'd had the power turned off and the water disconnected when his mother died. And though some part of him wanted to be rid of the house, another part tugged at him to keep it. The crazy part of him.

"Why don't you let the house go back to the county for taxes?" Cailee asked the morning after his mother's funeral. They had gathered what few things he wanted to keep that were hers, and Cailee had shuddered visibly on leaving the house. "That tree." She'd pointed to a bare-branched cottonwood his grandfather had planted in the front, its gnarled fingers reaching skyward to an unseen god. "It gives me the heebie-jeebies. And no offense, but your mother didn't keep the place up very good. It just isn't worth keeping."

"I'll go back there someday and fix it up."

"When? You don't have time for our own house."

"Someday," Arn had promised her. And promised himself. He had imagined then—and many times since—that he'd restore the house to all its former splendor. Even in the years since Cailee's death, he kicked the idea around of driving up from Denver on weekends to work on it. But he never did. Even after he'd retired from Metro Homicide and had the time, he never did. Yet when Ana Maria called and lined up this consulting gig with the TV station, he told himself he finally had the money to restore it. And the time.

He downshifted. The Oldsmobile's mellow pipes announced his arrival as he pulled to the curb in front of the house. When he looked at it, he realized he might have to go back for more plywood to board the place up. Most of the ground floor windows had been broken last time he was here, and now even those windows on the upstairs gables needed boarded up. Graffiti had been spray-painted across the stuccoed front of the house, and one limb of the dying cottonwood had broken off and crashed through the bay window. The fallen mailbox in the shape of a caboose—the only thing Arn's father had contributed to the house—lay rusting and nearly hidden in two feet of overgrown weeds.

Arn grabbed the door handle and started to climb out, when he paused. Perhaps he should do what his wife suggested years ago: abandon the house. Let it go back to the county. He was certain it would need to be gutted, between the rain and snow that had rotted the insides and the critters that surely must have set up camp in there. He wasn't sure he had that much time on his hands. Or the skill. He could swing a hammer. But not well. He could even measure a line. Though he was usually off. This place required more talent than he possessed, and he slid back behind the wheel of his car.

He hit the ignition and shoved the clutch in, then dropped his head on the steering wheel and turned the car off. He climbed out and grabbed his work gloves before slamming the door. "I might not be Bob Vila, but I'll do my best."

As he walked to the back of the trailer and dropped the tailgate, he noticed a drop cord running from somewhere down the block into the house. Snow had nearly covered the electrical cord, bright orange peeking through patches of weeds that was the lawn of his youth.

He stepped away and traced the cord. Music came from the house, rising and falling, heavy drums and screeching guitars, as Iron Butterfly belted out "In-A-Gadda-Da-Vida" from somewhere deep inside.

Arn carefully opened the car door and grabbed his .38 snubbie from the glove box. He approached the front door and ducked to avoid the sagging porch beam, the volume getting louder. He grabbed onto the door knob and it broke off in his hand. Tossing it on the ground, he squeezed past the one-hinged front door.

He paused just inside the door to allow his eyes to adjust to the semi-darkness. As he suspected, water had damaged the walls and ceilings. But now was not the time to lament. He shuffled through a snowdrift that had blown in through a broken window, careful not to scrape against the wall and make noise. Not that it would have been heard over the blaring music. He stepped over broken beer bottles, past the carcass of an unidentifiable animal that seemed to grin up at him from what had been his mother's sewing room. He placed his hand on a musty, moldy, mildewed wall that reverberated from the heavy bass in the next room and kept inching closer to the sound. Light from the adjoining room cast eerie shadows on the blackened and weathered paisley-papered walls. He tightened his grip on the gun and breathed deeply. He peeked around the corner of the wall into the kitchen while holding his gun beside his leg.

An emaciated, gray-grizzled man lounged in a torn bean bag chair in front of a boom box. His stringy ponytail bounced on his thin chest in time with the music as one slippered foot tapped the floor. He read from a book by the light of a single naked bulb overhead. It swayed from wind that blew past the cardboard he'd propped against the broken windows.

The man grabbed a can of Pepsi and sipped, then returned it to the top of a plastic milk crate beside a half-eaten pack of Oreos. He leaned back, reading, his feet catching heat from a space heater positioned under a wire strung across the room. Socks and tattered Fruit of the Looms dried on the cord.

Arn stepped around the corner, his gun still concealed beside his leg. "What are you doing here?"

The old man jumped. His book flew across the room and hit a wall. He scrambled to stand. His arms flailed the air and he knocked over his can of Pepsi. His eyes darted in the direction of the back door.

"I said: What are you doing here?"

"Don't come any closer," the man stammered. He jammed one hand into the pocket of his sweatpants and thrust it toward Arn like a lame erection. His other hand held his sweats up over his meatless hips. "Don't come any closer or I'll shoot."

"You got your finger in your pocket."

"I got a gun."

"No you don't," Arn said, and brought his snubbie from beside his leg. "*I've* got a gun."

The man's shoulders slumped and he brought his hand out of his sweats. "All right. You want this place, I guess I'll have to move on."

"What? Turn off that racket!"

The man bent and flicked the power button on his ghetto blaster. "You got something against quality music?"

"I got something against squatters in my house."

"Your house?" The man straightened to his full five-feet-and-change and tossed his ponytail over his back. "Did you buy this rat trap? I wouldn't."

Arn slipped his gun into his trouser pocket and stepped closer. "Well, you thought it was a perfectly fine house up until a moment ago." He waved his arm around the kitchen. "What *are* you doing here? And just who the hell are you?"

"Danny."

"Danny who?"

"Just Danny."

29

"Like Liberace?"

Danny smiled a set of perfect pearlies that contrasted with his dark complexion. "More like Fabio."

"Still doesn't answer what you're doing here."

Danny rested his hands on his hips and pouted his lips like he owned the house. "This was my house until you busted in here." He grabbed a pillowcase inside the milk carton and walked to the make-shift clothesline. He snatched underwear and socks from the line and stuffed them inside. "What I'm doing—*was* doing—is keeping out of the cold." He threw on a faded green Army field jacket with the zipper broken and closed it with the solitary button remaining. He exaggerated a look past the cardboard to the broken window. "Hope I don't freeze out there tonight." He warmed his hands with his breath. "Gets cold when the sun sets. Not sure if I'll make it out there—"

"Don't guilt-trip me into letting you stay. And just who are you, to break in here?"

Danny's mouth drooped in profound sadness. Like he'd practiced it a time or two. "I'm just some old Indian making his way in the world ..."

Arn groaned. "Just what I need, to adopt some homeless Indian."

"I wasn't homeless until you came along. And after all the work I've done to the fix the place up."

And he had. Arn looked around in disbelief at Danny's remodel job. He'd cut an empty cat litter pail to make a dresser of sorts, underwear and a clean shirt folded neatly inside. An antique stainless steel bedpan-turned-wash-basin rested atop an overturned trash can, a jug of water beside it. Toothbrush, razor, and can of Barbasol were arranged neatly beside it.

On the opposite side of the room, Danny had covered a thin mattress with a wool blanket. A stuffed cat sewn to the pillowcase seemed to wink at Arn with its one sequined eye, the other one missing.

"How long you been squatting here?"

"I resent—"

"How long?"

Danny shrugged. "Since this summer when I put the run on some kids who snuck in here to smoke some weed. But I didn't bust the windows out. And I didn't tag the house with that crappy spray paint. This"—he exaggerated waving his arm around the room like he was introducing Arn to his castle—"is what I did to the place." He jerked his thumb at the door. "Now all I get for my efforts is tossed out in the cold. The so very cold…" He trailed off.

Arn leaned against a wall. He took off his hat and ran his fingers through his hair. "When was the last time you ate?"

Danny's eyes darted to the half-pack of Oreos. "Been a while."

"Would you eat a burger and fries if I bought some?"

The old man held up his hands as if to ward off charity. "Danny don't accept handouts. Now if you had some job…"

"I got a load of plywood and nails on my trailer I could use a hand unloading. I'd ask you, but—no offense—you don't look like you're in any shape to work."

"I'm thin, but I can work."

"All right then," Arn said. "You help me unload and board up the windows, and I'll spring for some groceries."

Danny grinned. Those perfect teeth reflected the swinging bulb. "Now that's more like it. Where's the wood?"

———

Arn teetered on a milk crate Danny had produced from another room. He'd finished his Whopper and fries while Danny was only three bites into his meal. Arn thought the man was stalling, soaking up as much warmth from the space heater as he could before he got evicted. But as Arn studied him, he realized he wasn't stalling. He was just a finicky eater. He'd laid one napkin across his ragged sweatpants, another to cover his milk crate. He would take a small bite of burger and dab at the corners of his mouth. Small bite and dab. He was midway to another nibble when he caught Arn staring at him. "What?"

"You're taking an awfully long time for someone who hasn't eaten for a while."

Danny carefully set his burger on the napkin. He picked up his soda and sipped daintily. "I eat slow and enjoy my food. It's how I keep lean and trim."

"And your physical condition has nothing to do with you having no job, no income, and after tonight—*if* I let you stay—you have nowhere to go?"

Danny finished the last of his Pepsi and leaned back in his bean bag chair. "My economic condition has nothing to do with lean genes." He slapped his chest hard enough that Arn thought he would knock himself out. "We Indians have made do with what the white man gives us for a long time."

Arn finished his own soda, trying to summon enough courage to give Danny the bum's rush when he finished eating.

"What are you going to do with this place?" Danny asked.

"Do? After I fix it up, I'm going to live here."

"This century?" Danny shook his head as he looked around the room. Plaster fell away in chunks from moldy walls. Water-damaged floors had turned mushy and threatened to drop into the crawl space.

The kitchen was the best room in the house, Danny had said, and still it reeked of moisture. "You handy enough to renovate it?"

"It wasn't my profession, but I can swing a hammer."

Danny laughed and wiped his mouth. "I don't know when you last swung that hammer, but this dump—no offense—is going to take more than what you got. I saw how you tried nailing that plywood to the windows. A carpenter you ain't."

"And I suppose you are?"

Danny thrust out his hand. "Go ahead, shake my hand."

Arn shook Danny's hand.

"What do you feel?" Danny asked.

"No instant attraction, if that's what you're getting at."

"I'm not." Danny jerked his hands free. "My hands are rougher than a cob while yours are smooth. Soft."

"Your point?"

"These"—Danny held up his hands—"have been used for hard work all my life. Yours haven't seen a day's work since, when? Your school days?"

Arn wanted to tell Danny he'd hired out to local ranches during school: springtime calving, summers haying and branding. Arn had developed into enough of a horseman that he'd gotten as much work as he wanted around Cheyenne. But Danny was right: nowadays, his hands were soft. "And you think you know more about houses than I do?"

"You recall when we boarded up the windows, you had to take five and six swings to my one?" He wadded up his empty burger wrapper and tossed it into a Walmart bag. "I've swung a hammer a time or two in my life. And pulled wire. And sweated pipe. I've done it all. And I could do it here, if I had the materials."

"I sense a proposition coming."

Danny took a half-smoked cigarette butt from his pocket and lit it. "I'll swap some honest hard work for a place to crash out of the cold."

"Honest like that drop cord you ran from the neighbor's house?"

"They're on vacation," Danny said. He blew smoke rings toward the ceiling. "And it's only illegal if you get caught."

"When was the last time you were caught?"

"Who says I ever was?"

Arn ran his hand over a faded design inked on Danny's forearm. "You didn't get this from a shop: It's a jail house tat. Not like this one." He traced a tattoo of an Army First Infantry patch that adorned Danny's other forearm. "And every time I got close while you ate, you moved your food away slightly. Like I was going to steal it."

"I figured someone as big as you had to have stolen food now and again." Danny smiled, but it faded when he saw that Arn was serious. "I never did hard time. Honest Injun." He held up his hand like an anorexic Tonto. "Just county time, years back."

"And by the time they figured out you gave them a false name, you were long out of their jurisdiction."

"How would you know that?"

"'Danny,'" Arn answered. "'Just Danny.' And no mention of a last name."

"Like I said, how would you know that?"

Arn stood and stretched. "Because I was a cop for thirty years."

Danny rolled off the bean bag chair and his eyes locked on the back door.

Arn moved to block him. "The operative word is 'was.' I got no cause to check on you."

Danny eyed him warily before he felt behind himself and eased back into the chair. "Fair enough. But what do you do nowadays, besides scare old men?"

"I'm retired Metro Denver Homicide. I'm here as a consultant to look into the deaths of three police officers ten years ago."

Danny snapped his fingers. "That's where I saw your mug, on the television at the library. That television babe Va-Va-Voom Villarreal talked about you." He stood and tramped around the room. His fuzzy slippers slapped the bare tile floor like a beached seal. "I got a regular celebrity here." He faced Arn. "But you look better in that picture on TV. And twenty pounds thinner."

"It's an old photo."

Danny dropped back into the chair. Plastic stuffing poofed up out of the ripped bean bag covering; tiny white beads flew upward. Some stuck to his gray hair before he flicked them off. "So, you're going to find out who capped that jerk?"

"Why does everyone call Butch Spangler a jerk?"

"He ever arrest you? Well, he did me. And he was way too aggressive for old Danny. Young Danny at the time." He slapped a hand against his leg. "Hot damn! We're going to catch a killer."

"We?"

"Sure. With me renovating this place, that'll give you more time to focus on catching the killer."

"Who said anything about renovation?"

"You going back on our agreement?"

"We don't have an agreement. What makes you think I'd let you stay here?"

"You know how you knew I spent some time in lockup? Well, ol' Danny's got street eyes, too. And I read you pretty good. You need someone to work on this place. You can't hire a construction firm: too expensive on a cop's retirement. Especially with everything that needs to be done. And I repeat"—Danny tapped Arn's thumb where he'd hit it with the hammer—"by your stellar performance swinging that hammer today, you don't have the skills to do it yourself." He grabbed his pillowcase and unpacked his clothes back into his makeshift dresser. "So, we got a deal here?"

Arn wanted to turn down Danny's offer, but the old man must have been clairvoyant. It was true that Arn couldn't afford to hire a professional to get the work done. His consultant fees from the TV station would all go into materials. And as he massaged his throbbing thumb, which had begun to turn black, he wondered if he was throwing away a lifetime of caution by letting a complete stranger stay in his house. Had Butch also let his guard down that night he was murdered?

"Oh, what the hell," he said. "Here's the deal: I'll have Capital Lumber drop off a construction dumpster for demolition and ask them to bring along a generator, so you don't have to steal electricity from the neighbors—"

"Borrow."

Arn ignored him. "You can crash here."

"Where'll you stay?" Danny asked.

"Well, it's a place with heat and lights. I've got a motel room. And if you've made progress by the time I stop around tomorrow, I'll let you stay here until the work's finished."

Danny smiled and sank back into his bean bag chair, his holey sweatpants conforming to his bony butt. "It's a deal. But don't worry about the generator for now. The neighbors got three more days before they come back from Vegas."

Six

ARN DROPPED THE TRAILER at the curb and started for Little America and a hot shower when his cell rang. "Whoa, Doris. Take a breath. Tell me slowly."

"I tried to call you."

"My phone's been in my car. What's wrong?"

"That man called for Ana Maria again," Doris wheezed, "just after she left for the day. He said if she wanted to know who murdered Butch Spangler to meet him at the Archer Fairgrounds. By the stables."

"There's nothing going on there this time of year except a horse show. And they don't go into the night."

"That's what makes me so scared."

Arn hung up and tromped the foot feed, the 4-4-2 fishtailing along the street. By the time he reached I-80, he was sliding seventy in the snow. At the on-ramp, he nearly slid off the road before he managed to get the car under control just before entering the eastbound lane.

The ten miles to the fairgrounds seemed to take a lifetime. Arn slid sideways when he took the Archer off-ramp, and he killed his headlights. The half-moon reflected just enough light off the new snow to navigate, and he slowed to an idle as he entered the park. Deserted. No signs of anyone. Including Ana Maria's car.

He stopped and turned off his car. He rolled his window down and stuck his head out the window. The wind blew the snow in stiff eddies that pelted his face as he strained to hear . . .

A scraping . . . hard . . . metal perhaps against pavement, rising on the wind, coming from the far side of a barn fifty yards in front of him.

Arn squinted while his eyes adjusted to the darkness, and he finally made out a Volkswagen Beetle parked in front of the barn. Someone moved inside the car.

Ana Maria opened the car door, her face framed by the dome light for the briefest moment before she stepped out and closed it. Arn cupped his hand to his mouth to yell when he froze, words trapped between his hand and his racing heart.

Movement off to Ana Maria's right. A white-garbed form blended with the snow. It moved between the barn and Ana Maria's car, quietly advancing on her.

Arn jumped out of his car and walked quickly toward her. The figure continued to advance, nearing her, closing to grabbing range. Arn broke into a run, as much as a fifty-five-year-old man can run. He slipped and silently cursed his cowboy boots, which were more at home on the back of a horse than running on slick ice.

Ana Maria turned toward Arn.

"Get in your car!" Arn yelled, huffing, his side burning from a stitch as he ran.

The figure stopped mid-stride, ten yards from Ana Maria, and seemed to be thinking his next move.

"Get in and lock your doors!"

"What?"

"That." Arn jabbed the air in the direction of the man, and Ana Maria's head snapped in the direction of the figure. The yard light over the office reflected off a long blade held at the man's side.

"Get the hell inside your car!"

Ana Maria flung herself inside and clawed at the door locks.

The man ducked inside the barn just as Arn reached Ana Maria's car. "I'm all right," she said. "Go!"

Arn grabbed his aching side and ran, half bent over like a big, blond Quasimodo. He reached the open barn door, breathing hard, his heart threatening to burst from his chest. He groped for the snubbie .38 in his pocket, took a final deep, calming breath, and button-hooked into the barn.

Here inside, all light was captured at the entryway, and the farther inside Arn walked, the darker it became. When he'd worked as a street cop, his eyes had adjusted quickly, his night vision saving him more than once. He squatted in the barn and waited for his night eyes to develop. He was kneeling in a narrow alleyway, stalls on either side. A horse chomped on hay or alfalfa. Another whinnied as if it welcomed him, the pungent odor of horse dung telling Arn they'd been stabled since the horse show ended for the day.

A snort. A stomped hoof off to his right. How many times had he hunted someone who needed hunting, needed taken off the street, sometime with the help of a K-9 officer? Except this time he had something better than a dog: he had a nervous horse to alert him to where Ana Maria's would-be attacker was. In the horse's own way.

A fabric brushed against the side of a stall farther inside, sounding louder in the frigid night air than it should have. Arn wiped his sweaty hand on his jeans and clutched the gun tighter as he inched his way along the stall. He stayed away from the side, careful not to brush the stall like the man he hunted had just done. Step and stop. Listen. Step and stop. Cock an ear, strain to hear.

The horse stopped snorting.

The man was gone.

Arn walked to the opposite end of the barn and peeked around the door.

Nothing. The man had made it out, and a terrible thought crossed Arn's mind.

He ran outside and around the barn toward Ana Maria's car. She sat behind the wheel, engine running and lights on. An expression of relief came over her as she watched Arn approach. She unlocked her car door and he jumped in.

"You scared me to death. What was that all about?"

"Didn't you see him?" Arn asked.

"I saw the guy I was here to meet walk out of the shadows. And now you scared him off. So much for finding out who killed Butch Spangler."

"The man had a knife, and—"

"No kidding? This is Wyoming. Everyone carries a knife."

Arn leaned his head back on the head rest. "Tell me about this guy you were supposed to meet. He give a name?"

"No. He called the station right when I left. He *knew* who killed Butch. I heard it in his voice. And he was going to tell me. Now he's not."

Arn took in gulps of air, his side still aching. "I don't want you to meet anyone alone until this is over."

Ana Maria turned in her seat. "Maybe you forget, but I've been doing investigative reporting for some years now. I think I can take care of myself. What I don't need is you to butt in when I got a witness that's willing to come forth." She rested her hand on Arn's forearm. "I know you just want to protect me. I'll be fine." She checked her watch. "I've got to run home. I recorded tonight's installment and I want to see how it went."

"With you," Arn said, "it always goes well."

"Well, it might not go any further without that witness talking to me."

"Sorry. But your safety comes first."

"I won't even dignify that." Ana Maria clicked her seat belt. "We still on to go over reports tomorrow?"

Arn nodded. "Drop me off at my car?"

"The one I heard the exhaust and the noisy tappets from a block before I saw you pull up?" she asked as she idled toward his 4-4-2.

"The same old Beast I had when you were in Denver."

Ana Maria stopped beside Arn's car. "Bring the Beast by the house this weekend and I'll adjust those lifters. And maybe do something about that obnoxious exhaust."

Arn waited until Ana Maria drove out of the complex before he turned his attention back to the barn.

Seven

ANA MARIA JUST STARES out her windshield like she expects me to mosey up and hop in her VW. Tell her who killed Butch Spangler. But I never intended to do that. What I wanted to do was put a scare into her. Make her stop her television special and let me get back to my life. But do I really want her to stop or not, drawing attention to killings that were out of my control ten years ago?

She lights a cigarette, her face momentarily illuminated by the glow of the Zippo. A frightened face, wild-eyed staring out the window into the darkness, fearful of someone she will only know as the Five Point Killer. And I notice I have begun to tremble myself, not from the cold, but from anticipation of the delightful fear in her eyes up close.

As I approach her, I slide my knife from the sheath that rides on the small of my back and lay it beside my leg. She looks away. I steady my shaking hand as I approach her, ready to bring the knife out at just the right time, flick a piece of flesh from her lovely cheek, hear her screams. And her disbelief as I melt back into the night. My warning complete: stop the television special and let me live my comfortable life in peace.

She glances my direction and I freeze, an immobile white sheet that blends in with the snow. After a moment, she looks in the opposite direction, and I take another step toward her car when ...

Loud exhaust approaches off the interstate. Someone pulls into the complex. I squint and see an old car idling toward us. Right off I make the driver as a cop: He doused his lights before he pulls into the fairgrounds and uses his emergency brake to stop—no brake lights. A cop. Or, as I see when he pulls to a stop, that Metro Homicide detective the television station hired to find me.

Ana Maria slips from behind the wheel and turns in Anderson's direction.

I inch toward her, using her car to shield me from him when—

"Get in your car!" he yells at her.

I freeze mid-stride. He's out of his car. He spots me. I look about the deserted fairgrounds. The empty barn I waited in is thirty yards away. I turn back just as he yells at Ana Maria again.

"Get in and lock your doors!"

"What?"

"That." He jabs the air. Ana Maria's head snaps in my direction, and I pull the white hood tight around my face.

"Get the hell inside your car!"

Ana Maria throws herself inside her car. The glow of her cigarette still illuminates her face as she hits the door locks.

The cop comes on a dead run. But even though I wear hospital booties over my shoes, I run faster. I reach the safety of the barn in time to strip the sheet off me. It exposes black pants and sweater and ski mask, the perfect garb for hiding in a pitch-black building.

The detective's wheezing precedes him, and I squat down. The doorway momentarily frames him. But for only a moment, as he ducks inside. A cop.

Used to entering buildings after bad guys, keeping out of—what was that term they used?—the fateful funnel.

I risk a peek up over a wood railing and narrowly avoid a hoof thrown my way from a big bay gelding. The cop walks slowly, checking each stall on the far side of the barn, and I wait my chance to sneak out the other way. I duck-walk and he freezes. He stares in my direction. My sheet has brushed against the side of the stall, loud in this cold air, and gave my location away.

He starts toward me.

I duck-walk faster toward the opposite end and keep stalls between us. As I reach the open end of the barn, I buttonhook the door just as he clears the stalls. He walks my way. Slowly, deliberately, his hand thrust out. I have no doubt it holds a gun. And no doubt he will use it. That excitement rushes over me again, and I pause: do I wait in the shadows and prove that you can bring a knife to a gun fight and win? Or do I silently slip away in the darkness?

I need Ana Maria to get the message to drop her TV special. But I cannot get to her, and the cop is mere paces behind me. He'll emerge from the barn at any moment. He'll see my black form stark against the backdrop of fresh snow. But she needs a warning. I really don't want my life interrupted.

I shuffle across the lot. Ana Maria stares at the barn where the cop disappeared, looking away from me. I reach his car and fumble in my pocket for a souvenir. A warning. I toss it through his open driver's window onto his seat before I run cross country to the safety of my hidden car.

Eight

ARN GRABBED A FLASHLIGHT from his glove box and retraced where he'd seen the man disappear inside the barn. In the dust and horse droppings on the barn floor, indistinct footprints showed where he'd stood against a stall. For how long? Had he watched Arn approach, or had he waited until the blackness swallowed Arn up before sneaking out the opposite door?

A chestnut mare hung her head over the top rail of the stall as if to say hello, and Arn cradled her head in his arm as he stroked her head. "Where the hell did that guy run to?" The horse nickered her reply—which was no help at all to Arn—and he left her to resume munching hay.

He bent and ran his hand over the marks in the snow and dust: faint and indistinct. He could tell nothing from the footprints, except their direction toward the open opposite end of the barn. As if the man wore no shoes at all.

He stood, his back popping, and played his light around inside. Light reflected off something white against one wall. A strip of sheet, perhaps six inches square, hung on a protruding nail that had snagged it.

Arn snatched it from the nail: It looked like any other sheet he'd ever seen. Except it was from the sheet Ana Maria's stalker had worn when Arn first spotted him outside, nearly blending in with the snow. The stalker was no dummy: he'd stripped off the white sheet after entering the darkened barn.

Arn slipped the patch of sheet carefully inside his jacket pocket. The smallest shred of evidence often was the piece he needed to complete the puzzle. He started out the back end of the barn when he caught a whiff of some overpowering odor. Horse liniment? Cologne, perhaps? Then it was gone, as quickly as the wind had blown it past his nose.

He hobbled away from the barn and followed the indistinct tracks in the snow. No tread pattern. Nothing sharp enough to indicate the shoe size or type. But the shuffling in the snow headed directly for his own car.

Arn approached his car from the blind side, the trunk side, leading with his gun. He crouched under the driver's window. When he stood, he turned on his flashlight and shone it inside the car. He breathed deeply when he saw no one and slipped his revolver back into his coat pocket.

He looked around a final time before climbing inside his car. When he sat on the seat, something jabbed his butt. He leaned over and grabbed the small plastic object before he turned the dome light on and held it up for a closer look.

Nine

ARN TOSSED THE SMALL plastic five-point star badge on Johnny's desk. "That look familiar?"

Johnny picked it up and turned it over in his hand. "So it's a plastic badge. Our DARE officers used to give some like those out to little kids. What's your point?"

"You failed to mention yesterday that all three dead officers had worked on two cases where the killer left those at the scene. Why did you keep that from me?"

"It's not material. It was just coincidental. We checked that angle at the time, *ad nauseam*." He handed the badge back to Arn. "It looks about like any other badge our community service officers give out at schools."

"But not exactly the same kind?"

Johnny shrugged. "What's your point, besides being a pain in my rectum?"

"You still got the crime scene photos of the Five Point Killings?"

Johnny absently grabbed a pencil from his desktop and began to nibble on the eraser. "I can't show them to you."

"I'm not asking. Just pull up the photos of the badges left at those two crime scenes and compare them with this one."

"They're not the same. I don't know how you got this notion in that thick head of yours, but the Five Point Killer is long gone from these parts."

"Humor me."

Johnny pushed his chair back and it rolled into the wall. "I got better things to do than prove your bullshit ideas wrong." He tossed the pencil in his desk drawer. "But I will."

He slammed the door leaving his office, and Arn could hear him asking Gorilla Legs for the Five Point Killer case files. Their voices muted, then, as they moved down the hallway. In minutes, Johnny returned. His lip quivered and his voice wavered. "So, it is the same kind of badge—"

"When did the department stop giving them out?"

Johnny walked to the window and looked out. "Ten years ago," he said over his shoulder. "About the time Butch Spangler was murdered." He faced Arn. "Where did you get it?"

Arn explained that he'd driven to the Archer Fairgrounds after Ana Maria got the call from the man who claimed to know who killed Butch. "The guy must have worked his way around and set it on my car seat."

"Toying with you," Johnny said. "That's all. Somebody having some fun."

"It was a warning."

"If it was," Johnny said, "why didn't Ana Maria share information with us about a potential witness?" He sat at his desk and looked around for that pencil to nibble on.

"It's in your drawer."

"What?"

"Your pencil," Arn said.

"Piss on the pencil! I got half a notion to arrest her for withholding information."

"What are you afraid of?" Arn asked.

Johnny looked away. "Nothing."

"Now it's my turn to call bullshit. You're afraid I'll see something in those reports that links the Five Point Killer to Butch and the other two detectives."

"Drop it." Johnny nibbled on his upper lip and his foot tapped the floor.

"Tell me, what *are* you afraid of?"

"The damned Five Point Killer!" Johnny threw his pencil stub against the wall. "You happy now?" He turned his back on Arn. His hands trembled as he got up to straighten a picture hanging on the wall. "At the time of the murders, the killer scared the hell out of most of us with any common sense." He turned back around, and his eyes locked on Arn's. "The son-of-a-bitch was a ghost. We never picked up even one tiny piece of physical evidence. Except those silly badges."

"After last night, there's all the more reason for me to look at those cases."

"Someone was just screwing with you last night. Either way, I'm still deferring to Ned Oblanski. If he wants to give you those case files, he can. And"—Johnny leaned closer—"if he feels like I do about your reporter friend, he just might arrest her."

"If you think she's withholding information, you must think she needs protection."

"Protection from some guy who *might* have information?"

"If I hadn't interrupted him, he might have got to her."

"So you say."

"He had a knife—"

"What kind of knife?" Johnny asked. "And what did he look like?"

Arn dropped his eyes and somehow found that same piece of lint still on the carpet. "It was too dark. I never got close enough to see. He made it out of the barn before I got a good look. But I swear he had a knife—"

"I recall you were always quite the tracker. Like a lot of cowboys. Did some elk hunting. Deer and mountain lion, as I recall."

"And your point?"

"My point"—Johnny dropped into his chair—"is that there should be tracks enough for an experienced hunter like *you* to see something."

"The tracks were indistinct. Like they were ... brushed away. Or something."

"Because there was no one there."

"That badge—"

"Proves nothing," Johnny argued. "Anyone could have put it there on your seat anytime. It just took a while to work its way into your imagination. And your butt."

"You forget, I interviewed people all my life. And just now—when you came back from comparing that badge with the old crime scene photos—you *knew* they were the same. So let's cut the crap, and maybe we can find out who the Five Point Killer is. And find out who killed Butch in the process."

"There's no connection." Johnny nibbled through another eraser. "Can't you get that through your head?"

"Then why this?" Arn picked up the plastic badge and held it for a moment before he tossed it back onto Johnny's desk. "I was hired to find out who killed Butch. If this wasn't a warning to back off, why risk putting the badge on my car seat?"

Johnny grabbed his mug and walked to the coffee cart. Stalling. He sniffed the day-old coffee and dribbled some into his cup before turning back. "Butch and Gaylord worked the Five Point Killings. I worked patrol when those murders happened, so I wasn't privy to a lot. All I remember is Butch coming into shift briefing and asking us to shake down our snitches. See if anything dropped out. 'I'm so close to finding this son-of-a-bitch,' he kept telling us, 'I can smell him.' Apparently he was. The killer found him first."

"So you *do* think those killings and Butch's murder are connected?" Arn asked.

Johnny looked away, and Arn had his answer. "Have you talked with Oblanski?" Johnny said.

"He wouldn't tell me anything about the Five Point cases," Arn replied. "But I know Gaylord died an autoerotic death. And Steve died in a house fire."

"How did you find that out?"

Arn didn't answer as he ran his fingers through his hair. "Awfully coincidental, those two dying just as the Five Point cases were close to being solved. And not a month before Butch's murder."

"If you talked with Oblanski, then you know he still thinks Frank Dull Knife would be good for Butch's homicide. Not some killer passing through here with a pocketful of toy badges."

"Either way, Ana Maria's television special just might bring some witnesses forward."

"After all these years?" Johnny shrugged. "I doubt it."

"Well, it got someone spooked enough to send me a little warning last night to back off." Arn stood and walked to the coffee pot. The same donuts were on the cart that were there yesterday, as stale as the coffee, and he passed on both. "If Gaylord Fournier died by an auto-erotic death, maybe his death wasn't an accident. Maybe he was murdered for what he knew about the Five Point cases. Same as Butch."

"So how do you connect Steve DeBoer? He didn't work those cases."

"He was their supervisor," Arn explained. "They had to report to him about their progress. He knew what they knew. "

"Enough!" Johnny swiveled in his chair to toss the rest of his coffee into the trash can. "Gaylord's and Steve's deaths were accidental. Live with it."

"Then let me see the reports. Maybe there's something there—"

"We missed?" Johnny said. "We didn't. You'll have to do your mercenary gig without those files."

Arn leaned forward. "I was loathe to mention it before, but you're in the running for the permanent police chief job."

"That's no secret."

"And it might make you look ... inept ... if an outsider waltzed in here and solved a crime that your agency's worked on and off for ten years."

Johnny stood. Though thirty pounds lighter than Arn, he was several inches taller, intimidating in his glare as he came around the desk. He stood close enough that Arn smelled his coffee breath and stale cigarette smoke reeking from his blue blazer. "What's your point?"

"I'm not here to make you look bad, Johnny. But ... " Arn shouldered his briefcase. "The mayor *insists* your department cooperate."

Johnny looked down at Arn, inches away. His jaw clenched; his fist balled and slapped his leg. "It's been years since anyone's threatened me without getting an ass beating. Only reason I don't now is because we worked together once. And we were friends. Once. Now get out of my office. Mercenary bastard."

Arn hesitated just long enough to let Johnny know he wasn't intimidated before he started for the door. Then he stopped and without looking back said, "If you won't order your lieutenant to give me their files, the least you can do is point me to someone who may know something."

"No one in this department's going to help—"

"Anyone?"

"Georgia Spangler," Johnny blurted out.

"Butch's sister?"

"Ah, that's right," Johnny prodded. "You two had a thing in high school."

"Until I quit the team to go work cows and she dumped me. I didn't know she still lived here."

"She's a chef at Poor Richard's. You know she was the first one to call Butch's murder into dispatch."

"I didn't realize that."

Johnny smiled. "You would if you actually took the time to read the police reports."

Ten

ARN SAT IN THE Poor Richard's parking lot. He leaned back in his seat and closed his eyes as he thought about what he would say to Georgia. He'd called her when he left Johnny's office and was surprised she remembered him from their brief fling in high school. "I'd be delighted to visit with you," she said. He tried reading her tone of voice, her willingness to talk. But even after a lifetime of reading people for a living, he came up blank with her.

He walked into the restaurant and spotted Georgia. She leaned on a podium as she talked with the hostess. An apron encircled Georgia's waist, as small as Arn remembered from her cheerleading days. Her black hair fell to her collar, and her hazel eyes twinkled through crystal-rimmed glasses. She smiled when she spotted him. She wiped her hands on her apron and smoothed her top. "Arn Anderson. It's been what? Thirty-five years?"

"Thirty-seven." He'd done the math on the way over. "You don't look a whit different from the last time I saw you."

Georgia laughed easily. "You mean that night when we … broke up?"

Arn nodded.

"Well, you've got some bad memory, 'cause I'm not that pretty girl that dragged you into the back seat of that old Mercury of yours."

"I thought I was doing the draggin'," Arn said.

She hooked her arm through his and led him toward the back of the restaurant, past two couples sitting on either side of a half-eaten birthday cake sporting enough candles to start a forest fire. The elderly birthday girl looked up and smiled as they passed. Blue frosting smeared her bright pink lipstick and mixed with her red rouge. The younger man next to her dabbed ice cream off his cardigan sweater before he turned his attention to wiping the old lady's mouth.

Georgia seated Arn at a table in back and promised to return. When she did, she was cradling two plates in the crick of her arm and a carafe of coffee. "People claim I have the best rhubarb pie." Heat from the pie had started melting the vanilla ice cream, a small drop spilling onto the table in what Arn recognized as a low velocity spatter. Just like blood, he thought, and cursed himself for thinking like a detective at a moment like this. He unfolded a green linen napkin and spread it over his lap. "Johnny White said you take offense when folks call you a chef."

"That's right." Georgia frowned. "A little too pretentious for me. Around here, I'm just the cook. And sometimes baker. Dig in. But don't go to sleep."

Arn stopped his fork mid-mouth. "Sleep?"

"Folks say I put so much sugar in my pies that they drift off to sleep." She laid her own napkin over her lap. "I hate wimpy ingredients." She poured each of them a cup of coffee. "I wondered when you'd come around. After Ana Maria Villarreal brought up your name as a consultant that first night on television, I figured you'd stop by and ask me about Butch."

"If this isn't a good time … "

Georgia waved the air. "I've told the story so many times, I can do it in my sleep. The first few times gave me more grief than you can imagine, but I'm all right now."

Arn ate his last bite of pie and spooned up the remaining ice cream until he couldn't put it off any longer. He set his plate aside and grabbed a notebook out of his briefcase when he caught her snicker.

"That's some purse you got there." She smiled. "They issue you that down in Denver?"

"A friend thought I needed to … expand my horizons. Said I'd feel young again. It's a man bag."

"Suit yourself. But here in Wyoming—and you should know—it's still a purse."

Arn flipped to a clean page and leaned back in the booth. "I'll read Butch's incident report tonight, but give me the headline version of what happened the night your brother was murdered."

Georgia took a deep breath to steel herself. She wasn't as numbed to the incidents of that night as she professed. "Pieter called me at 1:30 that morning. Crying. He asked me to come over right away. When I got there, Butch was slumped over in his chair. I learned later he'd been shot twice in the chest."

"I remember when Butch brought Pieter along on patrol when I worked at the PD here. Cute little fella. Where was Butch's wife that night?"

Georgia closed her eyes and rubbed her forehead while Arn waited for her to continue. "Hannah was out partying. Like always. She usually came home long enough to sleep it off and put on fresh clothes before she went out cattin' around again. She was still out bar hopping when I got to the house that night. But then, she had a few more minutes drinking time before they closed." A slight smile tugged at the corners of Georgia's mouth. "The gutter slut died in a car accident the year after Butch was murdered. Guess the booze finally caught up with her." She held up her hand. "Sorry if I don't sound too upset by Hannah's death."

Arn said nothing and flipped pages in his notebook. "Johnny said a Detective Madden assumed Butch's murder investigation."

"Bobby Madden." She nodded. "But don't expect to interview him unless you got a clairvoyant on retainer. Detective Madden died in a retirement home in Aurora four or five years ago. I remember he was a good detective. Thorough. He interviewed me multiple times." She looked away and took off her glasses, which had started to fog. She dabbed at her eyes with her napkin.

"We can do this another time."

"I'm fine. It's just that Madden interviewed Pieter a half-dozen times, too, like he was a suspect. A boy who just lost his father."

"Standard procedure with homicides: look first at the family and work out," Arn explained. "Most times, the killer will be close to the victim. But to bring Pieter in that many times does seen excessive. Unless . . ."

"Unless Madden had something? All he had was rumors around the police station that Butch abused his son."

"Did he?"

Georgia stirred cream into her coffee while she thought. "Not physically. He wouldn't want anyone to think Butch Spangler abused his own kid." She leaned closer and her hand brushed Arn's. "Don't get me wrong—I loved my brother. But he was terribly vain. He abused Pieter emotionally. I don't think he even realized that he did."

Arn refilled their cups and jotted in his notebook. "How so?"

Georgia motioned to Arn's face. "Because Pieter looks more like you: blue eyes, blond hair. Tall. Unlike the Spanglers, with our black hair and dark eyes and stubby short legs. Butch told Pieter he must have been someone else's son."

"Then you can see why Madden naturally thought Pieter resented his dad. Maybe even hated him."

"I can." Georgia wrapped her hands around her coffee cup and sipped slowly. "But Pieter put Butch on a pedestal. He was proud his father was the department's top detective. And when Butch started dragging Pieter along to work—"

"Because Hannah was rarely there to watch him?"

"Because she was *never* there for him. It doesn't mean it was right for Pieter to see what he did when Butch drug him to those crime scenes. You ask me, that's abuse. But under the circumstances, what could Butch do?" Georgia looked askance at the birthday girl as the young couple helped her into her wheelchair. "Detectives got called out at the drop of a hat back then. When I wasn't working, I'd come over and watch Pieter until Butch came home. But just as often I was at work and couldn't get away."

"You both must have been eliminated as suspects fairly quickly."

Georgia frowned. "We should have been that night. The crime scene tech who worked with Madden ran some chemical over our hands."

"GSR test: gun shot residue. Standard procedure to eliminate people as shooting suspects. Or confirm them as the shooter. I'd guess the tech bagged Butch's hands?"

"They taped paper bags over his wrists."

"In case Butch got off any shots of his own," Arn explained.

"His service gun still hung over a chair in the kitchen." Georgia gripped Arn's forearm tightly. "Now *you're* not thinking Pieter could have killed his dad?"

"I'm not thinking anything. But I'd like to talk with Pieter too, if he still lives close."

Georgia sat back and smiled wide. "He's one of Cheyenne's top architects." She grabbed his notebook and jotted an address down. "I'll tell him you'll stop by." She handed the pen back. "Now, when do you want to go to dinner someplace besides where I work?" Her hand shot to her mouth. "I'm sorry. I assume you're not married."

Arn automatically rubbed his naked ring finger. "Not to worry. Cailee's been gone for fifteen years now. Breast cancer." He couldn't believe himself, opening up to this woman he'd only dated for a month back in high school. "And you?"

"Always the bridesmaid, never the bride. So are we on one of these nights?"

Arn's neck warmed, and he hoped the lights were dim enough to hide his blush. "You've got a date. Just as soon as I'm settled in."

He quickly stuffed his notebook into his briefcase and started for the exit and then noticed the restaurant had filled with noon patrons. And he hadn't even been aware of it. Had he lost his edge? Is that what had happened to Butch: Had he become complacent and let someone walk in on his space? Because if he was letting his guard down, this was no time for it. Not if plastic badges kept popping up on his car seat.

Eleven

"**HAND ME THAT FRAMING** hammer," Arn said.

Ana Maria tucked her notebook under her arm and grabbed the hammer hooked on a nail jutting out of the bare wall.

"Did you do what I told you on the phone last night?" Arn asked.

"I doubled checked the doors and windows before I went to sleep," she answered. "And this morning, I got up in a pissy mood. That guy I was supposed to meet out at the fairgrounds never called back. Now I might never know who killed Butch."

"Well, if he does call, I don't want you to meet him alone again. You understand?"

"I'm doing an investigative story. If that's the only way he'll talk— with no witnesses—I'll have to."

Arn swung the hammer, missed, and hit his thumb. He dropped the hammer and cursed under his breath as he shook life into his digit. "Just what I need, another damned appendage bruised."

"Maybe this will take your mind off your owie." Ana Maria sat on a metal folding chair and opened her notebook on an overturned drywall bucket. "I asked around the police department—"

"Someone there actually talked to you?" Arn didn't hide his amazement. He'd tried talking with other officers but got the same cold treatment Johnny and Oblanski had given him.

Ana Maria winked. "A couple of good-looking officers who worked there during the time of all three officers' deaths talked with me."

"What did they say about Butch?"

"That he was an overbearing jerk. But he was their sharpest detective in investigations back then. They were both amazed at the time that Butch hadn't been able to solve the Five Point cases."

"How about Gaylord and Steve?"

"They said the same thing about Gaylord. That he was a little prick."

"Prick could be good in the police business." Arn stuck his thumb in his mouth. It didn't help the throbbing or his thumb turning black.

"When you were in football, did you ever have a manager who was some little geek everyone hated?"

"Darrin Mays," Arn said immediately. "Little peckerwood wasn't tough enough to play, so he made our lives miserable. Switching play books. Writing us up late for practice when we weren't. Just a little piss ant."

"That's just how these two cops described Gaylord: a 'piss ant.' They said if his wife hadn't been Steve DeBoer's sister, Gaylord would never have gone back to investigations. They weren't surprised when he accidentally hung himself."

"You mean, if he hadn't died spanking his monkey while hanging from the rafters in his basement," Danny chimed in. He dragged a sheet of plywood across the floor of the kitchen and propped it against a wall.

"Where did you hear that?" Arn asked. "It's supposed to be confidential."

Danny's thin shoulders bounced under his bib overalls as he chuckled. "Nothing's confidential if you know who to talk to. I lived here back then. And I listened to talk on the street. About the fourth or fifth rumor I heard that Detective Fournier died buffing his banana, I started believing it."

Arn turned his back on Danny and leaned closer to Ana Maria. "Those officers you talked with get any vibes, any rumors that Gaylord's death was connected to Butch's murder? Or Steve DeBoer's for that matter?"

Ana Maria grabbed a cigarette out of her purse. She fumbled around for her lighter when she caught Arn's scowl and put it back in the pack. "They thought it odd that Butch's supervisor died in a fire, and a month later his partner hung himself. Butch suspected something wasn't right with those accidents. They were certain of that."

"Maybe Butch killed them," Danny said, coming back into the kitchen.

"Don't you have home remodeling to do?"

"I would if someone helped me." Danny fished a snipe out of his pocket, along with a wooden match. He sat and struck the match to the butt just as he caught Arn's look of disapproval and snuffed it out. "Can't even smoke in my own home."

"Danny—"

"I know," Danny said, grabbing the wall to help him stand. "Get to work and earn my keep."

"Why don't you go out and start the generator. It's cold in here."

Ana Maria waited until Danny had walked out of the room before she asked, "Who's the old dude you adopted?"

"Danny."

"Danny who?"

"Danny LNU," Arn answered. "'Last Name Unknown,' as we used to write on arrest sheets when we didn't know someone's name."

"Are you saying the law wants him?"

Arn shrugged. "All I know is *I* want him. The man looks like he'll keel over with a big heart attack any moment. But he works me into the ground, and he knows near everything about home construction."

"Then why isn't he out making good money?"

"Probably just doesn't want to be found."

The generator kicked in. The bare bulb overhead flickered to life, and the two space heaters started to spew heat.

"Couldn't you just call Cheyenne Light, Fuel & Power and get electricity turned on?" Ana Maria asked.

"They'd need to inspect the house first. And as long as this place has been left abandoned, with the squirrels chewing the hell out of the wiring, it's a mess. Until Danny rewires the place so I can get an inspector over here, the generator will have to do."

Danny came back into the house and headed for the front room with a bag of drywall screws under his arm. Ana Maria leaned closer. "Do you plan to move in here? To this—" She waved her arms around the room.

"Until Danny gets it renovated, I can't afford to live in a motel and at the same time shell out money for this … dump. So I *have* to move in here. Just to save a few lucky bucks. And speaking of which, if I don't get busy and work on Butch's case, I won't even have any money for another space heater." Arn slapped his hands against his thighs to restore circulation as he paced the room. "Butch and Gaylord and Steve all worked on the Five Point cases during that time. That's got to be the connection."

"Not that again. The Five Point cases were isolated." She held up her hands. "I know what I said about them all being connected somehow. Two men murdered the same year. The same way. And none after the last victim. But that was just for television. The cops I talked with think whoever the killer was, he moved on after that second victim."

"Then how do you explain that plastic badge in my car?"

"So someone tossed in a cheap kid's badge," Ana Maria argued, sounding a lot like Johnny White. "It doesn't mean the killer has returned."

"Maybe he never left."

"Maybe it's not a 'he.'" Ana Maria grinned. "Wouldn't that boost ratings?"

"Hey boss," Danny called from the bay window by the front door. He was looking out the one dirty pane of glass that remained. "You got company."

Arn and Ana Maria joined him at the window. A white Audi had pulled to the curb behind Arn's Oldsmobile. A man Arn's height, but lean, lithe, and athletic, stepped from the Audi and hopped over a snowdrift. A turquoise hair tie held his blond ponytail, which ended right at the top of his ski sweater. He stood with his hands on his hips as he looked at the sagging second story, working his way down to where Arn and Danny had shored up the porch with landscape timbers.

"Stay here," Arn told Ana Maria. "Danny and I will go out and ..." But Danny had already disappeared out the back door.

"Hello, the house," the man called out in a baritone voice that sounded as if he should be practicing for Christmas caroling next month. He stepped gingerly onto the rickety porch and stood by the door.

Arn slid his hammer from his tool belt and concealed it beside his leg. He opened the new solid oak door Danny had hung, and it swung open as smoothly as a bank vault. "What can I do for you?"

The man's pale blue eyes held Arn's for the briefest time before he worked his way from Arn's scuffed work boots to his Carhartt jacket with the one sleeve torn from an exposed staircase nail. "You look just as I remembered."

"You're the second person to tell me that. Explain."

"When you worked here at the police department, Dad brought me to work. You were a shift sergeant then, I believe." He held out his hand. "Pieter Spangler."

Arn fumbled to slip the hammer back into his tool belt. He wiped his hand on his trouser leg and shook hands. Pieter's grip was surprisingly robust for someone fifty pounds lighter.

Pieter peeked around the door to look inside. "I tried to buy this place a few years ago. All the windows were broken and the door was down, so I came in and looked it over. I figured I could pick it up for a song. But the assessor said the owner kept the taxes current and wouldn't give me any other info. 'The owner wishes to remain anonymous.'" He backed away from the door. "So, you're Mr. Anonymous?"

"I am." Arn shook his head and caught himself staring. "And you're Butch's little boy. You were so—"

"Cute? Another way of saying 'effeminate.' Until halfway through high school, that is." Pieter leaned closer. "Do you know how embarrassing it is when you're fifteen and your aunt pinches your cheek and brags what a darling you are?"

Arn tilted his head back and laughed. His own mother's sisters did just that. "Oh yeah, how I lived for the day my voice finally changed."

Pieter raised his hand in a high five, and they slapped palms. "To all us guys who were once cuties," Pieter said.

His smile faded and he became solemn. "Aunt Georgia said you wanted to talk with me. I thought I'd save you a trip to my office." He tapped the side of the porch. "Cool old place."

"You like old houses?"

"I buy historic old homes. And now and again I even restore one. This was one of the last of the carriage houses in Cheyenne." He stepped to the far end of the porch and looked up at the high drive-through where people used to pull their wagon in to unload supplies.

"Great Grandfather built it when Cheyenne was little more than an end-of-the-line railroad town," Arn explained. "Passed down through the family. I was the only one left alive who wanted it."

"Well, you've got a good start on restoring it."

Arn wanted to tell Pieter that Danny Last Name Unknown was the craftsman behind the new drywall, the demolition of half the house that had rotted through the years, and the plumbing he planned to replace later in the week. But if Danny was that paranoid, Arn wouldn't spoil it by telling on him.

"Aunt Georgia said you had some questions about Dad."

"If it wouldn't be too painful."

Pieter shook his head. "I've told it so many times."

"Come inside. I got two folding chairs that ... a friend acquired someplace."

They stepped inside and their breath frosted, the space heaters failing to reach this far. Arn led Pieter through the house to the kitchen, where Ana Maria leaned against the counter. She stood close to a space heater, and her hand was wrapped around a mug of hot coffee.

Pieter smiled and his eyes locked onto Ana Maria's. "You're the TV lady who's doing the special on Dad's murder."

"I am. Did you watch the first two installments?"

Pieter's mouth down turned. "I couldn't. No offense. Maybe it was linking Dad's death to Gaylord's and Steve's that put me off."

Ana Maria poured Pieter a cup of coffee and nodded to a metal chair beside where Arn sat. "You don't think they're related?"

Pieter sipped his coffee. Arn thought he hadn't heard Ana Maria, it took him so long to answer. "When Steve died in that fire," he said at last, "Dad was senior investigator, and he assigned himself Steve's investigation. Same with Gaylord. All I know is Dad would have told me if he thought there was anything unnatural in the way they died. And believe me, he looked for it. Obsessively."

Ana Maria handed Pieter a mug of coffee. "I just hope my special will jog someone's memory about your dad's murder."

Pieter forced a smile. "I still think about him every day."

"Must have been hard."

"Hard?"

"Being with your father every day. Going to some of those crime scenes he investigated," Ana Maria said.

"I coped." Pieter finished his coffee. He handed Ana Maria the empty mug. His hand brushed hers and lingered there for several moments. "Are you married, Ms. Villarreal?"

"To my job."

"Bummer."

Pieter leaned on the piece of plywood that spanned two saw horses and functioned as a countertop. "By now I assume you've read the police reports on Dad's death. The autopsy report. The follow-up interviews with a hundred people who wanted him dead."

"I started reading them last night," Arn said.

"And you thought I might have some hidden tidbit of knowledge I might have forgotten that you'll be able to bring out?"

"Something like that."

"'Better to get it straight from the horse's ass,' was Dad's way of saying people don't realize they have some knowledge until asked in the right way."

Arn's eyebrows rose.

Pieter smiled. "It was something Dad thought he could do, too."

Arn took off his ball cap and ran his hand through his sweaty hair. "I've interviewed witnesses years later who didn't realize that the car they saw the night of the murder, or the phone call they got, or the kid walking his dog was significant. Until I walked them through it."

Pieter smoothed his slacks and tugged the cuffs over his wingtips, old and worn on the outside but polished. "Dad had that quality, too. Something good investigators develop, I suppose."

Some men were just born with that ability, Arn thought: the ability that put them at the top of the food chain. By all accounts, Butch had been top dog in his world, just as Arn had been in his when he was in Metro Homicide, innately sensing weaknesses in others that told him when to pounce. And if Butch was anything like Arn, he'd developed the same instinct to bring that information to the surface. Sometimes to be used against them.

Pieter stood. "May I have a refill?"

Ana Maria poured from the percolator, and Pieter's hand brushed hers again. He smiled as he sat back down. "I was on Christmas break from school, and Brothers Medical Supply had given me more deliveries. Between that and getting ready for basketball practice that month, I was plumb worn out and hit the hay early. So when I heard arguing downstairs, I wasn't sure how long it had been going on. Then I heard a shot." He looked away. "I later learned it was two shots to Dad's chest."

"If you don't expect them, two or three shots can sound like one." Arn had responded to a robbery in progress in Denver's East Colfax area one night for what they called a stop and rob: quick in at a convenience store, intimidate the clerk, and quick out with all the cash. Usually took only minutes. Sometimes it went sour. Like that night. When Arn had stepped from his unmarked car that evening, he swore he heard only one shot. But the shooter had gotten off three, she shot so fast before she burst from the store directly toward Arn. Scratch one robber, and the crime scene techs had to pry her gun from her cold, dead fingers still curled around the grips.

"I came down the stairs and there was Dad," Pieter continued, looking at the tip of his shoes, "sitting where he always did in front of the TV. Pants undone like he always did right when he got off work." Pieter swirled the coffee around in his cup. "Did I mention how vain my dad was? Kept his pants too tight because he thought it made him look thinner? He was having a hard time growing older."

"Lot of guys getting on in age have a hard time," Ana Maria said, a twinkle in her eye. "Some guys buy sports cars. New clothes out of their generation. Some even buy goofy purses and pass them off as man bags." She winked at Arn.

"That was Dad. Living a midlife crisis in his own way." Pieter pinched his nose between his fingers and closed his eyes. "I've thought of that night a hundred times. That if I'd have come down the stairs a few moments sooner, I might have scared the killer off. Or he would have drilled *me*." He opened his eyes and leaned closer. "Aunt Georgia says sometimes God spares us for something better. What do you think, Mr. Anderson?"

"I've known people who—for no logical reason—lived through some terrible trauma. It's how we handle it once we're spared that molds us. And your aunt says you've made the most of your life since then."

"I've tried, Mr. Anderson." Pieter stood and walked around the room. He looked up at exposed roughhewn timbers most old Western houses were built with. He ran his hand over a rafter and it caught on a splinter. He jerked his hand away and stuck his finger between his teeth to pull the sliver out. "I called Aunt Georgia right away that night. I knew Dad was dead—Lord knows he took me to enough crime scenes. I could spot a dead person a block away."

"Why didn't you call 911?" Ana Maria asked. She sat on the chair beside Arn, the two huddled together around the space heater looking like they were watching some Grade B movie.

"Dad had serious words with other cops over the years, so I didn't trust them. I just didn't know who else to call except Aunt Georgia."

Ana Maria flipped through her notes. "The police report said she called 911 at 1:45 a.m."

Pieter nodded. "She lived fifteen minutes across town. When I got down to Dad that night, I recall that the big Felix the Cat clock's tail ticked off 1:30." He pulled his trouser cuffs over his wingtips. "Are you going to find Dad's killer?"

"When I worked Metro," Arn said, "I solved every homicide assigned me."

Pieter took a deep breath. "All right, then. What else can I tell you? After the police left that night, I went with Aunt Georgia, and I didn't leave her house until I went off to college."

"Where was Hannah all that time?"

"Where Mom always was—getting hammered in a bar and getting laid … " He turned to Ana Maria. "No offense."

She waved it away, and Pieter continued.

"Mom came home while the police were conducting their investigation. Aunt Georgia told her she was taking me to her place for the night. Mom never objected. Never came around to bring me home the next day. Or any day. She just didn't care. And when I went to her funeral the following year, I couldn't even bring myself to show any grief. That's cold, I know."

Pieter stood and walked the room. He eyed the old rafters exposed after Danny tore plaster down, old wiring frayed from age and rats, the old hardwood floor made squishy from moisture. He turned to

Ana Maria. "Do you really think your TV special will yield any new evidence?"

"I'm optimistic. Already we've gotten calls in on the tip line," she said. Then: "Who do you think killed your dad?"

"Frank Dull Knife," Pieter answered immediately. "I've always thought that. It was just too convenient, him having an affair with Mom, and his court hearing scheduled the week after Dad was murdered, with Dad the only witness."

Arn thought so too. In Butch's file were the interviews Billy Madden and Ned Oblanski conducted on Frank. Along with Frank's rap sheet: two stints in the Wyoming state penitentiary in Rawlins, a dozen local lockups around the country for petty crimes. Frank had been around the horn. He would have known the police would zero in on him for Butch's murder, and he would have had his lies together.

"You ever run into Frank?" Arn asked.

Pieter smiled wickedly. "In Kmart once. He saw me two aisles down and promptly beat feet the other way. I slinked around and came face-to-ugly-face with him. I didn't say a thing to him. Didn't need to. The look of terror that crossed his face was priceless." Pieter hit an exposed rafter. Blood trickled from a lacerated knuckle, but he paid it no mind. "I thought many times about hunting him up. Making him pay for killing Dad. But as satisfying as it would be, it would only hurt Aunt Georgia if I was in prison. No, someday he'll be linked to it." He smiled at Ana Maria. "Maybe this TV special of yours will be his downfall."

"Johnny White thinks the Five Point Killer murdered Butch," Arn said.

Pieter's jaw muscles worked overtime, and his teeth clenched. "All Dad ever talked about was those cases. He was obsessed with them. 'I'm so close I can smell him,' Dad told me before he died. 'All I got to do is match some pieces of the puzzle.' But we know he didn't have time to match anything."

"It's the only case that linked all three officers," Arn said.

Pieter leaned back against the wall and crossed his arms. "I hung with Steve and Gaylord later on, when Dad was working and I got old enough to care for myself. They talked about the Five Point cases now and again, but not to the extent Dad did." Pieter looked to the ceiling. "God, I wish I hadn't."

"Hadn't what?"

"Hung with Steve and Gaylord. I got to be the ultimate jinx. First Steve passed out with a cigarette and died—"

"Fire marshal's report ruled it accidental," Arn said. "So did Butch's incident report."

Pieter looked away, and Arn thought he saw a tear form at the corner of his eye. "Steve was like an uncle to me. Good man." He wiped his face with the back of his hand. "And Gaylord was like a crazy older brother."

"One that trusses himself up and whips his willy to a porn mag," Ana Maria added.

Arn and Pieter looked in amazement at Ana Maria.

"No offense." She smiled.

"Gaylord's death wasn't your fault either," Arn said.

"I told myself that." Pieter stood and brushed drywall dust off his trousers. "Thanks for listening to my ranting, Mr. Anderson. And Ms. Villarreal." He smiled at her. "If you think you need a man's perspective for your story, drop by my office. Or over dinner."

Pieter started for the entryway. He passed the front room and the staircase that led to the second floor. As he grabbed the stair railing, it pulled away from the wall.

"I've got to fix that," Arn said.

Pieter looked around. "Among other things."

Arn held the door for him. Pieter paused on the porch to wrap a scarf around his neck. "And if you need any help making your way through the maze of municipal codes on your remodel, feel free to ask." He slapped the side of the house and grinned. "Someday I'll have time to restore my old houses. But for now, I'll have to admire those who do."

Ana Maria and Arn waited until Pieter had pulled away from the curb before going back inside. "Something's bothering you," Ana Maria said.

"Does it show?"

"You didn't take a solitary note all the time talking with Pieter."

"I wanted to … observe, as we talked," Arn said.

"And what did you observe?"

"What did you observe?" Arn asked.

Ana Maria led him into the kitchen and poured more coffee. "He hit on me."

"Is that surprising? Men often hit on you."

"Besides me being just a little old for him, he had a promise ring on one finger."

"Guess I missed that," Arn said. "But then, I have no idea what a promise ring is."

"He's spoken for."

"Ah. And nothing else?"

Ana Maria laid a piece of cardboard on the cold metal folding chair before she sat. "What *are* you getting at?"

"Frank. Pieter's not as convinced Frank killed Butch as he lets on. If the prime suspect in your father's death lived in your town, how long would it be before you found a way to, say, kill him in a staged self-defense?"

73

"About a week…"

Arn sipped his coffee, oblivious to Ana Maria. "What did you say?"

"I said, there's something else, isn't there?"

Arn studied the hot steam rising from his coffee cup. "How did you know where my mother's house was located?"

"How? That's a silly question. You gave me the address yesterday when you said to meet you here."

"But I didn't tell Pieter. Or Georgia."

"Why's that so important?"

"By Pieter's own statement, he'd asked the assessor's office about the place, but they wouldn't tell him anything," Arn said. "A search of county land records would also show the owner of this place as anonymous."

"So?

"So how did he find out where I'd be?"

Twelve

WHEN NED OBLANSKI WASN'T in his office the following morning like he promised, Michelle smiled knowingly. And lied like a good secretary does to protect her boss. "Lieutenant Oblanski unexpectedly had to go out to the shooting range for qualification." She began writing directions on a notepad when Arn stopped her.

"I know the area well." As a youngster, he'd hired out to the Rocking W spread just west of where the police shooting range now stood. His horse had thrown him in a rattler-infested pasture at the ranch, breaking his ankle and sidelining him for the summer. "I think I can find it."

He drove west of town on Happy Jack, past the windmills with their slowly turning blades, and finally spotted the black range flag at the entrance to the police range. Past the gate, he followed a dirt road another quarter mile before crossing the security fence.

As he drove by the long-range benches, an officer touched off his sniper rifle and Arn jumped. He stopped his car and hastily wadded up a Burger King napkin from his glove box. He stuffed it in his ears before continuing to the pistol deck.

He parked at the classroom beside two unmarked police cars. Oblanski faced a row of turning targets on the firing line, while another officer stood beside him holding a stop watch. When the targets turned, Oblanski pulled his coat back with one hand and drew his gun with the other, the whole effect efficient. Smooth. His two shots sounded as one, and he holstered just as smoothly. Oblanski did this twice more, each time quicker than the last. Arn counted to himself: on his best day as a young officer, he was never as good as Oblanski. But then, he reasoned, he'd always made up for it by his superior tactics. Like any good hunter.

Oblanski waited until the range officer marked his score on a clipboard before squaring up to the targets once more. This time when the range officer called out, Oblanski dropped to one knee and drew a gun from an ankle holster. He fired nearly as fast as with his duty gun. Quicker from an ankle rig than Arn had been from a belt holster when he worked the street.

Holstering his ankle gun, Oblanski spotted Arn leaning against the classroom building. He dipped his head to the range officer and whispered. The range officer took off his ear muffs and headed for a thermos bottle that sat atop a shooting bench at the fifty yard line.

Oblanski thumbed cartridges into a magazine as he walked toward Arn. "What do you need this time?"

"We had an appointment."

"Gosh. I guess I forgot." Oblanski grinned. "I must be losing my mind."

"Or getting sloppy." Arn motioned to Oblanski's trouser leg riding over his ankle holster. He bent and pulled his pant leg over his gun. "I need those files on Gaylord Fournier and Steve DeBoer."

Oblanski ignored him and nodded to a uniformed officer who climbed out of his car. "If you want to throw a few rounds, the range officer, Greg Smith, will let you—"

"Those files?"

Oblanski walked to a shooting bench and brushed snow off the seat before he sat. He grabbed a range bag and took out cleaning gear. "Chief White was gracious enough to give you Butch Spangler's file." He threaded a bore brush into the end of an aluminum rod. "The chief and I feel that the DeBoer and Fournier cases are so unrelated to Butch Spangler's murder as to be of no use," he said as he field-stripped his duty gun. "I'd hate to have the surviving families harmed by your ... meddling."

"But it's all right for me to look at Frank Dull Knife's file because you think he killed Butch?"

"I'm not alone in that opinion."

"You're just pissed 'cause Frank didn't roll over when you interviewed him."

Oblanski seemed not to hear him as he separated the slide and barrel of the Glock .40. He dipped a copper brush into Hoppe's cleaning solution and ran it down the barrel. "Bobby Madden sent me to Frank's mechanic shop the morning Butch was killed." Oblanski held the barrel to the light. "Hannah came home while Bobby and the crime tech were working the scene. She'd been out drinking with Frank that night, but he left a couple hours before the bars closed."

"I read in one of the reports that Hannah was dancing with some other guy who was never identified," Arn said.

"Bobby interviewed Hannah, but she didn't give a name. We turned the town upside down, but we never ID'd the guy. But it sure as hell wasn't Frank Dull Knife."

"So you talked with him at his shop that morning?"

"More like noon when he finally showed up." Oblanski dribbled a spot of oil on the slide rails before he put the gun back together. "When he finally dragged into his shop it was around midday. Said he was out test-driving a car."

"But you didn't believe him?"

"Not then, and especially when the car owner filed a complaint against Frank later." Oblanski grabbed his ankle gun and field-stripped it. "She said when she got her car back from his shop it had a hundred miles on it. That's some test drive, and I called Frank on it but he wouldn't come off his story."

"I read where Bobby Madden interviewed Frank later that day as well."

"Bobby screamed 'dumb-ass Polack' at me when I came back empty. 'I'll squeeze the information out of Frank myself.'" Oblanski laughed and ran a Q-tip down the magazine well. "Bobby's interview lasted exactly eight minutes before Frank lawyered up. Now why would a man just out for a hundred-mile test drive need a lawyer?"

"You must have talked with Pieter Spangler. He thinks Frank is good for Butch's murder too. But the Five Point Killer is at the top of Johnny White's suspect list."

Oblanski snapped the gun back together and leaned over the bench. "You want to be of some use, pin Butch's murder on Frank and forget the Five Point cases. That'll just muddy the waters. You prove Frank killed Butch. That is, if you actually want to do something besides cash an easy paycheck from the television station."

Arn picked up Oblanski's backup gun, a Colt Mustang .380, lighter and flatter than any backup gun Arn had carried when he worked the street. "The murder weapon was never found."

"We pulled a search warrant on Frank's place but came up empty," Oblanski said. "We figured he drove someplace to ditch the gun."

"Might account for those hundred miles on that lady's car."

"That's what we felt at the time. Especially since he refused to say where he drove to."

Arn nodded at Oblanski's trouser cuff that had ridden back over the empty holster. "Everyone here carry Colts for backups?"

"No," Oblanski answered. "Officers carry whatever they can qual with. Never used to be that way."

"We used to be closed-mouthed about backup guns," Arn said. "In case the administration here found out about what we carried."

"Same now." Oblanski laughed. "Now look at me: I *am* the administration."

When Arn worked in Denver, most officers carried backup guns. Each weapon was put through a ballistic print; in case multiple guns were used in shootings, the coroner could determine which gun killed the suspect. "Where does Frank live?"

Oblanski zipped his range bag up. "He still lives by the oil refinery, in a one-room affair in back of that greasy, noisy, ratty, smelly old Quonset he calls a repair shop."

Arn started for his car and then paused. "I'll have to go over your head to get those case files on Gaylord and Steve."

"Like how?"

"The mayor promised the TV station full cooperation. If you and Johnny refuse to hand them over ... well, you understand, I got no choice."

Spittle flew from Oblanski's mouth. "There's no connection—"

"I'll be the judge of that. After I read them."

Oblanski's fist slapped his leg, and his jaw clenched as he stopped inches away from Arn. "Don't screw with me, Anderson. Drop it."

"Or you're going to use that little backup gun on me and toss it away?"

Oblanski slung his range bag over his shoulder and stomped toward his car. Arn called after him, "We're not done yet."

Oblanski stopped and waited for Arn to catch up. "Now what the hell you want?"

"Ana Maria Villarreal. I want you to assign a marked unit to check on her at night. With this special she's airing, I'm afraid for her."

"Is it because of the phantom man you chased the other night? Chief White told me about that cockamamie story of yours."

"I did chase after someone. Or rather hobble after someone. At least check on Doc Henry's status."

"That's right. The guy you suspect has been calling Ana Maria."

Arn walked around and faced Oblanski. "Doc Henry stalked and raped three women in Denver thirteen years ago. Raped and killed as many as four others, though we never found the bodies. Ana Maria's coverage helped catch him. But not before he raped her, and nearly killed her before I found the two in a park in Lakewood."

"And now you think this Doc Henry's hunting her?"

"I can't say. He was paroled from Four Mile in Colorado last year. Humor me, and just verify he's current with his parole officer and still in Colorado."

Oblanski jotted the information down. "That I can do. And I'll assign an officer to babysit her. If she needs it."

"She won't know she needs it until something happens."

Oblanski shrugged. "I'm in a reactive profession. So sue me."

"I will, if anything happens to Ana Maria."

Thirteen

ON HIS WAY TO Frank Dull Knife's shop, Arn passed Poor Richard's and pulled into the parking lot. The afternoon crowd was gone, and the parking lot deserted as if catching its breath before the rush of dinner patrons who would arrive in a few hours. Arn breathed deeply a final time before he entered the restaurant. He felt more like a high schooler sniffing around the class queen than a widowed over-the-hill ex-cop.

He stepped through the door and let his eyes adjust to the dim light. He spotted Georgia reading the morning copy of the *Wyoming Tribune Eagle*, and he watched the way her lips moved silently as she read, the way she took off her glasses now and again to study a picture. She looked up and saw Arn by the front door and waved him over.

"I thought someone was watching me." She smiled and patted the booth beside her. "Like those Nat Geo documentaries, where the wildebeest sense that lions watch them and bound away just before they're pounced on. You going to pounce on me, Arn?"

He'd kicked that very thought around many times, and he quickly changed the subject. "I used to deliver this before they merged when I was a kid." He tapped the newspaper.

"*Eagle* or *Tribune?*"

Arn groaned. "*Eagle*. I had to get up at o-dark-thirty before school. Dad would have killed me if I missed junior football just to deliver the paper."

"How can I forget, you in your red-and-black Indians uniform that always seemed a size too small."

"I think the coach purposely issued uniforms smaller to make us look more buff." Arn laughed and fidgeted in his seat. "But all it managed to do was give us snuggies."

Georgia laughed as she folded the newspaper and set it aside. "Like my Aunt Bethany, who was ten years older and more like a big sister. She convinced me that if I wore a training bra a size too big and stuffed it with tissue it would make me appear more … mature."

"Did she ever answer that old question: why is 'panties' plural and 'bra' singular?"

"You are a romantic."

Arn blushed, and Georgia let him off the hook. "But you didn't come here to talk about panties and bras."

"I'm here strictly on business."

"Liar." She grinned. "But I'll let you tell me what your business is."

Arn opened his bag and Georgia smiled. "You always cart around that purse?"

"Man bag. And it was a gift," Arn lied. He took out his notes and set them on the table. "I'm headed over to talk with Frank Dull Knife."

"You talked with Pieter."

"He stopped by Mom's old house yesterday. I moved back in. At least, I'm renovating it while I hang my Stetson there."

"I think Pieter has as big an obsession with Frank as he does with old houses. But Frank won't tell you anything. He's never confessed yet."

"I've got to try." The waitress brought coffee and Arn waited until she was out of earshot. "Tell me what you know about Frank."

Georgia sipped her coffee and studied the ceiling. "Butch told me most of what I know about Frank and Hannah. They had an affair for a couple months before Butch died. It just happened to be Frank's turn at her. Before him, it was someone else, and before him, someone else…you get the picture. She made it a career to sleep with everyone except my brother." She refilled their cups, and her hand shook as she continued. "Their problems began right after Pieter was born. Hannah saw her life drifting by on the cloud of cleaning and cooking and taking care of a kid she never wanted. And putting up with Butch."

"Sounds like Butch is the one who put up with a lot."

The coffee fogged Georgia's glasses and she took them off. "I loved my brother, but he was no saint. Typical Type A personality. Demanding. Perfectionist. Vain as hell. And if anything upset that in his home, Butch could get…pushy."

"With Hannah?"

"They argued. Good Lord, they argued. Yelling matches so loud, that old busybody next door—what was her name?"

"Police report says Emma Barnes."

"Yes, her. She'd call the police at the slightest hint of an argument between them." Georgia wrapped her hands around her mug and stared into the cup. "But Butch never would have hit Hannah. He was too concerned what others would think if he had. And he wouldn't have been *physically* abusive to Pieter, either—might have showed marks. But it didn't mean he didn't abuse him up here, of course." She tapped her head. "Never a day went by that Butch didn't tell that boy how worthless he was. Or how he was someone else's kid. Or how he'd never amount to anything." She frowned and her voice became louder. "And dragging Pieter along to work. That was abuse enough, don't you think, in Butch's warped way? He thought he'd get Pieter interested in going into law enforcement when he got older. That if he tagged along to often-gruesome scenes it would peak his interest."

Arn thought it was abusive as well. He recalled a serial killer a decade ago who'd worked his way across the country. He'd begun killing in Arkansas and made his way west, killing farm couples in four states. He slipped up when he deviated from his MO and killed a single woman in downtown Denver, all the while dragging his preteen daughter along when he raped and murdered his victims. By the time Arn retired from Metro, the girl was still in residential treatment for the trauma she'd witnessed. He couldn't imagine dragging your son along to work. But smaller agencies, he knew, bent over backward to accommodate their officers. "It must have been hard for Pieter."

"It was," Georgia said, "until he was old enough to escape."

"He run away?"

Georgia shook her head. "Not that kind of escape. When Pieter got old enough, he went out for every sport he could. The more time he spent in school activities, the less he had to be around his dad. Pieter loved Butch, but he had to get away when he could."

Arn filled their cups again and grabbed the sugar. He quickly swapped it for Sweet'N Low packs. "Why didn't Hannah just file for divorce?"

"And lose her meal ticket?" Georgia laughed. "She knew Butch was too worried what others would say to divorce her. She had it made."

Arn sipped his coffee and thought what might not be covered in the police reports he'd read. "Did Butch talk about the Five Point cases to you?"

"Incessantly. He bragged he was so close to catching him, he could smell him. He even suspected Frank. I could see why Ned Oblanski thought Frank killed Butch."

"But why would he have opened the door for Frank that night?" Arn asked.

Georgia stopped her coffee cup mid-mouth. "Who says he did?"

"Johnny White said Butch was paranoid. That he was worried about bad guys he'd put away hunting him down."

"He was always worried that one of those nasty bastards would find him with his guard down," Georgia said.

Arn knew how Butch would have lived. He had lived in that world for thirty years: Looking through the peephole before he opened the door. Glancing in the back seat of his car before he climbed in. Checking the rearview mirror more than he should have. Arn knew the hunter could easily become the hunted if caution was thrown out. So he couldn't see Butch answering the door for Frank Dull Knife.

"Butch would have had to let his killer in," he said.

"How so?"

"The front door." Arn shuffled through papers before he found Pieter's statement. "Pieter told the investigators that his dad always—and he emphasized *always*—locked the door when he came home from work." He fingered the papers until he found the call log from that night. "Butch called out at home on the radio at 10:40 p.m. Between then and when Pieter called you at 1:30, Butch let his killer inside the house."

Georgia's eyes widened. "Pieter had to let me in when I came over. The front door had one of those spring-loaded locks that a person could lock back. But Butch never did. But ... someone inside could have tripped the lock and gone out the front, and it could have looked like Butch had locked it like he always did."

"That makes it easy. All I got to do is find out who Butch let in that night."

Arn gathered his notes together and stuffed them in his briefcase when Georgia stopped him. "Thought anymore about that dinner date?"

"Every minute, it seems."

"Then when…"

Arn rested his hand on Georgia's forearm and squeezed gently. "Cailee's been dead fifteen years, and I've never been able to…get close to anyone else. But I'm working on it. Believe me when I say I *want* to call."

"Then do so soon, Arn Anderson, before I waste away behind the grill."

Fourteen

ARN PULLED INTO THE downtown Depot Museum parking lot beside Ana Maria, who was sitting in her thirty-year-old Volkswagen. He squinted against the bright light reflecting off the ten-foot-tall horse and rider galloping in slow motion atop the Wrangler store.

A man in a torn and faded camouflaged parka stood from his corner spot and approached them with his hands hidden inside his jacket pockets. Arn grabbed his gun from under the seat and set it between his legs. The man stopped abruptly, as if seeing something in Arn that didn't make it worthwhile to bum drinking money. He turned around and rejoined another bum in a heavy tan coat waiting for an easier mark.

"Shut the Beast off," Ana Maria said. "Those noisy tappets are killing me."

Arn turned off the ignition. "Better?"

"It is. Did I interrupt anything?" Ana Maria asked.

"I was just headed over to Frank Dull Knife's shop," Arn said.

"Don't let that coyote touch your car. The last person I knew who took their outfit there ended up walking home a mile from his shop."

"You're the only one that'll touch the Beast." Arn had bought the Oldsmobile 4-4-2 after Cailee died. He figured every man should have a midlife crisis and buy a vintage muscle car—especially when the love of his life dies prematurely. "What do you have?"

Ana Maria handed him a copy of an ER form dated two weeks before Butch's death. The bum who'd approached them fell to the pavement. He tried standing but had little luck. Arn didn't really care. He wasn't a cop anymore.

"I'm not sure if it's significant, but two weeks before he was murdered, Butch was rushed to the ER to have his stomach pumped," Ana Maria said. "Seems he OD'd on his Xanax."

"I won't ask who you sweet-talked to get this."

"It cost me lunch and an afternoon of listening to a rookie brag about the radio calls he got last week."

"What a trooper you are." Arn grinned. "But everything is significant right about now." He held the ER form at arm's length and reached into his pocket for his glasses. "There was something in the evidence sheet about a prescription bottle … " He thumbed through the stack of papers in Butch's homicide file. He found the evidence sheet and donned his reading glasses.

"Who sold you those paisley frames anyway?" Ana Maria asked.

"Some kid at Walmart. She said it would go with my man bag and make me look ten years younger."

"More like ten years goofier."

Arn paraphrased from the evidence sheet. "The bottle of Xanax was nearly empty when the tech bagged it. 'For anxiety' the prescription bottle read." He thumbed through other pages. "There's no mention anywhere that Butch suffered from depression." He gave Ana

Maria the ER form back. "If anything, he should have been on cloud nine if he was close to solving the Five Point cases."

"Wouldn't you be depressed if your wife was hosing half the men in town?"

Arn pocketed his glasses. "You didn't call me over here just to tell me this."

"Chief White's going on the air with me tonight," Ana Maria said.

Arn leaned out the window and cupped his hand to his ear to shield it from a train passing through the depot. "Did I hear you right: Johnny is cooperating with the media?"

"I think the phone call the mayor got from our station manager had something to do with it, though Chief White denies it. He said he was coming on air with me because his agency doesn't need an outside consultant to solve their cases."

"What's Johnny going to say?"

"He's going to renew his appeal to the public for any information on the Five Point killings ten years ago, and say that the reward money is still in escrow. He's going to tell the public his agency is starting to man the tip line twenty-four/seven and that he's assigning two investigators to run down any leads that come in."

"That might get something moving."

"Especially since he's personally heading up the renewed investigation," Ana Maria said.

"Johnny working the case?" Arn said. "I bet he hasn't worked an investigation since he went to administration. He must want me out of his hair pretty bad."

"Or he wants to shine when the city council makes a decision on the permanent chief position next week."

Arn started his car to leave when he saw Ana Maria made no effort to drive away. She looked at her rearview mirror, her head on a swivel looking around the parking lot. Arn turned off his car and started to speak when another Union Pacific train blew its horn, passing fifty yards on the other side of the old Union Pacific Depot. "What's bothering you?" he asked when the train rumbled on in the distance.

"He … he called again."

"The guy from the other night?"

"Doris said it sounded like him. He wants to meet again."

Arn grabbed his pen. "Where?"

"He'll call me at seven, right after tonight's airing."

"Johnny and Oblanski both blew me off when I told them about what happened with him the other night, so they won't be any help. If we're going to trap him—"

"There's not going to be a 'we,'" Ana Maria said. "I've got to meet him alone."

"I won't have it. You have no idea who this guy is."

"What if he has something that points to Butch's killer?"

"If that happens, you might get that national exposure you want," Arn said.

"There you have it. I want this story to go viral. And the only way I can is if I earn this man's trust."

"And if you're wrong, and you *become* the story? You may get national exposure for that, too. Didn't Doc Henry's attack teach you anything?"

"It did," Ana Maria answered at last, her voice quivering. "That's why I called you for help."

"I thought you said you were meeting this guy alone?"

"I am," Ana Maria said. "But I need your gun to take along to the meeting."

Arn felt a migraine coming on, and he closed his eyes while he rubbed his temples.

"Are you going to let me use your gun or not?"

"Maybe I can hide in your back seat, at least?" Arn asked.

Ana Maria laughed. "You hide in my Bug? That's a joke. Now can I use your gun?"

Arn looked around the parking lot. People came and went into the restaurant in the Depot Museum, and the Albany restaurant across the parking lot, but no one paid them any attention. He reached between his legs and opened the cylinder. His palm concealed the gun as he handed his snubbie through the window. "It's got five shots."

"Same as the one you taught me to use in Denver?"

Arn nodded. "Same gun."

Ana Maria stuffed it into her purse.

"I can't talk you out of it?" Arn asked.

"I'll be all right." Ana Maria started her car. "And if you and that old guy you're rooming with have nothing better to do tonight, tune in and catch Johnny's debut television appearance."

Fifteen

*THE DAMNED **U**NION **P**ACIFIC* engineer blowing his horn deserves ...
*okay, maybe not what the others got. But he deserves something, for tooting
right when I'm trying to hear Ana Maria's conversation with that old cop.*

"I don't know you."

"What?"

*A bum in a camouflaged parka pulled tight around his dirty neck walks
up to me. His hands are deep in his pockets like he's hiding something. A
weapon perhaps? I can never tell with these street people, and my hand goes
under my own parka and rests on the handle of my knife.*

"Who the hell gives you the right to work this parking lot?"

"Get lost," *I tell him as I look around him at the parking lot.*

*The bum stops a few feet in front of me. His morning breath has carried over
to the afternoon and just about knocks me out. But I've smelled worse, I tell
myself. Those men ten years ago were worse, and I survived. I always will.*

*The man's hands come from inside his pockets. He has no weapon, and I
walk over, closer to Anderson's open car window.*

"I always work here. This is my corner!"

The man won't go away. In another time, I might have set him up and flayed him. Just for fun. But this is the reformed me, and I motion him close. "You know me?"

The man shakes his head. "Never saw you before."

I bring my knife out, careful to keep it hidden in the folds of my parka. "I'm the one who's going to gut you. After all"—*I smile wide*—"it's hunting season."

The bum's eyes widen. And I see that utter fear in his eyes as he realizes I intend to cut him.

I shake. Just a mild tremor at first. But it builds. The more frightened he becomes, the more I quiver with anticipation of what I could do. And I stand. I take a step toward him, and he falls. His legs backpedal. His arms scrape the pavement getting away. I have no desire to hurt the man. I am, after all, reformed, and the only thing I want to know is how close they are to finding out about me.

I pull the strings of my hood tight, and my watch cap down nearly covering my eyes, as I slowly step nearer to them when—

Anderson looks my direction. I turn my head, staring at the ground like I'm looking for loose change, and he turns his attention back to Ana Maria. She hands him a manila folder. It can only be police case files she's somehow ripped off from the cops.

He passes her something through the window of his car. Damn that bum all to hell! If he hadn't come along, I might have been able to inch closer to see what passed between them. It could only mean more information for the special she's airing. I guess my little warning call to her meant nothing. I guess I'll have to talk with her in person as soon as I talk to the bum. In my own special way.

Sixteen

ARN DROVE PAST THE oil refinery, the acrid odor seeping through the Oldsmobile's windows so thick he could taste it. Arn wondered how Frank put up with the smell, wondered if Frank's eyes watered like his own did as he neared. But then he knew career criminals could put up with most anything. And Frank qualified as a career criminal, if Arn was to believe his rap sheet. Frank was sentenced to the State Boy's School in Worland at thirteen for jacking one too many cars, and he'd gotten out of there just in time to begin his formal career: a strong-arm robbery of a Denver porn shop, which netted him two years at Colorado's Four Mile Correctional Center, where he'd learned just enough to be a mechanic for a local gang.

Frank must have missed confinement, because the year after he was paroled, he was nailed at a Cheyenne home he'd burgled. The eighty-one-year-old lady living alone held Frank at gunpoint until police arrived. That was good for three years in the Wyoming State Pen in Rawlins. He'd remained out of trouble ever since—except for the burglary charge Butch had worked up on him, the charge that had disappeared when Butch died.

"Since he was released from Rawlins," Oblanski had told him, "Frank's been seen in and around a dozen residential burglaries, but nothing's proven."

"And your street contacts yielded nothing?"

Oblanski leaned back in his chair and thought about that. "Seems like everyone's afraid to talk about Frank Dull Knife. Every scroat in Cheyenne has clammed up about him. Only thing I picked up from my snitches is that Frank went the straight and narrow after Butch was killed. Just one more reason I know he murdered him."

Arn checked the map and turned south, away from the refinery. He had no argument for Oblanski's reasoning. Most serious criminals he'd dealt with had begun their careers penny ante and graduated with honors to more serious crimes. Arn had arrested several who'd committed their first homicide, and it had scared them so badly they wilted from the mean streets they'd lived on all their lives, cowering in their cribs, waiting for someone like Arn to hunt them down.

Perhaps Oblanski was right that Frank killed Butch, accidentally or in the heat of the moment. Perhaps Frank had actually huddled whimpering in one corner of his shop that night, frightened at the thought of what he'd done. Or frightened of a lethal cocktail being injected into his veins if he was caught. Perhaps that had been Frank's come-to-Jesus moment. Still, Arn couldn't see how Frank could get inside Butch's house to kill him. Unless Butch let him in.

A block past the refinery, Frank's dirty Quonset loomed higher than the dead pine and cottonwood trees drooping over the lot. A fenced area behind the shop housed a dozen beater cars and trucks awaiting repair. Or awaiting the crusher, by the looks of them.

Arn climbed out of the car. He fished his bandana from his pocket and used it to open the door to Dull Knife Auto and Truck Repair. He closed it with his elbow as he stuffed the bandana back in his pocket.

A dented and stained gray metal desk with something caked down the front sat ready to greet patrons as they entered the shop. And if that wasn't enough to make customers want to hang out in Frank's little piece of heaven, there were the papers overrunning the desk, vying for space with a half-empty bottle of Ten High whisky, complete with an empty Welch's grape jar just waiting to be filled up. *Yum. Yum.*

Sounds of a motor in the work area rose and fell and sputtered. Arn walked past one of those cheesy dollar bills that gets hung on the wall when a business first opens, and past a Snap-on Tool nudie calendar showing Miss November with a crescent wrench sticking out of her thong. Her eyes seemed to warn Arn not to step through the shop door.

Frank was leaning over the fender of a Dodge sedan, his head buried under the hood as he tweaked the carburetor. The chain hanging from his biker wallet clanged against the car's fender. Scratches in the faded paint coincided with the chain, but Frank made no effort to pad the fender against the metal assault. War wounds.

Hearing movement in the shop, Frank half-turned his head. "You can't be in here," he yelled over the drone of the engine. "Insurance company will drop me like a hot hooker." He disappeared again under the hood.

Arn remained where he was, careful not to rub against a scarred work bench with oil dripping down the jaws of a bench vice, parts of a carburetor scattered across it. He cupped his hand over his nose. Exhaust permeated the shop as it seeped through a gaping hole in the tail pipe extension running out of a cutout in the overhead door.

Frank looked up from under the hood and saw Arn still there. "I said, get the hell out of the shop area! You want something, I'll be done in an hour after I take this beater for a test drive."

"Another hundred-mile 'test drive'?"

Frank pushed away from the car. The motor returned to idle, and he approached Arn. "Maybe your dumb white ass didn't hear me." He tossed his oily skull cap on the shop bench and squared up to Arn. His fists clenched and unclenched, his chest rising and falling atop a beer belly his greasy Levis barely contained. The top buttons of his red flannel shirt were missing, revealing stubby chest hairs that matched the chin whiskers he hadn't shaved this week.

He took another step closer. Arn took a step back from the smell of his breath, either Ten High or feces. Could be either. "Not until I talk to you, if you're Frank Dull Knife."

Frank grabbed Arn's arm and tried to shove him toward the door, but Arn was forty pounds heavier. And sober. He jerked away from the man and Frank staggered back, eyeing Arn suspiciously.

"I'm not here to fight," Arn said. "If that were the case, I'd be wiping this dirty floor with your greasy butt."

Frank took another step back. "What you want to talk about?"

"I think you know. Or did you forget that BS story about your one-hundred-mile test drive the morning Butch Spangler was murdered?"

One of Frank's booze-bleary eyes twitched at the mention of Butch's name, and Arn pressed a bluff. "I can always get a subpoena issued to have you testify at a deposition."

"I got work to do," Frank blurted out. "Damned hospital dropped my contract. I serviced their vans for years, and now I got to make up for it." He jerked his thumb at the decades-old Dodge barely idling. "I'm a working stiff."

"Must not have worked hard enough, if the hospital dumped you."

"It was you bastards," Frank said between clenched teeth. Or at least through what few teeth remained. "You guys told the hospital I was drunk when I dropped off one of their rehab vans." He pointed to the door. "I got no time for your crap."

"Maybe we could take that deposition at the county attorney's office."

Frank spun around and nearly fell reaching for a large crescent wrench on the fender of the Dodge. He grabbed it with his left hand, and Arn noted his wristwatch on the right, his belt cinched opposite from a right-handed person. He thought back to Butch's murder: the photos and autopsy never mentioned if the killer might be right- or left-handed.

Frank took a step closer to Arn, and as Arn's hand went into his pocket, he realized he'd given his gun to Ana Maria. His hand came to rest instead on a spanner wrench teetering on the edge of the work bench, and he braced himself. But Frank merely tossed the crescent wrench under the hood of the Dodge and shut the car off. "We can talk in the office. Five minutes. Then you can go get your damned subpoena."

Frank staggered past him through the office door. He dropped into a one-armed captain's chair with *Cap. Ahab* gouged on the one arm remaining. Guess no one had told Frank that Ahab lost a leg, not an arm. He reached for the Welch's Grape jar. Dust swirled around his bleary eyes when he blew the dirt out before pouring three fingers of Ten High. Three very thick fingers, and he downed half of it before slamming it on his desk. Whisky spilled onto a work order, and Frank grabbed a dirty shop rag from his back pocket. He dabbed at the invoice for the Dodge. The printing on it was as neat as Arn's writing was sloppy.

Arn took off his cowboy hat and hung it on a deer antler coat rack. When he turned back, Frank stood abruptly, knocking over another nudie calendar from his desk. Miss May ended butt-crack up while Arn backed away from Frank's dragon breath.

"Now I recognize you, without that cowboy hat. You're that retired Denver cop the TV station hired to stick his nose in Butch's murder." Frank polished off the rest of his whisky and grabbed for a refill. "You look a lot younger on TV. And thinner. But you're no cop now."

"Oh, you're good." Arn grinned.

"You can just do an about-face and get your ass out of my office."

"I can still get that subpoena. You understand what that is?"

Frank remained silent as he glared at Arn.

"It's four o'clock now. Say I come back with a sheriff's deputy and serve you at around five. Isn't that happy hour?"

"All right." Frank refilled his glass. "All right. But I got nothing new to say that I haven't told you guys ... the cops ... a dozen times. I had nothing to do with Butch Spangler's murder."

Arn picked out the cleanest part of the dusty wall to lean against and grabbed a small pocket notebook and a pen. "Then you won't mind telling it again. To avoid that deposition."

"All right then. Ask your damned questions so I can get back to work," Frank said, backing away and plopping back down as if to get distance from Arn's questioning.

"Let's start by you telling me when you first hooked up with Hannah."

Frank leaned back and scratched his testicles as he smiled. "Her and Butch came into the shop with an old Studebaker Lark. Who the hell's got a Studebaker as their only car? Cheap-assed Butch Spangler, that's who had one." He swirled the whisky around in the glass. "Joey Bent over at Import Motors didn't want to work on the Lark, so he sent them to me. I was hungry. I needed the work. That was before I undercut the hospital's regular mechanic and got that contract. Now look at—"

"Hannah?" Arn pressed.

"Hannah. Sure. First time I saw her," Frank continued as he took another gulp, "was when she stepped out of that Stude, halter top and short shorts begging to be stared at. It was love at first rub, which is what I did when Butch wasn't looking—rubbed that itch Hannah was born with. That racist bastard was livid when he found out an Indian was pumping his old lady."

"Maybe he was mad because *anybody* was messing with his wife." Arn flipped a page. "Then there was the matter of Jerry Shine selling you a gun three weeks before Butch's murder."

"Jerry sold me nothing. Prove it."

"Then you admit you knew him?"

"Of course I knew him. He ran a sleazo pawn shop down by the tracks. Just ask him."

"Bobby Madden tried. His report says Jerry fled the country. Or came up missing a week before the murder."

"That's right." Frank snapped his fingers. "I heard Jerry left. But then he was always talking about going to parts warmer. Jamaica, I think, *mon*." He held his empty glass to the light and drained the last drops of whisky. "Hannah was just someone to have fun with. An all-right lay." He wiped his mouth with his greasy sleeve and scratched his testicles again. "But she was getting long in the tooth. All those years of drinking and partying wear on women."

And some men, Arn thought, looking at the specimen of manhood sitting in front of him, with his late-forties-going-on-sixties teeth as green as any spring meadow, the weary, bleary, bloodshot eyes trying to track Arn as he paced the room.

"Aside from screwing his wife, you must have had it out for Butch for working up that burglary case on you. You had"—Arn flipped pages for emphasis—"a preliminary hearing scheduled for the week after Butch was murdered. How convenient, the only witness suddenly dying."

Frank leaned back and locked his hands behind his head. "I can't lie, I would have been the recipient of good fortune with him dead. Fact is—if you check my case file, you'll see—Butch got the county attorney to drop charges the week *before* he was killed."

Arn had skimmed the reports again last night, but he recalled nothing about Frank's charges being dropped. "Now why would he do that?"

"How the hell should I know?" Frank said, looking away for a micro-second that told Arn he knew exactly why. "All I knew is I was home free. So I had no reason to kill the man."

"There was still his hot wife. And the fact that Butch could refile the burglary charge any time."

Frank stood and knocked his glass to the floor. It broke, and he kicked glass aside with his boot. "Okay, Mister Detective, you tell me how you'd argue I killed him."

Arn tucked the notebook back in his pocket and stared at Frank, feeling smug as the man plopped back down in his chair. In another life, in another time, he might have taken Frank out and throttled him. He was certain that he would have. "All right, how's this: You left Hannah at the bar that night, presumably to go to sleep, as you had a job early the next morning. But you didn't come back to this little Shangri-La." He waved his arm around the filthy office. "You drove over to Butch's and somehow talked him into letting you into the house. Maybe he wanted to avoid his nosy neighbor hearing an argument and calling police dispatch again. Once inside, you shot Butch twice with that gun Jerry Shine sold you."

Frank smiled.

"Some speculate that the next day, instead of working at your shop, you were taking a little drive somewhere. About fifty miles one way to dump that gun. But me ... " Arn paced the room. "I don't believe that. Call it the suspicious cop in me. I think you put those hundred miles on *before* you killed Butch. I think you took Jerry Shine for a one-way ride where he couldn't say when he sold you that gun."

Frank's smiled faded. "Hell of an imagination. Except Jerry couldn't have sold me a gun. I'm a felon. Felons can't possess firearms."

"Jerry knew that. That's why he sold it to you under the table, and left a note in his safe that was opened by his wife a year after he went missing."

Frank stood and slowly walked around the desk. "Maybe I took the customer's car that night after I left Hannah at the bar. Maybe I was pissed 'cause she was dancing with some other dude, and I went out snagging without her. Maybe I spent the night in some babe's house and drove home after I woke up."

Arn took out his notebook again. "What's her name?"

"Who?"

"The woman you claim you hosed all night."

Frank frowned, and liquid courage kicked into high gear. He picked up a breaker bar from the desk and cocked it back. "And maybe I'll crack that big Gumby head of yours. Then we'll see how far your imagination gets you."

"You'll look damned funny to the ER docs."

Frank looked wary and lowered the wrench a couple inches. "Why would they be looking at me?"

"When they try to figure out how to extract that wrench from your ass."

Frank dropped the wrench and it clanged on the floor. "I got to get to work. And you"—he jabbed his finger at Arn—"should be looking up that dude Hannah danced with that night. He could have brought Hannah home and offed Butch after she let him inside."

"The detectives never found out who he was."

Frank tapped the side of his head. "I know who it was."

"Then I'll interview him."

Frank smiled wide. "You just do that. You ask that fine Officer Oblanski how it was dancing and rubbing against Hannah that night."

For the first time since he'd entered Frank's domain, Arn stood speechless. He thought about Ned Oblanski and Hannah the night Butch died, and the reason the identity of the man she'd danced with never came up on reports. It had been Oblanski's job to run down dead-end leads, and that would surely have been one of them.

"We'll be seeing one another again." Frank ran his finger across his throat. "And next time, I'll be sober."

Seventeen

THE SPOTTING SCOPE is beginning to hurt my eyes, and I set it on the seat while I grab a thermos of coffee from the floorboard. But I can't let it set for long. Ana Maria's broadcast is over for the night, and she'll get into that crappy brown VW Bug and drive to meet me.

I'm certain she didn't tell Anderson where we plan to meet. She's convinced she blew it the last time, when Anderson butted in. She assured me she will not let the same thing happen tonight. If I could just reason with her, tell her those deaths back in the day were necessary. And that I've been sinless ever since. Maybe that will convince her to back off. We need some quality face-time, Ana Maria and me.

The knife in the sheath along my back rubs me, and I reach back to move it aside. I sharpened it tonight before I came out. But I doubt I'll need it. Ana Maria will drop her series once I talk with her tonight. In my own special way.

Movement in the TV station parking lot, and I grab the spotting scope again. Ana Maria stands just outside the back door, looking around like I'm just sitting in the parking lot waiting to speak with her. But she knows better.

She knows to meet me a mile through town at Frontier Park. For my own special rodeo.

I bring the scope away, and taillights a block down from the station flick for a heartbeat, then go dark. I put the scope to my eye once more and adjust the focus. There's only one vintage Oldsmobile 4-4-2 in Cheyenne. Anderson is staking out her car. He'll follow her to the park.

I hit the steering wheel. And hit it again. And again. Anderson is making it harder for me all the time to discourage Ana Maria. Now I'll have to get serious. Now I'll have to use more persuasion than I'd intended. But on the plus side, she'll be frightened to death tonight. And that will frighten Anderson even more. I begin trembling with the ecstatic thought. What a bonus.

Eighteen

"HAND ME THAT BAG of chips," Danny said.

Arn passed Danny the Fritos. He laid a handkerchief over his lap to protect his holey sweatpants and began crunching on the chips.

"Chew any louder and everyone will hear us." Arn picked up his binoculars and looked at Ana Maria's VW Bug parked in the dark lot behind the television station. He checked his watch: the evening broadcast with Johnny would be wrapping up any minute, and Ana Maria would soon leave to meet her caller. Providing he'd phoned again tonight.

"You got another Orange Crush?"

Arn half-turned in his seat. "I got half a notion to let you off here. Whatever possessed me to bring you along?"

"Something about not leaving me at the house where I could freeze? If you haven't noticed, it's colder than a well digger's butt out here."

"Well, as soon as we're done, we're going to AutoZone and grab some new points and plugs for the generator."

Danny grabbed the bottle opener from the dash and popped the cap on his soda. "That's all I wanted. A warm place to sit until we could get to the parts store. Not my fault you have something else going on."

"Shush."

Arn scooted down in the seat, and Danny took his lead. "That her?"

"It is." Arn handed Danny the binos. "Looks like she's backing out."

Arn waited until Ana Maria had left the station lot and turned west on Lincolnway before falling in several blocks behind her.

"You'd have thought she'd want you to come along." Danny closed the chip bag and set it on the floorboard. "After all, she's not big enough to take care of herself."

"She's big enough to take care of herself, all right. Trust me. But I'm afraid she might be getting in over her head with this story. Especially if it connects to the Five Point murders."

"That was something back then." Danny finished his soda and stuffed the empty bottle in a Walmart bag on the floor. "I drifted into Cheyenne the year before all that. First time I ever felt the need to hang with anyone was when those killings were happening." He shuddered and drew his collar up. "I fell in with a couple guys from Montana that came here every year during Frontier Days. Best panhandling they ever had, they said, with the rodeo-goers flocking to town. Concerts just begging to have some professional work the crowd. But the two victims were ... different, as I recall."

"Random."

"Yeah. Random. No one that I hung with felt safe."

Arn pulled to the curb when Ana Maria caught a red light. "So you and these two guys you just met and split a place?"

"Split a place?" Danny chuckled. "If you call setting up housekeeping in an abandoned home splitting a place."

"Like you squatted in my house?"

Danny straightened in his seat. "I resent that label."

The light turned green and Ana Maria turned north toward the Capitol, Arn and Danny hanging back. "As much as I detest the police—no offense—wouldn't it be smart for her to get them involved?"

"In what, meeting a man who has information he wants to give her? Johnny and Oblanski already made it clear they'll assign an officer for protection *if* she demonstrates a need."

"In other words, if she's attacked?"

"And only then. Being shorthanded, I'm afraid they're reactive."

"I really detest the police."

Ana Maria drove across 8th and started into Frontier Park. Arn had spent many summers in the park as a kid competing on the high school rodeo team. He'd been a fair saddle bronc competitor, but when the rodeo coach suggested he try bull riding, he started to shine. Until a bull gored him and broke his arm. That sidelined him from the rodeo team and the football team, and in his ambitions to make Georgia the one to break his cherry.

Ana Maria parked across from the entrance to Frontier Park while Arn pulled along 8th and doused his headlights. Danny put the binos to his eyes, straining like he was born to surveillance. "Her dome light just came on for a second."

Arn grabbed the binoculars. "She's out of her car. Where the hell's she going?" Ana Maria had parked in the one spot not illuminated by any street light, her white blouse the only thing bobbing in the darkness. "She's walking into the park. There." He pointed and handed Danny the binos.

"But there's nothing there."

"Someone's there," Arn said, zipping up his coat. "I'm certain." He handed Danny his cell phone. "Keep watching. If anything happens to me, call 911."

"Sure," Danny said. "But how do I use one of these things?"

Arn gave him the quick and dirty class in using the cell to call 911. "Hold your hand over my dome light."

He opened the door and silently closed it after he slid out. Squatting beside his car, he waited for a pickup to drive by on the street before he cut across the snow-covered grass. He entered the park, using the street for cover, anticipating where Ana Maria was heading.

A half-moon peeked between storm clouds and vaguely illuminated the park. Arn stopped behind a tree and squinted in the darkness. A hundred yards away, something white flickered between trees and bushes: Ana Maria's white blouse.

Nineteen

ANA MARIA PARKED JUST where I told her, the darkest spot in the park, away from any streetlights. She gets out of her car and looks around, unaware that Anderson has pulled his car along 8th and is walking this way. Nor is she aware that I crouch under this pine tree, ski mask pulled tight, waiting for her to walk close enough to grab her.

Anderson is gaining, running into the park toward where Ana Maria makes her way closer, yet too far to yell a warning. For the briefest moment, I entertain the notion that I will kill him. Then toss that great idea aside. I like my life the way it is. I don't want to complicate it by killing again and having the entire weight of law enforcement come down on me, looking for the Five Point Killer. I don't want to explain I was right in killing those men. All I want to do is get Ana Maria off her crusade to find me.

Ana Maria walks toward the Botanic Gardens. Just like I told her. "I'll tell you just who killed Butch Spangler that night," I reassured her when I called. "But come alone," I repeated. "I don't want to get drawn into court testifying against the killer." I thought that was a nice touch. A convincing touch. No one wants to go to court, especially if they have to look over their shoulder for some psycho.

Ana Maria is near, now twenty yards along the path.

I squat behind the tree, legs trembling with the anticipation of what terror she'll soon be feeling.

She doesn't know that I won't hurt her. This time. If she drops the special.

Ten yards. She picks her way carefully in the dark.

Five yards.

She stops, looking my way, her hand going into her purse. I cautiously look down at my white garb that blends with the snow, wondering what could have set her off. Then I realize she saw nothing. She heard nothing. It's that damned woman's intuition again, and I just have to wait it out.

After a full minute, she resumes along the trail.

I crouch. Legs drawn tight against my chest.

Waiting.

And I pounce.

Twenty

ARN RAN FROM TREE to tree, using them for cover, following Ana Maria, until...

Gone. Ana Maria disappeared, and Arn strained to spot her.

He ran toward a huge ponderosa pine where he'd last seen her standing, watching, looking into the darkness. At what?

He reached the tree, his breaths coming in great gasps as much from the running as from his impending feeling that something had happened to her. He left the cover of the tree and stumbled. He bent and picked up Ana Maria's purse, its strap broken. He tucked it under his arm as he fished out his gun, which was still inside the purse.

White flutters. Off to one side. Just a momentary flash under drooping branches another twenty yards farther in. He bent over while making his way past trees. He snatched a piece of white fabric stuck on a branch of a bush. He held it to what little light the moon afforded: the fabric had been sliced, not torn.

Arn pocketed the piece of cloth and squatted, looking at the light snow that had accumulated last night. He picked up drag marks heading off toward the Botanic Gardens.

Whimpering suddenly. Off to his left. Hanging in the stiff wind. Then it faded when the wind died.

Arn cupped his hand to his ear. Silence.

He strained, looking around the park, but saw nothing. Had he imagined it?

He cocked his ear again, his head pivoting like a miniature sonar, and the whimpering once again rose and fell at the whim of the wind, this time coming from beside the Gardens. Arn walked, then ran, toward the sound, louder the closer he neared, gun thrust out in front of him.

He grabbed his side when a stitch overcame him. He gasped frigid night air until he'd caught his breath enough to run doubled-over toward the noise.

White movement on the ground under a pine tree, and Arn hobbled toward it. Ana Maria lay on the ground beneath the tree, hands and legs and mouth duct-taped. When Arn broke through the trees, her eyes widened. She tried screaming through the tape, thrashing against her bound hands and feet, when—

A short, stout tire billy, like those truckers use, arched out of the night and crashed down on Arn's shoulder. He dropped to the ground and his gun skidded across the snow, Ana Maria's purse sliding away. He staggered to his feet, his head swaying, struggling to turn. A man in an oversized hoodie and ski mask swung the bat, and again Arn fell when it cracked into the back of his leg.

He tried standing, but his leg gave out. He fell back onto the frozen snow and matted grass as a heavy weight jumped on his back and forced him to the ground.

A blade reflected moonlight, and a heartbeat later his attacker flicked a piece of flesh off Arn's cheek. His hand came up to protect his face, but not before another flick of the knife sliced off a piece of his ear, blood trickling down his neck, onto his shirt front.

Then the attacker was gone, as if he had made his escape on the wind.

Arn groped for his gun. Found it. He turned over, backpedaling, getting his back against a tree, expecting his attacker to return for a rematch. When he barely caught the sound of crunching footsteps in the snow running away from him, he knew the attacker had left for good.

He tried to stand but fell back, his leg muscles failing to cooperate with his effort. He crawled atop sticky pine needles jabbing into his trousers. When he reached Ana Maria, he set the gun on the ground beside him and gently peeled the tape from her mouth.

"Good God, are you all right?" she said.

"I've been better," Arn said as he cut the tape from her arms with his pocket knife.

She wrapped her arms around his neck. Her mascara had run with her sobs, making her look as if she were auditioning for a bit part in *The Rocky Horror Picture Show*.

Arn let her cry into his shoulder until she stopped. "Give me your bandana," she said. She wet it with snow and dabbed at his cheek and ear. Then she looked wildly around and spied his revolver. She grabbed it and swung it around in the direction the attacker had gone.

"He won't be back tonight," Arn said. He gently wrapped his hand around his gun and eased it out of her grasp before she could accidentally shoot him. Setting it in the snow, he peeled the tape from her legs. "Give me the headline version of what happened."

For the first time, Ana Maria seemed to realize Arn had followed her. "And just what are you following me for?"

"Damned good thing I did."

"I'm not so sure he actually wanted to hurt me."

"What the hell kind of assessment is that?" Arn asked.

She looked away, wiping her cheeks with her coat sleeve. "He could have hurt me any time. I think he wanted … *you*."

"Bullshit."

She dabbed his cheek with the bandana again before putting pressure on his sliced ear. "How else do you explain superficial cuts when he could have killed you?" She smiled for the first time. "My purse goes better with your outfit than that one you carry, by the way. Hand it here, and hold the bandana."

Arn slid her purse over to her, and she fumbled inside for her cell phone. After dialing 911, she sat back against the tree trunk and rubbed her wrists. "He said to meet him at Frontier Park. He said he'd call again once I was here and give me further instructions."

"To the Botanic Gardens?"

Ana Maria nodded. "I had your gun in my purse, so I felt safe—"

"It's only useful if you can get to it."

"But I never had a chance. This guy came out of nowhere. He choked me. Slapped tape across my mouth before I knew what happened. When I tried reaching for the gun, he wrapped duct tape around my wrists like he was tying up a steer. Drug me off." She stood when the sounds of the sirens neared.

Arn pointed to her ripped blouse. "When did he cut this off?"

"A few yards into the woods. He cut it off and hung it on a tree like he wanted to make sure you followed."

"All I had to do was follow his cologne," Arn said.

"I thought I was imagining it."

"It was the same cologne as the night at the fairgrounds. I'm trying to place it."

"Old Spice," Ana Maria said. "I dated this old fuddy-duddy in Denver who went through about a gallon of the stuff a week. That doesn't help us. Unless we find a suspect dripping in Old Spice."

"Did he say anything?"

"Just 'drop the television series,'" Ana Maria answered.

"Would you recognize his voice if you heard it again?"

She waved her arm for the ambulance crew and police who had just pulled into the park. "I doubt it. But next time I'll have a better plan in mind."

"Next time!"

The ambulance stopped thirty yards away, and paramedics hauled a gurney from the back.

"What do you mean, 'next time'?'"

"I'm going to find out who killed Butch Spangler. And the guy I talked to tonight knows who it is," Ana Maria said.

"Didn't you learn anything tonight? This guy doesn't know a thing."

"Ever heard of woman's intuition? I just *know* he can tell me who killed Butch."

The paramedics wheeled the cart next to Arn. They lowered it and unloaded a jump box with their equipment. "My car's parked on 8th," Arn told Ana Maria. "Do me a favor and drive it home for me. Along with Danny. And keep my gun."

"You two out for a date?"

"I'll explain later. But you'd better have the paramedics check you out first."

Ana Maria waved the suggestion away. "I'm not hurt. Besides, I got other things to do. Like figure out who this guy is."

Arn tried standing, but his leg had begun swelling already. He was letting the paramedics load him onto the stretcher when one of them stopped. He bent and picked up a chain. Eight inches long, shiny chrome. He handed it to Arn. "You must have dropped this."

116

Twenty-One

ARN HOBBLED INTO JOHNNY'S office and shut the door. He tossed the piece of Ana Maria's blouse onto his desk. "Now maybe you'll provide her some protection."

Johnny stuffed papers in his briefcase without looking up. "I read the officer's report from last night. I'm taking it under advisement."

"Advisement!" Arn slammed his fist down on Johnny's desk. A tin cup stuffed with pencils bounced several inches high. It overturned coming back down, spewing pencils and pens across the desk, but Arn made no effort to pick them up. "By the time you get your head out of your rectum, the shithead from last night could kill her."

"What more do you want me to do? Oblanski's assigned an investigator to look into the assaults on you two last night." Johnny closed his briefcase and started for the door. "We have a dozen assaults a week. Do you think we got the manpower to assign a personal body-guard to all of them? Get real. This isn't Denver, big shot."

Arn leaned over, inches from Johnny's face. "Not every assault victim is airing an investigative report on three police deaths. All which may be connected to the Five Point cases."

Johnny stopped and hung his head. "Not that again."

"Someone doesn't want me—or Ana Maria—looking into those deaths. Someone sent us both a message last night—"

"Some message." Johnny pointed to Arn's jeans bulging at the leg from the wraps, and at the butterfly bandages on his ear and cheek.

"This guy last night could have killed us both. He didn't. He wanted to warn us off the case."

Johnny's face grew serious, his eyebrows coming together in a pronounced frown. "What it tells me is someone's toying with you. I can't offer any protection. But I can offer advice: if this guy is good enough to make you look like a fool twice now, he's good enough to finish the job any time the notion strikes him. If he's more than just toying with you."

He started out the door when Arn called after him. "I need those files on Gaylord and Steve. And the Five Point cases. I've already had the mayor's office grease the wheels with the city legal advisor."

Johnny paused, turned around, and kicked the door shut with his boot. The veins in his neck throbbed, and spittle flew from his mouth. "I don't appreciate being held hostage in my own office—"

"You don't want me finding Butch's killer?"

"What the hell kind of question is that?"

"The way you're keeping me out of the loop makes me wonder. I shouldn't have had to go to the mayor. You can expect a call from his office any time," Arn lied. He had called the mayor, who told him he couldn't force the police chief to release official reports. In time, Arn told himself, he'd tell Johnny the truth. But not today.

Johnny sat on the edge of his desk. He closed his eyes and pinched his nose together. "What do you need?"

"Everything. Incident reports, interviews, photos. Any follow-up reports that were filed over the years."

Johnny picked up the phone, and Arn wasn't sure if he was calling a uniform to toss him out or not. But Johnny asked for the city attorney, and they spoke for a moment before Johnny hung up the phone. "Gorilla Legs will have everything copied in a couple hours. But don't ever push me like this again or I'll haul you into the mayor's office personally and demand you be canned. He's got just enough pull with the TV station he can make it happen."

"Fair enough," Arn said.

"You get what we have with one caveat: you keep this office informed as to what you learn. If anything."

Arn nodded. He thought he'd start by telling Johnny that Oblanski was the one dancing with Hannah the night Butch was murdered, the one who'd given her a ride home. It wasn't so much that he mistrusted Johnny; he just didn't want it getting back to Oblanski. And Arn wanted to confront him in person. He needed to gauge Oblanski's reaction for himself. His life and Ana Maria's life might depend on it.

Twenty-Two

ARN CLOSED THE CANVAS drop cloth he'd stapled over the doorway leading to what had once been his mother's sewing room. He wrestled a piece of plywood on top of two sawhorses and broomed dust off it. When he finished, he moved the makeshift table close to the new drywall Danny had hung yesterday. He separated Gaylord and Steve and Butch's incident reports in order of occurrence, and then set aside photos taken of all three deaths. He grabbed a box of push pins and began tacking photos on the wall.

"I hope you know you're the one going to fill in those pin holes before I paint," Danny said.

Arn spun around and did the best he could to hide the pictures. "You can't see these!"

"Already have. I accidentally knocked them over when I was spackling in here earlier. They're pretty gruesome."

"Leave."

"And miss out helping you solve these cases?"

"I don't need help," Arn said.

Danny smiled and sat on a chair missing the back. "Like the Lone Ranger didn't need Tonto? Or Hopalong Cassidy didn't need Gabby Hayes? You need me. We got some time before dinner's ready, so let's see what we got."

Arn started to argue, then gave up. "What the hell," he said. He finished pinning photos. "No one would believe I shared this with ... "

"A formerly homeless man."

"Something like that."

When Arn had pinned the pictures on the wall, he wrote in pencil each officer's name on the drywall above and returned to the reports.

Danny stood to look at the photos from a different angle. "Aha." He pointed to a series of photos. "I told you Detective Fournier slapped his monkey to death," he said almost gleefully

Gaylord Fournier hung naked from his basement rafters by a flimsy cotton rope. *Hustler* and *Playboy* magazines were strewn about in front where he could get a good look as he masturbated. A full-length mirror reflected his body back at the camera.

"I just don't understand how he could have died." Danny ran his finger over Gaylord's hands, which hung beside his bare legs. "Looks like he could reach up and save himself."

"That's if he realized he needed saving," Arn said. He laid out the police reports. "Most men—and just men seem to be involved in this—put a ligature around their neck that applies pressure to the carotid as they masturbate. At just the precise moment when they're about to lose consciousness, they pull the ligature and release the rope. Their safety knot."

"Some safety knot," Danny said. "Why didn't Gaylord use it?"

"Who knows? Maybe he didn't realize he was that close to losing consciousness. Maybe his safety knot got sweaty and didn't allow the rope to slip free."

Danny wiped his hands on his jeans like he'd actually touched Gaylord's dead body.

"I saw that happen before," Arn continued. "There's only about a ten-second window between pulling the safety knot and saving yourself, or ending up like Gaylord."

Danny grabbed a follow-up report from Gaylord's pile and moved the lamp closer. "It looks like Butch Spangler was the investigating officer."

"He was the primary. Bobby Madden assisted."

Danny turned the page. "Butch believed Gaylord had been doing this for some time."

Arn took Butch's report. He'd interviewed Adelle Fournier, who was out shopping at the time. Butch quoted her as saying Gaylord had his own little man cave in the basement that she never ventured into. "Too many filthy magazines," she said. "Too embarrassing."

Arn laid the report down and approached the photos. He donned his reading glasses and turned the floor lamp to illuminate them better.

"Find something?" Danny asked.

Arn held up his hand. He needed quiet to think, before the thought vanished as easily as the drywall dust had settled.

He bent to the reports and shuffled through them until he came up with Gaylord's autopsy report. "'Everything was consistent with accidental hanging in the commission of an erotic event,' the coroner ruled," Arn said. "The medical examiner noted that the rope 'had cut through the outer dermis as a result of hanging.'"

"I'd think you'd expect that with a rope," Danny said.

"Adelle said her husband must have been doing the wild thing with himself for some time. But..." Arn ran his fingers over Gaylord's bulging neck encircled by the rope. "Men who do this never—and I repeat, never—use just a rope. That would result in just what the ME noted: cutting into the neck. These people always use something between..." He looked around frantically and grabbed a shop rag from the chair. He rolled it up around a length of twine he'd snatched from the floor. "Between their neck and the rope: a towel or a pillow. Something so they can go to their work and function. The last thing they want to do is draw attention from people noticing rope marks on their necks."

"I still don't understand why you got your panties in a wad," Danny said. "If the ME said it was accidental ... "

"He might have been wrong. Like Butch may have been wrong."

"So you think someone did the hanging for ol' Gaylord?" Danny laughed.

"I need to get into his old house."

"For what?" Danny asked.

Arn hefted the piece of rolled-up rag. "I need to get a look at where his little self-love nest was."

"How are you going to do that?"

"Find out who bought the place and ask them. It's not rocket science."

"Neither is it rocket science that Steve DeBoer's death was 'unquestionably accidental,'" Danny said, reading aloud from another report. "Passed out in his own home with a cigarette between his fingers."

Arn sat across from Danny and picked up the fire marshal's report. Steve DeBoer had passed out in his recliner with a cigarette in his hand that ultimately set the curtains on fire. "Accidental," Arn breathed. "Smoke inhalation killed him."

"Good," Danny said. "Then we can scratch one death off as an accident."

"Not quite yet," Arn said. He put on his reading glasses again and stared at the picture of a semi-blackened Steve DeBoer, recliner parked under heavy curtains that were little more than burnt shards. "There's something odd about that scene ... I need to talk to Pieter. He said he spent some time with Gaylord and Steve. If anyone knows more about them, he should."

The timer went off and Danny stood. "How about you check with him after we eat."

Twenty-Three

DANNY SLIPPED A HAND inside an oven mitt and took dinner out of the toaster oven. He set the casserole plate on top of a trivet on the makeshift counter and turned to paper plates stacked neatly on one end. The tuna casserole smelled good, especially since Arn had only eaten on the run today, in more ways than he liked. He'd slipped through the drive-through at Dr. Zhivago's Russian and Mexican Exotic Grill, and the vodka chili burrito had given him Montezuma's Revenge. He prayed it was out of his system.

"Where'd we get the card table?"

"Dining table."

"Okay," Arn said, "where'd we get the dining table?"

"Same place we got the toaster oven." Danny nodded to the front door. "In the dumpster."

"If you're going to lie," Arn said, flipping the receipt taped to the bottom of the toaster box, "you're going to have to do better than that." He leaned over the casserole dish, but Danny shooed him away. "Where'd you get the money?"

"I had to go begging, 'cause some tightwad won't spring for appliances for the place."

"I don't see why we couldn't just keep eating out."

Danny laid the oven mitt inside a milk crate atop kitchen towels. He stood with his hands on his hips, just like Arn's mother used to do when she was preparing to scold him. Or educate him. "We need to get some nutritious food into us. We can only eat so much McDonald's and Taco John's and … what's that place that's always giving you the Hershey squirts?"

"Dr. Zhivago's Russian and Mexican Exotic Grill," Arn groaned.

"That's the place. Waiters dress like Cossacks in sombreros." Danny unfolded another chair he'd acquired someplace. "We got to start eating healthy. Besides, with company coming over we needed something besides milk crates to eat on."

"Company? Danny, we don't even have a running toilet in here."

"I replumbed the bathroom today." Danny beamed. "So we won't have to keep using that smelly, barbaric thing you picked up at the camping store. And the shower surround will be delivered tomorrow, so we won't have to go to the Rec Center."

"What makes you think you'll be around long enough to use the shower?" Arn asked.

Danny waved his arm around the room. "You think this place is going to get finished anytime soon? I'm here until the last of the paint dries. That was our deal."

That had been their deal, Arn told himself, and he was glad they'd made it, too. In the four days since Danny had started renovating the old house, he'd torn out the moldy plaster and lath, with Lowe's delivering more drywall tomorrow. He'd pulled half the wire in the house and planned to finish that and install a new breaker box by the weekend. A working toilet and shower would be welcome, and the furnace people were scheduled to install a new unit tomorrow afternoon after city inspectors checked Danny's wiring. Arn could pick up an Army cot at surplus, and the four-hundred-a-week that went into the roach trap he was staying in would go toward materials for the house.

"If you're that far along, I might just move in to my old room after the furnace is installed."

"Your old room over the carriage garage?"

"Is it ready?" Arn asked. "'Cause it beats sleeping in the hallway."

"I haven't hung a new door yet, but the drywall's up."

Arn had grown up in the room just above where his great grandfather, and later his grandfather in a moment of nostalgia, had pulled their buggies to unload. As a kid, he would lie back on his wafer-thin mattress, close his eyes, and file the faint odor of horse dung that lingered into his imagination. Bad guys came and went, chased by sheriffs in white hats, inside Arn's imagination back then. What happened back in buggy days underneath his boyhood room offered an escape from the painful abuse from his father, and his thoughts returned to Pieter. Like Pieter's father, Arn's father had been a city policeman. And also like Butch, Arn's father had been abusive, though in other ways.

"You never said who's coming to dinner," he said to Danny.

"Ana Maria," Danny answered. "I told her the least I could do for her giving me a ride home last night was invite her over."

"All right, but make sure the generator's running. I'm getting tired of working with no city electricity. We need some amenities. Like a TV."

"Crap!" Danny snapped his finger. "They're re-airing Chief White's segment in three minutes."

"So you *have* a TV? Where'd you get it?"

"Dumpster." Danny started down the hallway devoid of plaster on the wall studs, bare lath sticking out in places, dangling wires taped off, and passed through the door into what had once been the living room. A thirteen-inch television sat on a plank spanning two concrete blocks.

"I don't recall getting the cable hooked up yet."

"You didn't," Danny answered, plopping into his bean bag chair.

"Then where … ?"

"Two houses down." Danny leaned over and adjusted the volume. "They came home long enough to grab fresh clothes, then took off again."

"You can't tap into their cable," Arn said.

"Sure I can." Danny held his finger to his lips as the camera panned from Ana Maria to Johnny standing nervously on the Police Department steps. His eyes darted between Ana Maria and the camera. His blue tie contrasted with his starched white shirt in the glare of the floodlights.

"I understand there have been new developments in the Butch Spangler murder investigation," Ana Maria said, thrusting the microphone at Johnny.

"I thought you weren't getting anywhere with Butch's murder?" Danny said.

"We're not. Johnny must have uncovered something he's not sharing with us."

"Even if he didn't learn something new, the killer—if he's still around—will think so."

"That's what I'm afraid of," Arn said.

Ana Maria asked Johnny about the Five Point killings. He looked around like he was planning his escape route, nervously switching his weight between feet. Johnny wanted to be anywhere other than talking on television about the Five Point cases. "There's never been any connection between Butch Spangler, Gaylord Fournier, or Steve De-Boer and those murders," he said.

"But all three officers died around the same time. And all three men were working those cases."

Johnny looked directly into the camera. "Mere coincidence."

A knock on the door made both of them jump, and Arn reached for his ankle rig that wasn't there. He promised himself he'd go gun shopping tomorrow. Right now, Ana Maria might need the gun more than he.

He hobbled to the door and grabbed a claw hammer from beside a box of drywall nails. He peeked through the hole, careful to keep to one side of the door. Ana Maria stood on the porch cradling a bottle of wine and stomping circulation into her feet. Arn dropped the hammer on the floor and opened the door. She walked in and surveyed the improvements to the house. "You've done quite a bit since I was here last."

"Make that Danny's done quite a bit."

"Maybe you ought to marry him." Ana Maria drew in a long breath. "Especially by the smell of dinner," she said as Arn led her into the kitchen.

"Your episode looked good tonight," Danny said. He'd turned off the TV and stood at the doorway waiting for her like a maître'd. He took the bottle of wine and held the label to the light. "A Chardonnay from one of the Mendocino wineries. Excellent choice to go with tuna casserole."

He opened his pocket knife and withdrew a corkscrew, which he worked into the cork. It popped coming out, and the bouquet was pleasant and sweet wafting past Arn's nose. Danny grabbed red SOLO cups and poured Arn and Ana Maria three fingers. He noticed Ana Maria eying the cups. "Best we can do until someone"—he exaggerated a look at Arn—"springs for some regular glasses."

"You're not having any wine?" Ana Maria asked when she saw Danny replacing the cork. "You sounded like you're knowledgeable."

Danny smiled and took off the foil covering the casserole dish. "That was my trouble: I was too much a wine expert back in the day." He laughed. "And it wasn't this fancy kind, either." He dished them each a serving and joined them at the card table.

"Are you feeling okay?" Arn asked Ana Maria.

She picked at her casserole with her fork. "DeAngelo threatened to take me off the television special and pass it to someone else." She swirled the wine around in the cup. She sipped lightly and set it down. "He said high ratings weren't worth me getting hurt."

DeAngelo Damos has been the TV station manager since before Arn could remember. Perhaps before electricity was invented. The old Greek had a reputation of being hardnosed but fair with his reporters. If he threatened to pull Ana Maria off the special, he must have thought there was something to the threats. Especially after last night.

"DeAngelo got a call from a man this morning telling him to stop my series. That's actually the only reason I'm still involved with it. DeAngelo hates to be told what to do."

"What man?"

Ana Maria shrugged. "DeAngelo didn't recognize the voice, so he called the police."

Arn downed the wine in a gulp, like he did with beer. He was more a beer man. "I'd bet a paycheck the station records every incoming and outgoing call."

"DeAngelo's line is always recorded. He made a copy and gave it to the detective. Now all we have to do is go around asking people at random to give a sample of their voice." Ana Maria pushed her plate away, her casserole only half eaten. "The bad thing is that if he's now getting threats to drop the special, I must be getting close. But ... "

Arn finished his casserole and Danny dished up another helping. "Is there something to that 'but'?"

Ana Maria finished the last of her wine and dropped her fork on her plate before scooting her chair back. "I hate to admit it, but I'm scared shitless. Last night in the park … he came on so unexpectedly. I had no time to react."

Arn understood. When he was working the street, he could see danger long before it visited him. But when he retired, the same danger could come up and kick him in the behind and he wouldn't see it coming. He'd been out of the police business just long enough to be losing his edge. And he couldn't seem to get it back.

"I thought, with your gun … " She wiped a tear on her napkin. "But I was helpless last night. Now I'm not sure if I should go back to my apartment." Arn saw her eyes water for the first time since she'd survived Doc Henry's assault. She looked around the room. "Could I stay here? I don't feel safe at my place."

Danny choked on casserole. Arn spilled the rest of his wine on the table. He quickly dabbed it with a paper towel while he regained his thoughts. "Maybe you missed something, but this place is barely livable for a couple old guys. I don't know what we'd do with a—"

"Girl? Damn you, Arn Anderson, I'm not some twenty-two-year-old girl on her first assignment for that Denver station. If you think I haven't seen men in their whitey tighties, you're mistaken."

"Well, you haven't seen *me*. In *mine*," Danny blurted out.

"I'd rather be living in this place than cowering in my apartment waiting for that guy to jump me again."

"I guess it would be out of the question to ask you to hand the special off?" Arn asked. "Surely DeAngelo has someone in mind to take over?"

"Nick Damos. DeAngelo's grandson," Ana Maria answered without hesitation. "He practically begged DeAngelo to let him run with it." She tossed her napkin in the garbage. "After *I* developed it, Nick wants to run with it. What an assuming little prick. I'm seeing this through. Now whether I get any sleep at night, or stay awake with your gun pointed at the front door, is up to you."

Danny stood and tossed his paper plate in the garbage. "You two sit and visit. I'll be in one of the other upstairs bedrooms. I think if I move some lumber around I can squeeze another Army cot in there."

Twenty-Four

NED OBLANSKI STARED OUT the window, his lip quivering with rage. "What do you take us for, a bunch of rubes? Of course we checked out everyone Butch had sent to the joint over the years. And Gaylord and Johnny too, in case there was a connection. You come to my office and accuse us of incompetence."

Arn moved out of spittle range. "I didn't accuse you of anything. There's just nothing in Butch's files that noted it was done."

"Well, it was. Now if that's all you came in here for—"

"You pissed at me for something besides this?"

Oblanski sat with his arms crossed, and Arn remained silent. He often learned more from someone by keeping quiet and waiting for them to vent. Like Oblanski was about to do now. "You hear Johnny in that TV special?"

"I was busy getting sliced up."

"So, I read the report. Too bad." Arn thought a slight smile tugged at the corners of Oblanski's mouth. "I'm pissed because Johnny went out of his way to praise Gaylord on the Five Point cases on television last night. Butch was so close to catching the son-of-a-bitch ... " Oblanski zinged a paper clip off a chair across the room. "That piss ant Gaylord was as useful as a condom machine in a convent. Butch did the heavy lifting on those cases."

"Sounds like you admired Butch?"

"He was a brilliant investigator."

"But he treated you like crap," Arn said. "You even threatened to beat the snot out of him."

"Who told you that?" Oblanski asked, then snapped his fingers. "Chief White."

"No comment. But you admit you hated Butch."

"He was an arrogant jerk, and I was the junior investigator then, so I caught everything that rolled downhill. I would have kicked the dog shit out of him, except ... there was something about him that made me stop."

That something, Arn knew, was Butch's temperament, his aura he projected as the alpha male. If Butch felt cornered, he'd come out swinging and snarling, and God help the man on the receiving end. Even someone as big as Ned Oblanski.

"Now if there's nothing else, I gotta do some police work."

"There is." Arn opened his briefcase and took out his notes. "You're still convinced Frank Dull Knife is the most likely suspect."

"He had the most to gain by Butch's death."

"You don't feel that way because you were both screwing Butch's wife?"

Oblanski stopped midway to stuffing Red Man tobacco in his cheek and his head dropped slightly. "I don't understand."

"I think you do." Arn set his papers on the chair, expecting Oblanski to lose his temper as he had a minute ago. "You were the phantom guy Hannah was dancing with that night. The one who gave her a ride home after the bars closed."

Oblanski spit the tobacco out in the garbage and rocked back on unsteady legs. "It was my night off. The Rusty Nail had a live band, and I danced whenever I got the chance." He grabbed the back of his chair to steady himself and eased himself down. "There was this hot chick rubbing a greaseball's leg, but the greaseball wasn't paying her any attention."

"Frank was the greaseball?"

Oblanski nodded. "Hannah was a bit old for me at the time, but she looked... itchy. So I took her to the dance floor, and she came on to me."

"Did you know she was Butch's wife?"

Oblanski shook his head. "I never saw her before that night. I thought she was just another hottie needing to get short-dicked."

"But you knew Frank?"

"I knew he had that chickenshit mechanic shop by the refinery, is all," Oblanski said. "Frank got pissed and grabbed me on the dance floor. Wanted to fight me. I'd have gladly obliged if the bouncers hadn't given him the bum's rush." Oblanski stared at the floor, never looking directly at Arn. "I never took Hannah to bed. After we left the Nail, we found a place to park. We were pretty heavy into the necking when she asked what I did for a living. When I told her I was a cop, she burst out laughing and told me who she was. It took me about twenty seconds to zip my pants and fire up the car. I drove directly to her place. When I came around the block, I saw the lights of the coroner's wagon and the squad cars. I kicked her out at the end of the block and drove home." He stood and faced Arn. "She didn't tell anyone about that night. Except Frank, I guess."

Arn closed his notebook. "Frank thinks you had a good reason to kill Butch: Hannah."

"Because I picked up a chick at the bar who happened to be another detective's wife? Who the hell are you, accusing me—"

"And the way you resented Butch, the way he treated you like crap, would be motive in any investigator's book," Arn said, bracing himself should Oblanski lose his temper once again.

Oblanski pulled the blinds aside and stared out the window. "Are you going to tell Chief White what you just told me?" he said at last.

"Let me sit on it for a while. There may be a conflict of interest if you're in charge of reopening Butch's murder, but it's not for me to determine."

"Thanks for that," Oblanski said over his shoulder.

Arn shouldered his man bag and started for the door when the phone rang. Oblanski answered it and closed his eyes tightly, his face scrunching as he held up his hand for Arn to stop. "Of course," Oblanski said. "I'll come right away."

He hung up and grabbed his sheep skin coat. "Want to take a ride?"

"Where to?"

"The hospital. Johnny's been shot."

Twenty-Five

ARN SAT IN THE thin vinyl padded chair in the ER waiting room, sipping hospital Starbucks while he waited for news about Johnny. Oblanski had left the waiting room when the mayor's office called, leaving Arn alone with a young couple huddled together in one corner. They were awaiting word on their infant, who was fighting for her life after crawling under the sink and ingesting rat poison. Every time someone in hospital scrubs walked by they jumped, expecting the worst, then settling back when the scrubs walked on through the room.

Across from them an elderly mother slumped in her chair, eyes puffy from crying. Arn had sat with her earlier as she told him her middle-aged son had overdosed on sleeping pills and Thunderbird wine. The emergency room doctor had given him a fifty-fifty chance. Arn had held her hand until she reassured him she was all right. And she had been, until the ER doctor entered the room, and Arn knew by the graven look etched across his weathered face that the mother would have no good news tonight. Arn had delivered many death notices in his thirty years as a lawman, and he never got used to it. Apparently the doctor hadn't either, as he cried along with the mother while she buried her face in his shoulder. The doctor softly rocked her, stroking the old woman's head until a nurse entered the room and led the woman away, freeing the doctor to attend to another tragedy.

The emergency room door opened and Arn caught a glimpse of another doctor, covered in blood, trying to save a woman Arn heard was run over by a car in front of the Air Guard base. Blood caked his gown, and his splash shield was smeared so badly he could barely see through it. A nurse pulled a sheet over the dead woman while the doctor stripped off his gown, mask, and paper booties. He tossed them into a biohazard container by the door. When he emerged from the trauma room a moment later, he wore jeans and a white shirt with no visible sign he'd been covered in a victim's blood moments ago. But Arn knew the effects would stay with the young intern long after this night ended.

Oblanski re-entered the waiting room and the young couple jumped in anticipation. When they saw he was no physician, they returned to praying softly in the corner. Oblanski motioned to Arn, and he followed him into an empty room a couple doors down from the waiting room.

"I didn't want it this way, but the mayor says I'm the acting chief until … " Oblanski looked at the wall, as if he could see Johnny lying in his bed in intensive care. "Until he comes out of it." He rubbed his forehead. "God, I hope he pulls through. I may have had words with Johnny, but I'd give anything … "

Arn laid his hand on the man's shoulder. "I know you would. And every other officer does too." He gently led Oblanski to a chair beside an empty bed. "What did the doctors say about Johnny's condition?"

Oblanski looked up, his forehead furrowed, mouth down turned. "He's in an induced coma. Docs gave him a better than fifty-fifty chance if they can keep the pain under control. He's a strong man. I have to believe he'll beat the odds."

"I hope so." Arn scooted a chair close beside Oblanski. "Give me the headline version of what happened."

Oblanski leaned back and white-knuckled the arms of the chair. "Johnny pulled into his driveway after work. His wife heard the car door shut, and he started talking with someone, but she paid them no mind. He often talked with neighbors when he got home, she told the responding patrolman. She went back to cooking supper when she heard two, maybe three shots. By the time she got to the door, Johnny was down in the driveway and the shooter was gone. Doctors dug one slug out him, a .380. Too deformed for any ballistic match, but enough to know it was a hollow point. 90 grains. My crime scene tech thinks the state DCI Lab could enhance it."

"You're sure of the caliber?"

Oblanski rang his hands together. "We found two spent .380 cases in the driveway." He stood and walked to the sink. "The one that did the damage was a contact shot. Powder stripling on Johnny's chest, muzzle imprint. Meaning someone surprised him. Shot him before he could react."

"Or the shooter was someone Johnny knew."

"Either way," Oblanski said, "Johnny must have sensed something wrong with whoever he was talking with."

"Is that the wife's opinion?"

"No," Oblanski answered, "it's mine. Johnny's pant leg was pulled up from going for his backup gun. Only reason for him to go for it is if he felt threatened." Oblanski bent to the sink and splashed water onto his face. He patted dry with a paper towel. "What the hell did Johnny do to make someone mad enough to want to kill him? He hasn't worked the street as an investigator in years. He hasn't put any-one behind bars in a decade. He's the proverbial good ol' boy."

Arn stretched out his legs and tilted his head to the ceiling, thinking just that. There was only one thing in his mind, and it wasn't coincidence. "It's got to tie in with his TV appearance."

Oblanski nodded and tossed the paper towels in a trash bin. The wad hit the rim and fell out, but he made no attempt to pick it up. "I've been kicking that around. Maybe Butch's killer *is* still here in Cheyenne. Maybe I was right all along—maybe Frank killed Butch and he doesn't want the case reopened." Oblanski buried his face in his hands. "Why shoot Johnny? Now?"

"Because he was the most visible face of the reopened investigation," Arn said. "Except me and Ana Maria."

Oblanski nodded.

"Are you ready to admit she needs protection now?"

"All right." Oblanski threw up his hands. "So I made a mistake. I can spare one officer to keep guard either at your house or Ana Maria's. Your pick."

"She's staying at my place until the TV special blows over."

Oblanski raised his eyebrows. "You old dog, you."

New drywall hung on the walls of the entryway as Arn entered, but he barely noticed. Nor did he pay much attention to heat from the new furnace as he staggered, dog-tired, to the coat room and opened the door to hang his jacket up.

"Your boots muddy?" Danny yelled from the kitchen. He came around the corner wearing an apron adorned with a rooster and wielding a pepper mill menacingly in Arn's direction. A new floor lamp cast an evil glow over his anorexic face. "Take 'em off."

"Take them off?" Arn looked around the room. "The carpeting is gone. All that's left is the subfloor—"

"Take them off. I don't feel like sweeping any more floors today."

Arn leaned against the wall and tugged off his boots.

"And don't lean against there. I just taped and mudded that wall."

Arn set his boots on a piece of cardboard and hobbled into what was shaping up to be a usable kitchen. Danny checked a meal in the toaster oven before grabbing butter from a fridge that hadn't been there that morning. "Where'd that come from, and don't tell me the dumpster."

"Of course not," Danny answered. "It's too big to fit in the dumpster. It came from the fridge fairy."

Arn started to protest, then gave up. Danny had his own way of acquiring things. Arn just hoped the police didn't come knocking on the door wanting to recover them.

"Where's Ana Maria?" Danny asked. "Supper's ready."

"She's staying late at the station," Arn answered.

"Is that a good idea, her leaving work in the dark?"

"Oblanski finally admitted she needs police protection. He's assigning an officer to her." Arn pulled a chair out from under the card table and plopped down. He closed his eyes and rubbed away a migraine forming at the fringes of his temples.

"You look like hell." Danny grabbed a pie plate from the oven and set it on the impromptu counter. "Have a hard day?"

"The hardest." Arn leaned over and grabbed the pot of coffee. "Somebody shot Johnny White today."

Danny stood holding a serving spoon over the chicken pot pie. "I saw it on the news. Tell me the SOB's in custody."

Arn shook his head. "Oblanski has no clue who shot him. Every detective in the division's been rattling doors all day, but not a solitary neighbor saw a thing."

"Johnny alive?'

"Barely," Arn answered. "Oblanski wanted to question him for a moment, but the surgeon said bringing him out of his coma for even a brief time might kill him."

"Dammed shame. Johnny was a nice guy."

"I didn't realize you knew him."

Danny served up supper and set the plates on the table. "After a sort. He'd stop me when he saw me walking the streets downtown. Ask if I needed anything. I guess he felt obligated, him being an Indian too." He grabbed a plate of buttermilk biscuits and set them beside a stick of butter melting on a plate.

"This is pretty good," Arn said after he'd blown on hot crust enough to sample it. "How'd you find time to cook between hanging drywall?"

"The drywall was easy. Getting the water heater hooked up was the hard part."

"Great," Arn said. "So we can take a shower tonight?"

"Not together, if that's what you're hinting at."

"It isn't."

"Good." Danny carefully spread his napkin on his tattered sweat-pants. "Who does Oblanski think shot Johnny?"

"Frank Dull Knife."

"Indian down by the refinery?"

"Do you know *everyone* who lives here?" Arn asked.

"Unfortunately, I know him." Danny filled their coffee cups and sat back down. "When I first blew into town years ago, I met Frank at a bar. He's a Cheyenne from Lame Deer, up in Montana, and I'm Oglala Lakota, from South Dakota. We're practically relatives, so I thought we had a lot in common. We had a few too many beers one night in a bar and Frank went nuts. He wanted to fight every white guy there, which I think we did." Danny rubbed his misshapen nose. "After that night, my scrawny butt couldn't take any more of his hospitality. Do you think he's the shooter?"

"I just don't know, Danny. It would make things so easy if he were." Arn finished his pot pie and tossed the paper plate in the trash. "I feel someone wants the spotlight dropped on those three officers. Tell me, you were here when the Five Point murders happened. Could one of the street people have been the killer?"

"Anyone could have been," Danny answered, dabbing at his mouth with a napkin, "as many street people as we get every summer. The newspapers could just as well have dubbed him the ghost killer. Not a single clue was left, if you believe the newspapers."

"Same thing with Johnny's shooting."

"Then you better find this guy before he kills again."

"Just what I intend doing," Arn said. "As soon as I get a good night's sleep."

Twenty-Six

*I **WOULD HAVE LIKED** to use my blade on Johnny. Taking my time. Watching his reaction to dying slowly, his pain prolonged. But blades, though lethal, take time to make someone bleed out. I couldn't chance someone walking by. Seeing me in his driveway plunging the blade in while he screamed and coughed blood over me. I had to kill him quickly. A part of me is furious that I reverted to my old self. Furious that I failed in fighting off the urges that lay dormant the last ten years. Another part of me is convinced I killed Johnny because he was spearheading the reopened investigation into the Butch Spangler death and the Five Point cases. He was allowing the investigation to re-open, so I had to kill him. It was the ultimate warning to drop the investigation. They'll have to drop the cold cases now and work overtime finding Johnny's killer.*

Or so I thought until tonight, when Ana Maria came on air from the hospital. There was no update on Chief White's condition, she reported. She said an anonymous hospital employee had said it looked grim for Johnny. "But this changes nothing." *Ana Maria looked into the camera, and seemed to be looking at me. Challenging me.* "We will continue investigating the killings of the three officers a decade ago and the Five Point Killer cases."

I slip my ski mask in my pocket. In case they wake up.

I stop two blocks from Anderson's house, the crunching snow under my tires louder in the frigid night air than I would have wanted.

I step out and bundle my hoodie around my face, leaving my heavy coat in the car. Where I'm going, I don't want to risk a bulky jacket scraping against anything.

I walk through back yards of this neighborhood, the downed rotted fences making it easy to go from house to house. Only a few people brave enough to live in this part of town, with so many abandoned and run-down houses providing the homeless and bums off the railroad places to crash. And a place to rob or beat the unsuspecting passerby. But this late at night, the hobos have long ago succumbed to the booze they had for dinner.

I reach the alley in back of Anderson's house. Yesterday I walked by, figuring out the best way to get inside, and I avoid clumps of frozen snow as I make my way around the side where I wait at the corner of the house by the front door. I pause, listening. A dog barks the next block over, and in a cottonwood overhead an owl says hello. But no one stirs in the house.

I take out the ring of try keys from my pocket, wrapped in a rag to keep them from rattling against each other. They'll fit most old door locks, and many dead bolts manufactured in the last few years.

I put one foot atop the rickety porch and slowly put weight down, testing. But Anderson has replaced much of the wood, and it takes my weight.

At the door I stop and listen. I put my hand against the door. Even if I can't hear someone walking around, I'll be able to feel vibrations on the door. It remains as lifeless as a tombstone, and I unwrap my ring of keys. They have served me well in years past, and I know there'll be one that fits this lock. I work my way around the ring—perhaps ten or twelve keys—slowly inserting each until ...

The lock clicks open. I pocket the ring, and listen a final time before cracking the door open. It creaks ever so slightly and I raise up on the knob, taking weight off the door, and open it wide enough to slip by. Inside, I close the door and stand against a wall, allowing my eyes to adjust to the darkness. And more importantly, waiting for my heart to slow. I fear nothing being inside this house. What I fear is that my excitement will override my instincts. And I will make a mistake.

I breathe deeply, aware that the throbbing in my head is slowly lessening, and I start for the staircase. Off to one side a light glows, another room, perhaps a night light, and I turn to the staircase railing. I reach for it, then pull my hand back. Just one more opportunity to make noise. I know. I have experience.

I step to one side of the stairs, knowing that more noise is possible if I put my weight in the unsupported center, and carefully put my weight down. Step by step I test each rung before I ascend another. When I reach the top floor, I once again pause. I feel my temples throb, my heart race, and I breathe deep as I look around the hallway.

Three doorways open into the hallway, but there are no doors on any room. When I feel composed, I once again keep to one side of the hallway and inch down. I feel the floor beneath for any sign of it giving me away, and peek around the first door. Ana Maria. What the hell is she doing here? She sleeps on her side. Almost in a fetal position, like a child. But she is no child. She wants to find me. She wants to destroy me.

I pull back, wondering what she's doing in Anderson's house. I become angry at myself. Back in the day, I would have never taken anything for granted. I would never have entered any of the victims' houses without thoroughly checking. Everything. Including what cars were parked in the neighborhood. But it will never happen again. I will never again leave anything to chance. Ever.

Ana Maria snorts and I freeze. When she settles back again, I debate what I should do with her. But I stick to the plan. I'd decided to visit Anderson and send him a message before learning she slept over. As much as I would like to see the terror in her eyes once again, I stay on plan and continue down the hallway.

The next two rooms have been stripped of lath and plaster. Bare wires dangle from the walls. A light fixtures swings in the center of the rooms. I pass by on the way to the room at the end of the hall.

The last room, like the other three, has no door and I look around the corner of the jamb. Anderson sleeps on his back. Even in the dark, his wispy blond hair is tussled and lies off to one side of his balding head. His feet stick out of the comforter, big, oversized feet, and I smile. What I wouldn't give to tickle his foot. And when he awakened suddenly, carve another throat under the one he's got. But I have an agenda. I really don't want to hurt him. I want him off my case.

I step inside his bedroom and listen intently. His breathing is deep, consistent, and I know he's in deep sleep.

I approach his bunk—a camping cot, really—and squat down five feet from it, studying him. Even at his age, he would be a handful, with his thick shoulders and arms, his heavy, muscular hands outside the covers. But I have to send a message, and I spot that message under his bunk.

I crawl on my belly, spreading my arm out until I can grab his slippers. I carefully pick them off the floor and stand up. I look a last time at Anderson sleeping, almost regretting that all I want to do is send a message, and backtrack my way out of the old house.

Twenty-Seven

DANNY'S DRYWALL HAMMER SLAP-SLAP-SLAPPING on fresh wallboard jolted Arn awake. He rubbed the sleepers out of his eyes, just as he'd done a thousand times as a boy in this same room over the carriage garage. He stared at the ceiling, remembering cowboy posters he'd collected and hung there: Gene Autry and John Wayne and Roy Rogers, heroes all to a young boy who just wanted to be like them. And wanted to be like his grandfather and great-grandfather who'd settled here when Cheyenne was a whistle stop for the Union Pacific.

But the dark side of those men had frightened Arn growing up as well. His great-grandfather had been arrested and narrowly escaped a hangman's noose for rustling cattle west of town. His grandfather had shot and killed a man on the steps of this very house when the man demanded money from a poker game. Which his grandfather had cheated in.

And his own dad. His father had so wanted to carry on the family tradition of lawlessness, but somehow fell into a position as a policeman for the city. The brutality he could never exert over the people he arrested spilled into his home life. And onto his only son, who'd found solace in this room from a father who beat him for small infractions of the household rules.

As miserable as those days had been, Arn never had to contend with Danny's hammering at six in the morning. He sat up on the edge of the cot and looked out into the hallway. When he'd jumped on Danny last night about hanging a door, the old man had stood with his hands on his hips. "What you want me to do? Just tell me. Lay floor tile or pull wires or texture drywall, 'cause I only got so many hours in a day." It was great to be home again.

Arn grabbed his jeans from a nail sticking out of the wall and slowly, painfully, put one leg in at a time. Between working on the house and fighting with the man in the park, he felt every muscle like he was back competing on the rodeo circuit. Danny had found him a foam camping pad—the pad fairy, he claimed—which helped Arn's aches some. Still, resisting a midlife crisis didn't extend to sleeping on cots. His next check from the television station, he told himself, would go to buy a bed. Make that three beds: for him, for Danny, and for Ana Maria.

Arn unplugged his cell from the wall and called the hospital, but there was no change in Johnny's condition. "Who shot you, old friend," Arn said aloud as he used the chair to help stand. His leg still throbbed from the beating in the park. He'd iced it to ease the swelling after he'd gotten back from the ER the other night. Still, it took him a moment to catch his breath before reaching under the cot for his slippers.

"Shouldn't you at least zip up before you parade around in morning wood?" Ana Maria walked by his door, toothbrush in her smiling mouth, exaggerating a once-over of Arn's open trousers. He turned his back to the hallway and zipped up. He looked a final time for his slippers under the cot before tiptoeing around drywall dust that seemed to float on the floor.

He tested the bare steps for exposed nails as he picked his way downstairs. A board creaked under his weight loud enough he thought it would give way, and he moved to the side to cling to the rickety railing for support.

In the living room downstairs, Danny squatted over a box of drywall nails. His arm was poised to swing his hammer again when he saw Arn, and he put it in the nail bucket. "Ana Maria and I have been starving to death waiting for you to wake up."

"Sorry," Arn said, crow-stepping over drywall dust. "I guess I was more beat than I thought."

"If you hadn't been sleepwalking, you might have woke up a little refreshed."

"I don't sleepwalk."

"Hell you don't," Danny said. "I heard you upstairs when I was sleeping."

"I sleepwalked once." Arn drew in a deep breath. "But it wasn't last night. What smells so good?"

"Flapjacks. They've been warming in the oven for an hour."

"Toaster oven?"

"No, a regular oven."

"Don't tell me: the stove fairy?"

"You're catching on." Danny smiled. "It was delivered early this morning."

Arn followed him into the kitchen. Ana Maria poured coffee and dished flapjacks on their plates.

"You see my slippers?" he asked Danny.

"They're a little big for me," the old man replied. "Besides, they're a little threadbare."

"Well, someone took them," Arn said.

Danny grabbed the butter and syrup and sat across the card table from Arn. "No, it means you're getting forgetful like the rest of us."

"Let me know when you find them," Arn said. "They're like old friends to me."

"I would, "Danny said, "but I'm taking a break."

Arn looked approvingly around the kitchen. "You've done a lot this week."

"Question," Ana Maria said as she dribbled syrup on pancakes. "If you can do all this, how come you're not out making serious bucks?"

"Like work a steady job? With a contractor?" Danny held up his hands like he was giving up. "I'm better than any contractor."

"Then start your own handyman business," Ana Maria said.

"I got no time for that," Danny said. "I'm too busy right here. Besides, we're not prying, remember? And since this is a Saturday, I'd like to watch football."

"Then do it."

"I can't," Danny said between bites of pancake. "Those tightwads two houses down don't even subscribe to ESPN."

"The one you're stealing service from," Arn reminded him.

"I prefer to think that we're just using service that they pay the cable company for anyway. Besides, I'm taking a breather and helping you with those cases you got tacked up on the wall."

"I told you to stay out of there." Arn had ordered Danny to stay out of the sewing room, where he had written on the fresh drywall with a Sharpie, perfect for organizing his thoughts.

"I needed my toolbox I left in there," Danny explained. "Excuse the hell out of me if I glanced at your precious wall while I was there."

"I got nothing else to do this morning either," Ana Maria said.

"What, did I adopt you two?" Arn tossed his paper plate in the trash and grabbed his coffee cup. "Let's go."

He led them down the hallway to the sewing room. "The Situation Room," as Danny had started calling it. Arn pulled aside the sheet hung across the doorway and led them in. Even though he had already seen the pictures—seen them and had nightmares about them—the photos cried out in all their gruesomeness, some black and white, others in murderous color.

Ana Maria stopped at the doorway. She swayed and caught herself on the door jamb. "You don't have to come in here, you know," Arn said.

She steadied herself before overturning a plastic milk crate. She took in deep breaths and sat in front of the wall. "If I'm going to help solve this, I need to man up."

Arn gestured to a new door waiting to be hung that Danny had propped against one wall. "Grab some saw horses we can lay this door on."

Arn waited until Danny left the room before sitting beside Ana Maria. "I never heard you come in last night. I told you to wake me up."

"You were sleeping as soundly as that policeman assigned to watch me."

"The officer was sleeping?" Arn fumbled to open his cell phone. "That's bullshit. Oblanski's going to have to replace—"

Ana Maria rested her hand on his arm. "It's all right. Don't you remember what it was like to be a young officer? Full of piss and vinegar and wanting to be in on all the action you heard come across the radio? Not parked in a television station lot waiting to follow some reporter home, only to sit for hours watching a dark house. If it happens again, then you can report the guy."

Arn hesitated a moment before closing his phone. "If it happens again—"

"You'll be the first I tell."

Danny returned with folding sawhorses and helped Arn place the door across the sawhorses as a makeshift table. He ran his hand over the surface. "I'm a reluctant participant in messing up this nice door."

"If I do," Arn said, "I'll buy another."

He handed Ana Maria the manila folders. "You up to this? First look-see of crime scene photos can be nasty if you're not used to it."

Ana Maria nodded. "Just let's take a look."

Arn spread the Five Point case files across the door. His eyes darted from Joey Bent's file to the photos on the wall.

Danny leaned over Arn's shoulder. "Joey and this Delbert Urban were sure cut to pieces. The papers didn't do them justice back then."

Both victims had their throats slit. Joey sat slumped in his chair wearing no pants. Blood had dripped down onto his bare legs, and his ear-to-ear slice seemed to smile at the camera as he still clutched a bottle of lotion.

"Remember I mentioned I got into a bar fight along with Frank?" Danny said. "He cut hell out of two cowboys before the bartender waylaid him with a tire billy."

"You saying he might have done this?" Ana Maria asked.

"All I'm saying is, Frank loved his blade," Danny answered.

Arn shuffled through the file until he came upon Butch's field notes. He'd written the word "helpless" across the top. "Butch figured Joey died with no struggle," Arn said as he thumbed through the incident report. "I've investigated deaths where victims got their throats slit. They thrash around like ... well, a chicken with its head cut off."

"I'm no trained investigator," Danny said, "but except that he's damn near decapitated, it looks like Joey died a pretty easy death. Not like someone killed him in cold blood. More like *cool* blood—like the killer eased Joey into his death."

153

"You're sharp." Arn walked to the photos. "See that beer can just sitting on the side of the coffee table? If Joey had struggled with his attacker, it would have been spilled. And the coffee table would probably have been overturned."

"The killer must have sneaked up behind him?" Ana Maria asked. "No other way to kill him without a struggle."

Arn put his glasses on and held Butch's hen scratching to the light. "Butch underlined 'acquaintance' and 'date,'" Arn said, tapping the lotion in the picture. "He must have thought the killer wanted to give Joey a happy ending."

"Kind of sexist," Ana Maria said. "Who says the killer was a guy?"

Arn jotted that in big letters across the top of the wall. "Good point. No reason he wasn't killed by a woman."

"I don't know about you," Danny said, "but looking at these pictures makes me feel a little queasy. I'm going to make some coffee."

He left, and Ana Maria scooted closer. She flipped through the second folder and laid out Butch's field notes on Delbert Urban. "'Same as Joey Bent,' Butch wrote. 'But different.' What do you suppose he meant by that?"

Delbert had been killed on the couch in his office at the Hobby Shop, his crimson Speedo pulled down the crack of his butt and failing to camouflage more blood than Arn had seen at a crime scene. The soaked couch cushions lay scattered across the floor, and the end table was smashed.

"Rules out someone sneaking up when he was passed out. Delbert must have put up some fight. Looks like two cats that got into a fight in the back yard, crap scattered all over the room." Ana Maria ran her finger over Butch's notes. "The 'same' must mean that both men were killed when someone slit their throat."

"Or this." Arn pointed out that the crime scene had been staged: the bodies moved so the first thing anyone saw inside the door was a gaping hole under their chins. "The killer staged it this way to shock anyone seeing it."

"Why?" Danny asked, munching on a cookie. He'd walked back into the room with a plate of sugar cookies and a carafe of coffee. "Just 'cause he's a sicko." He bowed to Ana Maria. "Or she's a sicko."

"The killer had no history with his victims," Arn explained. "If he had, he would have covered them after he killed them. Protect their dignity."

"Or it could be they were the same because of this." Ana Maria pointed to the small five-point star badge pinned to Delbert's bare chest, matching the one on the floor in the background of Joey's house. "But what was different?"

"Besides that bottle of Johnny Walker Black Label on the floor?" Danny dunked his cookie into his coffee cup. "Winston Churchill's drink of choice."

Arn and Ana Maria looked sideways at him. "How you know that?" Arn asked.

"Maybe in another life I got an education. Point is, besides drinking like old Winston, Delbert was as big as Winston was, by the looks of him."

Arn flipped through the papers until he found Delbert's toxicology report. "Delbert tipped the truck scales at 262. And he had a blood alcohol of only .04—two drinks for someone as big as he was. Rules out a scenario that Delbert was killed after he passed out."

Arn scanned both victims' particulars: Joey lived alone in a modest part of town, while Delbert had an upper scale place on Cheyenne's north side. "So that's why Delbert entertained at his shop: to keep it from his wife. You wouldn't want your wife finding out."

"I'm not married," Danny answered.

"Were once?" Ana Maria asked.

"I was," Danny said, "but we're not prying." He held Delbert's file to the light. "What's NAMBLA?"

"North American Man/Boy Love Association," Ana Maria said. "Bunch of sick bastards that like young boys. Pedophiles. I did a special on them some years ago in Denver. The local chapter president came on sweeter than honey until I told him I was with the news. Then he clammed up so tight you couldn't drive a stickpin up his keister with a jackhammer. Needless to say, I didn't shake his hand." She finished her fourth cookie, and Arn marveled that she still maintained her figure even though she ate like a horse. "Looks like ol' Delbert liked little boys."

Arn leaned back in the folding chair. He straightened his leg out and rubbed it, grateful it wasn't broken. Then again, he thought, the guy with the tire billy could have broken it if he'd wished to. "Maybe that's how the killer got close, by posing as a boy?" Arn looked at Danny. "What do you weigh, 110? 115?"

Danny hitched up his jeans, which had slid down what passed as his hips. "This morning, 117. And I know what you're saying. Someone my size could have passed as a boy."

"Or a woman could, as Ana Maria pointed out."

Danny walked to the wall. "That's odd."

"What's odd?"

"That." Danny traced a faint footprint left in blood on Delbert's nude back. Arn put his glasses back on and bent to the photo. He'd seen that same footprint in the last couple days. Somewhere. Or maybe because a hundred people in Cheyenne might wear that same tread pattern.

He shut his eyes, imagining how the scene looked during the crime, something he'd often done when he was investigating the very worst of human nature. He envisioned Delbert and his killer drinking. Perhaps Delbert had impressed the other with his expensive taste in whisky. They may have agreed to have sex: Delbert was partially nude, and a condom lay on the floor beside the couch in anticipation. Perhaps Delbert drank a little too much—the killer slipped behind him. But when he started the death slice, Delbert came alive. They fought. The killer wrestled him to the floor, stepping on his back. Just like Butch had speculated.

Arn tilted the lamp to the photos and squinted through his reading glasses. "There!" He pointed to a tiled spot outside Joey's front door. "There's that same shoe print. I think." He motioned to Ana Maria. "You don't need glasses like us old farts. Come see if those tread patterns are close?"

Ana Maria stood next to Arn and leaned close to the photos. "They're the same. Not conclusive enough for court, but they're the same pattern."

"But we already know the same person killed them both," Danny said. "He left his calling card: that five-point star badge."

"Then where's the other shoe prints?"

"What prints?" Danny asked.

Ana Maria's head swiveled between photos. "You're right. There are no other prints."

"That's just my point." Arn grabbed a cookie and dunked it into his coffee. A chunk broke off and bobbed like a miniature life preserver. "As much blood as there is at both crime scenes, there should have been a trail of bloody shoe prints all the way out the door. But there's only that single print in each photo."

"I don't get it." Ana Maria grabbed the initial reports from both murders and scanned them. "Butch mentioned it was the same tread pattern. So?"

"Whoever killed these victims put the print there on purpose," Arn said. "He *wanted* a single shoe print to be found. There's no other explanation for the killer not to have left a bloody trail."

"So what did he do?" Danny asked. "Get beamed out of there? Climb the walls like a fly so he wouldn't touch the floor? He had to have laid down more tracks."

"I don't know," Arn said. "I'm going to have to study on that."

"What's bugged me as I was studying the old newspaper clippings," Ana Maria said, tapping the photos with her pen, "is why were there only two Five Point victims?"

"That's easy." Danny beamed. "Delbert frightened him."

"How you come to that conclusion?" Arn asked.

Danny nodded to the photo with a piece of cookie. "It looks to me like the killer had it easy with Joey Bent. But when he went to kill Delbert, he was too big for his attacker to handle, and it was Katy bar the door. A real knock-down-drag-out fight." Danny punched the air. He feinted a jab and nearly fell down before Arn caught him. "I think Delbert scarred him so badly he called it quits. Or moved out of the area."

Arn clamped a hand on Danny's stooping shoulders. "You would have made a good detective if you weren't a wanted man."

Twenty-Eight

THE PING OF THE elevator outside the hospital waiting room woke Arn from a light nap. He sat up and looked about before standing and stretching. He'd stopped at the nurses' station this morning to ask about Johnny: he was still in an induced coma, but his vitals were improving.

He walked to Johnny's room to talk with the officer sitting in the hallway. Arn remembered such duty, and figured the officer must have pissed off someone to draw the boring assignment of sitting outside the room. "I don't know how the chief's doing," the officer said, clutching the latest edition of *Guns and Ammo* magazine. "Only thing they told me is to keep everyone out except hospital personnel."

Arn returned to dozing in the waiting room when an angry voice rose from the nurses' station. A woman was yelling at two nurses, their blue scrubs barely visible as they cowered behind the safety of the counter separating them from the crazy woman. "This is bullshit!" the woman screamed. "I demand to see Chief White!"

The charge nurse walked around the counter and laid her hand on the woman's fleshy arm. She jerked away. "I'm Adelle Dawes, bitch. Dr. Dawes' wife. I pay your wages."

"Then you're the person I need to talk to about a raise." The nurse's lip rose slightly in a Mona Lisa smile before she became serious again. "And you still can't go into his room."

One of the nurses caught Arn's attention, the panicked look on her face asking for his help as if he still wore a badge.

"Are you Adelle Dawes?" Arn asked, sliding between her and the nurse like a boxing referee. He recognized the name of Gaylord's ex-wife, who'd married Dr. Dawes after Gaylord's death. "I'm a friend of Johnny's too. Can we sit for a moment?"

Adelle glared at the floor nurse before stomping past Arn into the empty waiting room. The nurse mouthed a "thank you" just before he turned and followed Adelle. He walked to the coffee pot and grabbed a Styrofoam cup. "Would you like a cup?"

"Is it as crappy as all other hospital coffee?" she asked as she wiggled and struggled to fit between the arms of the chair.

"It is."

"Then count me out."

"Can't blame you." Arn counted himself out on the crappy coffee as well and sat in a chair opposite her. He told her what the nurse had said of Johnny's improving condition, and how only hospital personnel were allowed at his bedside. "Are you a friend of Johnny's?"

"He was friends with my brother, Steve DeBoer." Adelle took off her coat and tossed it on a chair.

Arn sat quiet, like he often did, waiting for someone to tell him things. All sorts of things. Which Adelle did.

"Johnny always treated Steve well," Adelle volunteered.

"It must have been hard, losing a husband and brother the same year."

Adelle laughed. "The husband was no great loss. He did pretty much whatever he wanted to do." She flipped open a silver cigarette case and stuck a Virginia Slim into her mouth, then spied the *No Smoking* sign and stuffed the cigarette case back in her purse. "You're that retired cop the station brought in to find Butch Spangler's killer."

"I am."

"And to come up with a connection between Gaylord and Steve and Butch." She laughed again. "That Villarreal woman's come up with some doozies to boost her ratings, but this has got to take the cake."

"You don't see a connection between all three officers' deaths?"

Adelle leaned forward for effect, and Arn backed away. Something about vodka breath at ten in the morning. "I watched Johnny on TV claiming that the Five Point Killer could be the link between them. That would leave Gaylord out. The little piss ant couldn't find elephant tracks in the snow, no better investigator than he was. If it wasn't for my brother, Gaylord would have been working animal control."

"But he must have known as much as Butch about the cases, them being partners."

"Only because Steve ordered Butch to take Gaylord under his wing. He would swagger through the front door every night, bragging. 'We're so close to catching the killer,' he'd say. 'By this time next week we'll have an arrest.' Big shot. But in reality, *Butch* was close. Gaylord was just along for the ride."

Arn reached around the chair and grabbed his bag.

"What's that?"

"My briefcase," he answered digging for papers.

"Looks like a purse."

Arn took out a notebook and flipped pages to notes he took about Gaylord's death. "The initial report says you found Gaylord the evening he died."

Adelle took out her cigarette case again. This time, she stuck a cigarette into her mouth. She aimed her shaking hand, holding a diamond-studded lighter, to it. She drew a deep breath and looked in the direction of the nurses' station. Daring them. Blowing smoke rings their way. "When I came home from shopping, that damned fool Gaylord was in the basement. In that room he called his man cave." She laughed nervously. "Except there were no men ever came around. Only Butch's little kid now and again. Or Steve when he needed to ask Gaylord something. But yeah, I found him swinging. Butter smeared all over his little bitty *cajones*. Eyes bulging out like he was still looking at those porn mags. A connection with Butch and Steve? That Villarreal woman is really nuts this time."

A tall, fit man entered the room, the graying around his temples setting off his nearly black hair. He seemed to glide as he walked, lithe, sure of himself. He glared at Adelle, who hurriedly snubbed her cigarette out in a coffee cup. "This is my husband," she said quickly. "Doctor Jefferson Dawes." She tailed out "doctor" so that Arn knew he was in the company of royalty. "What are you doing here?" she asked him.

"I'm a doctor. Doctors frequent hospitals. Especially when their damned nurse claims she can't read my orders and I have to come here and tell her in person."

Adelle looped her arm through his. "Jeff is in demand as an orthopedic surgeon."

"I doubt Mr. Anderson is interested in my life history," Jefferson said.

He was turning to leave when Adelle stopped him. "Lunch?"

"I can't," he answered. "I've got to prep for that marathon."

"Then what time should we have dinner?"

"Don't wait for me. I'll be late checking on a patient here."

She looked after him walking down the hallway, as if expecting his return. "We usually have dinner," she volunteered. She shook out another cigarette. It dangled out the side of her mouth making her look like a drunken sailor about to order another Singapore Sling. When she turned back to Arn, her faraway look was replaced by one of desperation. "We have a good marriage," she blurted out. "You and that Villarreal woman remember that in your reports to the public. Jefferson has *never* had an affair."

Pieter Spangler appeared, walking down the hall alongside a young nurse in blue scrubs. He saw Arn in the doorway of the waiting room and waved. Adelle stiffened. She jabbed her cigarette in his direction. Ash fell on the carpeting, and she ground it in with her shoe. "That kid ... you watch out for him. He's creepy."

"He can't be too creepy with that good-looking lady on his arm." And creepy people don't rise to become one of the region's top architects, Arn thought.

"He hung around with Gaylord. A kid!" Adelle's voice was loud enough that nurses at the nurses' station looked her way. "And he bought our old house after I moved out. What sicko would want to buy a house where a man hung himself?"

Pieter stopped when he saw Adelle staggering toward the elevator. He bent and whispered something to the nurse beside him before they continued to the waiting room. Adelle dropped her cigarette into a Styrofoam cup and brushed past Pieter without acknowledging him.

Pieter looked at Adelle as she waddled into the elevator. "Adelle doesn't like me much," he told Arn.

"She's got bad memories of you spending time with Gaylord, by the sounds of it."

"I spent time with all dad's fellow officers." Pieter turned up his nose at Adelle's still-smoldering cigarette in the coffee cup. "As I recall,

Adelle never had any use for Gaylord when they were married. No, what she's mad about is that I bought that ratty old house of theirs for a song."

The elevator dinged and Pieter jumped, perhaps expecting Adelle to return. "Excuse my manners. Let me introduce my fiancée, Meander Wells. Meander, this is Arn Anderson."

"Pieter says you were a friend of his father's," Meander said, offering her hand.

"A long time ago," Arn answered.

"After Gaylord died," Pieter said, as if needing to clarify Adelle's hatred, "she boarded up the house and moved in with Dr. Dawes. It was the very week after Gaylord's death. She let the house go to seed, and I picked it up for taxes. That's why she's got it in for me. She thought it was worth a lot more because it was in that historic part of town south of the tracks the railroad used to own. Fact was, no one wanted a house where a hanging took place. Even if it was in a historic district."

"Historic or not," Meander said, "Pieter paid too much in taxes for that spooky place."

Pieter grinned and wrapped his arm around her shoulders. "Meander wanted to see where a man died … an autoerotic death." He gave her shoulder a squeeze. "I intend on restoring the place. It'll be our first house when we're married."

Meander swiped at his shoulder, but he drew back in time.

"Actually, I've got no time to restore any house now, as busy as I've been. So, I just replenished the boards that had rotted away, against vandals and homeless like I do all my old homes. Someday I'll get the time to restore them."

"Like I'm doing with my mother's old house," Arn said, leaving out that fact that the old place came with an emaciated homeless Indian.

Meander checked her watch. "Break's over. I have to get back to the floor."

Pieter looked after her as she disappeared down the hallway before turning back to Arn. "Are you here to see Johnny too?"

Arn nodded.

"Meander said they brought him out of the coma for a few minutes today. That's a positive sign." He checked his own watch. "Got a ten o'clock appointment with the developer of that new shopping center south of town." He started out the waiting room. "Meander's going to keep her ear to the floor. If there's any change in Johnny, I'll call you."

"Thanks," Arn called after him.

He walked to the nurses' station. The charge nurse saw him and came around the counter. "Thanks for taking Adelle away. She likes to throw her weight around. Which is considerable."

"Understood," Arn said. "Does a Dr. Delaney still work here?"

"Ralph?" The nurse sighed and picked up the phone. "He's been in the cafeteria for an hour. I'll tell him you're coming. And tell him his nurse called and said he's got patients waiting."

Arn took the elevator to the cafeteria and followed workers on their late lunch break, a cornucopia of colored scrub uniforms: blue and browns and green, intermingled with white lab coats here and there. Arn got in line at the salad bar and dished some greens onto a plate. He figured if he were talking to a doctor, it couldn't hurt to show solidarity by eating healthy. At least until the interview was over. "Could you tell me where Dr. Delaney is?" he asked as the clerk weighed his salad.

"That white-haired vacuum cleaner in the corner," she answered, handing Arn change for the salad. "Notice he's alone? That's 'cause no one can stand to eat with him. Bon appetite, big guy."

Arn picked his way through the crowd toward the corner table. Dr. Delaney, a thin man in his seventies not much bigger than Danny, sat shoveling food in. Stripped chicken bones were piled high on one plate as the doctor worked on his last drumstick. Two cheeseburgers waited on another plate. He saw Arn standing over him and wiped barbeque sauce from his lips. "They had a special on ribs."

Arn introduced himself, and Delaney shook hands sticky with barbeque sauce. He motioned to an empty chair. "Sallie called and said a knight in dull armor rescued her from Adelle Dawes." He striped the chicken leg and attacked one of the cheeseburgers. "You're that retired cop the TV station brought in as a consultant on Butch Spangler's murder."

"I am. I'd like to ask you some questions, since you were his primary care physician."

"What about patient confidentiality?"

"The man's been dead for better than ten years."

"Good point." Lips smacking. "If Butch don't like it, he can sue me." Lip smacking. "What do you want to know?"

"Butch was admitted to the ER a couple weeks before he died to have his stomach pumped."

"He OD'd on the Xanax I prescribed," Delaney mumbled, halfway through the first cheeseburger. "The man was a bundle of nerves. A patrolman brought in the empty prescription bottle the night they admitted him. Butch must have taken a month's worth—the bottle was near empty. That quantity should have killed him." Delaney motioned to Arn's salad plate. "You going to eat those?"

Arn shook his head, and Delaney grabbed his pack of croutons and opened them. "I ripped Butch's behind for that stunt once he came around. I told him to go easy on the Xanax, and he started bawling. First time I saw that in him. He said he needed extra Xanax to fall asleep. That he'd probably taken more than he should have with his nightly dose of Budweisers. I almost upped his dosage—the Xanax, not the beer. But then I thought better of it and just refilled the prescription. Two weeks later, he was worm food."

Delaney wolfed down the second cheeseburger and stood with his tray in hand. "If Butch loaded up on the Xanax that night and took a few too many beers, he would have passed out cold."

"And he might not have been aware if someone walked in on him?"

"That's almost a certainty," Delaney said. He was walking toward the tray drop-off when he stopped and turned back. "You want some free advice?" He nodded to Arn's plate. "If you have another salad, skip the cheese. Causes hardening of the arteries. You got to start eating healthy, Mr. Anderson."

————

Arn pulled out of the hospital parking garage as his cell phone chirped. He pulled to the side of the road and accepted it. When no one talked on the other end, he said louder, "Arn Anderson."

"It's me," Ana Maria said in barely a whisper. "DeAngelo wants me to go on air tonight again. Give an update on Johnny's shooting."

"And you don't want to?"

"Does it show?" she asked.

"It does if you connect Johnny's shooting with your television special. This morning you were gung ho about going ahead with tonight's airing. What happened today?"

"Your ratty old slippers," Ana Maria said, her voice trailing off, shaky.

"I lost them," Arn said. "What's that got to do with you not wanting to go on tonight?"

"I got your slippers. The ones you thought you lost," Ana Maria's voice wavered.

"What do you mean, I *thought* I lost?"

"They were on the front seat of my car when I came out of San-ford's restaurant today. You didn't lose them. Someone took them—"

"Sometime last night," Arn breathed. "While we were sleeping."

"I'm scared, Arn. I don't know if I should treat this as a warning to back off the special or be on notice that the killer can take us any time."

"Or he's toying with us," Arn said. "Maybe you ought to turn it over to Nick Damos."

"I need this. We need this, to catch this guy."

"All right," Arn said. "Do you want me to hang around the station until you get off work tonight?"

Ana Maria paused, her breaths coming in quick gasps. "I'll be all right. I've got police protection sitting in the parking lot. And I still have your gun."

"I'll call Oblanski and ask him to beef up security."

"Don't," Ana Maria said.

"What?"

"Don't," she repeated. "There's just enough investigative reporter in me to want not to scare him away. Or her. Besides"—she waited while footsteps walked by—"Nick Damos will jump on this like a crazed dog if he thinks I'm too scared to finish the series."

"All right. It's your call."

"But if you happen to replace your doors and window locks in the house, I'd be a happy woman."

"I'll get Danny on it. Just as soon as I go to Frontier Arms and buy a gun."

Twenty-Nine

ARN PULLED HIS TRUCK beside Pieter's white Audi parked in front of the large *Pieter Spangler, President* sign in front of Spangler and Associates. He walked past the splashing waterfall that sprayed water on duck and swan sculptures, and on a trout that appeared to be leaping out of the water after a dragonfly. It was flowing freely despite the freezing temperature.

He ascended marble steps that were devoid of the recent snow. They were polished to a high shine, yet had a slight pebbly feel that made walking safe. The entry doors opened automatically, split so that one half dropped into a slot in the floor and the other shot up to disappear into a slot overhead. As soon as Arn walked through the opening, the doors came together like a clamshell trapping its prey.

Halfway down the thirty-foot-high ceiling, an indoor terrarium bigger than a car hung suspended by invisible wires. Bonsai trees grew beside native Wyoming grasses growing beside wildflowers sprouting out of lush green vegetation on the terrarium floor. Lightning bolts and a mini rain shower highlighted the effect.

Arn walked to the receptionist's desk. Her lips moved, but he couldn't hear her. Yet nothing separated the lady from Arn. He moved to one side, but could not see an attached headset on the receptionist.

"May I help you?" she asked, suddenly audible.

"I'm here to see Pieter Spangler."

"One moment," she said. Then once again her muted voice talked with someone for a brief moment. "You may use the elevator," she said, "or the staircase."

A clear glass spiral staircase connected the ground floor to the next, the steps appearing to disappear into the wall. They didn't look like they'd hold his weight, and he opted for the elevator.

Arn expected a futuristic time machine that would whisk him upstairs at warp speed. But when the elevator door opened, he was greeted by an old freight lift like those he'd used in Denver warehouses years before. He stepped in and pushed the only button: the second floor. The elevator struggled upward, chains overhead clanging against supports. It shook and rumbled like an amusement park ride. When the door opened, he stepped out and looked thirty feet down to the lobby through clear glass. He felt his legs buckle and grabbed the elevator door for support.

"A little over the top, isn't it?" Pieter leaned cross-armed against a secretary's desk, broad smile gracing his face. He chin-pointed to the glass floor. "I got that idea from the Hualapai Tribe's glass walkway at the Grand Canyon. What do you think?"

"I think I might throw up if I get any dizzier."

Pieter laughed. "This building's my laboratory." He came off the desk and stepped closer. "And my showroom. I employ my vision of what I think people will want in their future."

"Like the receptionist downstairs? Try as I might, I couldn't spot the microphone or how she controlled her speakers and phones."

"That one was a real brainchild, one of my favorites," Pieter said, his hands animated as he talked. "I got that idea from watching old reruns of *Get Smart*. There are no speakers or phones per se. I call it my Cone of Silence. Pretty cool, huh?"

"It is." Arn chanced a look down. His stomach churned and he closed his eyes. "Particularly in contrast with that old-school elevator."

Pieter motioned for Arn to follow him. "Don't look down and you'll be all right." He led Arn to his office. Once inside Pieter's office, all sounds from the outside were blocked—even though there was no door.

"I salvaged that old elevator from a hotel in Salt Lake City they tore down a couple years ago," Pieter said. A dreamy look crossed his eyes. "And until I get the time to restore one of my historic houses, I'll have to settle for riding that old lift every morning."

Inside Pieter's office, Arn felt as if he'd walked through a time bubble. The room stood in stark contrast to the rest of his building. Pieter's graduate degree from Pratt Institute in Brooklyn hung beside his picture of the Cheyenne South basketball team when they won the state championship. Filing cabinets lined one wall, marked *Codes* and *Future Proposals* and *Upcoming Bids*. A horizontal rack held dozens of cardboard cylinders packed with, Arn guessed, a hundred building layouts. Plain Berber carpeting cushioned heavy footfalls, and the office was furnished much the way he was furnishing his mom's old house: Walmart Modern.

"I don't spend much time with clients in my office." Pieter seemed to be reading his mind. "I figure there's no sense in spending money on furniture and office accoutrements when it's just me. If you saw the house I grew up in, you'd know where my frugality comes from." He motioned for Arn to sit.

"The sign said Spangler and Associates. Where are the associates?"

Pieter laughed. "There are none. Just me. It just sounds more ... professional."

"I'm impressed," Arn said. "How does one go from graduating Pratt Institute of Architecture to three years later owning one of the region's premier firms?"

"I've always had an interest in architecture." Pieter beckoned Arn to a four-foot-square piece of plywood butted against the far wall. On top of the plywood stood a miniature office complex, each building showcasing a different architectural concept. "My junior year science project in high school."

"Can I?"

Pieter nodded and Arn carefully picked up one of the tiny plastic buildings.

"That features a cantilevered roof. My science teacher had never heard of such a thing on that type of building until I brought this model in."

Arn set it back in the same dust spot, counting the sixteen buildings that formed Pieter's idea of an office complex clustered around a central fountain. Arn recognized many of the concepts in Pieter's office building displayed in the model. Each miniature building had been glued together so carefully, Arn thought they'd come from a kit.

"No kit here." Pieter picked up another building and held it to the light before blowing dust off and setting it back. "All of this is from scratch. Made in my bedroom." He chuckled. "I must have used a gallon of modeling glue putting it together. People down at the store must have thought I was huffing, as much glue as I bought."

Arn turned over a placard that had tipped over. It was the grade of C-minus that Pieter's teacher had given him. Pieter had encased it in plastic to display next to his project.

"My teacher gave me a bad grade because he thought the concepts would never work. Said I'd never make it into the architectural world."

"What's he saying now?"

"I wish I knew. Mr. Noggle left his wife for some banker's secretary my senior year. Rumor was he went to the Bahamas and drowned in a boating accident." He grinned. "Serves him right." He bent to a small office fridge and handed Arn a bottle of Perrier. "But you didn't come here to ask about snobby old Mr. Noggle."

"I didn't." Arn took a sip and the fizz shot up his nose. "I've been losing sleep over your dad's anxiety."

"You? I'll bet you sleep like a log and snore just as badly."

Arn laughed. "You've been talking to my … friends." He was careful not to mention Danny. "I spoke with your dad's physician, Ralph Delaney. Butch had taken much of his Xanax by the time he died. Much more than was prescribed."

Pieter swiveled his chair and looked out the window. In a vacant field across from the building, a mother pulled her young daughter down a snow-packed slope on a sled while a Yellow Lab barked as it kept pace with them. "Dad was reluctant to take too many Xanax. He was afraid taking too many would take the edge off finding the Five Point Killer. But he drank too many brewskies and took too many pills."

"And had to be rushed to the hospital?"

Pieter nodded. "A couple weeks before his death, he had to be carted to the emergency room." Pieter swiveled back around. "Catching the Five Point Killer was his obsession, and he said he was so close he could taste him."

"Is that why he needed Xanax?"

"That, and Dad would become livid thinking about Frank Dull Knife being out with Mom. Especially since he suspected Frank was the killer. Pretty soon he'd take more Xanax and chase it down with more beer." Pieter paused, and Arn waited for him to tell it at his own pace. "You'd pop Xanax like candy too, if your partner died within a month of your supervisor. Add to that the Five Point cases."

"Did your dad ever talk with you about those?"

"Talk about them?" Pieter tilted his head back and laughed, but Arn recognized it as a laugh of pain. Not pleasure. "Dad bounced his ideas off me, even though I didn't want to hear his gruesome details. But you want to know if Dad told me something that never made it into any report. He didn't. And I'd know, too. 'Cause by the time I started high school, I'd been to so many calls with Dad that I was more knowledgeable about crime scenes than any of those boobs on CSI. I'm just lucky I turned out reasonably sane."

Pieter finished his Perrier and lobbed it into the trash across the room. "Still got it," he said. "You asked about Dad's Xanax. You on to something?"

"Dr. Delaney said if a person took too many Xanax along with alcohol, he'd pass out. Butch had four beers that night and was working on a fifth when he was murdered. Did you hear anyone else downstairs with your dad that night?"

"Like company?" Pieter shook his head. "But then I always slept sound. If Dad had invited someone over that night I wouldn't have known. Dad really had no friends except ... " Pieter looked out the window again. "Other cops. Why?"

"There's another possibility I've been kicking around. Maybe Butch invited someone into the house. Maybe for a beer. Maybe just to talk. And maybe this person saw his Xanax in the bathroom and slipped them into his drink. And when Butch passed out, shot him and fled. All without a struggle."

"But that would rule out Frank Dull Knife. If he came around, Dad would have climbed his frame and the place would have been torn to hell. I can't see Dad letting him in."

"So of the officers he worked with, which ones did he invite over regularly?"

Pieter's face went pale. "Johnny White."

———

By the time Arn started for the parking lot, it was nearly dark and Pieter insisted on walking him out the building. He stayed with Arn until he opened his car door. "I get the impression you want something," Arn said before he climbed in.

Pieter shrugged, looking around the deserted lot. "Johnny was shot because he went public on reopening Dad's murder case. At first I thought it was a good idea. Finally catch the killer. Now I'm not so sure."

"Johnny's a professional. He knew what the consequences might be in going public. But he felt strongly that your dad's murderer could be caught—with the right person coming forward. That's why he agreed to go on air with Ana Maria."

"What's the chance that someone will remember something new after all these years?"

Arn started his car and turned the heater on before stepping out and closing the door. "I've worked many cold cases where information comes to light years later. In Butch's case, someone may think there's been enough time since the murder to feel safe going to the police now. I'd say there's a good chance that someone out there has information. Johnny's plea to the public just might jar something loose."

"Then that's all the more reason for you to watch your back." Pieter looked around the parking lot a final time before Arn climbed into his car. "'Cause I'd sure hate to see a friend of my Aunt Georgia's hurt by Johnny's shooter."

Arn slapped him on the back. "Thanks for your concern."

"Hey, you up for a cup? I'm just locking up."

"Ana Maria Villarreal's on television for another installment," Arn said, "in thirty minutes."

"You can come to my place and watch it. Beats sitting around that thirteen-inch TV of yours."

"Thanks, but I got to see to a homeless man."

Thirty

AS ARN PULLED TO the curb in front of his house, his headlights shone off a forest-green Impala parked at the curb. Pieter's warning rang in his head, and he grabbed the gun he'd just bought today, a snubbie .357 revolver, from the glove box. His hand clutched his gun inside his jacket pocket as he approached the house. He bent his ear to the door. Muffled voices rose and trailed off inside: Danny's and a woman's. He took his hand out of his jacket pocket and chided himself for being so jumpy. But as his hand rested on the door knob, Arn reminded himself that women can be just as deadly as any man. And as ruthless. He shoved his hand back into his pocket, his finger finding the trigger, as he stepped cautiously inside.

He followed the voices into the kitchen. Danny was laughing beside Georgia as they leaned against the new countertop frame that waited for Danny to finish it. Arn bent and slipped the gun into his ankle holster and then stepped into the kitchen. Clusters of candles illuminated the new folding kitchen chairs Danny had "found," and he'd thrown a blanket over the card table as a quick tablecloth. An aria playing from Danny's one-speaker stereo filtered through the room, and odors of something special wafted past Arn's nose. They stopped laughing when they spotted Arn.

"Mr. Danny was just telling me how you two met." Georgia smoothed her skirt. "But he won't tell me his last name."

"That's Danny Boy. Mr. Mysterious." Arn motioned to the table set with flowered plastic Chinet, not the pauper's paper plates they'd been using. "What's this?"

"It's your gourmet meal for the evening." Danny grabbed a flashlight and opened the oven door. "Buffalo stew with corn bread."

"Where'd we get buffalo?"

Danny's hand covered his heart. "We Lakota always know where the buffalo roam."

"You in on this?" Arn asked.

"It's Danny who thought of a nice impromptu dinner." Georgia sat on a folding chair. "It just happened to be my day off when he called."

Arn bent and whispered to Danny, "Where'd you get a phone?"

Danny covered his mouth with his hand. "Those folks two doors down. They're still not home. And they got a landline. Now sit."

Arn took a seat across from Georgia and waited for Danny to serve them. "It's going to be hard to impress a chef. I mean a cook."

———

"I'm impressed." Georgia scooted her chair back from the card table and laid her napkin beside her plate. "And full."

She picked up her plate but Danny stopped her. "Until we get the kitchen set up, it's easy to clean up after meals." He grabbed the plates and stuffed them and the plastic utensils in a garbage bag. He tied the drawstring and slipped his coat on.

"Where you going?" Arn asked.

"Take out the trash and then to bed. Unlike some people"—he exaggerated a look of scorn—"I got work to do here tomorrow."

Danny disappeared out the back door and Arn stood to refill their coffee cups. "I'd say let's sit in the living room, but it's full of things. And I have no sitting room yet."

"This is just fine." Georgia sipped her coffee and leaned back in the chair. "How's Chief White doing?"

"Doctors are hopeful. They brought him out for a few moments today. I stopped by, but they wouldn't let me see him."

"Pieter said he ran into you. And that witch Adelle."

"She was there with her husband."

"I'll bet he told her he'd be busy jogging?" Georgia said.

"You psychic?"

Georgia laughed. "Meander gets all the dirt at the hospital. The only running Dr. Dawes does is into the arms of other women. Makes Adelle madder'n hell. She deserves him. Just like Hannah deserved what she got."

Arn refilled their cups and sat back across from her. "You never did explain what happened to her."

Georgia scooted her chair closer to the space heater and hugged her cup. "The year after Butch was murdered, Hannah took a double gainer off the bridge outside Laramie. Drunk."

"So she never straightened out?"

"Just 'cause her husband was dead?" Georgia laughed. "Hannah hit the sauce even harder after Butch died. She collected the hundred thousand bucks the feds give spouses for line-of-duty deaths and drank through it by the time of her wreck. If I hadn't insisted she set some aside for Pieter's college, he never would have been able to attend."

"Must have been devastating for him to lose both parents inside a year."

Georgia stood and emptied the grounds in preparation for brewing another pot of coffee. "After the police were through working Butch's crime scene, I took Pieter to the house to gather his things. He moved in with me, and Hannah never saw him after that. She never even went by her own house that I know. It went back to the bank when she didn't keep up payments."

Arn laid his hand on Georgia's. "You must have done something right, by the way he turned out."

Georgia smiled wide. "I guess I did."

A key rattling in the door caused Arn to jump, and he bent and grabbed his ankle gun. He put his finger to his lips and tiptoed toward the door. He stood off to one side and unlocked the deadbolt, flinging the door open in one smooth motion. Ana Maria's eye widened and her legs buckled when she saw the gun pointed at her, and Arn quickly stuffed it in his back pocket.

"My key won't work," she sputtered.

"Danny installed a new lock today. I got a key for you in the kitchen."

Ana Maria followed Arn into the kitchen and stopped when she saw Georgia. "I'm sorry to interrupt."

"You're not interrupting anything," Arn said and introduced them.

"I'd know that face anywhere." Georgia stood. "I see you every night doing the news. How's the special coming along?"

"We've got tips coming in every day. I'm optimistic we'll find your brother's killer."

Ana Maria fidgeted, her eyes darting to the door, wanting to tell Arn something. Georgia picked up on it and nodded to Arn. "I have to turn in. Got the day shift tomorrow."

They walked through the house, and Arn held the door for Georgia. She stepped gingerly off the steps and froze when she saw the police car parked across the street under the light. "Are you in trouble?"

"Just a precaution to keep Ana Maria safe. She been getting threatening calls over her TV special."

Georgia reached out and brushed his cheek as she touched the bandage dangling from his ear like an oversize gypsy earring. "Connected with that?"

"I believe it is."

Arn opened her car door. "This is our first one," she said.

"First one what?"

"Dinner date, thanks to Danny. Now all I got to do is talk you into taking me on a real date."

Arn was certain he blushed even in the darkness. "As soon as I make some headway in this case and can take a breather, I'll call."

"Understood."

He waited until Georgia pulled around the corner before walking up to the police cruiser. The officer's head slumped against the headrest, and even with the windows shut, Arn heard snoring. He slapped the window and the officer jumped. He grabbed his flashlight and shone it into Arn's face. "Who the hell are you?"

"I'm one of the people you're supposed to be protecting." Arn shielded his eyes. "Now if you can't keep awake, maybe Lt. Oblanski can find a replacement."

"Please don't do that, Mr. Anderson." The cop rubbed his eyes and sat up tall in his seat. "I won't go to sleep again."

"We'll let it slide this time," Arn said and walked back into the house.

Ana Maria huddled around the space heater in the kitchen. "He was at tonight's taping."

"Who?"

181

"The guy who grabbed me. The one who attacked you." She used the chair to steady herself as she sat. "I was interviewing Lt. Oblanski at the front entrance to the police department. He'd just started connecting Johnny's shooting with Butch Spangler's case when that man walked in back of my cameraman. Just enough on the periphery I couldn't see his face."

"You're sure it's the same man?"

"You know that woman's intuition thing you always hammered into me? Well, mine went off louder than gunshots in a closed room." Her legs trembled and her foot tapped nervously against the leg of the card table. "It's the same Old Spice I noticed before. And I smelled it in spades tonight. The guy must bathe in it, it was so strong."

"We need more than that to go to Oblanski."

"His black drawstring on his hoodie. Same as the guy had the other night. How many guys go around wearing white hoodies with black drawstrings?"

Arn tried to come up with an argument to refute her logic, but knew it was a lost cause. Ana Maria was right.

"He came around to say hello," Ana Maria said. "To let me know he was still thinking about me."

Arn slipped his gun out of his boot and set it on the table. "We know someone got in the house last night. He could have killed us right then if he'd wanted to."

"Except he didn't want to." Ana Maria's hand shook holding her coffee cup. "He wants to play with us a little first."

"Which is why I had Danny hang that new door yesterday, and install a new lock this afternoon."

"And there's a cop out front."

Arn forced a laugh. "If you can wake him long enough to do something."

182

Thirty-One

ARN HAD STAYED UP half the night going over the reports, comparing photos of all three officers' deaths, racking his mind for the connection. It was there. He just didn't spot it. Yet. And when he dropped exhausted into the cot with the lumpy camping mat and covered himself with an old comforter the bedding fairy had left for Danny, Arn slept sounder than he had in years. And that scared the hell out of him. With the person who'd knifed him and shot Johnny still roaming the streets, the last thing he wanted was to sleep soundly.

Danny's music awakened Arn just as the sun crested the horizon, melting the new snow that had fallen on his scrub lawn last night. He put on the slippers Ana Maria had returned to him and trod down the stairs. Danny had covered the steps with carpet remnants, but they still creaked under Arn's weight.

The smell of coffee hastened him to the kitchen, where Danny stood over a pan frying bacon, poached eggs waiting in small bowls and a bright flowered apron protecting his torn sweatpants. The old man hummed along to some rock song playing on the mono-speaker ghetto blaster he'd rescued from a downtown dumpster. He slapped the side of the pan with a spatula in time with the music. "Grab a fork and paper plate," he called over his shoulder.

"Aren't we going to wait for Ana Maria?"

"She left an hour ago. I think. I heard her walking around and covered back up." He dished up food on plates and sat across the table.

Arn speared bacon with his fork. "You outdid yourself this morning."

"Figured you needed cheering up."

"How so?"

"Someone slashed your tires. And keyed your Oldsmobile."

"What!"

"Yeah, sometime between when Ana Maria left the house and when I took the dog out for a crap."

"What dog?"

Danny finished his bacon and seemed to ponder if he should have seconds. "Those folks a couple doors down saw the cable line tapped into theirs and followed it here. They threatened to go to the cops on you."

"On me!"

Danny waved the air. "Don't worry. I smoothed it over."

"What did you tell them?"

"I traded walking their dog while they're on another vacation for cable time." Danny's appetite won out and he impaled another piece of bacon with his fork. "Aren't you going to check on your car?"

Arn dropped his knife and fork and headed for the door.

"You'll freeze your Little Johnson out there unless you put something on," Danny called after him. "My robe's in the closet."

Arn grabbed the flowered, terry-cloth robe with *Lucille* embroidered over the pocket, which was big enough for two people plus the woman who'd donated it to Goodwill. He wrapped it around himself and slipped on his boots, then cracked the door and peeked out. The marked cruiser was gone, following Ana Maria as directed. Arn waited until a car had driven past the house before he stepped outside and shut the door.

His car hugged the ground on flat tires where he'd parked it behind Georgia's last night. He ran his hand over the knife cuts to the sidewalls, careful not to get cut on the exposed steel cords. Standing, he studied the footprints in the melting snow, indistinct as the paw prints that ran from the neighbor's house to Arn's.

He continued to examine the footprints, hunched over, following them. When he reached the far side of his car, he froze. *Drop the Case* had been gouged in the side of the door, probably with a sturdy knife.

Arn warmed his hands with his breath as he walked to the porch. The door had locked, and he banged on the side of the house. He banged again just as an elderly couple drove by slowly, pointing and laughing at the odd man wearing the woman's flowered bathrobe.

Danny opened the door and stopped him. "Knock the snow off first."

Arn knocked one boot against the other before setting them on cardboard. He slapped the door. "One of those spring-loaded ones. I hate them."

"It was the best lock they had."

"Remember me telling you about Butch's lock just like that?"

"Vaguely," Danny said.

"Replace it with a dead bolt."

"You paranoid?"

———

"You paranoid?" Oblanski asked, and Arn could almost hear his snicker over the phone.

"After someone grabbed Ana Maria and attacked me? You bet I am. After somebody came into my house—into my room—and stole my slippers, just to make a point? You bet I am. And after my tires got slashed and the side of my car sliced up? You bet I am. And don't forget Johnny. All I'm asking you is to do your job." Arn felt growing anger; not so much at Oblanski but at himself. He'd let his guard down—that guard that had saved his bacon more times than he could count when he'd worn a badge—and his complacency now could have cost him his life. As well as Ana Maria's and Danny's.

"I've assigned a man round the clock to keep watch over Ana Maria," Oblanski said. "That's about as much as I can do with the manpower we got."

"Well, someone got into my house past your steely-eyed patrolman."

"And now *you* want protection, too?"

Arn wasn't sure if his pride would allow police protection, but Oblanski's arguments made his case. "If someone wanted you dead, why didn't he just walk up and shoot you like Johnny?" Oblanski asked.

"He's toying with me. Wants me to keep looking over my shoulder."

"Like a deer looking for the cougar who'll pounce eventually?"

"Something like that."

"I'm sorry all to hell I have budget constraints," Oblanski said. "I don't know if you've heard, but every available man is running down leads on Johnny's shooter. You'll just have to keep looking over your shoulder until—"

"Until the killer decides to make his move?"

"I got to run to the hospital," Oblanski said. "They might bring Johnny out of the coma for a few minutes. If they do, I want to be there to talk with him."

Arn hung up his phone and accepted the coffee Danny handed him. "You're on your own, by the sounds of the fine Lt. Oblanski."

"You mean *we're* on our own," Danny said.

"That's why I need you to reinforce the windows and stick extra screws in the boards over the windows we haven't replaced yet." Arn grabbed a Bounty towel and jotted a number down. "Get a security system installed."

"What do I use for a phone?"

Arn handed him his cell. "And tell them we don't want those stickers plastered over the doors and windows advertising we have a system."

"What are you going to be doing?"

"Before I call the insurance and a tow truck? I'm going to take a shower to cool off."

Thirty-Two

ARN STOPPED THE VIDEOTAPE of Butch's crime scene. He'd watched it a half-dozen times, but nothing jumped out that wasn't noted in the police reports. He ejected the tape from the obsolete VCR Danny had "acquired" somewhere and turned to the white wall. He stood studying the photos of the three officers pinned beside those of the Five Point Killer's victims, his mind playing with the variables. And with the constants.

Danny pulled up a chair and set his coffee cup on the makeshift table. "Let's see what we can brainstorm this morning."

"This doesn't concern you."

"A fresh set of eyes can help, if I recall you saying that," Danny said. "And as many times as we've both seen them, our eyes are getting a little weary. But let's try it again."

"Don't you have drywall to hang?"

Danny looked sideways at Arn. "I would if someone else in this house would help me. But right this moment, I'm on break." He rested his elbows on the table and leaned to look at the white wall. "So what we got?"

Arn sighed. "Both Five Point murders were committed in late summer, but a year apart."

"Damn," Danny said. "I never noticed that."

"That's why I'm a PI and you're a sidekick." Arn munched on a cookie from the plate Danny brought. "I thought it might be someone whose business slows down after the summer: bricklayer. Construction worker."

Danny leaned back in his chair sipping coffee. "Maybe the killer was a teacher. School janitor. Someone who's gone for the summer."

"Or a student just returning from living with a custodial parent away from Cheyenne."

"Can you see some kid overpowering grown men?" Danny leaned back and caught Arn staring at the dog biscuit Danny gnawed on. "I just finished walking the neighbor's dog. It was a leftover treat."

Arn dropped his pen on the door. "No one reported anyone suspicious walking away from either crime scene. And again, with that much blood, the killer would have been covered in it." Arn had read in one police report that two patrolmen responding to Delbert Urban's homicide had puked the moment they saw the amount of blood covering the office. "Delbert Urban especially, killed in the middle of a business district in the afternoon. Why?"

"Beats me."

"What are sidekicks for?"

"Okay." Danny stood and walked to the white wall, looking at the photos from a different angle. "Maybe the victim showered before coming out. Does the Hobby Shop have a shower?"

Arn made a note to ask Oblanski if the Hobby Shop had a shower. And if it or Joey Bent's house was checked for blood in the drain. "Good idea."

"That's what sidekicks are for."

Arn sifted through Butch's field notes and located one he found interesting. "An angle that Butch and Gaylord were working was that both victims were killed by prostitutes."

"Because both were almost nude?"

Arn nodded. "Cheyenne's not exactly the mecca for street flesh. Where would someone find a hooker around here?"

Danny laid his hand on Arn's forearm. "You're good-looking enough you don't have to pay."

Arn jerked his arm back.

"All right," Danny said. "But do you want male or female?"

"With someone as fat as Delbert Urban, and effeminate as Joey Bent, I'm leaning toward male. Especially with that NAMBLA letter at Delbert's."

"I agree. We'll take a drive by a place in a little bit that used to cater to gays when they were open. But break's over. I got to get back to taping drywall."

Danny had just risen to leave when Arn stopped him. "Thanks for hanging that new door. The place is shaping up. Just wondered where you learned your home improvement."

Danny faced him and rested his hand on his thin hips. "Home improvement? Try old world craftsmanship. I wasn't always a derelict."

"You're not one now."

"Thanks," Danny said and nodded to the photos on the white wall. "One other thing: the media at the time also called this guy the Full Moon Killer, as both victims were killed under a full moon. Think that's just coincidence?"

Arn walked to the white wall and put his reading glasses on. He could almost feel the knife rip into soft flesh; feel sticky blood spurting over the victims, the cast-off blood spattering the walls and floor. He could hear bones break, lungs filling with fluid to snuff out life before their time. He could smell the stench of rancid blood and putrid feces as they died.

"That SOB didn't do anything by coincidence. He planned it that way," he said. When he was a young officer, Arn's shift sergeant had warned his men to be especially vigilant during full moons. And it was true. People did crazy things during a full moon.

He started gathering the police reports and then whirled around. "There!" He slapped Delbert Urban's picture. "That's where I saw that shoe print before." Arn scrambled to look through Gaylord's case file. He tossed a picture in the center of the door. "Right there! It's the same print."

Danny squinted and put on his own glasses. "I don't see any shoe print."

Arn traced a single, faint shoe print found in the mud in front of Gaylord's house the afternoon Adelle found him hanging. "There's no mention of this print in any police report."

"Meaning?"

"Meaning Oblanski was the first officer on scene and secured it until Butch arrived. Yet Oblanski made no mention of it."

"Because another officer put it there?"

"Or because he didn't think it was germane to the case." He held Gaylord's photo next to Delbert Urban's. "The same tread pattern outside Gaylord's house is on Delbert Urban's back."

"I've seen it, too." Danny pocketed his glasses and backed away, his lips quivering. "You remember that morning you lost your slippers? That shoe print"—he nodded to the photo of Gaylord's house—"was

191

in the drywall dust *right* outside your room." He laid his hand on Arn's shoulder to steady his trembling legs. "I thought it was yours. Maybe you're right. Maybe the Five Point Killer has returned."

Arn pried Danny's hand from his shoulder. "And maybe Gaylord's hanging wasn't autoerotic after all."

Thirty-Three

"FRIGGIN' GLASS!" I DESERVE everything I get, stepping on what's left of my television. How juvenile, picking it up and slamming it on the floor. And how juvenile was it slicing Anderson's tires and gouging the side of his nice old classic? But when I went right past that policeman again and to the front door, the try keys wouldn't work. I needed to get inside once more. The last time was just too much fun, watching him sleep. Knowing I could take him any time I wished. I'd been thinking of that all day, anticipating. Short of my head exploding and waking the cop sleeping in his car, I had to do something to bleed the anger off. But vandalize a car? And on a full moon, when the cop could have awakened and seen me. It's not like when I planned the killings on a full moon to give the cops something to ponder. Send them in a different direction. Tonight the policeman could have spotted me. Tonight luck favored the foolish. Again.

I take off my shoes and wrap them in a plastic bag before hiding them above my loose ceiling tile. I've read some people have a favorite weapon they use. Some a ritual they go through before heading out to hunt. My superstition is my shoes—they've been good to me all these times, and will continue to be in the future. Because they have a future with me.

Tonight. Tomorrow at the latest. With Johnny surviving and coming out of his coma immanently, I can't chance that he'll remember me walking up to him in his driveway. I can't chance he'll remember me thrusting out my hand to shake his, clutching my small auto.

I'll have to pay him another visit. And I'll wear my lucky shoes when I do.

Thirty-Four

ARN TOSSED THE PHOTOS from Delbert Urban's crime scene and Gaylord's hanging onto Oblanski's desk. "Same tread pattern at both scenes."

Oblanski picked them up and held them to the light filtering through his window. "It was muddy that day. So some patrolman walked in the slop with Vibram shoes. We all wore them back then." He tossed the pictures on his desk and went back to sorting through his messages.

"Damn it, Oblanski. Can't you get off your high horse for just a moment and admit the same person who killed Delbert Urban and Joey Bent might also have hung Gaylord—"

"Enough!" Oblanski slammed his fist on his desk. A small framed wedding picture bounced to the floor. The glass shattered, but he made no effort to clean it up as he glared across his desk at Arn. "You want to sensationalize this. Make your name pop into people's minds. What kind of gig you looking for, some talking head at CNN or Fox?" Oblanski took several deep, calming breaths before continuing. "I've heard enough of your lame theories these last few days to last me a lifetime."

"They weren't lame."

"A murderer didn't grab Ana Maria and cut you when you went to help her. It was some damned fan obsessed with her, is all. Then there were the slippers you forgot you left in Ana Maria's car that you claim someone sneaking into your house grabbed. And don't forget some neighborhood kids slashed your tires. Keyed the side of your car." Oblanski skidded a pencil off the rim of the trash can. "It's not as sensational as you make it out to be."

Arn stood and shouldered his bag. "All right. Blow me off. But mark my word, Acting Chief: anything happens to Ana Maria Villarreal because of your complacency, and I'll come hunting *you*."

Oblanski stood suddenly and rushed around his desk, fists clenching, jaw muscles working overtime. "You come in here and threaten me, I'll ... "

Arn stepped closer and tossed his bag on a chair. "Just what the hell you gonna do, Acting Chief? I hope it's something, 'cause I'm butt-tired of your petty horseshit."

Arn counted to five—the number that experience told him bullies usually took to realize their threats could lead to an ass-whooping—and Oblanski backed away. "I got nothing else to say to you. Do not come into the police department again."

———

Arn passed the Air Guard base on his way to pick up Georgia for a lunch date. She lived with Pieter in a part of town that was the exclusive part of Cheyenne in the 1940s and 1950s. Doctors and lawyers, railroad tycoons and cattle barons lived there when Cheyenne was booming. And that part of town now boasted one upstart architect.

Arn drove past massive brick homes large enough for multiple families. His father had told him stories about this area, where the police responded to calls about minor thefts and vandalism, about people hopping guarded fences to steal exotic flowers grown in the summer. Occasionally a designer dog or cat. Not like other parts of town, where it might be dangerous just to step off your porch at night. Like where the house Arn grew up in was located.

He pulled off Carey into Pieter's wide circular driveway. Arn's tiny rental car looked out of place beside the red brick tri-level, twin frozen waterfalls caught in mid-flow on the edge of the back yard. The fan-shaped stained glass balcony window above the portico seemed to smile at Arn as he stretched, and twin colonnades on either side of the front double doors were accented by cast-iron lion heads with the bodies of horses.

He used the car door to steady himself, working the stiffness out of the leg the attacker had struck the other night. If he had been more limber, he would have kicked himself in the butt for buying the ghetto car insurance policy that had given him this tiny widow-maker until his 4-4-2 was fixed. What he needed was his car back. Something with leg room. "We'll be done with your Olds in a week," the manager at the body shop told him. "Give or take a week."

The garage door opened and Georgia stood with her arms wrapped around herself, breath frosting as she waved him into the driveway. "Car doesn't much fit you. Yours?"

"Not any longer than necessary." He explained the tire slashing and the car getting gouged with the warning, and how he was at the mercy of a Denver insurance agent whom he'd arrested for fraud some years back. And who was so gracious as to authorize him the go-cart sitting in Pieter's driveway.

Georgia stood in the doorway looking up with concern in her eyes. "The damage to your car is connected to Johnny's shooting and to your investigation, isn't it?"

"Naw," Arn said without conviction. "I just live in a bad neighborhood, is all."

"That's for sure," Georgia said.

Arn had grown up living next to blacks whose fathers worked as porters on Union Pacific passenger trains, and Mexicans whose dads worked as firemen oilers. It hadn't been easy for him, with his ice blue eyes and nearly white blond hair. More than a few days he'd gotten jumped on the way home from school. And more than once his dad had to set his broken nose. He waved his hand around the front of the house. "Our place wasn't like this."

Georgia looked around with a smile. "Pieter said if he ever made it big, he wanted a place along the old Cheyenne to Black Hills stage route."

"It used to go right by here," Arn said. "My great-granddad drove for the line when it first cut through Indian country in 1876. Cracked a whip for two years until he realized it was safer punching cows than become part of a Lakota ambush."

Georgia looked to the north, as if she could envision the stage rolling by on muddy roads. "That's where you must have gotten your love of horses."

"Actually," Arn said, "my granddad passed that along. He came to live with us when he got too old to run a branding iron or cut nuts."

Georgia scrunched up her nose. "That sounds barbaric."

"That's calves' nuts. And it's not as barbaric as sitting on his lap, listening to his stories, knowing I could never really live them like he did." Arn unbuttoned his coat. "The old boy even fought in the Johnson County War in 1892." He laughed. "With all the things he got into, it's a wonder he lived until he was 94 rather than dangle at the end of a posse's rope."

"Enough talk of death for one afternoon." Georgia led him through Pieter's garage. Arn stopped and admired a canary yellow Karman Ghia under a car cover. "Great shape for a ... '74?"

"You know your imports." Georgia ran her hand along the top. "This is Pieter's baby. He doesn't drive it much. Can't hardly find anyone to work on them anymore. It was his first car as a kid, and he's been nursing it since."

Arn shook his head, hoping his own baby would be out of the body shop soon.

He followed Georgia into the house, which was filled with antique furniture. Georgia hung his Stetson on a hall tree that reached nearly to the ten-foot ceiling. It was topped with a carved elk head resting on intricate maple leaves.

They walked past twin oak secretaries on either side of double stained glass doors, past a standing Tiffany lamp illuminating a rolltop desk as long as Arn's bed. At least what he remembered his bed being like back in Denver. He stopped and lightly traced a hunting scene carved in the back of the desk.

"Pieter got his love of old things from Butch," Georgia said. "Who never owned anything new, what with following Hannah around town and paying her bar tabs. Pieter said when he became successful, he'd start collecting."

"I got old stuff," Arn said.

"Antiques?"

"No. Just old stuff I should have gotten rid of instead of sticking it in a storage unit in Denver."

Georgia nodded knowingly. "I got some of that old stuff myself that's hard to toss out." She motioned with a finger. "Keep me company while I finish putting on sheets."

Arn followed her across polished mahogany floors, nails and gouges showing through a satin finish and giving the floor character. As they walked past an iron-grated fireplace, the pine pitch crackled and spit, and Georgia paused just long enough to toss in another log before heading up the winding staircase. She looked at Arn trailing after her. "I just need to straighten Pieter's things up a couple times a week. If I don't, he'll sleep in the same sheets for a year."

"Sounds like you won't be doing it much longer."

"How so?"

"Pieter's fiancée will be taking over those chores," Arn said.

"Meander?" Georgia laughed as she grabbed a set of sheets from a hall closet and headed into Pieter's bedroom. "I don't look for them to be tying the knot anytime soon. Grab an end." She tossed the fitted sheet across the bed to open it. Arn was never able to do much with fitted sheets. Or much else domestically related. Cailee had done all that, and Arn was always amazed at the hours she put in around the house. He wished she were here so he could say how much he appreciated her. He made a mental note to tell Danny how much he appreciated what he did every day around the old house.

"I thought they were engaged?" Arn lost his grip on the fitted sheet. It swatted the side of his head like a giant rubber band.

"Pieter and Meander have been engaged since high school. Pull that corner."

Arn did as he was told.

"I think it's more comfortable for them to claim they're spoken for than fight off suitors." Georgia shooed him away. "You're not much with sheets, are you?"

"Guess I do more harm than good."

"You got that," Georgia said. "Let me finish so we can get a bite to eat."

Arn dropped his end of the sheet and walked around the spacious room. For as many antiques as the rest of the house had, Pieter's bedroom was bland. Like his office. A simple rag rug lay in front of a four-drawer dresser. A single photo hung over the dresser, and Arn put on his glasses. It was the same picture Pieter had in his office.

"Nike and Pepsi sponsored the team the year they won state." Georgia came around the bed, smoothing the sheet. "Everyone got a new pair of Nikes and Pepsi for a year." She stood with her arms crossed in front of the picture. "It was his junior year, and you'd have thought he won the lottery." She laughed. "I think that was the year his voice changed. Kid grew up faster than Butch wanted."

She dusted off the picture with her handkerchief. "I told you he spent as much time in sports as he could to keep away from Butch." She tapped the picture. "But then he's always been competitive. And generous. Hell, he gave the Nikes away to Meander's little brother. Stayed with New Balance. Pieter said Nikes hurt his feet. Generous."

"You sound just like a proud ... "

"Mother?" Georgia smiled. "I am. In a sense. He's more like my boy than my nephew. Sure, I was proud, the way he always worked his tail off at that freight company after school. Or helping Meander's little brother out when he could. Pieter wasn't afraid to give as much as he made. Sure, you can say I'm just a little proud."

She brushed past him and tucked the comforter in, leaving Arn to roam the room again. A scarred green footlocker with *US Army* in faded black letters on the lid guarded the foot of Pieter's bed.

"That was Butch's," Georgia said from somewhere on the other side of the waist-tall mattress. "Pieter stores a few things of his dad's he wanted to keep after the murder. I took the rest to Goodwill, and his police equipment down to the police department."

"I saw Butch's old uniform hanging behind the glass down in the lobby."

Georgia slapped the bed to knock the last of the wrinkles into submission. She came around and looked down at the footlocker. "Pieter donated Butch's uniform and Sam Browne belt from when he worked the street. He thought people coming into the police station might see it and remember who his father was."

She stepped back and surveyed the room with her hands on her hips. "Finished. At least until next week. Hungry?"

"Famished."

"Then I'll pick the spot," she said as she flicked the lights off in the room.

Thirty-Five

GEORGIA ASKED THE WAITER at Sanford's Grill to seat them in the back. Arn followed her past wall-to-wall junk hanging off the walls and suspended from the ceiling. Bicycles more at home in a 1950s commercial dangled overhead, while old dented and rusted hubcaps dotted the walls between more old-time sports pictures than Arn recalled seeing before. Shiny hood ornaments from the 1960s accented cracked, wafer-thin baseball gloves. As the waiter showed them to their table, Arn thought the only thing missing was Fred Sanford faking a heart attack while LaMont looked on skeptically.

"I think I had a unicycle like that once." Arn pointed to a single-tired contraption missing a seat. "I wrecked every day after school trying to get away from the Ortiz brothers."

"They were ornery, as I remember," Georgia said as she opened the menu.

"Ornery, hell. They were purely mean little bastards. They weren't very big but they hunted in a pack."

"And that might have been mine." Georgia pointed to a cracked Louisville Slugger balanced on top of a rusted milk can.

"You played ball?"

"Don't sound so chauvinistic. I played Little League shortstop before I filled out enough to become a cheerleader."

Arn wanted to comment on how aptly Georgia had filled out, but he wisely kept quiet and opened his own menu. "What's good?"

"I love the Rusty Hood. Reuben smothered with wine sauerkraut and pickles and—"

"If it's so good, why don't you serve it at Poor Richard's?"

"Shush," she whispered. "They'll shoot me as a spy if they hear I cook there."

A waitress arrived at their table wearing a red-and-white-striped skirt and bobby socks with patent leather pumps. She was smacking gum. Georgia motioned to Arn, and he ordered the Rusty Hood and vegetable noodle soup. She the Cobb salad.

"I thought you said the Rusty Hood was good?"

"It's great. But if you only knew how many calories there were in that, you wouldn't have ordered it."

"Just what I need." Arn tugged at his waistband. "Another new belt."

"How's Chief White?" Georgia changed the subject. "Meander says the floor nurses up on the seventh floor have high hopes for his recovery."

Arn filled Georgia in on what Oblanski had told him: Johnny wasn't strong enough today, but by tomorrow the doctors expected to bring him out of the coma to see how he handled the pain. "If Johnny's up to it, Oblanski hopes to be able to talk with him then."

The waitress brought their orders, and Arn was only vaguely aware that he broke his second pack of crackers and sprinkled them in his soup.

"You sure you're hungry?"

"What?" He looked up.

"You've been reading the alphabet soup in that bowl for five minutes like it was the newspaper."

"Sorry." He brushed crumbs off his hands. "I hate to admit it, but I have other reasons for asking you to lunch."

"I figured as much." Georgia dribbled vinaigrette over her greens. "You needed to ask me more questions."

"Damn woman's intuition."

She smiled and picked up her fork. "Don't worry about it. I'll take a date any way I can get it. Ask away."

"Okay." Arn took a deep breath. "Here goes. Butch and Hannah's neighbor, Emma Barnes, placed you at the house at 12:45 the morning Butch was murdered. But you didn't call 911 until 1:45. An hour later."

Georgia sipped her tea, twirling the tea bag around in the hot water. "I called 911 at 1:45 because that's when I arrived. Pieter called me at 1:30 and I drove right over. As soon as I saw Butch, I called police dispatch."

"How do account for the hour discrepancy?"

Georgia speared an olive, and it bounced on the end of her fork as she gestured. "Butch constantly complained to me about that old busybody. Always calling the police about things."

"I saw on the call logs how many times she reported them fighting."

Georgia put her fork down and seemed to be studying an old ball bat resting on a milk can screwed to the wall. "When Bobbie interviewed me that morning, we talked about it. He thought like I did: that Emma must have seen someone else going into Butch's house. He never had a yard light, and she was older than dirt ten years ago. Bobby was convinced Emma saw the killer, and that he went inside the house at 12:45, shot Butch, and fled. Bobbie doubted she'd ever had a clear view of the front door from her house."

"Then I'd better talk with her."

"Good luck getting anything from her," Georgia said, picking onions off her plate. "She sold the house a year after Hannah lost hers to the bank. Emma is soaking up air at the Shady Rest Retirement Home."

"Why do they always give old folks' homes names that sound like the residents should have one foot in the grave?" Arn asked.

"Because Emma does."

"Then I better drive on over there sooner than later."

"And one other thing," Georgia said, leaning her arms across the table. She squeezed Arn's arm and winked. "She dislikes men. Especially if you tell her you were a retired cop."

"So you're saying I should go in drag and hope her eyesight's crappy?"

Thirty-Six

ANA MARIA SQUIRMED TO get comfortable in the tiny car. "We could have taken my Bug. At least there's *some* room in it."

Arn pulled his bad leg away from the steering column and flexed it. "As you can see, the Clown Car's not exactly smooth driving for me, either."

"Clown Car?"

"Clown Car. Damn thing reminds me of those miniature cars at circuses toting a dozen clowns around the arena. Friggin' Clown Car."

They drove past Frontier Mall—what else would you call a shopping center in Cheyenne, Wyoming, Arn thought—and past strip malls farther up the road. "Turn at the next light," Ana Maria said. "Shady Rest is the next block."

She directed Arn into a cul-de-sac. A scrub field sat on one side of the retirement home, a Toyota pickup up on blocks on the other side. With no trees in sight, the Shady Rest waited at the end of the turnaround. "Just where I want to spend my last days," Arn said.

They slid to a stop in a parking lot that probably hadn't been scraped of ice and snow since last winter. Arn opened his door and began the ritual he'd developed to get out of the car. He used his hands to pull one leg past the steering column and set it on the ground before using the door jamb to haul himself erect. He stood for a moment stretching his back and legs before grabbing his bag when he caught Ana Maria staring at him. "What?"

"I don't feel one bit sorry for you," she said. "If you'd upped your policy, you'd be driving something comfortable now."

"You mean, if I hadn't arrested the agent who sold me the policy?"

"That too."

They made their way slowly across the pavement, passing a picket fence broken down from the weight of the snow and time, a few rotting boards all that was left to show there'd even been a fence once. As they climbed the ice-and-snow-packed steps leading to the retirement home's office, Ana Maria started to slip and grabbed Arn's arm. Arn wasn't sure who would fall first as he grasped the bent railing loose in the concrete. His cowboy boots skidded, and he grabbed the railing again. It pulled loose from the crumbling concrete and he flailed his arms to keep his balance.

"Of all the times not to have my cameraman here," Ana Maria said. "Or my phone. I could have made a mint posting that little dance to YouTube."

When they reached the top of the steps, Arn stomped snow from his boots before entering the office. A television sat in one corner of a small commons area, four residents huddled around it. Sleeping. "I've seen test patterns with better picture quality than that," Arn said.

Ana Maria looked at him. "What's a test pattern?"

Arn shook his head. "Just something I used to study for."

He walked across the commons to the front counter. A pimple-faced kid wearing jeans with the knees blown out and sporting an AC/DC cap perched backwards on his purple hair looked up from a computer. He made no attempt to hide the porn flick he was engrossed in. And he made no attempt to see what Arn and Ana Maria wanted.

Arn slapped the ringer hard enough that it bounced on the counter and nearly fell to the floor. But it got the kid's attention. "I dammed near fell on your steps out there."

The kid looked over his shoulder briefly before going back to watching every bump and grind on the video. "And your point?"

"Snow and ice is packed in your parking lot. That's my point."

The kid swiveled in his chair and faced the counter. His eyes settled on Ana Maria's chest for long moments before he nodded at the door. "Did you notice that snow shovel leaning against the door? I leave it there. If anyone's offended by the snow, they can shovel it. Just what are you and this hot mama here for besides bitchin' about our sidewalks?"

"We need to see Emma Barnes."

"You family?"

"No. We'd just like to visit with her."

The kid looked over at a roster of residents tacked to a wall. "Go pack sand, mister," he said, and started turning back before Arn reached over and clamped a hand on the kid's shoulder. He recognized the world of authority the kid was king in—he was a bully like Arn had dealt with a hundred times. In another life, this geek might have worn a gun and badge and ordered people around just to watch them squirm.

"You denying the authorities access to Ms. Barnes?" he asked.

"You are …"

"The authorities," Arn answered. "Now if we need to get a subpoena just to talk to her"—he waved his hand around the shabby lobby—"we might as well call in the state inspector to look at this dump."

Pimple Face threw up his hands in resignation. "No need for that. We just like to protect our clients."

Arn looked around. "So you're all about their welfare here at Shady Rest?"

"You could say that."

"No, I couldn't," Arn said, "with any conviction. Her room number?"

The kid pointed down a long hallway on the other side of a door. "Hall B. Room 107."

Ana Maria waited until they'd started down the hall before she chuckled. "A subpoena? Is that your standard threat for everything? And the state inspector was a nice touch."

"If that didn't work, my next threat was probation and parole."

They walked the hallway, which was mushy from a recent ceiling leak, black mold forming down on one wall. They found Emma Barnes' apartment next to a three-foot gap where the drywall had been torn out. Arn rang the doorbell, but didn't hear it chime. He punched the bell again and it fell to the floor, wires dangling out of the wall waiting for a repairman. Someday.

He rapped on the door, and was ready to knock again when it opened.

"Who the hell are you?" Emma Barnes stood little more than five foot, with trifocals that caused her to constantly move her head up and down as she focused on Arn. Wind whistled through ill-fitting dentures, and she shifted her weight between legs swollen with fluid. "I said who the hell are you?"

"Arn Anderson, ma'am."

"That supposed to mean something? You ain't selling seed packs, are you? 'Cause the last zucchini seeds I bought never came up."

"We're here looking for information…"

Ana Maria stepped in front of Arn and smiled broadly. "I'm Ana Maria Villarreal, from News 5."

Emma's eyes lit up and she shook Ana Maria's hand. "I see you every night at six. Cuss you out, now and again." She held up her hands. "Nothing personal."

"No offense taken. May we come in? We would like to visit for a moment."

Emma turned painfully and hobbled into the living room of the tiny two-room apartment.

"It wasn't going too well," Ana Maria whispered. "Thought I'd better jump in before you blew it."

"So much for my natural charm."

Emma motioned them to a three-legged couch, a brick jammed under where the fourth leg should have been. Like the Captain Ahab of the couch world. She craned her neck up at Arn. "You were just at the door."

"I was."

"Who are you?"

"I'm working with Ms. Villarreal. We'd like to know about Butch Spangler."

"He's dead."

"We know that." Arn forced a smile. "May we visit?"

"Suit yourself."

She sat in an occasional chair and picked up a tatting shuttle from a TV tray beside her. She wrapped a ball of string around one hand and began making lace, ignoring them. She looked up as if seeing them for the first time. "You were just at the door."

"We were," Ana Maria said.

Arn watched in fascination as the old woman bowed her head to her string. His mother had knitted for hours, much as Emma did now, everything from sweaters to tablecloths to baby booties. And every year at Christmas, Arn would get a knitted stocking cap and matching pair of gloves, both too porous to keep out the cold. Usually in a pink or pastel. Which gave the Ortiz brothers more fuel to pick on him.

Beside Emma's ball of string, an empty plate with crumbs of some sort indicated she'd just eaten. "What did you have for lunch?" Arn tried loosening her up.

"How should I know," Emma said, not looking up from her tatting.

Arn's uncle, his mother's brother, had deteriorated much as Emma had. He couldn't remember what Arn wore to school that morning, but he remembered every person's name who'd helped him brand cows for the past fifty years.

Arn took out his notebook and pen. "What do you recall about the night Butch Spangler was murdered?"

Emma laid her tatting shuttle and string on the TV tray. "I'm half blind. Not deaf. You don't have to yell. Now what the hell you want to know about?"

Arn looked to Ana Maria for help. She rested her hand on the old woman's arm. "We just want to know what happened the night he was killed."

Emma turned in her seat to face Ana Maria. "What do you need to know?"

"When the police talked with you," Ana Maria said, "you reported that Georgia Spangler got to Butch's house—"

"At 12:45."

"You're quite sure about that?"

Emma glared at Arn. "I'm old. Not dumb. Of course I'm sure. Oh, I didn't see her face, but that sister of Butch's was the only one who ever came around. She'd pick up that little guy of his ... " Emma trailed off and grabbed her shuttle and string again. "I was sitting there"—pointing like she could see it in her mind's eye—"by the window facing their place. I thought she was coming to pick up the boy again."

"Were you usually up at that time?" Ana Maria asked. "Because it was pretty late."

"I was always up late. Damned trains a block away always blowing their fool horns. Sure, I was always up, keeping an eye on that Spangler house in case I needed to call the law." She looked at a corner of the ceiling with a faraway look. "Sitting right by my bay window. Wish I was there. Sitting and making doilies."

"Could anyone have come to the house before the sister got there?" Emma shrugged. "I don't think so."

"So someone might have?" Ana Maria pressed.

Emma looked longingly at the bathroom door. "I've got bladder issues. Always have. I can't seem to drink a cup of joe that I don't have to pee. That was the only times I left that window that night, when I had to take a whiz."

As if to punctuate her explanation, she used the arms of the chair to stand and shuffled into the bathroom. Ana Maria leaned over and whispered, "You think someone was there that night before Georgia came over?"

Arn checked his watch. "We'll see."

Emma was in the bathroom long enough to tat several doilies, Arn thought, checking his watch. When she finally emerged, she pulled her dress over her legs.

"Eight minutes is long enough to kill anyone," he whispered to Ana Maria. He jotted in his notes that someone could have come to the house before Georgia did while Emma was in the bathroom. "Did anyone come to the house after Georgia?" he asked.

Emma tatted lace.

"Besides the police?" he pressed.

"That no-account Indian she was sparkin'," Emma said.

"Frank Dull Knife?"

"Yeah. Him."

"He came that night?" Arn asked.

"Don't try to confuse me!" Emma grabbed a small pair of scissors and snipped the string. She spread the doily across her lap, her head bobbing as she focused through her trifocals. "Of course he didn't come that night. He came around after the cop was killed. To see Hannah."

"Often?" Ana Maria asked.

Emma stopped, working her fingers out of the scissors. "That's the odd part. The Indian came around quite a bit before the cop died, when he was out working. But after the murder, I only saw the Indian once."

Ana Maria moved closer and met Emma's eyes. "When was that, Emma?"

"Couple weeks after it happened. Hannah chased him into the yard, grabbing his greasy hair. Slapped him. He turned and knocked her to the ground. 'If you don't come back,' she screamed, 'I'm going to tell.'"

"Tell what?" Arn asked.

"How the hell should I know?" Emma wheezed between her dentures. "I'm not nosy."

———————

Pimple Face was knocking snow off his Nikes, and a stocking cap had replaced his AC/DC cap. "Guess he actually thought you'd call the state inspectors," Ana Maria said as they stepped onto a clean walk.

The kid had sprinkled snow melter on the steps, and Arn was grateful that Ana Maria wouldn't have another YouTube moment as he picked his way down.

He held the car door for Ana Maria and walked around to the driver's side. As Arn was halfway through his entry ritual, he froze. A solitary shoe print—distinct among other shuffling prints that were not his—had been set in the snow beside the door.

He crawled out and looked closer at the print. It was placed a few feet beside tire treads that had pulled up to Arn's rental. Someone had stood where Arn stood, but there was no damage to his car. Nothing taken.

"What is it?"

He motioned for Ana Maria. She climbed out and walked around the car. As soon as she cleared the trunk, she spotted the print. She paled when she realized the implications. "It's that same print that was at Gaylord's house." She trembled noticeably as she looked around the cul-de-sac. "And on Delbert Urban's back. And Joey Bent's house."

"And just outside my car when it got vandalized."

"Another warning?" Ana Maria asked.

"Or the killer's throwing down the gauntlet. Let the games begin," Arn said to himself. "I'm tired of being the hunted."

Thirty-Seven

*"**PISS ON YOU.**" I give some prick backing out of his driveway the middle finger. This is a public street. I can sit here as long as I'm not blocking his drive. And if he thinks I'm looking at some babe with my spotting scope—I am. I lower it. Now's not the time to throw caution to the wild wind just because I want to see Anderson's reaction. And watching Ana Maria's reaction to seeing the shoe print is a bonus. Still, it wouldn't do for the police to get a call about a long-distance window peeper sitting on the street, and I drive away.*

This is the second time I acted impulsively today. The first when I followed Anderson and Ana Maria to the Shady Rest and, on a whim, drove the cul-de-sac and turned around. I stopped next to Anderson's rental car and grabbed my shoes from their box. Did I put that single shoe print by his car door to warn him? I thought I did. Until just now, when I saw how he nervously checked the area when he found it.

I hope he doesn't take it as a warning.

For excitement's sake, I hope he takes it as a challenge.

Come find me, Mr. Metro Cop.

Thirty-Eight

DANNY CAME DOWN THE stairs, drywall mud caked to his sweat-pants and the front of his T-shirt. "Cop out front."

Arn moved the blanket masquerading as a curtain aside. A white Crown Vic had pulled to the curb across the street. "How you know it's a cop?"

Danny stopped at the coat closet long enough to grab his field jacket. "Trust me, it's a cop."

"Where are you going? I'm sure he's not here for you."

"I've got to walk the dog."

"By the back door?" But Danny had disappeared by the time the knock came.

Oblanski stood in front of the door with his hands in his pockets, looking like he'd pulled an all-nighter at the local bar. He craned his neck around the door and looked inside. "I love what you've done with the place." He nodded to the bare walls, seeing where insulation on old wiring had flayed to reveal exposed ends that needed taping off.

Danny had wired a single naked bulb that dangled in the middle of the room with a drop cord that strung from the kitchen for power. The bare subfloor hadn't been covered yet, and the staircase railing lay where it had fallen down the night before. "Is this what I got to look forward to in retirement?"

"You should have seen it when we started."

"We?"

"Handyman who's helping me." Arn looked to the back door. "He had to leave for a minute. Come in."

Arn led Oblanski through the house to the kitchen. Danny had hung and taped new drywall and routed the countertop edges yesterday. Arn motioned to chairs around a small table he'd bought at Walmart last night. "This will have to do me until my furniture arrives from storage." He offered Oblanski a cup of coffee, but Oblanski declined.

"This isn't police coffee," Arn pointed out.

"In that case," Oblanski said, accepting the cup.

Arn sat across from him and slid a sugar bowl over. "Must be important for the chief to come around."

"Acting chief."

"You sound like Johnny now."

"Hope I don't wind up like him," Oblanski said.

"How's he doing?"

Oblanski sipped lightly at first, then took a deeper drink. A smile crossed his face. "This is pretty good. Maybe I'll marry you." Arn debated telling him that Danny had made the coffee and the old man was already spoken for.

"Johnny's still stable," Oblanski went on. "The docs say he's doing better than expected. They'll probably bring him out of the coma late today just long enough that I can talk with him for a bit." He cupped his hands around the mug and was silent for long moments before he looked up. "With Johnny out of it, I'm the one who has to go on air with Ana Maria tonight. Gonna be different going on being the acting chief. What do I say on TV?"

Arn kicked his bad leg back, the stiffness slowly leaving these last days as the swelling subsided. The doctor had taken the stitches in his ear out yesterday, and his sliced cheek was healing as good as expected for a fifty-five-year-old man. "Tell the viewers we're close to solving Butch's murder. Tell them some new evidence has come in through the tip line that connects Butch to the Five Point Killer cases." Arn stood to refill their cups. "And tell them we have a strong suspect in Johnny's shooting."

"But we *don't* have anything new."

"You ever do much hunting, Ned?"

"I go to a pheasant farm every year, is about all I have time for."

"Well, I've hunted everything in this state, and most in other places. I especially liked to hunt bear when I was younger."

"I detect a moral to this parable?"

"No, but there is a lesson." Arn wiped coffee dripping down the side of his cup. "When you hunt bear, you bait them. I've hunted over elk or deer gut piles. Sometimes sweet gooey things like donuts and syrup, and I sat over the bait. Either way, you make the bear think you have something. You lure him in from the woods with the thought of that bait going down his hungry gullet." He downed the last of his coffee and set the cup on the counter. "If you convince the killer we have more, he'll want to come in and see for himself. We'll make him hungry with our bait."

"If he'll be watching."

"He'll be watching all right. He can't drag himself away from the television," Arn said. "If you make the killer think we have something substantial, it'll bring him in from the woods. Like the bear. Then we'll have him."

Oblanski stood and finished off his coffee. He stood, thinking. "Why do I get the impression you know more than you're telling me?"

Arn remained silent.

"You still don't trust me, do you? You still think I was hiding something because I never told anyone I danced with Hannah that night."

"It does look … odd," Arn said. "But that may be the only thing it is: odd. And you're right, I do have something."

"What is it? We had an agreement to share information."

"I haven't put it straight in my head yet. There's something I'm missing." Arn tapped his temple. "This damned thick Norwegian head of mine, I guess. But I'll figure it out just as soon as I make a few more inquiries."

————————

Arn pulled through the circular driveway that lapped the front of Jefferson and Adelle Dawes' house and parked under a pine tree twice as tall as the power pole at the edge of the property. He extricated himself from the Clown Car and was hauling himself out by the door when his hand slipped and he fell in the snow. He grabbed the side of the car and stood. He brushed himself off, looking around to see if anyone had seen him making a fool of himself. But there was no one else visible on either side of the tree-lined street. Arn figured that by the looks of the neighborhood, they were probably busy online with their stockbrokers.

He ducked his head inside the car, rubbing his sore leg. He grabbed his man bag and shouldered it as he started up the winding pathway to the house. Native grasses coexisted with winter-blooming wildflowers lining one side of the walkway, dwarf orange and apple trees the other side. Arn was gawking at the foliage when he came around the corner of the garage and nearly collided with Jefferson Dawes. The doctor stood with one leg against the side of the garage, stretching, wearing running shorts despite the frigid temperature.

Jefferson straightened up and arched his back. He grinned at Arn's man bag. "Adelle said you were coming over to talk with her. I'd stick around, but I got to get run time in when I can." As Arn looked after him jogging down the hill toward the outskirts of town, he wondered where Jeff was running to. And to whose arms he was running.

"Who the hell gets drenched in cologne before a run," he said to himself as he walked toward the massive front doors.

The front door opened before he reached it, and Arn stopped in his tracks. Adelle stood framed in the doorway wearing an oversized Denver Broncos sweatshirt and baggy shorts big enough to fit Arn. She was barefoot, with purple polish caked to her scaly toes. She wore no makeup to hide the triple bags under her bloodshot bleary eyes, and her hair looked like she'd just stuck her head in a blender. You didn't have to get fixed up for me, Arn thought. Adelle was looking a lot like his Uncle Tony, with his scaly elbows and beer belly that cascaded over his belt, and Arn couldn't imagine why Jeff would ever want to mess around on the hunk of burning love gracing the doorway.

"You set off the security cameras coming up the walk," she spit out. Where the entryway smelled like it had been drenched in Old Spice after the doctor left, Adelle's breath smelled like she'd drunk some. She stood aside to let Arn into the house, waving the air with a cigarette. "I was wondering when you'd come around asking your fool questions."

Adelle's morning breath had carried over into afternoon breath and reeked of last night's bender. Arn's first thought was of that gut pile he'd told Oblanski he hunted bears over. "This way," she said, as if directing a servant.

Adelle had definitely traded up from Gaylord, Arn observed as he followed her waddling through twelve-foot-high hallways adorned with original art on either side, past a gas fireplace that disappeared somewhere in the ceiling. He sank in burgundy carpeting as they walked past double doors and into a den lined with leather-bound books along one wall, medical journals and reference books on another. Adelle motioned to twin leather chairs across from a matching chocolate leather divan. "Sit wherever," she said and staggered to a wet bar. "What you drinking?"

"It's a little early for me," Arn answered as he opened his bag and grabbed his field notes.

Adelle's double chin bounced as she laughed. "It's never too early."

Ice tinkled in a tall tumbler, and she struggled with a stopper before it finally popped out of the decanter. She took a long pull before pouring some in her glass and plopping into a chair, her fat folds blending with the folds of the overstuffed chair. She draped one beefy leg over the arm and surveyed Arn through the glass as she focused on him. "You married?"

"Widowed."

She looked in the direction of the front door as if she expected Jefferson to return. "Well, don't ever get married again."

Arn stood by a fireplace mantle, which was cold and lifeless this morning like Adelle and Jefferson's marriage. Two badges sat side by side, one labeled "Gaylord" and the other "Steve."

"That was Bobby Madden's idea." Adelle pointed with her glass. "He thought I might like to have my brother's badge. And when Gaylord hung himself, Bobby asked if I wanted that one too." She swirled the drink around in her glass. "I told him what the hell, I might as well retain some little memories from those days. Just too bad ... "

Arn sat on the couch and waited for her to continue.

"Too bad about Butch's badge," she said. "I thought it would be nice to have all three badges lined up there. Like they were ready for roll call. But Georgia told me to pack sand if I wanted his."

"I saw Butch's badge pinned to his old uniform down at the Police Department."

Adelle shrugged. "It would have been nice to have something from all three. They really were closer than ... a lot of the old guys at the department think." She took another swallow of breakfast. "How's Johnny coming along?"

"Doing well," Arn said. "I think he'll pull out of it."

"I'm glad to hear that. Any suspects?"

Arn hesitated. Up until now, he hadn't given Adelle or her husband a second thought. Until he smelled the Old Spice as he walked up to the Dawes' front door. "Ned Oblanski's working on some promising leads," he lied.

Adelle took a long pull of her drink. Some sloshed out of the class and spilled on her stained sweatpants. "Guess Johnny will be able to identify his shooter when he comes to?"

"Possibly."

"Well, he sure the hell wasn't shot in the back or anything. If he was shot in the chest, he'd damn sure know who did it."

Arn had been helping Danny hang ceiling drywall and hadn't caught Oblanski's interview. He'd have to ask him if he mentioned where Johnny was shot. "I don't know," he lied again.

"Well, why the hell you come out here and mingle with us ... neat and elite?"

Arn opened his bag. The fish under the glass aquarium coffee table skitted to the corners as Arn laid his notebook on it and flipped to his notes. "I need to ask some questions about Gaylord."

Adelle waved her glass, and her bourbon brunch sloshed down the front of her sweatshirt. She winked at Arn. "You want to dry it off?"

Arn remained wisely silent.

"Well, neither does Jefferson these days." She took another pull of her breakfast. "But I thought you were hired to find Butch's killer?"

"Gaylord and Butch were working on several cases together at the time. I'm just trying to put everything together, especially since they died so close in time to one another."

She downed her drink and waved her glass in the air. "Ask away."

"How long was Gaylord involved in the autoerotic practice?"

"How should I know?" Adelle used the side of the chair to stand and headed for the wet bar. "That sicko bastard may have always done it while we were married." She looked at the front door again. "Wives are always the last to find things out."

More ice tinkling, and Adelle tipped the last of her bourbon into her glass. She wrapped both hands around the decanter like she was wringing out the last drop, while Arn remained quiet. Waiting for her to tell him things. And she did. "I was eight years older than Gaylord when we married. At the time, people thought I was a real catch. What ya' think?"

Arn shrugged. Answering truthfully wouldn't get him the information he needed.

"Daddy wanted me to marry one of his junior loan officers. 'He'll be president when I retire someday,' Daddy said." She sucked an ice cube and her cheek bulged out like a squirrel storing up for winter. "But I didn't get along very well with my father. 'Piss on you' I told him one day when he pushed the loan officer on me. I ran away and married

Gaylord." She leaned forward and her loose sweatshirt dropped down. Arn looked away. That wasn't the only thing drooping down.

"Gaylord. What a dud he was. And you know what a kick in the ass is: that junior loan officer *did* make bank president when Daddy retired."

"Gaylord must have had some aptitude for police work if he made detective?"

Adelle laughed. "When Daddy put a call to the police commissioner, Gaylord made detective. And Steve promoted Gaylord over experienced officers." She spilled booze down the side of her mouth and Arn handed her a box of tissue. "Gaylord's background was robbing old ladies when he was a kid. Busting shop windows and stealing booze. He grew up north of Manhattan's Lower East Side. In the East Village."

Arn's college roommate had been raised in that area, in the Bowery. In that neighborhood infamously known as the Five Points. "Wyoming's a long ways from New York," he said.

"It is. But when the judge tells you to leave the state or he'll throw the book at you next time, you move. 'Cause the next time Gaylord would have been in court as an adult." Adelle ignored the tissue and pulled her sweatshirt up to wipe her mouth, exposing her belly. Arn looked at the ceiling. He was having too many nightmares lately as it was.

"Anyway, it scarred Gaylord, and he left New York. Came out west. Straightened out. Got his Criminal Justice degree, and that same year Steve hired him. Gaylord would have been Lieutenant of Investigations," Adelle spit out, "if he hadn't hung himself." She stood and staggered back to the wet bar. "If I'd caught him loping his mule like that, I would have killed him. Where does anyone even get the notion to do that?"

"Internet would be a good start."

"Dumb as Gaylord was?" Adelle chucked. "Use the Internet? Besides, he was just too lazy to research such things."

Arn had investigated several hangings in his career that were reported suicides but proved accidental. An underground community existed where men—usually white, usually blue-collar—exchanged tips: how to intensify their orgasms. Or how to escape detection by padding the rope around their neck with a towel. Or how to construct the perfect escape knot so that—at the moment of masturbatory orgasm—they could disengage the rope and save themselves. Apparently, Gaylord's had failed. Apparently, he should have done his research better.

Arn flipped to a blank page, expecting the worst from Adelle. "Tell me, did you know about Gaylord's dirty little habit, or you just didn't care because you had other things … going on?"

"I told you, I didn't know." She used the back of the couch to stumble across the room. "Just what the hell are you implying?"

"Just that you had your own little thing going on the side."

"How dare you … "

"Do you deny having an affair with Jefferson while you both were married?"

Adelle leaned over the couch and Arn thought she would tip over. "Maybe I was. His wife didn't care, running off to wherever the hell she went with that science teacher from East High. But to imply we did something illegal … "

Arn held up his hand, and she stopped long enough to take another swallow. "A week after Gaylord's death, you moved in with Jefferson."

"So we couldn't get married," she blurted out. "Until later. We thought it would look … "

"Suspicious?" Arn finished for her.

Adelle dropped into a chair across from him. "Look. Jefferson's wife left him before he could serve her with divorce papers. Ran off with that teacher, Noggen or something."

"Noggle?"

"That's him. Jefferson couldn't serve her because he couldn't find her. He had her declared dead years later and we married. But what's that got to do with Butch's murder?"

"It all is tied in."

"How?"

Arn poised with his pen above his paper. He'd written a full page of notes, talking with Adelle, and hadn't recalled doing so. "I don't know yet." He flipped to a clean page. "So you just boarded the house up when you moved out?"

When Adelle leaned over to set her glass on the coffee table, she farted. And chuckled. "After Gaylord hung himself in there, I checked with a Realtor. She said no one would buy a house where a man hung himself. 'Wait a while,' she told me. 'People will forget in a couple years and we can put it up on the market,' she said."

"But you didn't?"

Adelle shook her head. "Jefferson does quite well with his practice, so we didn't need the money. I forgot about it." Her face turned crimson. "Until that piss ant Pieter Spangler bought it from the county rolls." She shook her head. "I suppose it's really my fault. I should have kept the taxes up."

"You ever go back to the house after you found Gaylord ... hanging?"

She shrugged. "No. I turned everything over to an auction house to sell all our stuff. Not that we had much. Not like this." She waved her arm around the spacious room. "The weekend Gaylord jerked his root in the noose, Jefferson and I were to meet in a Denver motel—"

227

"I thought you went shopping?" Arn asked.

Adelle waved the air. "Did I? Don't matter now, does it? Anyway, I made our meeting. Jeff didn't. He called and said he had a patient emergency come up and couldn't make it down there. When I got home, there was Gaylord. Swinging like a naked Tarzan."

Arn jotted in his notebook, knowing that if he remained quiet he'd learn more.

"Jefferson and I have had our speed bumps," Adelle went on. "His marathons he insists on running take time away from us."

Arn thought of the sports Pieter went out for, not because he especially liked them but because it got him away from Butch. Arn could see Jeff doing the same, to escape the creature sweating bourbon in front of him.

Adelle sat quietly on the couch, rubbing her glass like she wished the booze genie would come floating out and take her away. When he was sure Adelle had gotten off her sagging chest what she wanted, Arn asked the questions he really came here to ask.

"Do you recall what Gaylord said about those Five Point cases?"

Adelle shuddered, and Arn wasn't sure if it was from the overdose of bourbon or from the fear of remembering. "That's all Gaylord talked about when he came home from work. How he and Butch were close to solving it." Her voice lowered to a whisper. "Gaylord became paranoid. He was outright terrified, I tell you. Afraid to death the killer would find him and Butch."

"Did he take any extra precautions?"

Adelle shrugged. "He bought a new vest, and even wore it at home most of the time. He started carrying a backup gun just like Butch's little automatic. Too small to do any harm, but it made him feel secure." She downed the last of her drink. "Except he wasn't secure from himself."

Arn stuffed his notes in his bag. "I'll let myself out," he said, not wanting to risk having to help Adelle up when she toppled over. When he was nearly out of the room, he stopped and turned. "Tell me, when Jefferson goes out running, does he always look like he's … going to work?"

"You mean, does he always fix his hair and gargle a quart of Scope?" Adelle asked.

"That and his cologne."

Adelle's eyes teared and she looked into the bottom of her empty glass. "That damned Old Spice. He just started wearing it lately. Almost like some … friend said she likes it."

Thirty-Nine

DR. WILLEM ROUGH ENTERED the examination room, and Arn was reluctant to shake hands with the proctologist. Especially one named Rough. But he needed information, and this was the only way to corral the doctor's time. Rough pointed to the examination table with a finger as big as a Polish sausage. When Arn seated himself on the table, the doctor scanned his information in a laptop on a counter. "My receptionist said you needed to talk about some cases I had when I was with the Coroner's Office."

"I do." Arn eyed Dr. Rough snapping on examination gloves and taking the cap off a tube of KY Jelly. "I had the finger wave when I retired two years ago," he said.

The doctor smiled. "Then it's high time you had another. Drop your knickers."

"But all I need is to talk."

"You'll drop them if you want information." Rough put the tiniest drop of KY on the end of his gloved finger. "Time is money for me.

Besides covering your ass, it covers mine. Now drop your socks or we don't talk."

Arn turned around and dropped his pants along with his whitey tighties. He gritted his teeth as he thought of the doctor's bulging knuckles.

"Say 'ah.'" Rough laughed, and Arn grimaced when he realized the doctor hadn't taken his wedding ring off. He withdrew his glove with a snap and deposited it into a specimen container before motioning for Arn to sit.

"Do I get a cigarette with that?"

"No," Rough said. "Even if you felt pretty good." He laughed again. "But don't take that personal. All I found was your prostate's as big as a bagel."

"I keep it in check with medication."

"Take this slip to the checkout desk." Rough handed Arn a piece of paper and typed on his computer. "Now what cases do you want to talk about?" he said without looking up.

"The Five Point killings."

Rough stopped typing. He swiveled his stool toward the wall, his breath quickening. When he turned back around and faced Arn, he'd composed himself. "Now I recognize you. You're that retired cop looking for Butch Spangler's killer."

"The TV station hired me as a consultant."

"Then forget the Five Point cases," Rough said. He snatched his paperwork and headed for the door.

"You haven't given me a chance to ask."

"You got questions, check with the police." As Rough opened the door, Arn grabbed his arm. Rough jerked away. "What right do you have—"

Arn nodded to the specimen jar. "Having some guy shove his finger up my keister gives me the right."

Rough paused.

"We had an agreement."

The doctor sighed and shut the door. "I don't talk about those cases." He walked back to the counter and set the jar down while using the edge of the counter to ease himself onto a stool. "Junior detectives used to come around for years and grill me like I was withholding information. I stopped talking with them years ago when I got out of the Coroner's Office."

"If you didn't want justice, why'd you get into forensics in the first place?"

"I was fresh out of med school and I didn't know what I wanted. I watched the old TV show *Quincy, M.E.*, and documentaries with Michael Baden. Henry Lee. They fascinated the hell out of me. I inhaled that stuff." He took out a pocket knife. He opened a blade and started cleaning under his nails. "So, when the ME's office offered me a position, I thought I'd died and went to heaven. I thought I'd be catching bad guys or finding hidden diseases that killed a loved one. Offering closure to survivors."

Rough turned away, and Arn was quick to point out, "I'm sure you helped a lot of families find solace."

"A couple." Rough's eyes lit up. "One was a twenty-seven-year-old runner who died at the finish line of the Casper marathon. I found she had near arterial blockage. Hereditary."

Arn kept silent, feeling more like a priest than an investigator needing answers.

"And a drowning at Glendo Reservoir they brought to me that same summer." He shook his head. "The family thought a fishing buddy had killed their son before pushing him out of the boat. But he'd experienced a cadaveric spasm: his hands were still clutching the reeds from the bottom of the lake when they snagged him and brought him up. When I told the family I thought his death wasn't a homicide, you should have heard the relief in their voices."

"An involuntary clenching of the muscles," Arn said. "I had a case in Denver years ago that had me scratching my head. Two brothers had been drinking at home when one got the call of the wild and went after the other one with a knife. Bad move. That brother shot the one with a knife. The dead brother still clutched the knife when they brought him into the autopsy room."

"And the ME had to break the victim's fingers to get the knife loose?"

Arn nodded.

Rough snapped his fingers and smiled. "It was things like that that made the job so fascinating. Figuring things out." He looked at the floor, his smile gone. "Then came the Five Point cases, and I thought I'd fallen into hell. That's when I knew I couldn't live with a job where you brought nightmares home at the end of the day." He stood and straightened a Pfizer calendar leaning to starboard on the wall. "Those cases caused me to get out of forensics and into something that didn't stink as bad."

"Anyone can become affected seeing homicides," Arn said.

Rough stuck his hands in his lab coat. "The Five Point cases weren't my first rodeo, Mr. Anderson. I'd been to shootings and knifings. One call where a son crushed his dad's windpipe with a rake handle. Another guy who killed his sister and propped her in a chair and went about his life like she still made breakfast for him every morning. But those were cases of spontaneity. Those I could understand. But the Five Point cases were so brutal. So … well planned."

"How so, Doctor?"

Rough paced the small examination room. "Butch Spangler and I went over those cases until I was sick of looking at him. The victims were either selected at random, or the killer met with each to have sex with them."

"Man or woman?"

Rough shrugged. "We had no read. Could have been either. But that was the only motive we could come up with."

"I've read Butch's reports. He almost seemed to admire the killer."

"Maybe because he—or she—was so thorough," Rough said. "We concluded with such a lack of physical evidence, the killer must have planned them to the tiniest detail. The total lack of evidence baffled us. Except … " Rough looked away.

"Anything you might remember could help."

"Okay then." The doctor faced Arn. "Think about this: we had partial shoe prints in blood on both crime scenes. We were convinced the killer put them there on purpose, because we found no other prints at the scene or leading away." He started for the door. "Now I got nothing else to say. I just want to forget."

Arn moved to block the door. He'd bared his butt and allowed himself to be violated, but he wasn't finished with the doctor yet. "Think: Is there anything at all you might remember … "

Rough nodded to Arn's notebook. "I'll bet you have every one of my reports in there. That should tell you everything I knew at the time."

"You assisted with Butch Spangler's homicide."

Rough rubbed his forehead. "That was perhaps the hardest of all. Other officers told me he was an egotist, but I liked him."

"There was a scribbled note in Bobbie Madden's report that you felt Butch knew his attacker."

"It was just an opinion," Rough said. "Would never have made it to court."

Arn waited for an explanation.

"I thought he knew his killer. Butch was killed with contact shots to the chest. I could imagine him spotting the gun the killer drew on him and grabbing it. Trying to wrestle it away, when the gun discharged. We did a GSR on his hands, of course, and he had gunshot residue on one. But Madden admitted he botched it bagging Butch's hands, so I couldn't even note it."

"And Pieter and Georgia's hands had a GSR test run also?"

Rough nodded. "The detectives tested them before I got there. Now if there's nothing else, Mr. Anderson, I got other poop chutes to look at today."

The doctor was out the door when Arn hit him with a final question. "You drew Butch's vitreous fluids in his eyes for a second test. Why?"

Rough stopped and dropped his head, taking a deep breath before answering. "Bobbie Madden asked me to," he answered without turning around. "He felt Butch had taken an undue amount of Xanax, by the near-empty prescription bottle he found in the bathroom. Madden thought Butch may have been sedated at the time he was shot."

"Did the second test pick up anything missed on the first?" Arn asked.

Rough slapped the door with his hand. "Nothing. But then, Xanax has a short half-life. If Butch took enough to knock himself out—or if someone gave Butch the medication without his knowledge—it wouldn't have shown up on the second test anyway."

Rough started down the hallway, then stopped. "My office will call you if anything comes back on your specimen." He forced a smile. "And maybe we'll talk again over an ice cold colonoscopy."

Forty

DANNY BROUGHT THEIR PLATES of meat loaf and potatoes and set them on the door-turned-table in front of the white wall. When Danny first suggested they eat their meals in front of photos of murder victims—an early working supper, he called it—Arn thought he was sick. Now it only seemed natural that they eat with pictures of graphic crimes as a backdrop. Like grotesque wallpaper someone should market, as Danny mentioned.

The old man opened a napkin and laid it over new jeans Arn had bought him. "Where did these come from? Because if you're giving me a handout—"

"I'm not."

"Good." Danny said. "'Cause Danny don't take charity. But where'd you get them?"

"The jean fairy," Arn told him.

Danny grinned and drizzled raspberry vinaigrette over the bowl of salad. He handed Arn the serving forks.

"I thought all you Indians were carnivores?"

"Even we carnivores need roughage," Danny said. "Or we'll end up like you did today at the proctologist's office."

"I don't know," Arn said. "It was pretty memorable. I might go back again tomorrow."

"No shit!"

"Shit," Arn said.

Danny sipped his tea and dabbled at his salad. "You sure you don't want to wait outside the TV station for Ana Maria tonight?"

"I told Oblanski if he didn't assign an experienced officer to Ana Maria, I was going to drop a dime to the mayor."

"And he reassigned him?"

Arn grabbed the mustard and began smothering his meat loaf. "The sleeper was a new officer who'd not yet been to the academy, he said. 'I don't have the manpower to dedicate an experienced officer,' he claimed."

"So?" Danny asked. "Is that officer still protecting Ana Maria?"

"He was replaced." Arn savored the buffalo meat loaf. "He's now working elsewhere. You'll probably see him running a street sweeper. Maybe a blade when it snows again. Something more suited to his demeanor. She's got decent protection now."

"Then I feel better," Danny said. "Not like I felt this afternoon when I was pulling wire in here."

Arn set his fork down. "What are you talking about?"

Danny pointed with a piece of buffalo still on his fork to a photo of Steve DeBoer. "What do you see in that photo?"

"Same as I saw yesterday," Arn answered. "Steve passed out in his recliner. Beer cans littering the floor a few feet in front of him. Overflowing ash tray partially consumed by the fire. What do you see?"

"I see something that isn't quite right." Danny dabbed at the corners of his mouth. "Do you believe Steve passed out and his cigarette started the fire?"

Arn had read and reread the incident reports, and the fire marshal's conclusions that were congruent with the autopsy findings. "Steve didn't have soot in his throat. If he had, that would indicate he was breathing at the time of the fire." He stood and walked around the makeshift table. He saw something, too. "But often as not, there's no soot. Especially after the firemen hose the room—and the victim—with pressured water."

"I didn't mean that." Danny dipped meat loaf in a spot of catsup on his plate. He ate it and held his fork like a weapon as he walked to the white wall. "That." He tapped his fork on one of the photos.

"That's a recliner."

"And what do you buy a recliner for?"

"What is this," Arn asked, "twenty questions? You buy it to recline. What else?"

"Then why did Steve move his recliner up tight against the wall?" Danny said. "He wouldn't have been able to recline while he was watching TV."

Arn paused, his fork near his mouth. That was the thing he was missing. Danny was right: Steve wouldn't have been able to recline his Lazy Boy. The wall would have stopped him.

He shuffled through the reports and pulled up the sketch the fire marshal's investigator had made of the scene. He turned back to the photos and dug his reading glasses out of his pocket, angling himself so the light didn't reflect off the glossy picture. "I'll be damned."

"What?"

"There." Arn used his Sharpie to mark off twin indents in the carpeting where the recliner had rested. Perhaps for years. Until the day of the fire.

"If I was a good sidekick, I'd suggest someone moved that recliner directly against those curtains at the wall."

"And a good sidekick might mention that those empty beer cans are right about in front of where the recliner always sat," Arn said. "Not back against the wall. And against the flammable curtains."

"Thank God the firemen responded as quickly as they did," Danny said, buttering his potatoes. "Or the whole room would have been consumed."

Arn checked his watch. Dr. Rough would just be giving the last finger wave of the day about now. On the fifth ring, his receptionist answered. "I'm sorry," the woman said—hired, as were most good receptionists, for their skills at running interference for their bosses. "Dr. Rough doesn't take personal calls."

"Would he," Arn said, sounding pained, "if I told you I was experiencing complications from my exam today, and I've retained counsel?"

"Just a moment," she sputtered, and Arn was put on hold. Listening to Barry Manilow was nearly as bad as the digit exam earlier, and Barry had belted out half of "If Tomorrow Never Comes" before Rough came on the line.

"Mr. Anderson, tell me what problems you're experiencing. If it's an emergency, I can meet you at the ER—"

"No emergency. No complications."

"But Abigail said you started having problems after the exam—"

"I lied. I'm not having problems. Though it's a little uncomfortable where your ring caught."

"I don't understand."

"I needed to ask you something, and I didn't want to wait until your finger was knuckle-deep in my behind to ask it."

"Is this about the Five Point cases?" Rough asked.

"No, it's not."

"Thank God."

"It's about Steve DeBoer. You performed the autopsy on him."

"I remember him well," Rough said. "He died a month or two before Butch Spangler. Fell asleep in his recliner, as I recall. Dropped his cigarette and passed out. Not uncommon."

Arn held the autopsy report to the light. He'd underlined a portion of Dr. Rough's report. "You specifically noted you found charred larvae in Steve's body."

"I remember that, too. Is there a point to all this, because it is Monday and tee-time is—"

"If that were true," Arn interrupted, "and I'm sure you were diligent in your conclusions—that would put the time of death twenty-four to thirty-six hours *before* the fire."

The line went silent for long moments before Rough came on again. "Flies have a natural life cycle, like everything else. The fact that they went through their first life-death cycle before the fire means the victim didn't die that day. I suggested that to Detectives Madden and Oblanski—that the larvae could not have gotten in there any other way. But they did."

"And with no soot in his windpipe?"

"Inconclusive."

"By itself," Arn said, feeling his anger rise. "And with all that, you ruled his death accidental."

Rough's voice rose an octave and his words came quick. Sharp. He wasn't used to being second-guessed. "My decision to rule Steve DeBoer's death an accident was based on the totality of the circumstances.

The fire marshal found no accelerant at the scene to indicate the fire was set intentionally. Steve simply passed out with a cigarette in his hand, which started the recliner on fire. It spread quickly to the curtains. He most likely died by smoke inhalation. I'm sorry that's not what you wanted to hear. Not with that television special linking all three officers' deaths."

Arn had worked with thorough pathologists and with sloppy ones, who took for gospel whatever investigators wanted on victims' death certificates. Perhaps, he thought, it was better that Rough had left the field of forensics. "I just had to satisfy my curiosity, doctor."

"Then if there's nothing else, we can conclude this charade."

"There is one other little thing," Arn interrupted him. "Remember we talked about how the medical examiner's opinion doesn't make it to the final report if there's nothing to back it up scientifically."

"My opinion stands that Steve's death was an accident."

"And I accept that. I know you conducted a fine autopsy," Arn lied, imagining Rough's head blowing up on the other end of the line as big as one of his examination gloves. "But was there anything at all you found inconsistent with your assessment? Anything that made you stop and wonder what the hell's this?"

There was a pause on the other end of the line, and Arn thought Rough had hung up. "A feather," he whispered.

"Feather from the recliner stuffing?"

"No," Rough said. "The recliner had batting material. This was a single feather that I found in Steve's airway that somehow was not washed away by the firemen's hose."

"What was the feather from, then?" Arn asked.

"What else?" Rough forced a laugh. "A bird."

Forty-One

WHEN I COME OUT *of the supply closet, two nurses pass me. One begins to say something, then stops. I look like every other doctor on the floor, coming and going, and she's certain she knows me under the mask. But not certain enough to stop and chat. Certainly not certain enough to poke fun at me for missing my flu shot and having to wear this thing. Thank God for hospital policy.*

Those two are just the kind of people I didn't want to run into. They almost stop me to talk, and I kick myself in the butt for doing this in the morning. I should have realized it wasn't visiting hours. I should have realized the only people in the hallway would be hospital personnel. If I'd done this in the afternoon, or early evening, the halls would be flooded with visitors. And confusion. But I'm committed now, and I pray my good luck—which has served me well all the other times—will hold out.

I head for the stairs. Johnny White's room's on the seventh floor, and I'd like to ride the elevator. But the security camera would pick me up the moment I stepped off. By taking the stairs, I have a dozen yards before I enter its field of view. And I know if I look behind me as I pass under it, the camera will only record my backside. And I'll look like every other doctor roaming the halls.

When I reach the seventh floor, I stop before entering the hall and check my watch. It's shift change at Cheyenne Regional. Thank God for them being so consistent. I wait for a few moments to make sure the nurses have huddled-up in their meeting room. And to let myself catch my breath.

I step out of the stairwell and into the hallway. The same police officer sits reading outside Johnny's room. I count the steps before I enter the field of view of the hall camera. Five steps. Six. Seven. Eight and I look over my shoulder, concealing my face.

I approach Johnny's room and I see the officer reading a Sports Illustrated. Except he's not doing much reading. He's doing more drooling than anything else. Gotta love that swimsuit issue. He looks up only briefly as I enter and close the door.

Tubes and IVs are stuck into Johnny. Monitors overhead produce a monotonous tone, green backlight bouncing off Johnny's slick forehead. His breathing is shallow but even. It's true what the doctors said: he'll pull out of this. I'm glad after all I didn't wait until later in the day. He might have been brought out of his coma. And I can't have Johnny talking. Damn you all to hell, Johnny White, this is just what I didn't want to start up again. But I got no choice. You know me.

I move to the far side of his bed and take off one paper booty covering my shoes, grabbed from the supply room.

I check my watch. They'll be in shift briefing for another five minutes, and I approach Johnny's bed.

I read once that more people die in the hospital than anywhere else. All I can say to Johnny today is "no shit."

Forty-Two

NED OBLANSKI'S VOICE THREW an edge that Arn picked up on immediately. "Meet me at the hospital. I need that outside set of eyes."

"What's going on?" Arn asked, but Oblanski had already disconnected.

When Arn arrived at Cheyenne Regional, a security guard stood by the entrance to escort him to a downstairs conference room. The guard shut the door, leaving Arn alone in the room not only with Oblanski, but also with a man he recognized as the hospital's chief of security and a gray-haired woman with an ID around her neck proclaiming her the hospital spokeswoman.

"Better sit for this one," Oblanski said. He didn't look like he'd slept for days as he introduced the chief of security, Captain Moore, and hospital public relations spokeswoman Hennessey.

Arn set his hat on one end of the conference table and took a chair across from Oblanski, who nodded to the security chief standing in front of a big screen TV. Moore punched a remote. A security camera monitoring a long hallway had recorded people walking by a uniformed policeman Arn recognized as the one he'd spoken with outside Johnny's room right after the shooting. The policeman kept his head buried in a *Sports Illustrated* as people walked by, and Moore tapped the screen. "This was a minute before."

"Before what?" Arn asked.

"Before that." Oblanski stood and approached the television. "Freeze it!" A doctor in a white lab coat, cap, and face mask walked past the policeman and entered a room. "He's in there exactly fifty-three seconds."

Moore resumed the recording, and Arn watched the tape counter. Fifty-three seconds later, the doctor emerged from the room. The man glanced nonchalantly to one side, his face away from the camera, before disappearing down the hallway and off camera. "Just what are we looking at?" Arn asked.

Hennessey looked at Arn like he was little more than an annoyance in the room. She smoothed her gray skirt and scowled at Oblanski. "We were informed that no extra security precautions were needed." She nodded to the chief of security. "Or we would have provided it." She leaned on the table and stared at Oblanski. "The hospital holds no culpability in Mr. White's death."

"Johnny's dead?" Arn said, sounding like so many people he'd given final notification to through the years: full of disbelief. Full of denial. "I just checked with the nurses' station a couple hours ago. Johnny was doing well. What the hell happened?"

"It was nothing hospital personnel did," the woman said.

"I think you'd better leave us now," Oblanski told her. "We really need to talk alone."

"Not if it involves the hospital."

"Please," Oblanski said, but it came out as a stern order rather than a simple request.

Hennessey huffed once before slamming the door on her way out.

"What happened?" Arn repeated.

"Like I said, this guy was in Johnny's room for fifty-three seconds. Twenty seconds after that, alerts went to the nurses' station that Johnny had coded."

"Our trauma unit rushed in," Moore said. "But Johnny was gone."

"When the nurses…" Oblanski closed his eyes and pinched his nose, breathing deeply to calm himself. "When the nurses called for the trauma team, Officer Blake went in there with them."

"The kid outside Johnny's room?"

Oblanski nodded. "He tried his best to preserve what evidence there was, in case Johnny's death wasn't natural. But the team tramped all over. If there was any evidence, it got wiped away quickly."

"The team had to get in there as quickly—"

"I know," Oblanski said to Moore. "I know. It's just that we don't have squat on the killer."

"Did Blake hear anything while the guy was in there?"

"Nothing."

"You sure it was murder?" Arn asked.

"Blake's down at the PD now making a statement," Oblanski said. "But in a nutshell, when he followed the trauma team in, the first thing he noticed was Johnny's pillow on the floor. It had bloody smears on the pillowcase." Oblanski buried his face in his hands. "The guy put the pillow over Johnny's face hard enough that it broke his nose. He bled all over the pillow."

"So Johnny was smothered?"

"Most likely," Oblanski answered. "We'll know at autopsy." He kicked the table leg. "If I hadn't gone on television claiming we were close to solving Butch's murder—and Johnny's shooting—" He glared at Arn. He said no more, but there was an unspoken accusation between them: if

Arn hadn't suggested Oblanski go on air with Ana Maria that second time with such false claims, Johnny may have been on his way to recovery. Rather than parked on a steel table awaiting autopsy.

"Tell me someone recognized this guy," Arn said.

Oblanski nodded to Moore, who aimed the remote at the TV and rewound the recording. "I had all my officers view the tape. Along with a dozen of the senior hospital staff. The mask and cap hid his features."

"So we're looking for a doctor?"

"Probably not," Moore answered. "He was dressed like a physician, but everyone agreed he wasn't any doctor working here."

Arn slumped in his chair, feeling as if life had just drop kicked him through goal posts he wasn't prepared for. "How the hell does someone impersonate a doctor and no one notice?"

"The mask," Moore answered. "Hospital personnel who fail to get a flu shot by the deadline date have got to wear a mask by policy. People saw him walking masked-up and just figured he missed his flu shot." Moore started the recording once again. "This guy knew where he was going even though he didn't work here. As you can see"—he pointed to the hallway—"he was in and out with no one paying him any mind."

Oblanski stood and paced in front of the television. "He went into Johnny's room at shift change when nurses on the floor are normally in their shift briefing. This guy knew his way around."

"Or studied hospital policy and procedure," Arn pointed out. "Can Officer Blake tell us anything about the guy?"

"He said he was taller than average."

"That's it? What the hell was he doing, sleeping?"

"Screw you," Oblanski said. "Not every officer sleeps on duty. Blake was ordered to keep everyone out of Johnny's room except hospital personnel. And"—he jerked his thumb at the television screen—"the guy was damned sure dressed like hospital staff."

Arn studied the screen again. The killer walked by Officer Blake and into Johnny's room as calmly as he would walk into Starbucks for his morning latte.

"We locked the hospital down as soon as this happened," Moore said. "And I pulled all the security tapes from two hours before that."

"There's nothing unusual on them." Oblanski anticipated Arn's question. "It's not visiting hours, so there weren't a lot of people: three construction workers coming in for a bite at the cafeteria. A nurse's assistant and a janitor tall enough to be our man. But all checked out."

"If he got into our hospital," Moore said, "it was from the only entrance with no camera."

"Could you play that again," Arn asked, and Moore rewound and started the recording. "This guy came up on the camera's blind side. And when he came out of Johnny's room, he looked to the side where the camera couldn't pick up his face. This guy either knows the hospital or he cased it." He turned to Moore. "Pull the security tapes from the day Johnny was shot until now."

"That's last Friday."

"It is."

"What do I do with them?" Moore asked.

"Sit down with your staff and review them. If this guy came in to get a lay of the hospital floor, he'll be on tape."

"But that'll take—"

"Moore," Oblanski said, and Moore nodded.

"You mentioned there was an entrance with no surveillance cameras," Arn said.

Moore turned off the TV. "First floor maintenance door. It's where deliveries are made. It's in the old part of the hospital. Most delivery people—UPS, Post Office, medical company suppliers—all have keys."

"And who would know that besides delivery folks?"

"Everyone at the hospital," Moore said. "It's even covered in first-day orientation."

––––––––––

When Captain Moore left to pull the tapes and make a copy for them, Arn turned to Oblanski. "Johnny's death was neither of our faults. Whoever this is"—he pointed to the freeze-framed killer on the monitor—"is calculating. He thinks things through. He's undoubtedly Johnny's shooter, and he knew if Johnny came to, he might identify him."

Oblanski stuffed his lip with Copenhagen, hospital policy be damned. "Moore's going to pull the tapes. But we don't have squat on this guy. Unless he's a sprinter and made it out of the hospital before it was locked down, he's common enough to blend in with everyone else here at the time. But maybe something will turn up with delivery companies." Oblanski had called the detective division and given them a listing of every company who delivered to the hospital, to find out which of delivery people had a key to the maintenance door.

He grabbed a pencil lying on the conference table and chewed the end until it broke. Just like Johnny did. "I had to call the mayor when this happened," he continued. "He's made an emergency appointment. I'm now the permanent police chief, though I wish to hell Johnny were still in that position."

Arn leaned back and rubbed his forehead. "I've been looking closely at Steve and Gaylord's deaths in relation to Butch."

"Go on."

"I can, with a degree of certainty, say that Steve's death was no accident."

"Bullshit! Bobbie Madden was there—"

"Every investigator makes mistakes. Even someone as experienced as Madden was." Arn explained about the single feather Dr. Rough

249

had found in Steve's windpipe. "The photos show two pillows—they look like couch pillows to me—partially burned and lying on the floor beside the recliner. I think someone smothered Steve with a couch pillow and started that fire. And he may have been killed a full day before the fire."

"What the hell's that?" Oblanski poured water from a pitcher in the middle of the table. "How did you come up with that conclusion?"

"Rough noted larvae found in Steve's throat, meaning flies fed on the body and went through their cycle. It would put the time of death at least a day before. Probably a mite more."

"You didn't know Steve DeBoer, but he was a stout guy. Someone just didn't smother him without a fight." Oblanski looked around for another pencil. "And the photos clearly show there was no struggle. How do you account for that?"

Arn shook his head. "I can't yet. But if I could look at the evidence . . ."

"It wasn't saved. Steve's death was ruled accidental and everything connected was destroyed years ago. Besides, right now I got too much to do worrying about Johnny's murder."

Arn stood and walked to the monitor. "There's just too much that points to all this"—he tapped the screen—"being tied in with Butch's murder. Whether it was Frank Dull Knife as you suspected, or the Five Point Killer like Johnny thought, you need to admit that ten years ago, someone killed Steve as well as Butch. And he killed another officer today."

Oblanski slumped lower in his chair. "What can I do?"

"Assign as many officers as you can spare to reopen Steve's case."

Oblanski tried rubbing new forehead wrinkles of responsibility. With Johnny's death, he'd inherited more headaches than he'd bargained for. "I have to talk with the crime scene tech working Johnny's hospital room. When I finish, I'll go to my office and start freeing up people to work on the connection between Butch and Steve."

Arn motioned to the monitor, which was showing the man in the mask and gown turning away from the camera. "And tell your guys to be on their toes. I wouldn't want to meet this guy unprepared."

Forty-Three

ARN WALKED OUT OF the conference room and started toward the parking lot when he spotted Jefferson Dawes walking down the hall toward him. He was rubbing shoulders with a twenty-something nurse in blue scrubs who giggled beside him, her hand brushing his. When he looked up and saw Arn, he stopped and bent toward the woman, whispering something to her. She headed down the opposite hallway, looking back and smiling at Jefferson before disappearing into an elevator.

"A running partner is all," he volunteered.

"None of my business who you're friendly with."

"What's that supposed to mean?" Jefferson glared down at Arn.

Arn shrugged. "Don't read anything into it. What you do is your affair. But while you're here, do you have a moment?"

Jefferson checked his watch. "You got about five minutes. A patient's waiting for me."

Arn motioned to an empty room, and they stepped inside. Jefferson stood by the doorway as if he wanted to escape. "Adelle said you drilled her about our affair. She might be ashamed to admit it, but we had that affair while we were both still married. So if you think you're going to use that against us ... " He trailed off.

"When did your wife find out?" Arn asked.

"She left me."

Arn kept silent, waiting for Jefferson to continue. True confession time once again, Arn thought.

"My wife cleaned out our checking account and left with that science teacher from South High." His eyes darted to the hallway. "At least that was the rumor around town."

"So Adelle told me. And the private investigator you hired came up short?"

"He never found her," Jefferson said. "Is this going somewhere?"

"You ever meet Gaylord?"

"Why do you want to know that?" Jefferson stuttered. Stalling.

"I'm just trying to get a handle on his death ten years ago."

"That's right. You're being paid to come up with some connection to Butch Spangler. But to answer your question, I met him once."

"At his house?"

Eyes darted to the door. Jefferson wanted to be anywhere besides talking with Arn about Gaylord Fournier. "Gaylord called me to his house a couple weeks before he ... died. He told me he didn't appreciate that I was having an affair with his wife." He laughed nervously. "But he didn't much object, either. He was more concerned with his image than his wife messing around. I didn't much worry about it at the time. Adelle said he had his own thing going."

"Which was?"

"Obviously, masturbating while he hung from the rafters," Jefferson said, then jerked his thumb down the hallway. "Ask that creepy bastard. He was pals with that sicko."

253

Pieter stood with his head bent, talking with Meander in the hallway outside the nurses' station.

"Now, if there's nothing else, make an appointment with my office if you wish to talk again." Jefferson kept staring at Pieter as he walked past him and into a patient's room.

Pieter and Meander walked toward Arn. "That guy gives me the creeps," Pieter said.

"He said the same thing about you." Arn motioned Pieter aside, and Meander stood on her tiptoes and kissed him on the cheek. "You boys gave a good visit," she said and headed for the elevator.

Pieter looked after her, a worried look on his face. "I should be grateful we can catch lunch now and again, with all the overtime she's been putting in." He looked around furtively and led Arn to a small break room, empty this time of day. "Meander said Johnny was murdered a couple hours ago."

Arn nodded. "By someone posing as a physician."

"Now *that* gives me the creeps." Pieter shuddered. "I'm worried to death for her. What if he's still in the building … " He gazed around as he walked to the vending machine. "Why would anyone want to smother Johnny to death?"

"Why would anyone want to shoot him to begin with?" Arn opened his bag and took out his notebook, jotting down what Jefferson had told him about Gaylord. "I'm convinced it all ties in with your father's murder. I got near-conclusive proof that Steve was murdered—"

"No way!" Pieter said. "Steve was the nicest man. When the team returned from the game in Casper the day after the fire, Dad told me about it. He said it was accidental. I just can't believe someone murdered him, too."

"But you believe Gaylord died an autoerotic death?"

"I do now." Pieter looked at the ceiling, and a sadness came with the remembering. "In Gaylord's basement, he had this long mirror propped against the wall. I asked if he needed help hanging it somewhere, and he snapped at me. He asked what I was insinuating. Like he got paranoid or something. Or on drugs. Anyway, he kicked me out of his basement and told me never to come back again. That was … " Pieter thought. "It was two weeks before Adelle found him hanging." He eyed the vending machine. "You don't think his death was anything but an accident?"

"If you call 'stupid enough not to work out an escape plan when you're hanging from your basement rafters' an accident," Arn answered.

Pieter walked to the Vending Machine of Death that offered sandwiches restocked once a week. Or every other week. Every squad room Arn had worked out of had a Vending Machine of Death, so-called because only the hungriest of men were brave enough stick their money in and chance E.coli. Or some other ailment. Pieter was such a brave man, and he ripped open the ham and cheese and wolfed it down. At least Pieter was within walking distance of the emergency room.

"I'd like to get into that old house of Gaylord and Adelle's you bought," Arn said.

"Why?" Pieter sat on a chair and washed the sandwich down with Mountain Dew.

"I'd like to get a look at Gaylord's man cave."

"Of course." Pieter wiped mustard off his mouth with a paper towel. "I can meet you there tomorrow afternoon."

"Can we get in"—Arn checked his watch—"sometime after six tonight?"

"Can't tonight. I'm taking Meander out for her birthday."

Arn looked down at Pieter, thinking about what Georgia had said about Pieter looking more like Arn than like Butch, with his blond hair and blue eyes. Except for the fact that Pieter was a couple inches taller and forty pounds lighter, he could have been Arn's son. "I'd really like to get in there tonight," he said again. "If my hunch is right, it might help solve your dad's death. And the Five Point cases."

"I don't know." Pieter paced the room, a concerned look etched on his face. "I had the power disconnected years ago when I bought it for taxes. I boarded it up right then, too, but the bums have been breaking in so regularly I gave up." He stood and paced the room. "It's not safe there at night. Aunt Georgia would just kill me if anything happened to you in there. I wouldn't feel right."

"I'm used to a little danger in my life." Arn smiled.

Pieter kicked the floor with the toe of his shoe. "I guess you could go in," he said at last.

"Do you have a set of keys I can borrow?"

"You won't need any. The locks have been broken so many times, I gave up replacing them. You can go right inside." He laughed. "As long as you don't spend the night with the hobos."

"Thanks," Arn said. "I'll go right after supper. There's just a few things I need to take a look at in the basement, and then I'll be out of there."

"Okay. But be careful. I've already called the police twice this month on some nasty-looking bums I caught squatting there."

"Thanks for the warning," Arn pointed to the rest of Pieter's sandwich tossed in the trash can. "I'll be in only slightly more danger than you were just now."

Forty-Four

"I'M BEING FOLLOWED," ANA Maria said as they sat looking at the crime scene photos.

"What do you mean, you're being followed? By who?"

"I don't know," she said. She nibbled the corner of a cookie. "It's probably nothing."

"And you didn't tell me before this?" Arn asked. "When did this start?"

"Today. I heard the coroner paged to go to the hospital just before Oblanski got there and called for his forensics team. By the time I arrived, they had the place locked down. I tried to get some on-camera interviews with the charge nurse on Johnny's floor, but she was too frightened—"

"Wait a minute," Danny said. He refilled their cups from a carafe and sat back down. "I thought you said the hospital was on lockdown. How'd you get in?"

"It was my cameraman's idea, actually," Ana Maria said. "We hung around the maintenance door and waited for someone to show up with a key."

"Like UPS or FedEx?" Arn asked.

"More like some guy dropping off a van he'd serviced and taking another one for an oil change. When he let himself in the door I kind of … sweet-talked him into letting us inside."

"You said were being followed?" Arn pressed.

Ana Maria shrugged. "Just a feeling. Enough that I found myself checking to make sure I still had your little gun. I shouldn't have even said anything."

"After the night the guy grabbed you"—Arn rubbed his cheek that was still sore from getting cut—"everything's important. Did you see anyone?"

"I was too busy trying to get a scoop on Johnny White's death. But every now and again I'd … just feel something. I know that's silly."

Arn didn't think it was silly. His first partner in Denver had been a woman. Young. Petite. Not much good in a bar fight, try though she might. What she did, though, was save both their lives when they responded to a silent burglar alarm at a residence one night. Arn had started into the house when Emily grabbed his arm. "Wait for a K-9," she said.

Arn had pulled away, saying "I don't need a dog to do my fighting," and started into the house again when she jerked him nearly off his feet. "What the hell you doing?" he said. "Let go of me so we can search this place."

"Someone's inside," Emily whispered. "And he's waiting for us."

Arn paused then. "How you know that?"

"I just got a … feeling. Do me that favor you owe me."

"I don't owe you anything."

"But you do owe it to your wife to come home alive," Emily said. "Just this once, throw that macho crap aside and wait for the dog."

Emily had been right that night. The dog made entry and immediately alerted on a man with a rifle crouched just inside the entryway. Emily had known that. Somehow. Just as Ana Maria knew she'd been followed. Somehow.

"I want you to stay home tonight," Arn said.

"In your dreams," Ana Maria said. "I've got to go on air with details of Johnny's murder, and then later with an update on Butch Spangler's homicide." She finished her cookie. "Besides, I have my new guardian cop right outside the house watching over me."

"I still don't like it."

"Neither do I," Danny said. "And I don't like you going out on an empty stomach."

Ana Maria smiled. "You know that guardian cop I mentioned? He gets off duty at eight o'clock, and he's taking me to Texas Roadhouse for supper."

———————

"When are you going to get your car back from the body shop?" Danny squirmed in his seat. As small as he was, the rental car cramped him, and his knees jammed against the dash. "I don't know if I can stand many more of your kind offers."

"You could have stayed home and finished that wiring job while I brought Mickey D's Happy Meals after I got done here."

"And risk you getting my order wrong?" Danny finished the last of his French fries and crumpled the bag.

"Just toss it on the floor," Arn said.

"Not a chance. This micro-limo is the next damn thing I'm going to have to clean for you."

259

"Then quit complaining."

"Speaking of complaining." Danny drew his knees to his chest and flexed his toes to get circulation back. "I need help with the wiring."

"I said I'd help sometime next week."

"I meant professional help. That old frayed crap in your home is a hundred years old."

Arn pulled to the curb across from Gaylord's old house and killed the lights. "Then I guess I'll have to hire a professional."

"That would cost you a year's wages," Danny said, "as much wire that needs to be pulled and replaced."

"Just great."

"But you're in luck. I got a friend who's a master electrician."

"What would that cost me?" Arn pulled his stocking cap over his ears and tugged at his gloves.

"Nothing." Danny smiled and hooked his thumbs in his patched jeans. "He just needs a place to stay."

"Like you needed a place?"

"Just like me."

"Forget it," Arn said. "I adopted you, but I can't afford to adopt another ... homeless person."

"A professional will cost a mint. Let him stay. Just for a couple of nights."

Arn grabbed his flashlight and opened his door. He tucked his notebook between his shirt and his jacket. "We'll talk about it another time. You coming in?"

"Where some guy hung himself?" Danny said. "Excuse me, but I'm just a little superstitious. Especially since old Gaylord did it not a block from a Catholic church." Danny pulled his cap down over his eyes and drew his coat around him as he leaned back as best he could.

"Besides, this will give me a chance to catch up on my sleep, since someone's snoring's been waking me up at night."

Arn started to argue, to tell Danny his own snoring was waking him up at night, but slammed the door before the wind took it off. He put his hand on top of his stocking cap and headed for the front door. It was much like his mother's had been: kicked in, hanging by rusty hinges that threatened to give way in the slightest breeze.

The windows had been broken, and the west wind had whipped the mold-crusted curtains to shreds. The rest of the windows had plywood nailed over them, one sheet ripped away and lying in splinters, halfway in and halfway out of the dilapidated house.

Arn shone his light on two sets of footprints, coming and going off the porch. It was hard to age them with the wind; they could have been made this morning, or they could have been made an hour ago. He patted his gun in his front trouser pocket and stepped past the broken door.

Adelle said she'd auctioned everything in the house after Gaylord's death, except for some junk no one would buy like the three-legged occasional chair leaning against one wall, waiting for someone to sit and relax. Just like a Currier and Ives postcard, Arn thought, playing his light around the living room. Empty Spam cans and chip bags littered the floor, and a wine bottle lay where it had been smashed against one wall. Colored light reflected Arn's flashlight, casting odd, animated shadows on the mold-blackened ceiling that brought his neck hairs to attention.

He tucked the flashlight under his armpit and opened his notebook on the occasional chair. Butch and Oblanski had investigated Gaylord's death, and Arn thumbed through the reports until he found the sketch Oblanski had made of Gaylord's house the night of his death. He turned around in the room until he oriented himself with the door leading to the basement stairwell.

Stuffing the notebook back inside his jacket, he walked to the stairs, stepping over a broken beer bottle. A used syringe crushed under his foot, and he stepped over a crusted condom. He put his hand on the knob and pulled, expecting the door to be stuck from years of disuse. But it swung open freely, the rusty hinges making a grinding sound like a casket lid being opened upon exhumation.

He caught sudden movement to his right. Coming at him. A blur in the darkness, just outside the periphery of his flashlight. Arn flattened himself against the wall and clawed for the revolver in his pocket when a calico cat—as large as a terrier—bolted past him. It swiped at his trouser leg in passing, ripping the denim.

Arn's hand came out of his jacket and clutched his chest as he bent over, sucking in air, his side aching like he'd just run a hard mile. The flashlight rolled on the floor where he'd dropped it, the beam illuminating the cavernous stairwell.

He snatched the flashlight and picked his way down the stairs. A step buckled under his weight and he grabbed for the stair railing. It ripped from the wall and hit him in the knee. He stifled a cry of pain out of fear of hearing his own voice loud in the creepy house. "Be careful of a couple bums I've run out of there"—Pieter's words of warning came back to him. But at the moment, he feared the wild cat returning for a rematch more than the bums.

He descended the rest of the steps more carefully, leading with his flashlight. He reached the basement, and dirty snow and twigs from a bush outside pelted him through a broken window.

Arn reached inside his shirt and took out the floor plan of the basement that Butch had sketched at the time. He turned it to orient himself and found the first room off the bathroom: Gaylord's man cave.

Oblanski had labeled it "Family Room" and Arn suppressed a laugh, thinking it some irony Gaylord masturbated in the family room.

The door swung in as easily as the basement door had, and Arn laid his hand on the butt of his gun, playing the light around, expecting the bums to rush him. But only the wind whipping dirt over a broken-down couch greeted him, and he breathed slowly to calm his heart.

He kneeled down and weighted the sketch with a rock on one corner, a broken water faucet on the other as he shuffled through the photos. Had he just now trembled when he found the picture of Gaylord hanging? He'd never been superstitious like Danny, yet the goose bumps along his arm competed with the hair on his neck to indicate otherwise.

He stood with the photo in hand, playing the light on the rafters above. Closing his eyes, Arn imagined Gaylord standing on a stool that had fallen out of the way, hand dangling at his sides, one hand on the escape knot that failed as he looked at porn propped against a full-length mirror in front of him. "Did you swing after you passed out?" Arn heard himself say, and he shuddered anew. The victims of his investigations often had a way of talking to him, and he to them. But this was one conversation he didn't want to have. Not right here. Perhaps I should have waited until morning...

Then his light fell on the rafter that seemed to be the one where Gaylord had secured his rope. He moved to one side as he compared the death photo with the exact area overhead. Shining his light from different angles, Arn raised up on tip toe and felt along the length of the beam, but he found no telltale gouge marks in the roughhewn wood. Then something fluttered overhead, and he saw that it was a single strand of cotton rope, the only thing remaining that marked where Gaylord had hung.

Arn looked at the pictures again, confirming that this was the very rafter that Gaylord used. Yet there was an absence of gouge marks, which would have indicated that Gaylord practiced autoeroticism while hanging regularly. But the photos showed hard-core porn propped against a mirror in front of where Gaylord hung, watching himself in the mirror while he reached the ultimate high.

The mirror. Arn strained his memory. The mirror. *Where the hell did the mirror hang? If I had been smart enough to bring the pictures of the rest of the house along...*

He snapped his fingers involuntarily, and the sound started him. "The damned mirror," he blurted out, finally recalling photos taken of the upstairs rooms. An intricately carved five-foot mirror, scalloped at the top, had hung in the Fournier's upstairs hallway. But the photos taken at the time of Gaylord's death showed a sun-bleached part of the wall where the mirror must have hung for years. And which was suddenly—at the time of his death—absent from that spot.

Arn walked bent over as he shone his flashlight around the basement floor, working slowly until his light caught a reflection of broken glass. He kicked a piece of cardboard blown against a wall. It flew across the room, revealing the scalloped frame of the mirror rotting beside a splintered dresser drawer. "No one takes a mirror down every time they use it, then puts it back," he muttered. He couldn't see Gaylord taking it down every time he did his dirty deed downstairs. He would have just bought another long mirror.

"I think you were murdered," Arn said aloud. "But who?" The answer came easily: the Five Point Killer, the only person who would think it through enough to set Gaylord up to look like his escape knot failed.

Arn stuck the flashlight under his arm, bending to put the pictures back in his notebook, when his light caught movement in a broken piece of mirror. Movement coming at him. Movement that might be the cat coming back for that rematch.

He turned at the sound of glass crunching under feet. Felt a strong arm encircle his neck. Quick. Sudden. Pulling him back off balance, lifting him off the floor. Arn yelled, but his cries were muted. He felt himself go under even as he clawed helplessly at his attacker's forearm.

He dropped his flashlight and it rolled aimlessly across the floor, reflecting in the shards of mirror some sinister figure behind him as he lost consciousness.

———————

Arn came to. Choking. Gasps coming in short spurts past the rope around his neck.

He kicked his dangling feet beneath him, struggling for something to stand on, something to relieve the intense pressure. He tried breaking free of the plastic ties that bound his wrists, but they held fast. Cutting deeper. But there was nothing to ease the impending loss of his life only moments away.

The figure walked around Arn, watching his agony from different angles. Through some type of mask across his face, Arn saw the person smiling, even in the blackness of the basement.

The man passed in front of him. Arn kicked out, his blow landing on his attacker's shoulder. The figure stumbled against a broken window, then growled with an intense fury as he picked himself up and moved behind Arn. He threw himself on him, his weight dragging Arn down tighter on the noose. No sound escaped Arn's constricted throat. His head felt as if it would implode with the loss of air, the life leaving him.

No. Air. Swaying. Like Gaylord swung. Legs twitched. Heart slowed. Chest heaved. Only. Seconds. Left …

Someone grunted in the darkness like a wild hog and rushed, knocking the attacker off Arn and onto the floor.

Danny yelled and kicked out. The figure avoided Danny's kick and hit him on the side of the head. Danny rolled across the floor and came to rest against a wall. The figure lunged at him, but Danny slashed the air with a knife as Arn lost consciousness once again.

He was only remotely aware of someone lifting him up, relieving the pressure on his windpipe. Air rushed in, searing his lungs. The awareness of pain returned as he sucked in great gasps of stale, basement-mildewed air.

"Here," Danny said as he put the knife in Arn's hand. "You're too damned big for me to hold you and cut the rope, too."

Arn stared, disbelieving, at the knife, his flashlight somewhere on the floor bouncing off the bright blade. "Cut the damned rope above your head!" Danny yelled.

Arn felt for the rope. Found it. Sawed it with both hands still secured by the plastic tie, thinking how the hell does Danny dull his knives so much …

Arn fell to the floor on top of the old man. Danny squirmed to get out from under Arn and then flopped back onto the floor. Arn rolled over, blood sticky on the back of his neck. Danny's blood, and Arn felt Danny's head. He squirmed, and Arn tried telling him to lie still, but no words came from his bruised throat.

He took off his jacket and stuffed it under Danny's head as he felt in his pocket for his bandana. Danny opened his eyes and forced a smile. "Did I ever tell you you're too damned big to hold up?"

Arn focused on the knife still in his hand, expecting his attacker to return. "I think you told me," was his guttural, raspy answer. The pain travelled along his throat and he struggled to stand, but Danny grabbed his shoulder and eased him back down.

Arn clawed at his trouser pocket; his gun still there, useless. "We need to get out of here," he said. It came out in little more than a whimper. "He might come back."

"I doubt it." Danny patted Arn's pocket for his cell phone. "I heard a car start up a few seconds after he ran out. Who was it?"

Arn shook his head, and even that slight movement brought pain. "Came up behind me. Didn't see him. Had a ski mask."

"That was no ski mask," Danny said as he punched in 911. "That was a surgical mask."

Forty-Five

ARN AWOKE AGAIN ON his way to the hospital as paramedics monitored his heart rate and adjusted a saline drip. The bag swayed over his head every time the ambulance hit a bump or took a turn. Arn tried talking to the medics, but his swollen throat had left his voice somewhere in Gaylord's basement. A lady paramedic rested her hand on his shoulder. "Don't try talking until you've been examined. Your friend showed us where you were hanging, if that's what you're wondering." Arn swallowed hard and managed to ask where Danny was before pain overtook him again.

"That little old fella?" she answered. "We cleaned the cut on his head and slapped a Steri-Strip over it. He refused to ride in and get checked out. Said the bandage was good enough for him. He said to tell you he was driving your car back to your house."

"But he doesn't have a license."

The paramedic grinned. "Then I guess you can ask the policeman waiting for you to ticket him. Here is where we go in."

The ambulance drove into a sally port and stopped. Nurses jerked open the back doors and hit the air ride. The ambulance slowly lowered as the air hissed out of the suspension until Arn's gurney could be wheeled off. "I can walk," he heard himself say, but he wasn't sure if anyone heard his raspy pleas.

Arn awoke from a light sleep, the product of something the paramedics had given him on the ride in. Or the product of an adrenaline dump from fighting for his life in Gaylord's basement. He tried sitting, but gentle hands eased him back down.

"Danny called and told me paramedics were transporting you to the hospital," Ana Maria said. "He told me what happened."

"I thought you had a date with your bodyguard?"

"He's waiting outside the ER. I thought you were more important than a free meal."

Ana Maria stepped out when an emergency room doctor who looked young enough to be Arn's grandson—if he had a grandson—pulled aside the curtain. He snatched a metal clipboard hanging from the foot of Arn's bed, scanned it quickly, and moved to the side of the bed. He deftly retrieved a small pen light from his pocket protector. "Open wide, Mr. Anderson. Not too wide, just enough so I can see what damage was done."

The doctor shone his light around inside Arn's throat, his glasses riding on top of his head. When he finished, he brought the glasses down and gently felt Arn's neck. He clicked off the light and it disappeared back into his pocket protector. "You're lucky. I see no permanent damage. But we're going to run x-rays just to be safe. You're going to be talking like you've been eating gravel for a while, but you'll recover."

"Thanks, doc," Arn heard himself say, but he didn't recognize his own voice.

The doctor nodded and pulled the curtain back. "He's all yours," he told Ana Maria, his eyes lingering on her just a bit longer. She pulled up a chair and sat beside the bed, while the doctor's voice trailed off as he ordered x-rays.

"If you played your cards right"—Arn forced a smile—"I think you could have a dinner date with that doctor, too."

"Naw," Ana Maria said. "He probably just wants his car tuned up." She grew serious and took Arn's hand, careful not to disturb the saline injection spot. "I think with this, along with everything else that's happened, I can convince DeAngelo to stop the special."

"I don't believe you," Arn said. He gagged and reached for a glass of ice water by the bed. He sucked slowly on the straw until he was able to continue. "We're close to finding Butch's killer. And probably Gaylord's and Steve's as well. And you want to pull the plug?"

"How do you know we're close?"

"What did you tell me when you started getting threats?" Arn said. "'We must be getting close. The son of a bitch is worried.' Well, the son-of-a-bitch must be worried if he tried killing me tonight."

Ana Maria's eyes welled up and she wiped them with the back of her hand. "But it's not worth you getting killed."

"Unless we find the killer," Oblanski said. He'd parted the curtain and glared at Ana Maria before pulling a chair close to Arn's bed. "I know you can't talk very good right now, but give me the quick and the dirty of what happened tonight."

Arn tried sitting, and Ana Maria propped pillows behind his back. "Me and Danny went to Gaylord's old house, the one Pieter Spangler bought—"

"Who's Danny?"

"Guy I hired to help me renovate Mom's house."

"We'll need a statement from him."

"I'll tell him." Arn ran his tongue across his dry lips and reached for the glass of ice water on the tray. Ana Maria handed it to him and angled the straw so he could drink. "We went to the house, but Danny got hinked and stayed in the car while I went in."

"Why'd you go there?"

"I wanted to see where Gaylord hung himself," Arn said between sips. "I thought his death might have been suspicious."

Oblanski shook his head. "I worked with Butch on Gaylord's case. I wasn't the most experienced investigator at the time, but I'd been on the street long enough to know a setup when I saw it. And Gaylord's was no setup. He died just like we noted."

"Even though I found evidence that he was probably murdered?"

"What evidence?" Oblanski stood and nodded to Ana Maria. "Is this something she put in your head, just to sell copy?"

"Maybe you're pissed 'cause Arn found something you missed," Ana Maria said. "Or doesn't the great Ned Oblanski ever miss anything?"

"I didn't miss a thing."

The ice water soothed Arn's throat, and he took another long sip before handing it to Ana Maria with a shaky hand. "There were no gouge marks in the rafters where Gaylord hung himself."

"I'm listening," Oblanski said.

"If Gaylord had been practicing his … autoerotic routine for any length of time, the rope's movement would have furrowed the wood."

Oblanski shook his head. "Now you're rambling."

"Am I?" Arn said. "Someone took that mirror from the upstairs hallway and put it downstairs. Scattered porn on the floor like Gaylord was looking at it while he hung, probably after they killed Gaylord."

"Adelle would have said something about the mirror."

"Your own report states Adelle never went back in the house after she found Gaylord," Arn got out. "And she turned everything over to the auction company. She would have no way of knowing about the mirror. If she was telling the truth."

Oblanski sat slapping a fist against his leg. "When we searched Gaylord's house that night, we did find books by the likes of de Sade and von Sacher-Masoch in his man cave. Books sick bastards like that read. I don't know—"

"Look at this." Arn winced when he ran his hand over where the rope had cut into the flesh of his neck. "Did you see rope marks on Gaylord's neck that night?"

"What stupid question is that? Of course I did. He was hanging by a rope."

"And did you ever see rope marks any other time you saw him at work?"

Oblanski thought for a moment, and his face turned ashen. "Never." He paced in the small space in front of Arn's bed. "You might—just might—be right on this. But why would someone hang Gaylord? The little prick was never a threat to anyone."

"Johnny was convinced the Five Point Killer was linked to Butch's murder. If Butch and Gaylord were working those cases together..." Arn trailed off. Ana Maria refilled his glass with ice water and handed it to him.

"If what you say is true, that Gaylord's and Steve's and Butch's deaths are connected, there's only one common denominator: the Five Point cases." Oblanski turned to Ana Maria. "I'm due to go on television with you again tomorrow night. What are you going to say?"

Ana Maria thought for a moment. "I'm going to speculate—on the air—that all cases are connected. That the killer returned to murder Johnny. And attack Arn."

"I'm not ready to try to connect Johnny's murder with the Five Point cases."

"I'd wager your forensics tech found a footprint," Arn said.

"Found a print where?"

"In Johnny's room."

"We found a lot of footprints in Johnny's room," Oblanski said. "The trauma team was in there for twenty minutes. They left a lot of prints. Couldn't be helped."

"The killer left a print that would be easy for you to find."

"You sound pretty sure of yourself," Oblanski said.

"This guy's predictable. And consistent. At every crime scene, he's left a distinct shoe print. The same print that was at Joey Bent's was on Delbert Urban's bare back. And our killer left it somewhere in Johnny's room where it would be undisturbed. He wants to make sure it's found."

"There was no ... " The color left Oblanski's face and he sat in the chair. "There was a single shoe print on the far side of the room. Away from the bed, near the window. Not even close to where the trauma team worked on Johnny." He stared at Arn. "This guy put that shoe print there just for us. Didn't he?"

Arn nodded. "He's thumbing his nose at us. Taunting us." He sipped more water. "Are your crime scene techs still at Gaylord's old house?"

"They're just about to wrap it up."

"Get on the phone and tell them to specifically look for the same tread pattern as was on that one print in Johnny's room. If the guy who attacked me left that same print—and I'm betting it's the same guy—then it was Johnny's killer who hung me tonight. And Steve and Gaylord's killer, and probably the Five Point victims' as well.

Forty-Six

AFTER X-RAYS, ARN LEFT the hospital the next morning AMA: Against Medical Advice. The ER doctor wanted to admit him for another day's observation. "I got a house to renovate," Arn told him, and he ordered a nurse's aid to help dress. A very young nurse's aide. But then, everyone looked young to Arn nowadays.

On his insistence, the woman turned away while he slipped his trousers on. "You can turn back around now," he said as he buckled his belt.

"Shucks," she said, handing him his wallet and car keys. "You mean I missed out on the male review?"

He pocketed the car keys. "Where'd these come from?"

"Some little old dude with a ponytail dropped them off this morning. He said, 'Tell Arn I pedaled as fast as I could.' Said he left your car in the parking garage."

"Thanks," Arn said.

"And that TV lady left a note." The nurse's aide handed Arn a handwritten note from Ana Maria. *Arn—call me when you're released and I'll come pick you up.*

274

Arn pocketed the note. Ana Maria didn't need him interrupting her day.

He stopped at the nurses' station to check out, and the charge nurse gave him two bottles of water and a prescription for salve to smear on the rope burns encircling his neck. "And we found this in your pants pocket." She handed him his revolver, cylinder open, with one hand, Ziploc containing the five rounds in her other. Anyplace else, a nurse would have freaked out finding a gun in a patient's pocket. But here in Wyoming, he was just one of many who came into the ER armed.

He rode the elevator with a mother and two screaming twin girls grating on his nerves. He dearly wished for the voice to scream back at the brats, but was rescued when the elevator stopped. Mother and urchins scrambled out, leaving Arn to ride the rest of the way down to the parking garage alone. And in quiet.

Icy wind blew hard pellets of snow sideways into him as he exited, and he turned his collar up while he marched around looking for where Danny had parked his rental. He spotted the car between a Ford Focus and Chevy Volt, two subcompacts that nearly hid the torture device the insurance company had given him. He tried opening the driver's door, but the guy who'd parked next to him allowed him to open the door only about eight inches, and he went around to the passenger side. He performed his entry ritual, folding himself in and struggling to move behind the wheel. A passing doctor and nurse stopped and watched the entertainment, chuckling to themselves until Arn finally dropped into the driver's seat.

Danny had left a note stuck on the steering wheel with a Band Aid: *This car sucks!!! I called the body shop and your Oldsmobile won't be done for two days. Pedal fast!!!*

Arn slowly drove out of the parking lot. With his bruised neck muscles stretched taut from fighting the hanging last night, he had to turn his whole body to check for side traffic. By the time he'd crossed the bridge over the Union Pacific depot, he felt as if he'd just finished a hard workout. From what he remembered of workouts.

He turned onto 5th Street, marveling that the city had designated this the South Side Historical District. A historic district with homes in disrepair, others abandoned, most much smaller than his mother's house. He remembered his father coming home from a tough day kicking the shit out of bad guys, sitting inhaling the swill he bought by the case, getting pie-eyed. "I wish we could move to the south side," he'd told Arn, who was sitting at his father's feet waiting for the order to fetch another beer. "The railroad built most of those houses for workers. Engineers. Conductors. We're going to get us one of those homes," he'd promised. "I just want to move out of Nigger Town," he said. "I hate it here." But Arn's father hadn't moved out of their part of town, mostly populated with blacks and Mexicans, railroad workers on their own when it came to finding a place to live. And as long as they lived within walking distant of the bar, his dad never would.

Arn pulled to the curb in front of Gaylord's old house and parked behind Pieter's Audi. Pieter was teetering on a ladder in front of a bay window, wielding a hammer like he was born to it as he tacked plywood over a broken window frame. When he spotted Arn, he backed down the ladder, taking off his work gloves as he walked to Arn's car. He bent to help Arn out of his rental, but Arn slapped Pieter's hand away. "I was hanged, not had my legs broken," he grunted. "I can get out by my lonesome."

"I heard about that," Pieter said.

"How?"

"The police called and wanted me to come down last night after you were attacked." Pieter forced a smile. "You want something to warm you up?"

"Like hot buttered rum?"

"Like coffee. I got a thermos inside."

"I'm not sure I want to go back in your house again."

"Understood."

"But I can take a cup. As long as it's not hospital coffee."

"God forbid."

Pieter had installed a new door lock and screwed the hinges tight. As Arn stepped inside, he realized the night had been kind to the old house. In the daylight, it was positively depressing. Gaylord's house had deteriorated since the pictures taken after his death investigation. The plaster walls were cracked and crumbling over wallpaper blistered by moisture. The ceiling drooped in some places enough that Arn had to duck to walk through, and the floor heaved with the settling foundation.

Pieter caught him staring at the basement door. "I decided to nail that shut. And I boarded up the windows in the back. Try as I might, I can't seem to keep the bums out. But this"—he pointed to Arn's neck—"is the final straw. I have to make sure no one gets in again. Like your friend."

"Friend?"

"Ana Maria. When I came here this morning to work on it, she was taking pictures in the basement."

"You'd think she was a reporter or something," Arn said.

"All I needed was for her to fall down those rickety steps and hurt herself. The one thing I don't have is homeowner's insurance on this dump."

"I take it you put the run on her?"

Pieter smiled. "Not that I wouldn't have minded spending time with her, but I just can't risk anyone else getting hurt here." He sat in the dirty three-legged chair Arn had noticed last night and motioned to a lawn chair, working his feet around in tight circles. "Sit. My hamstrings are a little tight from being up on that ladder."

Arn eased himself down, feeling far older than his fifty-five years. Pieter handed him a cup of coffee in a Roadrunner mug, and he wrapped his hands around it. "I don't much feel like the Roadrunner this morning. More like the Coyote."

Pieter cupped his own mug, the steam clouding his frowning face. "When the police woke me last night and told me to come down here, I knew something bad happened." He shook his head. "I knew I shouldn't have let you come here at night. I was afraid those bums—"

"It wasn't any bum," Arn rasped. He sipped slowly, the hot coffee feeling good sliding down his throat. "The guy who attacked me didn't ... smell like a street person." But then Danny didn't smell bad, Arn thought.

"What did he smell like?"

"Old Spice." Of all the things Arn remembered as his life was fading fast on the end of that rope, it was his attacker's overpowering cologne. "The man wore more cologne than a person ought to. Not like any street person working the corners around here. Besides"—he motioned to the trash on the floor—"he knew this place. Maybe that's his wine bottles or his chip bags. All I know is he was familiar enough to make it down the steps—in pitch black darkness, with no light. And making no noise."

Pieter nodded in agreement. "I'm sure you're right. Did you get a look at him?"

"It was too dark. I dropped my flashlight and got just enough of a look to see he was wearing a mask. Turns out it was a surgical mask."

Pieter uncapped the thermos bottle and refilled Arn's cup. "Someone connected to the hospital, perhaps?"

Arn gingerly rubbed the scab forming on his neck. "I don't know. I just have no idea."

"The police fingerprinted the place to death last night. Photographed and cast a shoe print outside."

"Shoe print?"

"Outside the house," Pieter said. "Ned Oblanski was pretty excited about it. The evidence technician showed him the plaster cast."

"All I know is the guy who attacked me was strong enough to choke me out. Lift me off the floor and slip that rope around my neck. If Danny hadn't come along, I would have been toast."

"Who's Danny?"

"Just some guy helping me remodel my house." Arn didn't feel like discussing the homeless man he'd befriended.

Pieter walked the room, stomping occasionally to keep circulation in his legs. "If your attacker wasn't a bum, who you figure it to be?"

"The same person who murdered Gaylord."

"But he died ten years ago of an accidental hanging."

Arn explained his suspicions about Gaylord and the absence of gouge marks where there should have been deep ones if Gaylord hung regularly. "I'm convinced his death was staged."

Pieter topped his own cup off and capped the bottle. "And you still think this ties in with Dad's murder?"

"More than ever," Arn answered. "Whatever your dad knew about the Five Point killings, Gaylord knew. I'm convinced whoever silenced your dad silenced Gaylord. And Steve as well."

"I can see Dad and Gaylord being murdered, but Steve?" Pieter set the thermos on the floor and paced again. "I stopped by Steve's that Friday before I went with the basketball team to Casper. His wife had divorced him the previous year, and I stop by to try to cheer him up. He had a six-pack chilling in the wings, and he'd just polished off another. I can definitely see him passing out and falling asleep with a smoke in his hand."

Arn stood slowly, painfully, and he wasn't sure what had beaten him worse, the guy last night or that inhuman rental car. "When you stopped by Steve's that afternoon, where was his recliner?"

Pieter shrugged. "In his living room, I guess."

"I mean, where exactly?"

Pieter looked to the ceiling for a long moment before answering. "Where it always was. Parked right in front of his TV. He was a lot like Dad—he watched a lot of television while he kept Budweiser in business. If I'd come home from the game that night, maybe checked on Steve..."

"But the team got snowed in at Casper," Arn said.

"The longest day of my life," Pieter said, "hanging with a bunch of immature kids in that motel room. Praying the interstate would reopen so we could get home before I strangled one of them. If I could just have gotten home and checked on Steve..." His voice trailed off.

"Nothing you could have done. Just like nothing you could have done about my attack last night."

"Except to steer you to Frank Dull Knife."

Arn turned his collar up and slipped his gloves on. "Your dad dropped the burglary charge against Frank a week before he was killed. And Frank broke it off with your mother after your dad's murder. And you still think Frank had a reason to kill Butch? Or is it just that you hate him?"

"Hate's a strong word." Pieter kicked the neck of the broken wine bottle. "But what would you feel if he was screwing your mom, and caused your dad to ... drink like he did?"

"I'd hate the man, too," Arn said. He headed for the door and the warmth of the Clown Car.

Forty-Seven

OBLANSKI CALLED ARN ON the way over to Frank Dull Knife's shop. "We picked up Jefferson Dawes a few minutes ago. Want to sit in on the interrogation?"

"Picked him up for what?"

"Johnny's murder." Oblanski outlined in a few words why: Jefferson knew Cheyenne Regional well, including the maintenance door devoid of surveillance cameras. And he would have known what angles the cameras were capable of recording. "He had access to caps and masks. And he's got a closet full of lab coats."

Arn rubbed his forehead, trying to get a handle on what Oblanski just told him. "Tell me you have more than that."

"We do," Oblanski said. "You were right—the crime scene techs found a footprint right outside Gaylord's house last night that was identical to the one in Johnny's room. It was the same tread pattern as we found on Delbert Urban's back." He paused. "And the same shoe print as the one I overlooked outside the house the night Gaylord hung to death." He went on to explain that Captain Moore had reviewed the hospital tapes, and one camera picked up Jefferson walking past Johnny's room ten minutes before he was murdered."

Arn had thought about Jefferson as he lay in his hospital bed last night: his wife running off with that science teacher sounded sketchy, as did his statement that Gaylord invited him to his house to warn him away from Adelle. What if Jefferson hadn't taken Gaylord's advice? What if he'd wanted Adelle enough to kill for her? Worse, Arn realized, what if he was looking for multiple killers for the officers? Then there was the Old Spice he was certain he'd smelled the night he and Ana Maria were attacked.

"We served a search warrant on Jefferson's car and found a pair of Nikes with what looks like the same tread pattern," Oblanski concluded. "We're having it compared with the others."

"Why did you search his car?"

"We received an anonymous tip that the shoes were in his Caddy," Oblanski said.

Perhaps, Arn thought, the anonymous tip came from the only other person who knew that Jefferson was the killer. Someone who would be pissed at their husband's activities now with younger women. "Better get someone over to interview Adelle," he said. Pain shot down his neck as he turned in the seat to check for traffic. "She told me that the night Gaylord died, she was to meet Jefferson for some heavy-duty lovemaking, but he was a no show. When you interview him, ask him to verify where he was that night."

"And if he can?"

"Then she was lying to me," Arn said. "And she might have helped Jefferson hang Gaylord."

The line went quiet for a moment while Oblanski jotted things down. "Can you think of anything else?"

"Lean on him about his first wife," Arn said. "I checked with customs and they have no record of her ever leaving the country. If Jefferson killed Johnny—and Gaylord, ten years ago—he'd be a good contender for the Five Point slayings."

"What's that got to do with Jefferson's first wife?"

"If she found out about him, she might have been afraid she'd be next and fled Cheyenne."

"Okay. But you're sure you don't want to sit in on his interrogation?"

"I got other things to do."

"Like what?"

"Remember, I was hired to solve Butch's murder."

————

Frank sat looking over reading glasses perched on his nose, bulbous with burst blood vessels from too many sessions with Jim Beam. When Arn walked through the shop door, Frank squinted at his computer screen. He wrote down parts numbers that Arn easily read upside down. Frank looked up and tossed his glasses on the desk. "Look what the cat drug in."

Arn nodded to the screen. "Hate to interrupt when you're dick-deep in some porno site."

Frank's face turned red. "I need a starter for an MG Midget. Wish people would just go to Import Motors." He leaned back in his chair, the chain of his biker wallet slapping the arm of the chair in time with his nervous foot. "What the hell you want now?"

"The truth."

"What planet are you living on?" Frank taunted. "Didn't you ever hear you'll never get the truth from a career criminal? Which I was"—

he grinned—"before I got religion. These days, I'm a legit business-man. Now what do you want?"

"Hannah suspected that you killed Butch, didn't she?"

"Where the hell did that come from?"

"She threatened to go to the police that night she chased you out of her house."

"She never chased me."

"Emma Barnes said otherwise."

"That old prune who lived next door—"

"Can remember the color of your shirt and the shine of your boots that night." Arn hung his Stetson on the elk antler coat rack. "Did Hannah threaten to go to the law because you killed Butch? Or because she could put you away on that burglary charge?"

Frank's lip quivered and Arn pressed his point. "The Highway Patrol ruled the cause of Hannah's fatal accident was brake failure. You work on her brakes?"

"You son-of-a-bitch!" Frank came off his chair, but Arn shoved him back down. Pain shot up his shoulders from the strain, but he wasn't going to let Frank know it. "Hannah could put you away. That's why you rigged the accident."

"I wasn't going back to the joint," Frank said, more in a whisper, as he slumped in his chair.

"Not with Butch dead, you weren't."

Frank reached into his shirt pocket and grabbed a pack of Marlboros. His hand shook as he brought the cigarette to the shaky match. "You know Butch dismissed the burglary charge."

"He could have refiled it any time, and you'd be back looking at a habitual criminal conviction."

Frank lit his smoke and looked around for an ashtray. He dropped his match in the same Skippy jar he'd drank whisky out of the last time Arn was here. "I didn't see Butch the night he was murdered."

"So you claimed. Some horse shit about having to get up early for a carburetor job. Except you weren't at your shop the next morning."

"I told you before I hooked up with another babe that night after Hannah started rubbing all over Ned Oblanski. I thought, what the hell, if she can come onto another guy, I can go home with another woman. We left the bar 'cause the little lady wanted some quality time at her house. Outside Wellington, Colorado. Exactly fifty miles from my shop."

"Why should I believe you now that you've had ten years to come up with some cockamamie alibi like that? Maybe because you want me and Oblanski's department off your case for Butch's murder."

"Enough!" Frank flicked his cigarette onto the floor and crushed it with his boot. "Sure I committed that burglary, just like Butch said. But he planted evidence, he wanted me so badly. If he'd done a little more digging, he'd have had me dead to rights." Frank shook out another cigarette and crumpled the empty package. "Hannah wouldn't have dared testify against me. She was with me the night I burgled that home."

"Hannah?" For the second time, Frank's statements had caught Arn flat-footed.

"You didn't know, big city detective," Frank grinned. "Hannah went through that window like she was born to break and enter. And we cleaned the house out. And a few homes the next week." Frank leaned in, smiling, remembering. "And you know why she loved it? She was an adrenaline junky. She fed off the excitement of getting caught. And she repaid me in bed every night."

"And Butch found out?"

Frank blew smoke rings toward his dirty ceiling. "When Butch brought me in for the burglary, he showed me a Rolex he claimed was stolen and said he found it in my car. I called bullshit on that. I never stole anything fancy I couldn't fence right off. So I dropped the bombshell about Hannah helping me."

"Because you knew he had you dead to rights?"

"Because he planted the Rolex, and I knew I couldn't get out of it. I told him Hannah and I were a team. If I went down, I'd drag her right down with me. He had no choice but to drop charges."

Arn regained his thoughts and grabbed his pocket notebook and pen. "If you weren't even in town when Butch was murdered, what's the name of the woman you went home from the bar with?"

"I can't do that. She's still married. I don't want to cause her any grief."

"And just what did you and Hannah argue about that night Emma Barnes saw her chase you out of the house?"

Frank shrugged. "After Butch was dead, there just was never a spark there. No intrigue any more. I needed some new babe. Know what I mean?"

Arn didn't. After eighteen faithful years with the same women, the spark had never left until the day she died. And it was still there for Arn.

"Hannah was on me constantly to stop by after Butch was murdered. I put it off as long as I could. The trips to Wellington took up a lot of my time. I told her I just felt odd screwing her in the same house her old man died in. I told her we needed to split. When I left the house, she chased me out onto the yard. Threatened to go to the law about our burglaries. But I knew it was a bluff. She'd never risk being charged along with me."

"Why are you telling me this now?"

"A former cop, and you've never heard of the statute of limitations? I can't be charged for those burglaries. It's too long ago."

Frank leaned forward and blew smoke in Arn's direction. "And I didn't have to kill Hannah *or* Butch. He sure as hell wasn't going to put his old lady away." He laughed. "What would people think?" He motioned to the door. "Now I got MG parts to order, so get the hell out."

Arn reached out with his pen and tapped a large welt on the back of Frank's hand. The man jerked his hand back and covered it with the other. "Where'd you get your knuckles scraped up?" Arn asked.

Frank held up his hand. "This? Work related."

"Are you sure it wasn't from hitting some old Indian alongside the head over on 5th Street last night?"

"Could be." Frank grinned. "Or it could've happened when I went to Wellington yesterday while a certain lady's husband was away. And the wrench slipped off while I was working on her Buick."

Forty-Eight

ARN WAS SEATED IN the lobby of the police department talking with the community service officer when Jefferson Dawes burst through the door. A thin, balding man in a herringbone suit followed on his heels as they headed for the exit doors. Jefferson stopped in front of Arn, jaw muscles clenching and unclenching. He started to speak, but the little man pushed Jefferson out the door onto the street.

Oblanski was warm on their heels. He ran through the lobby and stood looking out the door. Jefferson got into the passenger side of a Suburban parked at the curb, and it kicked up loose asphalt driving away. Oblanski waited until a white Crown Vic pulled out behind them before he turned and sat on the visitors' couch beside Arn. "Did Dr. Dawes say anything to you just now?" he asked.

"He wanted to," Arn answered, "but the little guy with him wouldn't let him."

"That's his attorney from Ft. Collins, and he didn't want Jeff to say anything in the interview, either. But Dr. Dawes doesn't listen to counsel worth a damn."

Oblanski turned to the community service officer. "Could you go upstairs and see if Michelle has any messages for me?"

When the officer left, Oblanski scooted closer and lowered his voice. "Dr. Dawes denied ever owning a pair of Nikes, even though we seized that pair in his Escalade. And when I asked if he went into Gaylord's house the night he was hung, his attorney tried to keep him quiet. It didn't work. I thought Dawes was going to throw a punch at me when he denied it. He claimed he was at the Denver Downtown Marriott in bed with an anesthesiologist the night Butch was murdered, and that's why he told Adelle he was tied up that night. He said he doesn't remember her name."

"Did he admit to being in Gaylord's old house last night?"

"He was pumping some nurse from Cardiac Rehab. We're running her down now."

"And Johnny?"

Oblanski looked to the double doors like he expected Jefferson to come stomping back in. "I showed him the hospital tapes. We'd done a height comparison between him and Johnny's killer in the video, and knew he had to be between six feet and six feet two. Dawes is six feet one inch. He says he was on the floor looking in on a patient. We verified he saw a man from Wheatland, but there's no way to know if he stayed on the floor after that."

"Did he ever clam up?"

Oblanski smiled. "When I started asking him about his wife that he went to court to declare dead, he went mute. I told him we checked with Customs and the Marshals, and she never left the country like he claimed. That got him shaking bad enough I thought he'd piss his pants ... you saw how angry he was when he came through here. Anyway, his attorney wouldn't let him answer that, and said they were leaving unless we were prepared to make an arrest."

"Which you're not."

"Not yet. I put one of my guys following him in case he goes to the hospital to talk with his alibi. But the girlfriend's off work today. We got an unmarked surveilling at her place, and I've applied for a phone tap. If the good doctor makes contact with her, we'll know when and what they talk about."

Oblanski kept quiet while a man went to the window of the records division to pick up a copy of an accident report. When he left, Oblanski asked how Arn's interview with Frank had gone. Arn told him that Frank claimed Hannah was his accomplice in numerous residential burglaries. "But it's impossible to check his story, with Hannah long dead."

"I hate to admit it, but it does make some sense that Butch kept it to himself," Oblanski said. "He wouldn't want anyone knowing the great Butch Spangler's wife was a common criminal."

"Unless she confided in someone else." Arn looked sideways at Oblanski.

The chief turned red. "I told you before, I danced with her that one night. We parked and made out until I found out she was Butch's wife. When I dropped her off down the block from her house that was the last I saw of her."

"I had to ask," Arn said. He pulled his collar away from his neck, which was scabbing up from the deep rope burn. The prescription was still in his pocket, and he needed to fill it.

"So, we're no further ahead," Oblanski said. "We're up against a stout brick wall. We got two solid suspects, Dr. Dawes and Frank Dull Knife. Either one could be our guy."

"You don't think they're all connected?"

"I'm leaning toward your theory: if we find the killer of any of the officers, we'll clear all three cases. And the Five Point cases as well. But just what the hell do I tell the public tonight when I go on TV with Ana Maria?"

Arn thought for a moment before answering. "You're asking my advice? Last time I gave it, Johnny got murdered."

"Like you pointed out, it was no one's fault. Including yours."

Arn wanted to thank Oblanski, but for some reason, the words never materialized. "Tell the audience that Johnny's murder shows just how close I am to solving Butch's death, and his connection to the Five Point murders."

"You mean *we're* close?"

"No. I meant *me*."

Oblanski shook his head. "I can't put a civilian in danger."

When Arn started to object, Oblanski held up his hand. "You were nearly killed last night. Pieter can say what he will about the homeless infesting that old house of his, but your attack was not the work of some bum wanting you dead because you uncovered his party house. If I come out and proclaim that you're a half step away from connecting everything—"

"But I am—"

"Your life won't be worth a nickel."

Arn stood and walked to the door. The sun set early this time of year, and his scarred neck was reflected back at him as he stared outside. "We need to force him out in the open. And I *am* close to connecting all these cases."

"Even Steve's?"

Arn nodded. "I read the report of Steve's fire. He ordered pizza the day before it happened. I need to double check on times to make sure I got things straight in my mind. I got to interview the pizza delivery boy."

Oblanski threw up his hands. "Is that all, just find some pimply-faced geek who used to deliver pizza ten years ago?"

Arn smiled. "Actually, Ana Maria found said geek. He's a night manager at the Flying J Truck Stop."

"I give up," Oblanski said. "Do what you need to do. Tonight with Ana Maria I'll say you are close to solving them. But you watch your ass. The last thing I need right now is another unsolved murder."

———————

Arn rushed home, late for his dinner date with Georgia. He was walking through the door and shaking off his boots when laughter erupted from the kitchen. Danny sat laughing with a man as emaciated as he was. The man nudged Danny and stood. He looked like a midget Abe Lincoln, with a long, dour face and a beard that rested halfway down his chest. He came to Danny's shoulders. And Danny was small.

"This is Erv," Danny said.

Erv wiped his hand on his tattered corduroy trousers and shook Arn's hand. Like Danny's, Erv's hand was rough. Callused.

"Erv's that old friend I was telling you about." Danny looked to the back door, and Erv put on a faded parka and disappeared outside. "We were going to talk about him, remember?"

"Better be quick," Arn said as he unbuttoned his shirt. "I got a dinner date."

Danny thrust his hand in his pockets, gathering his thoughts. "Erv needs a place to stay. He's homeless."

"Aren't we all?"

"But he's like me, he's got no place."

"Danny, I hate to break this to you, but I'm not running an adult orphanage here. If Erv needs a place to crash, tell him to contact some of the churches."

"He can't go to church."

"What do you mean, he can't go?"

"Erv's a sinner," Danny said solemnly.

"Aren't we all?"

"No, I mean he's got something wrong up here." Danny tapped the side of his head. "He's kind of titched. Not sharp like us. He thinks he's such a big sinner he'll burn up the moment he sets foot in a church."

"I find it hard to believe that a master electrician is an out-of-work electrician. He ought to be making six figures and living in a nice place."

"He did before he got titched." Danny tapped his head again. "He had to give it up. He couldn't go into churches for jobs. Now he goes from day job to day job."

"Well, he's not staying here."

"This is his chance to get back on his feet, if only some benevolent soul—"

"No."

"But Erv's got phenomenal hearing," Danny said.

"What's that mean?"

"Erv can hear a pin drop in the middle of a hurricane."

"I'd care if we had hurricanes in Wyoming." Arn checked his watch. "What's that got to do with him staying here?" He started for the stairs with Danny at his heels.

"Erv would have heard that person sneaking around the house the other night. And in light of recent events"—Danny rubbed the knot on the side of his head—"you might need someone to alert you if the guy comes back."

"We got a security system now."

"They can be overrode."

Arn stood with his hand on the new stair railing Danny had installed. "So you want me to let Erv stay because he'd make a good watchdog?"

"And because he can rewire this place."

"I don't have time for this." Arn checked his watch again. "Put him in the room between me and Ana Maria. There's no heat, but at least it's out of the wind." He bounded up the stairs. "Keep him away from the white wall. And Danny ... Erv better be housebroke."

———————

Georgia answered the door in a gray pantsuit, low pumps that brought her even with Arn's shoulders, with a simple turquoise neckless resting on her chest. She'd formed her hair in a French roll and held it back with a bone hair tie. She'd swapped her everyday glasses for a pair of wire-rimmed ones, and she had a petite watch on her right wrist. She looked to Arn as if she were going to a job interview. Then he remembered she had no more experience dating than he had. "You look sensational," he said, recalling that old Cary Grant line, leaving out "*Dahling.*"

Georgia handed him an Army field jacket, and he was taken aback momentarily. "It was Butch's," she explained. "When I'm thinking about him a lot, I dig it out of his old footlocker beside Pieter's bed and dust it off. You mind? It's not very dressy."

Arn smiled as he helped Georgia put on the coat. She'd rolled the sleeves to where they didn't engulf her hands, and she zipped it up against the cold.

She grabbed a clutch purse and looked a final time before turning off the lights and locking the door. "Where are we going tonight?"

Arn knew where McDonald's was, and Albertsons to pick up groceries for Danny. He suggested the only other place he frequented: "How about Dr. Zhivago's Russian and Mexican Exotic Grill?"

Georgia scrunched up her nose. "That the place where the waiters go around in those silly Cossack uniforms?"

"You know the place then?"

"Know it!" Georgia laughed. "Last time I ate there I was living in the bathroom for the next two days. That ever happen to you?"

"No," Arn lied as he held the car door for her. "No. I don't think it has."

She had to wiggle to fold herself into the Clown Car as Arn held her hand. "How about Poor Richards? That's as exclusive as I know."

"I work exclusive," Georgia said, hitting her head on the headliner. "Let's do Old Chicago."

"Quite a ways to drive in this go-cart."

"Old Chicago the pizzeria. Not the town, silly. Get in and I'll tell you where to go."

They drove past the Air Guard base just as a landing C-130 drowned out her voice, and Arn waited until it cut its engines. "There are a lot more places to eat than when we were kids."

"There are," Georgia said, and finally got her seat belt fastened. "Those were the good old days when places had character. Like that place over by the steam plant Dad used to take us for lunch. Run by a couple of colored ladies."

"Twin Sisters," Arn said.

"That's it." Georgia smiled. "I loved that place. Down from that dive my dad warned me always to avoid."

"Tippin Inn," Arn said as he waited for the light to change. "Dad used to tell tales about that, when it was called the Black and Tan—only people who felt safe were the blacks and Mexicans working the railroad. He used to get four and five calls a night on weekends for fights. Mostly someone didn't pay for their sex. They ran hookers in the basement. Not officially, but they rented rooms by the hour. Clean sheets extra."

"I heard it said you could buy most anything you wanted," Georgia said. "A nasty place."

Arn had worked around many such places in Denver, but they were spread out. When he worked the street, he and his partner would go from call to call putting out fires in just such places: a knifing here, a john stiffing a working girl there. Nasty places.

"On second thought," Georgia said, "maybe the good old days weren't so good after all."

———————

In Old Chicago, Georgia took the maitre'd aside and he led them to a corner booth. By habit, Arn sat with his back against the wall and looked over the packed restaurant. He was determined not to talk about his investigation, or the assault at Pieter's house. But Georgia didn't get that memo. "Pull your collar down." She winced when she saw the rope burn encircling his neck. The couple in the adjacent booth stared and looked quickly away, as if Arn had attempted suicide and failed. "Pieter called this morning. He said you came a hair's breadth from dying in that old house of his."

"So the ER doc said.

"I told Pieter to get rid of those old rat traps he buys up ... " She laid her hand on Arn's. "This ties in with Johnny's murder, doesn't it?"

The waitress brought their sodas and Arn ordered a hand-tossed. He waited until the woman was out of earshot to continue. "The PD crime scene techs matched a shoe print in Johnny's hospital room with an identical print found inside that old house of Gaylord's."

"It's good news, right?" Georgia sipped her soda through a straw. "Means the killer's getting sloppy."

Arn rubbed his neck. It didn't seem like good news to him. Especially after last night. "I wish he were getting careless. No, the killer left the print in Johnny's room for the police to find. And he did the same thing at Gaylord's. Purposely."

"How do you know that?"

"Oblanski said there was only that one shoe print inside Pieter's front door, placed so the police could find it easy. As dirty and dusty as that place is, there should have been a trail going into the basement and coming back out. As it was, there were only smudges."

The waitress brought their pizza and Arn opened a napkin on his lap. Danny would be proud of him.

"Maybe putting it there on purpose was the killer's way of reaching out. Maybe he secretly wants to get caught."

"I don't think so." Arn's eyes darted from table to booth to the front door. He couldn't shake the feeling that the killer was sitting here eating pizza, watching him and Georgia.

She laid her hand on his again. "There's something you're not telling me."

"I would have canceled our dinner date, but we made it a couple days ago..."

"What are you rambling about?"

Arn looked to the booth next to them, and a couple sitting at a table off to one side. He leaned in and lowered his voice. "I don't think it's safe to be seen with me."

"Just stop it and tell me what you're talking about."

The couple at the table stood abruptly, and Arn's hand went to his pocket. He felt the handle of his gun just as they abruptly headed for the door, and sighed with relief when they were gone. He'd become jumpy for good reason these last few days, and he struggled to get his cop-sense back. He debated whether he should say more to Georgia.

But she was with him in public, and whoever had tried killing him last night might be following him to finish the job. She deserved an explanation. "That shoe print in Johnny's room—and at Pieter's house—were the same impressions as the shoe prints found at the Five Point victims' crime scenes."

Georgia's reaction was delayed, but when she finally processed what Arn had just told her, she began shaking. Soda spilled over the side of her glass and she set it on the table. "Butch didn't tell me the details of those murders. He wanted to shield me. But he told Pieter, and he filled me in."

She took a deep breath, calming herself. "I was cooking at Little America back then, and we were all scared to death. Even the busboys. We'd walk to the parking lot after work in threes and fours. Waited around until everyone was safely in their cars and down the road. But there hadn't been a killing ... like the brutal killings of those men ... since, and I thought the murderer had moved on." She wrapped her arms around herself. "But the killer is still in Cheyenne, isn't he?"

"Him or a copycat."

"If it's the same one who killed those men ten years ago, why now?"

Arn noticed the couple in the booth to one side of them leaned closer to hear more, and he lowered his voice. "I got a couple theories. One is that the killer got away with those murders a decade ago, and Johnny's plea for the public's help set him off. In some twisted way he may think that killing the messenger—Johnny, and the attempt on me last night—will stall the investigation."

Georgia shook Parmesan cheese on her pizza. "And the other theory?"

Arn washed his pizza down with soda and glared at the couple next to them. They turned back around. "The other theory is far more disturbing. It involves some sick bastard getting his rocks off killing people a decade ago. And now he's remembered what a thrill it was. And wants to relive that thrill."

"Ana Maria reported tonight that Dr. Dawes had been brought in on suspicion of Gaylord's death."

Arn said nothing, hoping keeping his mouth busy with the pizza would deter Georgia. It didn't.

"Butch brought in Dr. Dawes on suspicion of murder when Gaylord was murdered," Georgia said between bites. "The doctor clammed up back then. He's not going to say anything now."

"Oblanski now has the pair of Nikes, and the positive match to Gaylord's crime scene and the Five Point killings." Arn polished off his slice of pizza and sat eying another. "But I'm not sure. Jefferson told Oblanski he's never had a pair of Nikes."

"What kind of shoes does he run in?"

Arn shrugged. "Haven't a clue."

"Find out. Runners are notorious for brand loyalty."

A man came in the door, his hand inside his coat pocket. Arn instinctively placed his own hand in his jacket until the man was seated at another part of the restaurant. "Now you're going to tell me you're a personal trainer as well as a chef."

"Cook."

"Whatever."

"I could have been, raising Pieter. He was fussy about his shoes, just like I'd wager Dr. Dawes is. Pieter went through Adidas and Nikes and New Balance until he found something that worked for a supinator like him ... " She paused mid-sentence and caught Arn's blank stare. "I thought you were in sports in high school. Didn't they teach you anything about equipment?"

"Yeah. Don't wear another's boy's jock strap." Arn broke down and grabbed another slice. "They never had fancy shoes like that when I played. We all wore Red Keds sneakers."

Georgia pushed her plate away and dabbed at her mouth with her napkin. "People with high arches and tight Achilles tendons wear the outside of their shoes badly. New Balance was the only brand Pieter could wear without hurting his feet. And Dr. Dawes might be a supinator, too."

Arn recalled Jefferson stretching his tendons that day he stopped to talk with Adelle. He made a mental note to ask Adelle what brand of shoes Jefferson ran in.

"Jefferson Dawes knew the layout of Gaylord's house," Arn said, connecting dots in his mind. "Gaylord asked him over there a couple weeks before his death, so he was familiar with the place. And he would have good reason to kill Gaylord, with Adelle in the picture."

"If you're talking about that witch, you should keep looking for reasons. Would you risk murdering a cop for *that*?"

"I see your point."

"But you really don't think Dr. Dawes killed Gaylord. Or Johnny. Or attacked you, though by the looks of him Dr. Dawes is plenty strong enough?"

Arn swirled soda around his glass, picking his words carefully. "It was just too convenient finding those shoes in Jefferson's car after an anonymous tip. And too handy that he was caught on a hospital surveillance camera ten minutes before Johnny was murdered." He held his hand up for a refill of their sodas. "And it's easy enough to check out his story that he was doing the wild thing with a nurse from cardio rehab when I was attacked." The waitress refilled their glasses. "My gut tells me I should be looking elsewhere."

Arn thought about asking Georgia about Oblanski. The last thing he wanted to do was taint the man's reputation. Still, in the short time he'd been reacquainted with Georgia, he'd grown to trust her. "Did Butch ever suspect Oblanski of fooling around with Hannah?"

Georgia laughed. "I wouldn't be surprised if she was doing the whole department." She lowered her voice as the couple in back stood to leave. "I can see Oblanski doing that just to get back at Butch. He had a way of belittling people. Including the low man on the investigations totem pole." She smiled. "Just the opposite of his son. Pieter treated everyone kindly. He was generous, giving away most of the money he made working for that freight company after school when he was a kid. But Oblanski and Hannah—don't discount it."

Arn steered their conversation away from his investigation to talking about Georgia. He learned she'd graduated at a small culinary school in Mitchell, South Dakota. She'd worked at several high-end steak houses in the region before returning to Cheyenne and eventually moving in with Pieter.

They finished and paid the bill, and both did the ritual of getting into Arn's tiny rental. On the drive back to her place, Arn learned she had been down the aisle twice but managed to flee at the eleventh hour both times. "'I need to take care of my nephew' was my official reason for breaking it off," she said.

"The unofficial reason?"

Georgia laughed. "I've never met a man I feel comfortable waking up next to in the morning with the covers reeking of beer farts and sweat."

Arn elbowed her. "You're still a romantic."

But she remembered how to kiss good night, Arn learned when he dropped her off. They sat in Pieter's driveway with the Clown Car running, not enough room for them to get really serious, just to touch on the fringes as most high schoolers do. What started as a good night peck turned into something that quickly frosted the windows over. When they finally came up for air, Georgia took an exaggerated breath. "You lied to me."

"Lied?"

"Lied," she repeated. "You have been keeping in practice all these years."

Arn wanted to tell her the only thing he'd kissed since Cailee died was his department goodbye when he retired. But why spoil the magic? "You've kept up on current techniques yourself."

"Thank God for *Cosmopolitan*." In the dark confines of the rental, lit only by green dash light, a twinkle shone in her eyes. "Want to come in for a drink?"

"Isn't that what Hedy Lamarr always said?"

"No, that's what I said." She stroked his cheek, which was just now healing from the knife slice. "Pieter's working late at his office every night this week, so we'll have the house to ourselves."

"Any other time ... " Arn truly regretted declining. "I *have* to look someone up tonight."

Georgia grabbed her purse and opened the door. "Don't promise to call if you're not going to."

He held up his hand. "I promise."

He waited until she was safely inside the house and had given him a short wave goodbye before he pulled away. He'd wanted to tell her he needed to talk with Steve DeBoer's pizza delivery kid. But even more pressing was the fact that he needed to lure in the car that had been following them since Old Chicago.

Forty-Nine

ON THE WAY TO the truck stop, Arn called Ana Maria. "Don't you know it's illegal to talk on the phone and drive?" she said, and Arn heard laughter in the background.

"You and Danny having a party there?"

She laughed again. "Me and Danny and Erv. Did you know he used to do stand-up comedy?"

"I'll bet he's a real riot. Get to another room."

"Let me grab my notes." Arn heard shuffling on the other end, and the laughter he'd heard grew faint. "I can talk now," Ana Maria said.

"What did you find out about Jefferson?"

"He was born a womanizer," Ana Maria said, "and he's apparently worked every day to perfect it. He was messing around on Adelle when he was married, and another woman at the same time."

"Any line on the first wife?"

"Nothing. Like she vanished into thin air."

"Or under the ground. How about that nurse he was supposed to be hosing when I got attacked?"

Pages rustled. "Jaine Barnes. According to neighbors, some tall good-looking guy—ostensibly Dr. Dawes—spent most of the night at her place. She moved out of her apartment this morning and checked in at the Plains Hotel under the name Jill Banister. Apparently she didn't want anyone finding her and asking about her relationship with the good doctor."

"That's why Oblanski's guys couldn't catch up with her," Arn said. "But it's not very original, using the same initials."

"What do you expect for a contract nurse?"

"A what?"

"A traveling nurse," Ana Maria answered. "They work at a facility for a specified time—six months is common—then it's *adios* to another hospital. The good Dr. Dawes has been screwing traveling nurses the last couple years. That way he's always got fresh babes. About the time he tires of them—"

"*Adios.*"

"You got it. But if he was with her, he couldn't have been at Pieter's basement hanging you."

Arn thought of that. Jefferson Dawes continued to lose his appeal as a suspect. Except for the missing wife. "I'll keep trying to find out about the wife," Ana Maria said. "Have you talked with the pizza delivery kid yet?"

"Heading there now."

"Good luck," she said. "I talked with him at the checkout for just a few minutes to verify his identity. He doesn't appear to be the brightest bulb on a branchless family tree."

Arn hung up then, concentrating on the maroon Chevy van a block back that followed him into the Flying J Truck Stop. He parked the Clown Car between a bull hauler and a fuel tanker and darked out, watching for the van. Within moments, it motored slowly by, the driver's head on a swivel looking for Arn's car. It parked on the other side of the bull hauler and killed its lights.

Arn began punching in Oblanski's number, then hung up before it could connect. He still had the gun in his pocket, and he wasn't an invalid yet. After he talked with the pizza kid, he'd figure out what to do about the van.

He pulled in front of the glass-fronted convenience store and used the car door to extricate himself. He stretched, looking at two clerks through the window: one at the register, the other making sandwiches at a deli.

Laun McGuire looked every bit his thirty years: thin build, with a premature widow's peak sticking through his dark hair. He operated the cash register in no apparent hurry as impatient customers stood waiting in a long line.

The other clerk looked younger than Laun as he made a sandwich in slow motion. The oversized rings in his ears reflected the neon lights over the deli.

Arn got in line, keeping the van in sight. When it was finally Arn's turn, Laun looked him over. "You buying something?"

"Not today. I'd like to speak with you for a moment."

"Hey asshole, keep the line moving." A trucker wearing a grease-caked stocking cap on the back of his head nudged him. "I said—"

Arn turned, and there must have been something in his look that stopped the trucker. He backed away a step. "Take your time."

"Now what's this about?" Laun asked.

"Steve DeBoer." Arn gave the trucker a last scowl before turning back.

Laun's legs buckled, and he leaned against the counter for support. "Can you take over, Worm?"

"Go ahead," Worm said, his pierced tongue clicking his teeth as he spoke. "I forgot what went on a ham and cheese anyway."

Laun came around the counter and untied his apron. "Is there some place private?"

Arn motioned to his car, and Laun followed him outside. Arn sandwiched himself behind the wheel. He hit his head on the visor and it tore off. The crumpled prescription fell to the floor, but he left it for now.

Laun squeezed into the Clown Car. Tall and lanky, he had to duck to enter, and he quickly shut the door. "What a POS," he said, slapping the rental's dash. "Is this what I got to look forward to when I dig myself out of that job?"

"If you work hard and live clean," Arn said with a smile, "you can get a car just like this one day."

"I've set my sights a little higher than you might think looking at me." The man shook out a cigarette and rolled down the window. "Mind?"

"Go for it."

The glow of the cigarette illuminated a face in the dark that wanted to be anywhere besides talking with a stranger about Steve DeBoer. "I've been taking night classes at Laramie County Community College the past six years. Working swing shift so I can make class." Laun exhaled and jerked his thumb at the store. "It's an all right place to work, but I want more." He blew smoke through the open window, flicked his butt onto the ground, and rolled his window up. "You want to ask me about that cop that burned to death ten years ago."

"Why do you think that?"

"I've watched Ana Maria Villarreal's special. I figured it would be just a matter of time before someone came to talk with me. But I already told some little cop years ago all about it, some gay fella."

"Detective Gaylord Fournier."

"Yeah. Him." Laun fumbled nervously with his lighter. "The paper said he died of a suicide not too long after Detective DeBoer."

Arn didn't tell him otherwise as he reached in the back seat for his notebook. He flicked the anemic dome light on; Laun's Zippo cast more light that it did. "You delivered pizza to Detective DeBoer the day before the fire?"

"I already told that Gaylord guy all this."

"Tell it again. Please."

Laun flicked open his Zippo and snapped it shut. Flicked it open, and snapped it shut. "The dude was drunker'n hell when I finally found his place."

"Finally?" Arn looked at his notes. "Should have been pretty easy to find."

"If he would have given the right address. Either he was too drunk to know his own place, or he gave the kid taking the order the wrong one. So I went next door to deliver it, and they steered me to the right house."

"You sound pretty sure after all these years."

"Wouldn't you remember," Laun said, "if the cheap bastard didn't even give you a tip?"

Laun didn't remember anything else significant, and Arn gave him a business card to call if he did.

After Laun left, Arn struggled with the seat belt, and it got hung up on the steering wheel. He was contorted, trying to free it, when Meander Wells opened the passenger door and leaned in. "Could a nurse come to the rescue?" She unhooked the belt.

"Thanks." Arn breathed a sigh.

"I've pictured you in a pickup. Something larger."

"Me too,"

"Pieter said your car got vandalized." She nodded to the Flying J. "Want tube steak or something?"

"Pardon?"

"Tube steak. They got great Coney dogs."

"I just ate," Arn answered, catching sight of the maroon van still in the back lot. The wait would do him good. "But I'd be up for a soda."

Meander smiled. "Be my treat. And don't give me that malarkey about Western man always paying."

After she'd paid Worm, they sat in a booth and she brushed crumbs off the seat with a napkin. She opened the paper wrapper and dribbled catsup on the foot-long.

"I thought Pieter would have sprung for a nice meal rather than make you eat a hot dog," Arn said.

"Tube steak," Meander corrected. "We go out a couple times a week." She bit into the tube steak. It squeezed out a bit of catsup that fell on the table and she wiped it away. "Like when you saw us the other day. He's always surprising me at work, taking me to lunch." Her smile faded. "That was the day Chief White was murdered." She put her foot-long down and leaned close. "All the nurses are scared to death," she whispered. "Security guards escort us to the parking garage after shift. And there's even a guard at the maintenance door now." She picked her foot-long back up and nibbled a bite. "But the killer's long gone, isn't he? We shouldn't have to worry, should we, Mr. Anderson?"

Arn sipped his coke. The maroon van was gone from its spot. "I believe the killer went in with the purpose of killing Chief White only. My best guess is he won't return."

"Good." She looked around. "But you be careful. The ER nurse told me how close you came to dying in that house of Pieter's. I told him the first thing we're doing after we're married is selling off those

308

old houses. He can collect something else from then on." She finished her foot-long and stood to leave. "Is there anything else I can do?"

"Just point me to the nearest pharmacy."

Arn left Meander to clean catsup off her top while he walked outside. The van wasn't where it had parked before, but he knew anyone determined wouldn't have given up for the hour he was inside the truck stop.

He pulled out of the parking lot, keeping an eye out for the van as he drove across town. He arrived at Walgreen's without spotting it, and his hand resting on the gun in his pocket was reassuring.

He entered the store and walked back to the pharmacy, where he handed his prescription to a white-robed pharmacist. A set of glasses was perched precariously on her long nose, and another set jammed into her beehive hairdo that looked as if she'd varnished it. "Only be a minute, hon." She disappeared behind the counter.

Arn walked away from the pharmacy to the window overlooking the parking lot. He cupped his hand to the glass and studied cars coming and going through the lot. But no maroon van.

He returned to the pharmacy when his name was called over the loudspeaker. "Do you take American money?" he asked when he stepped back to the pharmacy counter.

The pharmacist got a befuddled look on her face before she realized he was joking. "Of course," she giggled. She handed him his change and bent to another prescription, then looked up and saw him still standing there. "Is there something else I can give you, hon?"

"No," Arn answered. "I was just wondering what the half-life of Xanax is."

She fidgeted with the glasses in her hair as she tapped her foot. "Couple hours."

"How much would it take to knock someone out?"

"People don't take that much."

"But if they messed up and accidentally took too much—"

"I'm telling you, hon, people don't do that."

"Humor me."

"How big?"

"Little guy. About 160."

She tapped her foot again, as if calculating the dosage. "Normal dosage is one milligram. Five—crushed up—would put him out for about twenty minutes." She eyed Arn suspiciously. "You're not one of those who like to experiment?"

"At my age," Arn said as he started for his mini-coffin in the parking lot, "the only drug I experiment with is Geritol and Ex-Lax."

He paused outside, scanning the lot and the surrounding street for the van, but didn't spot it. He climbed into the Clown Car and struggled once again to put his seat belt on. As he turned onto the street from the parking lot, headlights a block back flicked on.

As Arn drove over the train tracks, the van kept pace with him a block behind. Arn turned at the first light and headed toward the darkened area north of the train tracks. If he were to confront this guy, he needed every advantage.

He tugged his gun out of his pocket and stuck it between his legs as he unwrapped himself from the seat belt. Then he turned the corner at what used to be the Leapfrog Bar, long closed, long darkened by time. It was here, according to Butch's reports, that Joey Bent had picked up a man with a slight limp and wearing a hoodie, the only clue Butch could put his finger on for the identity of the Five Point Killer.

When Arn passed the bar, the van had just turned off the overpass, a block behind him. Arn doused his lights and pulled behind the building. Fresh oil patch laid by city crews peppered the fender of the rental, but Arn had little time to think about the fee he'd pay when he turned the Clown Car in damaged. He used his emergency brake to stop, not wanting to trip his brake lights. He folded himself out of the car and hunkered behind a dumpster, clutching his gun tightly.

Squatting behind the dumpster, Arn listened to traffic passing by: a truck with loud stacks followed by the unmistakable clatter of an old Volkswagen followed by . . . the van passing the bar. It drove slowly; then the driver spotted Arn's rental and slid to a stop. The driver bailed out, playing a flashlight around the shadows, nearing the dumpster. His light illuminated Arn's tracks in the snow a moment before it was too late.

Arn's hand shot out and grabbed the man's collar, jerking him close. The flashlight dropped to the snow, and Arn jammed his gun barrel against the man's temple. "Even an old duffer like me couldn't miss. Who the hell are you?"

The man trembled but remained mute.

"My trigger finger is getting mighty cold. It might slip off any moment."

"Dan Long," he sputtered. "Sergeant Dan Long." His wild eyes were dimly lit by the street light on the next corner.

"Sergeant of what?"

"Police Department."

Arn relaxed his grip slightly. "Ease your badge wallet out."

Long pulled his coat out of the way and grabbed his badge from his belt. He held it to the light so Arn could read his bonafides. Arn released him and lowered his gun, but he didn't pocket it. "What the hell you following me for?"

Long stepped away and pulled his coat down over his badge. "Chief Oblanski," he said, as if that were the entire explanation.

"I'm waiting for the rest."

"The chief is worried you'll be attacked again."

Arn's hand went to his neck. "You think I'll drop my guard like I did last night?"

"I doubt it." Long blew into his hands to warm them up. "How'd you make my soccer van?"

"You'd be surprised what I used for surveillance in my day." But I'd never use something like the Clown Car, Arn thought. "Will you leave me the hell alone now?"

"And lose all this overtime?"

"Long…"

The sergeant raised his hands. "All right. I'll tell the chief you refused protection."

Arn wanted to tell Long that the best thing that could happen would be for his attacker to come around for a rematch. But he wouldn't do that if his quarry had a tail. And if Arn had spotted the tail, his attacker was most likely just as savvy.

Long picked up his flashlight and started back to his van when Arn called him back. "How long have you been with the PD?"

"Thirteen years in March."

Arn motioned to the Leapfrog. "You remember when this place was open?"

Long laughed and flicked his light on the back door, which had been boarded up with plywood. Someone had spray-painted a giant penis on the wood, and it had drooped with time and moisture. "Hard to forget the only gay bar in Cheyenne. 'Cept the owner never explained the name."

"Ana Maria said it meant two guys playing leapfrog naked," Arn said. "And one comes up short."

Long scrunched his face up. "I see now."

"Did you guys have any problems when it was open?"

"Not from them." The cop jammed his hands inside his pants pocket to warm. "But from every cowboy in the area who felt obligated to come to town and kick the shit out of a queer." He laughed. "Except sometimes the gays were a lot tougher, and they were the ones doing the shit-kicking. Why, you plan on reopening it?"

"You want me to?"

"Not on your life." Long shined his light on the bar again. "Do you know how hard it was to do bar checks without someone wanting to shake your hand?"

Arn realized he was still holding his revolver, and he slipped it into his pocket. "Do you recall the Five Point killings very well?"

"Like yesterday," Long said immediately. "Unfortunately." He kicked a clump of ice and watched as it rolled against the Leapfrog. "I was a rookie patrolman then. We stopped every homeless man we saw walking the streets. Rousted anyone who crashed in the parking garages. We had so many false leads we followed up on, but nothing even close." He nodded to the bar. "Except this place. The bartender had a hazy description of the guy when he left with the first victim ... "

"Joey Bent."

"Yeah. Him. Little dweeb who worked on foreign outfits over at Import Motors." Long looked at his boots, thinking. "Five foot ten to six two, the bartender claimed of the suspect. Medium build. Unknown hair because of a hoodie. Unknown age. Like I said: hazy. Nothing there ... except a limp." He shook his head. "God help the person who walked around town with a stubbed toe or pulled muscle back then, 'cause we rousted them all. Even checked out some vets hobbling to the VA center. No luck though."

"Do you ever think about those cases?"

Long's face lost its color. "Every. Damned. Night. And it's been especially bad since that Ana Maria began her horseshit special."

"You don't approve?"

"I wish to hell something would come of it," Long said. "But after ten years, there's nothing new that'll come to light. And a lot of people have already gotten hurt by it." He pointed to Arn's neck. "You ought to know."

Arn thanked him for what information he could provide and Long motored away from the bar, leaving Arn to wonder what the Leapfrog had been like back then. There were a few gay bars when he worked in Denver, but here in Cheyenne the Leapfrog had been a novelty. He'd read the interview Butch conducted with the owner when Joey Bent was murdered. "I'll be lucky to stay open the rest of the year," the owner had said. "Damned Internet. Gays have been hooking up with their computers. Next year, they won't even need a respectable place like the Leapfrog. Drives one to go straight."

The owner's predictions had been prophetic. Within the year, the Leapfrog closed shop, leaving gay men to hook up over the net. Perhaps, Arn thought, that was the reason the killer was seen with Joey and not Delbert. Butch had speculated the killer could have just as easily been a woman prostitute. But what if it was a man—a predator looking to fill his parameters for his next prey.

Fifty

I ASSUME ANDERSON SPOTTED the van trailing him. I picked him up right as he left Old Chicago. I don't know, but I would bet an unhealthy dose of lethal injection that it's a cop tailing him. He drives like a cop, keeping back a textbook block behind. Lately the police have been using old Crown Vics. This van has me thinking perhaps their learning curve is peaking. Perhaps I'll have to keep on my toes more from now on. I like that; the thought that things will become a challenge. About time. But in the end, I'll really never be in danger of that state-ordered lethal injection. I'm too good to get caught. If I keep my wits about me as I did back in the day.

Anderson darks out as he slips between two semi-trucks and trailers that hide his little car. Even if I didn't know he was a thirty-year cop, I'd know he's been around. Picked up tricks. Knows the little things that've kept him alive. I caught him off guard in the park the other night. And in the basement of Gaylord's old house. I suspect he'll be on high alert from now on. But that's okay, too. Anderson upping his game keeps me professional. Even if I wasn't seeking to get back in this game.

The cop in the van drives into the Flying J parking lot with his lights off. He's looking for Anderson somewhere in the maze of trucks idling against the cold. Only when Anderson pulls to the front of the place does the cop spot him. There's got to be a reason Anderson did that. He could have sneaked inside the back way. The cop would never have seen him. But what I've learned of Anderson—he doesn't do or see anyone by chance. There's always a reason.

Like the tall drink of water at the cashier counter. I walk in by the back door and stand with my back turned to the register. I try to listen to what Anderson and the cashier talk about while I wait for some pencil-necked geek with overgrown earrings to finish making my ham-and-cheese wrap. But there's too much noise in the store. I can't hear what Anderson and the guy are talking about. Whatever they say, they leave and cram themselves into Anderson's car.

I start out the back door. Perhaps I can get close enough to hear what they're talking about ...

"Hey!" Pencil Neck yells after me. "You need to pay for your sandwich."

I toss it back onto the counter, and it skids to the floor. The kid comes around the counter and stops cold. There must be something in my look that bores right through him that shuts him up. He backs against the wall and starts shaking. Candy-ass. If I had time, I'd come visit him when I got a spare moment. But not tonight. I need to know what Arn wants with this other clerk.

By the time I get outside, the guy is just hauling himself out of Anderson's car. I stand at the corner of the building, cars hiding me. Anderson goes through some contortions inside his car, stuck on the seat belt, when ... Meander Wells walks up and opens the passenger door. She dips her head inside and helps him untangle. What's she doing here?

Anderson shuts his car off and they go inside. Do I chance going in the back way and eavesdropping? Pencil Neck would surely call the law if I came in again. So I return to the warmth of my car to wait.

Anderson finally emerges. What they talked about for a half hour doesn't bother me. Their meeting spontaneously here was a fluke—Anderson making a special trip here to talk with the Flying J clerk is what concerns me. I think I'll ask him later. I got no time now. Anderson's pulling out. I lay back. I don't have to follow him. All I got to do is follow the cop in the beater van.

———————

The cop hits his headlight a little too soon. I'd bet that lethal injection again that Anderson's spotted it too as he motors west on Lincolnway. The cop hangs back, like he's overcompensating for his mistake with the headlights. If he doesn't pull out now, he'll lose Anderson.

I can't risk it. I pull onto Lincolnway. The cop pulls behind me. If he knew who was driving, I'm sure he'd pull me over. What cop wouldn't want to be the one who caught the Five Point Killer?

I hang back, judging the light ahead. When it changes to green, a truck with nasty exhaust stacks spewing diesel gets between us. The truck gives me cover, but I've got to slow up. When the truck turns off, I don't want to be parked in Anderson's rear-view mirror.

Anderson turns at the 9th. Streetlight and I get ready. But the truck also turns, and I fall in behind it. I can taste the diesel and am momentarily blinded by black smoke from its twin stacks. I lose Anderson. I can't slow, and I go to the next block before dousing my lights and working my way back to where I lost him.

In the parking lot of the old Leapfrog Bar, the cop's van sits idling, driver's door open. He must have spotted Anderson, and I park in the alley across the street watching the back of the building. I grab the spotting scope, but it's too strong at this close range, and I make a mental note to pack my binoculars the next time. All I can see is two men talking in the dark. And one appears to be taller and wider than the other. Anderson.

"What I wouldn't give for a listening device." *The words startle me in the darkness. Words startled Joey Bent in the darkness of the Leapfrog that night, too. He jumped when I sat beside him and said hello.*

"Come here often?" *He'd finally regained his composure.*

"I think I saw that in some movie," *I said.*

"You did. I'm not sure which one. I didn't know you were ... "

"Gay?"

Joey nodded.

"In Wyoming, it's wise to keep it under wraps."

Joey nodded again, and nervously took out a pocket knife and cleaned under his dirty nails. Like most mechanics. As if I wouldn't go home with him just because he had the dirty hands of an auto mechanic.

"It's kind of loud in here," *Joey said.* "I get my fill of loud noises in my shop every day. Cars running. Machines whining. Noisy."

"Then let's go somewhere." I gently laid my hand on the inside of his thigh. "Like your place."

I followed Joey out of the bar, hobbling in the shoes that hurt my feet so badly but which produced such a nice, traceable print for the police to find. At least that was my plan. And this being my first time, I'd planned things out meticulously. In a sense, Joey popped my cherry. He was my first.

And later, after I dragged the survival knife across his throat deep enough to sever his carotid artery, I sat down watching him as he thrashed about, hands clutching the gaping hole that he'd never be able to close. There had been something in his eyes as his fire died out, something between disbelief and hatred, even though he was drugged and drunk nearly unconscious at the time. That was something I tried to recreate in subsequent murders. But I never achieved it. It remained just out of my reach. But being back in the game, I'll try again. But I'm not sure I'll ever feel as good as I did the night Joey Bent popped my cherry.

Fifty-One

"WHERE'S ERV?" ANA MARIA asked. She sat rubbing the sleepers out of her eyes, hadn't put on makeup yet, and slouched at the table in a pair of Arn's sweatpants. He thought she still looked beautiful. "Is he still sleeping?"

"At seven o'clock?" Danny said. He put three eggs and a waffle on Arn's plate and a poached egg and one slice of whole wheat toast on Ana Maria's. "Erv was up at five, made his list, and went to Lowe's to get wire and a new breaker box."

Arn dribbled syrup over his waffle. "That's ambitious."

"I told you he'd come in handy around here." Danny sat down across from Ana Maria and slid a carafe of coffee her way.

Arn took a sip of coffee and settled back to inhale his breakfast. After the stress of luring what could have been a killer to a dark place last night, his appetite had exploded. "What did Erv use for money?" he asked. "He didn't strike me as a homeless man with lucky bucks in his pocket."

"He isn't," Danny said. "He used your Lowe's card."

"What! How did he get my card?"

"I gave it to him."

Arn dropped his fork on the plate, prepared to do battle with Danny, but the old man disarmed him. Somehow. Like he usually did. "Erv had to get supplies. And as you so aptly pointed out, he's broke."

"I would have given you the card if you'd have asked."

"You were sleeping like a log," Danny said.

"All right," Arn said. "I guess it was for the better. But did he call a cab?"

"You want bacon?" Danny asked.

"How did he get to Lowe's?"

"Let me put on another waffle." Danny stood up and bent over the stove.

"Danny!"

He lifted his face up and met Arn's stare. "Better and cheaper than a cab." He turned back to the stove and grabbed a pair of tongs. "He used your car."

"What! Erv stole my rental car?"

With his hands on his hips, Danny stood looking down at Arn. "That's pretty judgmental. He would have asked you, but he wanted to let you sleep in. I'd say he was being pretty considerate."

"And just how did he get my keys?"

"Do you know how soundly you snore when you come in from a date?"

"Relax," Ana Maria said. She wiped orange juice from her lower lip. "The way you gripe about the car, it might be a blessing if he did wreck it."

"Great," Arn said. "Just great. Erv's going to wreck the Clown Car and I can just imagine what the insurance company's going to give me after that."

"By then you'll have your Olds out of the shop," Ana Maria said.

"I called them yesterday." Arn sat back in his chair and sipped his coffee to calm himself. "They have the tires on, and they repainted the door. They just need to let it cure before I can pick it up."

"Look at the bright spot in all this," Danny said, daintily dabbing the corners of his mouth. "With Erv gone for a while, that frees you up to help me lay flooring."

———————

Arn's car crunched ice on the curb as Erv parked it. Arn started to get up.

"We got that last row left," Danny ordered, dragging the compressor hose and nail gun along the floor as he squinted to see his chalk line. They finished the last row of mahogany hardwood, and Arn grabbed a door jamb to stand. His knees popped in protest, and he kicked one leg out when it started to cramp.

Danny, on the other hand, jumped up easily. He stood looking smugly down at Arn, enjoying his predicament, and reached out his hand to help, but Arn slapped it away. "You're even older than me," Arn snapped. "I'd never live it down if anyone found out you helped me up."

"Suit yourself. I'll meet you downstairs for coffee."

Arn hobbled down the stairs just as Ana Maria walked into the house. She motioned him into the sewing room. "I found this on the seat of my car." She handed Arn a plastic badge.

Arn turned it over and handed it back. "It's different."

Ana Maria nodded. "This one's a six-pointed star." She slipped it into her purse. "I thought the killer might be running out of badges. Until I … happened to look in Nick Damos's desk. He's got a dozen of them stashed away."

"Are you going to go to DeAngelo about his kid?"

"No."

"Want me to have a come-to-Jesus moment with him?"

"No," Ana Maria answered. "I compared those scribbled threats someone put on my seat at work and the one under my windshield wiper. They match Nick's writing." She tapped her purse. "I'm not going to let him know that I know. But when the opportunity comes, Nick will get his comeuppance for sure."

———

Arn had been reluctant to fill out the intake form at Dr. Rough's office, remembering the memorable adventures in proctology he'd had last time.

"Your turn." The receptionist called to Arn in the waiting room. "You boys have fun." She exaggerated a wink.

He entered the examination room just ahead of the doctor. "Are you here for another happy ending?" Rough asked.

"Not if I can help it." Arn took a laptop from his bag and set it on a chair.

"That's not going to save you."

"I'm here to ask questions," Arn said. "Not for another finger wave."

"Ask away." Rough opened a drawer and took out a pair of examination gloves.

"You were the East High team doctor for the girls' basketball team for three years?"

Rough nodded as he took the end cap off a tube of KY Jelly. "I volunteered those three years. I did my internship at a sports medicine complex in Billings. I figured it was the least I could do since my daughter was on the varsity team at the time."

Arn powered up the computer and inserted a disc.

"What are we going to watch?"

"The person who killed Chief White."

"I told you I was out of that business."

Arn ignored him and paused the recording just as the killer came into view of the camera. "I looked over this a dozen times before I spotted it." He resumed the CD. The killer approached Johnny's room and walked by the policeman sitting outside in the hallway. Arn looked up at Rough. "See it?"

"See what?"

"He's got something wrong with the way he walks."

Arn turned the computer so Rough could better see it. Again, the killer walked the hallway leading to Johnny's room. "I caught it that time," Rough said. "He's limping ever so slightly. Let's see it once more."

Arn replayed the twenty seconds of footage another four times until Rough was satisfied. "He's got something wrong with either his knee or his foot. I can't tell from the video, but it could be either."

"Could he disguise that limp?"

Rough snapped on his latex gloves. "If he were to disguise a limp, wouldn't he exaggerate it so it could be spotted easily?"

"Good point," Arn said.

Rough put a miniscule dab of KY on the end of his gloved finger, and Arn clutched at straws, prolonging the inevitable. "Would a runner experience such traits?"

Rough paused, and Arn knew he was running out of questions. "If the runner was wearing old shoes, worn down, they could cause him to limp," the doctor said. "Or if the shoes didn't fit right—wrong brand, a size too small—it could cause this. Or an old injury."

"No way to see what brand of shoe he's wearing?"

"Not while he's wearing those paper booties over them. This guy a doctor?"

"We're not sure." Arn closed his laptop and slipped it inside his bag. He started for the door when Rough stopped him.

"Not so fast. I need payment for my time."

Arn nodded in resignation. He dropped his knickers and gritted his teeth.

Fifty-Two

ON THE WAY TO pick up Ana Maria at the television station, Arn called Oblanski. "I asked Dr. Rough to look at the hospital surveillance disc." He explained what Rough thought from a sports medicine angle.

"Jeff runs every day, though he said he wouldn't recommend it in icy streets like this. Too much chance of injury," Oblanski said. "I think we'll haul the doctor in again. Even if he won't talk under advisement of his attorney, at least I'll be able to gauge his reaction when I ask about any running injuries."

Oblanski planned to do what Arn often did: observe a suspect while he asked them questions. See if they became nervous and see if the suspect scratched. Or itched, as Arn called it. "Jefferson knows enough about injuries that he could easily conceal it if he thought people would notice," he said.

"I'll send one of my guys over to district court to have a subpoena signed for Jeff's medical records. We'll find if he's got a previous injury."

"Better go back further," Arn suggested. "All the way to when he started at the hospital."

"Why that far?"

"Remember the bartender at the Leapfrog saying the guy who left with Joey Bent that night had a limp?"

"I'm on it," Oblanski said.

Arn hung up just as he pulled into the TV station parking lot. Ana Maria came out the door and started for the Clown Car. Arn looked around the station lot and across the street. The police must be learning something. He didn't spot her security officer.

"You look pleased with yourself for some reason," he said.

Ana Maria smiled and took her stocking cap off. "Nick Damos is heading to Denver for the day."

"If it's only for a day, don't be so happy."

"It might be longer than a day if he's not careful," she added.

A team of horses trotted the street carrying a couple on a romantic tour of Cheyenne. The pair, in their eighties or perhaps nineties, sat in the buggy bundled up, laughing as cars passed them while the matched pair of Percherons trotted along, their massive hooves rattling bells dangling from their harness. Arn and Cailee had taken such a ride in the last year of her life. The last Christmas they'd spent together.

"Nick got an anonymous tip, absolute proof that the Five Point Killer is holed up under an assumed name in Denver," Ana Maria said.

"Why didn't you tell me this?" Arn asked. "Remember, we're supposed to be working together."

"Relax." Ana Maria smirked. "There's no new information. I just finagled around and had a friend from Denver place the call. Untraceable. Nick will be tied up for … some time. And out of my hair."

"Whereabouts in Denver?"

"I sent him to an address on Custer Place."

Arn had taken calls there through the years. Quite a few Indians lived there. And they wouldn't like a white man poking around. Even a Greek who looked as dark as any Indian. "He better be on his toes if he slinks around there."

Ana Maria grinned sheepishly. "Like I said, it'll keep him out of my hair. If he's scalped in the process ... "

"Understood."

"And I dug something else up." She took out a long, narrow reporter's notebook and flipped pages. "We're so hung up on Dr. Dawes being the one in the hospital footage, but I found out someone else who may walk with a limp."

"You going to tell me, or should I go through the phone book and guess everyone?"

"Or you can thank me for finding out Frank Dull Knife got busted up big time in a prison fight in Colorado. Seems like his knee was shattered by a table leg and just never quite healed right."

"Then I get a chance to visit him once again. How did you find this out?"

"You just gotta have the charm, baby," Ana Maria answered.

Arn drove past the intersection that would take them to Emma Barnes' house and continued toward the Holiday Inn. "Where we going?"

"Georgia's old house. Pieter called her at 1:30 the night he found Butch dead, and she said she arrived at Butch's place at 1:45. I'm just curious if she's right on the time, or if Emma Barnes was approaching senility even a decade ago."

Arn gave Ana Maria the slip of paper with the address, and she directed him past the Tortilla Factory. He slowed as he drove past, and Ana Maria slapped his arm. "If you're thinking about stopping there—"

"They have the best chili burritos."

"That's my point," she said. "I'd have to ride with you after."

They went another two miles and found Georgia's old neighborhood. Arn could see why she'd opted to move in with Pieter. Her house had seen better days, and it sat unoccupied. In another ten years, it would look like Gaylord's old house.

Ana Maria noted the time on the dash clock, and they drove to Emma Barnes'. "We have some traffic today," Arn pointed out as they passed the fifteen-minute mark. "Georgia wouldn't have had that to worry about at 1:30 in the morning. She'd have gotten there quicker—"

"If I didn't know better, I'd say you were building her alibi. Like you were sweet on her or something," Ana Maria said.

When they finally pulled off 10th Street, she jotted the time down. "Thirty-two minutes."

Arn pulled to the curb in front of Emma's old house and turned in the seat as best he could. "Maybe Georgia was wrong about the time. Or maybe Pieter looked at the clock wrong."

Ana Maria put her hand on his shoulder. "You taught me some years ago to go with my instincts. What do your instincts tell you about the time difference?"

"That someone's mistaken," he said immediately. "I just don't know who." He grabbed his Stetson from the back seat. "You up to doing some sweet-talking?"

"More like laying on the old Villarreal charm," she said. They'd planned to interview the owners of Emma's house and Butch's houses separately. Arn hadn't heard anything about the folks who'd bought Emma's, but the guy who'd bought Butch's bordered on reclusive. So many people through the years had come to the place wanting to see just where Butch Spangler had been murdered. It would take someone special to break through that crust. And Arn figured Ana Maria was a lot prettier than he was.

They climbed out of the Clown Car and she started for Butch's house. Out of the corner of his eye, Arn saw an unmarked Crown Vic parked where the officer could watch that house, and he walked toward Emma's old place. He passed a brown Buick with a badly crumpled fender parked in the driveway, and a one-ton Ford duly sitting halfway over the curb, two beer cans on the ground outside the driver's door. A man ran from the house and jumped when he saw Arn in his driveway. "Shit. You scared the hell out of me."

"Sorry."

"In this neighborhood, a man can't be too careful."

Arn agreed and handed him a business card. The man seemed to struggle with the name. "Arn Anderson. Like the old wrestler with the Minnesota Wrecking Crew? Got an autograph?"

It wasn't the first time someone mistook him for the pro wrestler. "I'm not him."

"Sure you are. No, wait—I seen you on TV." The man slapped his leg. "You're that guy who's looking into that cop's murder years ago."

"I'd like to look at your neighbor's house from that window." Arn pointed to a bay window facing Butch's house. He explained that he needed to check on angles, to verify Emma Barnes could see the house the night Butch was killed.

"Who that you're jawing with, Hilly?" a woman called from inside the house.

"Some feller investigating that cop's murder next door. Says he needs to see the house from inside ours."

A woman emerged from the house and rested her chin over Hilly's shoulder. She still wore a nightgown, despite it being eleven in the morning. "That right, mister? You need to come in?"

"If I could."

She slugged Hilly's shoulder. "Well, step aside and let him in."

"But I got to go to work."

Her grin widened and she winked at Arn. "I know you do."

Hilly stepped around Arn and climbed in his truck. He punched it and it crow-hopped jumping off the curb, leaving the little wife cradling a beer in one hand, a cigarette in a silver holder in the other. She looked Arn over and settled her gaze on his groin. "Come on in, Big 'Un."

She led him inside a house that looked as if the last time it had been cleaned was when Emma owned it. Everywhere piles of clothes narrowed the walkway, or reams of stacked newspapers, or garbage sacks bulging with crushed beer cans. "You want a drink?" she asked, smiling. "Or anything else?"

"I'm good."

"I'll bet you are," she said.

She shut the door, and Arn kept an eye on the escape hatch should he need it. "I'd like to sit at your bay window to the east."

"That's all you want?" She motioned for him to follow her. "See," she laughed when Arn followed her, "I made you come with one finger."

She led him down a short hallway cluttered with boxes labeled "underwear" and "socks" and "panties" as if they'd just moved in. She motioned to them, her can of Grain Belt sloshing on the floor. "Don't mind the mess, sugar."

"Can I sit?" Arn pointed to a chair in front of the bay window where Emma had claimed to see Georgia arrive that night, and where she'd sat most nights just waiting for some disturbance so she could call the police. He squinted through the dirty glass, and just caught Ana Maria's jacket disappearing inside the Spangler house.

The woman tipped the chair and a basket of dirty clothes tumbled onto the floor. "Are you married, sugar?"

"Happily," Arn lied.

"Then where's your ring?"

"Pawned it," he answered, moving the curtain aside.

"So we're not the only ones," she said and tipped her beer up. "You fool around?"

Arn ignored her and scooted the chair close to the window. He imagined how Emma had sat there practically every night, tatting doilies and watching the Spangler house. He could clearly see Butch's front lawn and front door through the window. Emma's memory was correct: she was able to see the Spanglers' place from anywhere in front of that bay window.

Cigarette smoke became more intense and Arn was suddenly aware that the woman had leaned closer, her face florid from the booze and only inches from his. "What we looking at, sugar?" She batted one eyelid, the other partially closed from a recent brown bruise rimming the eye. Probably last week, Arn estimated, when Hilly had tuned his dear wife up. "What we looking at?"

He pointed to Butch's old house. Ana Maria hadn't come out yet, and that worried him. "Why don't you sit here and see if you can spot it, too."

She giggled as Arn vacated the chair. He waited until she'd sat and put her beer can on the window ledge before hustling toward the door. "Thanks, ma'am," he called, and was out the door before she realized he'd escaped.

He walked to Butch's house, debating if he should give Ana Maria more time with the new owner. "To hell with that," he said, and walked to the front door. He stood looking up at the second floor, to what would have been Pieter's bedroom, when the door cracked open. "We're Mormon," a man called out.

Arn looked around. "Congratulations."

"We don't want any Watchtowers."

"Don't have any."

"Ain't you Jehovah's Witness?"

"I've been a witness to a lot of things, but never Jehovah," Arn said, thinking here was a twist, a Mormon putting the run on a Jehovah's Witness. "I'm consulting with the police department on Butch Spangler's murder."

"You're with the lady, then." The Mormon flung the door open. He wore the striped coveralls of a railroad man, with no T-shirt, his man boobs spilling out to the sides. His zipper was broken, revealing romantic off-brown underwear when he turned just right. Thank God he's not going commando, Arn thought.

"Come in quick."

Arn brushed past him. The man looked nervously around before slamming the door. "Jay-bos come around this time of day trying to give me Watchtowers."

"They come just about every day," Ana Maria added, as if she were there every day to witness this monumental event. She sat in a recliner, her legs gathered under her like she belonged to the house.

"Ana Maria told me her television station hired some old retired cop to help."

"That's me," Arn said. "The over-the-hill retired cop."

"Huber was just giving me a tour of the place," Ana Maria said, standing. "He's changed it some since he bought it at a foreclosure auction."

"Got it cheap." Huber beamed. "Guess no one wanted a house where a cop was murdered." He looked around the room. "But that didn't bother me none."

Ana Maria hooked her arm through Arn's and started a self-guided tour while Huber stood with his eyes fixed on her. Butch Spangler's house was small for a two-story. The front door opened directly into the living room where Butch had been shot. Arn could see the bathroom from the living room. A cabinet stood open, much like the crime scene photos showed. A side door was ajar, revealing a bed and dresser, while another room was piled high with a sewing machine and bolts of fabric. "Huber's missus takes in sewing," she said.

Huber walked beside them, scratching his two black chest hairs. "I put in a lot of work fixing this place up. It was in pretty bad shape. Replaced most of the wall board. The carpeting was so bad from all the blood, we had to bring in professionals." He smiled proudly. "They cleaned it so good you couldn't even tell where Butch Spangler died."

"Don't forget the staircase, Huber," Ana Maria said, and Arn caught her mischievous glance his way.

"The staircase was dangerous when I bought it. Took some fixing to get it right."

Arn knew dangerous staircases. He'd had one before Danny repaired it. "It looks nice."

"Think so?" Huber smiled wide, and Arn could count the number of teeth on one hand.

He walked to the staircase and turned around, imagining what Pieter saw the night he came down those steps and found his father dead in the chair. Butch would have been *right there*, slumped in his recliner, leaking over the dirty fabric that made up the recliner.

"It must have been a shock to the kid to find his dad shot right there." Huber seemed to be reading Arn's mind.

"I imagine so." Arn looked around again. Except for different paint on the walls and ceiling, and minor cosmetics, the house looked just like it did in the crime scene photos.

He walked to the front door. "You change the door, too?"

"Heavens no," Huber said. "You don't see a nice solid oak door like that very often. I had to keep it."

Arn grabbed the lock and turned it. The bolt retracted with protest, and he tried sliding the button to lock it back. It was nearly rusted closed, and it wouldn't budge. "Did you change the lock, or is it original?"

Huber walked to the door. He stuck his head out and looked both ways. "I couldn't change it. It's like the door: solid. Tough." He reached for the lock and finagled the button to close. "There's a trick to getting it locked. Took me a while to figure it out. But I needed a strong lock like this to keep the Jehovah's Witnesses out."

Fifty-Three

A SINGLE LIGHT SHONE through cracks in the plywood covering the window Danny had nailed up yesterday. Arn disarmed the security system and let himself in. A soft song played from the kitchen, and he walked through the house. Danny sat with his feet propped on a five-gallon drywall mud bucket, leaning back in an occasional chair the "chair fairy" had found for him. He turned pages in a book as he squinted under a reading light. He looked up when Arn entered and put his finger to his lips. "Erv's sleeping and he's got—"

"Phenomenal hearing," Arn said. "I know." He took his coat off and draped it over a chair.

"Why are you home so early?" Danny stuck a piece of toilet paper to mark his page in *1984* and set it on the counter. "I thought you'd still be out."

"Ana Maria and I just talked with the guy who bought the old Spangler house. He did some remodeling, but kept it mostly like it was when Butch lived there. Including a solid oak door with some antique-looking lock. That sound right?"

"Did he want to keep the door? I mean, does it have character?"

"It did nothing for me. But it's got some gouges and scrapes, if that's what you mean."

"Then I'd probably keep it. Old hardware is only slightly more difficult to come by than original doors."

Arn poured a cup of coffee and headed into the sewing room with Danny close behind. He parted the sheets hung over the doorway and stood in front of the white wall, studying the photos like he had every night since he'd tacked them up. He flicked on the floor lamp and shined it on the pictures. He pulled a chair close to the wall and sipped his coffee while studying the photos. He was missing something getting through his damned thick Norwegian skull.

"What are we doing?" Danny asked.

Arn ignored him and eyed the photos.

Danny started speaking again, but Arn held his finger to his lips. "Erv's got phenomenal hearing. In other words ... "

"Danny, keep quiet."

"Smart man," Arn said.

Suddenly, he slapped his leg. His coffee spilled over his shirt front, but he didn't even care. "You son-of-a-bitch."

Danny backed away. "Whatever it is I did—"

"Not you." Arn leaned over and tapped Butch's picture with his finger. "Hand me that remote."

Danny passed him the remote, and he turned on the television. He inserted the old tape of Butch's crime scene. Arn had run and rerun the video until he could memorize the scene. He'd never seen anything new. Until now. "There!" He stopped the tape.

Danny stepped closer to the white wall and shook his head. "What's there?"

"His hand," Arn said. "Look at Butch's hand." He ran the tape ahead a few frames and stopped it again. "See his hand? Now look at the still pictures."

Danny put on his glasses and squinted at the image of Butch Spangler slumped dead in his chair. "I still don't see what you're ranting about."

"About seventeen, eighteen years ago," Arn explained, "agencies began videotaping crime scenes. The first thing the crime scene tech did—or the video and photograph technician, when I was in Metro— the first thing they did was to walk through the scene. Before anything else was touched. Before anyone came busting in and destroyed evidence." Arn sat back in his chair, feeling exhausted and relieved both. "We'd use the tape to show the Watch Commander or the Battalion Commander, or the prosecutor, or anyone else who thought they needed to know what had happened. That way, they didn't need to go bull their way into the crime scene and contaminate things."

"It doesn't get you any closer to solving Butch's murder. The video shows what the still photos do."

"No, they don't," Arn said.

Danny put his glasses back on and blew drywall dust off the television screen, his eyes going from the television to the photos on the white wall. He took his glasses off and pocketed them. "I still don't see what you're so orgasmic about."

"This." Arn traced Butch's hand in the still photo. "The tape shows Butch's fingers are curled. But sometime after the video was shot, Butch's fingers got straightened out." Arn pointed to another photo with his pencil. "And look at his trouser legs."

Danny took off his glasses. "So he was a little sloppy. Give the guy a break, he was at home."

"With one pants leg halfway pulled up over his ankle? That"—Arn tapped it again—"is what I've been missing."

"Well, there you have it." Danny threw up his hands. "A dead man straightened his fingers out, and one pant leg is pulled up over his sock. Now why didn't I connect the dots? Now you can solve the puzzle of who killed Butch Spangler."

"I just did." Arn smiled for the first time. "Now all I have to do is prove it."

Fifty-Four

"I'VE GOT AN OFFICER bringing her in for the interview now," Ned Oblanski said. "The desk sergeant will let us know when they get here." He led Arn into his office and motioned to a chair. "Are you sure this is the only way?"

"It has to be," Arn answered.

"You know she'll never trust you after this?"

"I know that. She'll probably outright hate me."

"And I can't change your mind on recording the interview?"

"I have to insist on no recording," Arn said.

Oblanski nodded. He poured himself a cup of coffee and offered Arn one. Arn declined. "I'll be nervous enough as it is without caffeine messing me up even more."

"Then we'll just wait till she arrives." Oblanski sat and took out folders from his inbox that contained summaries of police reports he'd have to paraphrase for the press this morning.

"Looks like it was a busy night," Arn said.

"Ana Maria's been hounding my office already this morning," Oblanski said. "I told her she'll have to wait until the regular press briefing, but she claims she knows the victim."

"What victim?"

Oblanski kept quiet.

"Oh for God's sake, I'm not going to run and tell her. Besides, when you're giving your briefing I'll be busy in the interview."

"All right." Oblanski said. "A kid—hell, he was a thirty-year-old college student—was found by some joggers this morning in the pedestrian walkway under Yellowstone Avenue."

"A thirty-year-old college student?" Arn began feeling queasy even as he asked it.

Oblanski shuffled through the first responder's report. "Some McGuire ... here it is." He slid the report across his desk. "Some kid jogging found him with his throat slit. Bled to death."

Arn picked up the report. "Laun McGuire."

"Know him?"

Arn rubbed his head and handed Oblanski the police report. "I talked with him at the Flying J two nights ago. He was ... happy, I think, that he was getting an education. That he was going to make something of himself."

"Well, the only thing he's going to make today is the front page news." Oblanski gathered the incident report and tucked it in a folder. "Unlike this other poor bastard."

"What poor bastard?"

Oblanski fished another report out. "Press don't have this one 'cause we haven't made an identification yet." He slid the report across his desk, and Arn opened the folder. The victim, a homeless man in his forties who usually hung around the Depot bumming, was shown in his death repose under the railroad bridge by the Union Pacific Depot. Like

Laun McGuire's, the victim's throat had been cut and he'd bled over his camouflage parka. "I saw this guy."

"Him?" Oblanski tapped the picture. "Where?"

"Last week. By the Depot. I was talking with Ana Maria. He got into a little scuffle with some other bum."

Oblanski grabbed his notepad and pen. "What did the other guy look like?"

Arn rubbed his forehead. "I didn't pay any attention."

"Crap," Oblanski said. He tossed his pencil at the wall. "With a slice across his throat like that, I figured it might be the same one who offed Laun McGuire. Crap."

Oblanski's phone rang. He answered it and quickly set it back on the cradle. "She's waiting in interview room one. As soon as I finish with the press briefing, I'll be there. And I'll need a statement about what McGuire told you when you're finished."

Arn walked the hallway that seemed longer than it had ever been and entered the interview room. Georgia met him halfway across the floor. "What's going on? The patrolman who brought me in wouldn't tell me a thing."

"Chief Oblanski thought it'd be easier if I told you."

"Told me what?"

"He intends on arresting Pieter for the murder of his father."

"What!"

Arn motioned to a chair at a stainless steel table bolted to the floor. "Sit. Please."

Georgia stood defiantly for a long moment before sitting. Arn dropped into a chair across from her and opened his bag. He spread notes and folders on the table. "He wanted me to tell you."

"That's nonsense. Pieter loved his dad. How could Oblanski—and especially you—even think Pieter capable of that? What evidence do you have?"

"Emma Barnes—"

"That senile old bitty—"

"—was quite correct on the time that you arrived at Butch's house that night. She's got fantastic memory about all things … old."

"That doesn't explain why you think Pieter killed Butch."

"Pieter said he let you in that night after you arrived."

"Of course he did," Georgia said.

Arn turned a page in his notebook. "See, that's what's been bugging me. I should have realized it, living back in Mom's old house. It had one of those spring-operated door locks, where you push a button and the lock snaps shut and engages. The morning my car got vandalized, I locked myself out of the house. It was a new lock, and I hadn't thought to lock the bolt back with the spring button. The killer couldn't have engaged the lock on Butch's door—where it engaged on closing—because it didn't work very well. The guy who bought Butch's house said there's a trick to thumbing it back it so it'll lock. He showed me that it's near impossible to set it so it locks on closing."

"That's nonsense. The lock must have worked properly back then. That was ten years ago. Things rust up over time … "

"It was rusted and hard to work when the guy bought the place a year after Butch was murdered."

"The killer—the real killer—must have left the house after he killed Butch. And the lock naturally snapped shut like it's supposed to."

"That was the only logical explanation. It needs to be locked and unlocked, either from the inside or with a key outside, it's so worn and rusted. You told me you didn't have a key for the place."

"The guy must have changed the lock. He must have forgotten—"

Arn shook his head. "He's mighty proud of that heavy old door. And the stout old vintage lock." He leaned over and laid his hand on Georgia's arm, but she jerked away. "No one killed Butch and slipped out," he said. "Someone with a key needed to have locked it behind them."

"Frank," Georgia blurted out. "Hannah must have given him a key to get in so they could have their little bed-time."

"You even told me Hannah had gone out on the town to get laid. Frank would have no reason to want in. No, the only one who could have locked and unlocked that front door was someone from the inside: Butch or Pieter. And Butch was dead."

Georgia stood and paced the room. "Butch *must* have let someone in," she sputtered.

"Butch stayed alive in his job because he was paranoid. You told me that yourself. He wouldn't have let anyone in the house he didn't trust."

Georgia turned away from Arn and crossed her arms, her mother-hackles in full defiant mode. "The crime scene technician tested Pieter and me for gunshot residue."

Arn nodded. "And found no residue."

"There. That proves Pieter didn't shoot Butch."

"Except there was soap under Pieter's fingernails," Arn bluffed. He'd seen how close the bathroom was to the living room. If Pieter had handled the gun that killed Butch—as Arn had finally realized, looking at the photos—Pieter would have known the GSR test was standard practice. And washed his hands. "Now what fifteen-year-old boy wakes up in the middle of the night and thinks to wash his hands."

Georgia turned her chair away from Arn. "Then you tell me why he would have washed up that morning."

"Pieter hung around his dad long enough, went to enough crime scenes, to know the GSR test is mandatory on anyone at the scene. He washed up and scrubbed what particles were on his hands from the gunshots." Arn ran his bluff, like he often did, by the seat of his pants and pure cop intuition. He was banking on the fact that no matter how much two or more people committing a crime rehearsed their stories, in the back of their minds there was always something they'd missed discussing. "Pieter hated Butch for the abuse he heaped on him—"

"Pieter loved his dad." Georgia turned back around and spittle flew off her mouth, her neck a crimson color in the bright lights of the interview room. "He loved Butch!"

"He might have," Arn said, "but Butch took out his frustrations about Hannah on Pieter. Dragging him to those nasty crime scenes—"

"He wanted Pieter to be a law officer."

"I believe that." Arn softened his voice. "And I believed you when you said Butch never laid a hand on Pieter. But he abused him psychologically, just like you said. And Pieter finally cracked that night."

"He'd never hurt his father." Georgia's voice dropped to a whisper. "Pieter was always a good boy." Tears flowed down her cheeks, and Arn slid his bandana across the table. She hesitated before picking it up. "Does Oblanski know all this?"

Arn nodded. "And the prosecutor. There'll be an arrest warrant issued this morning."

He waited for that to sink in before continuing. He often felt elation when he was within a micro tic of gaining a confession. But he felt only a hollow in the pit of his stomach for deceiving Georgia. "Pieter doesn't have to be charged."

Georgia pulled the bandana away and met his stare.

"He didn't kill Butch," Arn said.

"That's what I've been trying to tell you." She leaned across the table. "But now you're accusing me. You think I had a key and let myself in? You think I got fed up with Butch abusing his son and killed him myself?" She tossed Arn's bandana at him. "You accuse *me*?"

"No," Arn said. "I'm accusing Butch." He turned to a sheet in his notebook he'd dog-eared. "Butch found out that Hannah—besides screwing Frank Dull Knife—had pulled a series of residential burglaries with him. Frank taunted Butch with that a couple weeks before he died. Butch couldn't bear the thought of people knowing his wife was a burglar."

"He was worried about something the last months of his life," Georgia admitted. "Maybe that's what it was."

"Butch took Xanax for anxiety ..."

"... he must have been worried people would find out about Hannah ..."

"... and he went to the ER to have his stomach pumped a week before his death. That was a false start."

"What are you rambling about?"

"He overdosed on the Xanax wanting to kill himself. Before he ultimately succeeded in doing so"

Georgia stood suddenly, and the chair overturned and skidded across the barren floor. "I'm outta here."

"You don't want to learn what I found out?"

Georgia hesitated before she set the chair upright and sat back down.

Arn took photos out of his bag and spread them across the table, along with still photos of freeze-framed video shots. Georgia turned away, and Arn waited until she turned back before positioning them so she could see. He traced Butch's fingers with his pen. "This was copied from the video taken the night he died. His fingers show they are curled. But around what? There's nothing there. Whatever he was holding at the time he died had been removed."

He laid another photo side by side. "And this is the still picture taken sometime after the video was shot, showing Butch's fingers straightened." He looked into Georgia's eyes. "Dead men just don't move their fingers willy-nilly. Butch shot *himself* with his own gun."

Georgia sat up straight and crossed her arms. "That's impossible. Butch's gun was hanging over the back of a kitchen chair. Still in his shoulder holster. He couldn't have shot himself fatally and walked back to his recliner."

"His duty gun was in the kitchen all right. But not his backup. Here." Arn thumbed through the photos and grabbed another.

Georgia looked away. "Does this make you feel good, showing me pictures of my dead brother?"

"Not particularly. But look at Butch's trousers."

Georgia bent and studied the photo. "So his pants are undone. I told you he was vain. Bought pants a size too small. He often loosened them when he came home after work."

"I'm not showing you this because his pants are unzipped. I'm showing you this because his trouser leg is pulled up. Got hung up on his sock."

She looked again. "And that proves what?"

"It finally dawned on me that Butch—like many officers—carried a backup gun. Some carry them in the small of their back. Some in shoulder holsters. Many, including Butch, carried one in an ankle rig. When I met with Johnny White, he had the same problem with his pants leg getting hung up on his holster. And Oblanski too, when his pants didn't fall all the way over his gun." Arn leaned across the table. "But Butch's gun is gone. Someone pried his gun from his fingers, and took off his ankle holster so no one would know. Was it you or Pieter?"

"That's bullshit. Butch was shot twice. The medical examiner said either would have been instantly fatal."

"A cadaveric spasm."

"A what?"

"That was another thing that finally penetrated my thick skull," Arn explained. "I talked with Dr. Rough about a drowning victim he had who still clutched reeds at the bottom of Glendo after death. It reminded me of a case in Denver where two brothers were fighting and one killed the other. The dead brother clutched the knife in his hands even when they brought him into the autopsy room. We had to break his fingers to pry the knife loose, they were held so tight."

"It still doesn't explain how Butch could have shot himself twice."

"Of course it does." Arn sat back in his chair, wishing he were someplace besides drawing a confession from Georgia. "Butch shot himself—my guess, he carried a small auto as a backup—and his muscles reflexed, tightening his finger on the trigger after that first shot. And he shot himself again. Either which would have been fatal by the ME's opinion."

Georgia forced a laugh. "Just who the hell shoots themselves in the chest? People shoot themselves in the head. Or didn't you learn that in Denver?"

"Someone as vain as Butch would." Arn flipped pages. "Butch always dressed well. Neat. Haircut once a week. And I'd wager his sister dyed his hair when he needed it, too."

Georgia looked away.

"You told me numerous times Butch was vain. Like many women. I've never investigated a woman's suicide by gunshot who capped herself in the head. Something about being afraid to look like hell when officers arrive. Vanity. And Butch wouldn't want that either."

Georgia stared at the corner of the room.

"But the kicker for me," Arn said, "was how you never once referred to Butch as being murdered. You always said he died. Like you knew what happened." He leaned over and laid his hand on her arm. This time she didn't jerk away. "You came to the house as soon as Pieter called you. He let you in. When you saw the gun in his hand, you knew immediately he'd killed himself." Arn rested his hand on Georgia's arm. "Butch tried killing himself by overdosing on his Xanax a week before he shot himself, didn't he?"

Georgia nodded. "I did my best to be around him after work. After that attempt. Anything so I could keep an eye on him. I was afraid he'd take more pills the next time."

"But you never imagined he'd shoot himself, I'd wager."

Georgia looked up. "I never thought, as vain as he was, that he would." She forced a laugh. "Guess he was just smart enough to get around looking like hell after he was shot. He just sat there in the chair looking like he'd passed out or something."

"And Pieter got involved, didn't he?"

Georgia's shoulder shook and she started sobbing. Arn slid his bandana across the table and waited. When she'd dried her eyes, she looked at him. "I ... I couldn't pry the gun loose from Butch's hand. His fingers were too tight around the grip. Pieter had to help me. He told me the detectives would do a Gun Shot Reside test on us both once they arrived. He said Butch always ordered that at shootings, and we washed up. I guess Pieter didn't get all the soap from his hands."

"That accounts for the discrepancy between when Emma Barnes saw you go inside and when you called 911. It took time to pry the gun lose and hide it. Then wash up so residue wouldn't show up on your hands. And take Butch's holster off his leg."

Georgia nodded.

"What happened to the gun?"

"I hid it in my purse. Bobby Madden was the first detective on the scene. He spotted Butch's hand still curled right off, and he knew what had happened. He just knew." Georgia blew her nose. "Sorry." She held up the bandana.

Arn forced a smile. "Under the circumstances, it's all right."

"Bobby told me to give him the gun, so I did. I told him he could keep it. I never wanted to see it again." She dabbed at her eyes with a clean spot and turned her chair around to face Arn, glad to finally tell the truth. "Bobby was going to open Butch's fingers, but the video tech shot his footage before he could. When the tech left to grab his 35mm for the still photos, Bobbie ... did it. He straightened Butch's fingers. He said if he didn't, the ME would spot that right off and ask what he was clutching at the time of his death."

"Was it Bobby's idea to rule it a homicide? There's nothing in any of his notes that mentioned suicide. Because he didn't want anyone to know?"

"There's always been such a stigma about officers committing suicide. I didn't want Pieter going through life with that." Georgia blew her nose again. "Bobby and Butch had worked investigations for years together. They were friends, as much as Butch developed friends. Bobbie said that if Butch's death were a homicide, Hannah—and Pieter— would get the hundred thousand dollars the feds give families for line-of-duty deaths. A suicide and they'd get nothing."

Arn shuffled through the papers until he pulled up Detective Madden's initial report. *The victim,* Bobby wrote, *must have struggled with his attacker because we found gun shot residue on one hand. Most likely when the victim grabbed his attacker's gun.* Arn knew that coroners and some medical examiners often went with whatever the investigating officer speculated. That explained the residue on one of Butch's hands.

"What did Bobby do with Butch's backup gun?" he asked.

"He gave it to the officer in charge of the Don't Ask Don't Tell gun buyback program the city has been doing for years. Bobby said it would be crushed into a thousand pieces along with every other gun turned in that winter." Georgia stood, hugging herself, and Arn sorely wanted to go to her. Tell her everything would be all right, now that the truth was out. But he wasn't going to lie to her.

"What will happen to me and Pieter now?" she asked.

"I'm guessing there'll be no charges filed, as there was no homicide committed. You've been misleading the public about Butch's death for a decade, but that's not chargeable. As for the hundred grand the DOJ gave Hannah for Butch's death, Pieter may have to repay it. But it's not for me to decide."

Arn nodded at the one-way glass, and Oblanski entered the room behind Pieter. Pieter ran to his aunt and wrapped his arms around her, hugging her for long moments before breaking away and facing Arn. "Those shots woke me that night, just like I said. By the time I ran downstairs, Dad was dead, and the only thing I could think of was to call Aunt Georgia."

Arn gathered up his notes and photos and put them back in his bag. "And all these years, you've been accusing Frank Dull Knife of killing your father."

Pieter frowned. "Frank never was any good. Finding out Mom and Frank were involved in house burglaries was the final straw for Dad. He was beside himself that last week. He didn't know what to do except ask that charges against Frank be dismissed. And no amount of Xanax could ease his pain. He did the only thing he knew to do."

Arn slung his man bag over his shoulder. "Now comes the tough part of being the police chief," he told Oblanski.

Oblanski kicked the carpet with his boot and finally met Pieter's eyes. "If we tell the truth, the feds come after you."

"And after Aunt Georgia?"

Oblanski nodded. "For fraud, possibly. You'll have to repay the money with interest at the very least, I'd wager. And the hardest part," Oblanski said, "is you'll lose your state builder's license.

Pieter's mouth drooped and he hugged Georgia. "What are you going to do, Chief?"

Oblanski shook his head. "I'll have all weekend to make a decision."

Fifty-Five

OBLANSKI SHUT THE DOOR, leaving Georgia and Pieter to fill out statement forms. "Now I see why you didn't want the interview recorded." He jerked his thumb at the interview room door. "Just what the hell do I do with *that*?"

"It's going to be a tough call." Arn waited until the secretary from Records walked past them in the hallway. "Sometimes, the right thing isn't always the legal thing to do."

"Criminally, there's nothing that can be done."

"The statute of limitations *has* run out on fraud."

"And the feds may not even pursue reimbursement for the money once they know why Butch killed himself." Oblanski sounded like he was trying to convince himself rather than Arn. "It could be argued that he committed suicide as a result of job stress." He led Arn into his office and shut the door. He found a victim from among the pencils on his desk top and began chewing the end. "If I keep my mouth shut, Georgia and Pieter will benefit, but you'll be hurt."

351

"How so?"

"If we don't go public with this, it'll mean the hot dog detective the TV station hired to solve Butch Spangler's murder failed. And failed to connect it to the other deaths, like Ana Maria claimed."

Arn groaned. "I forgot, I'll have to break the news to her..."

"Don't you dare," Oblanski said. "She's never kept her mouth shut about anything yet. This would be a huge story for her."

Arn thought of just that. If he told Ana Maria, there was a risk she would use it to catapult herself to national prominence. On the other hand, if he kept quiet, she'd go on spinning her wheels trying to solve a homicide that had never occurred.

"You've still got the deaths of Gaylord and Steve—and the Five Point cases—to solve," Arn said. "There's still a lot of news coverage she can get with your cases."

"You mean *our* cases."

"Not hardly."

"You're the one who uncovered them as homicides," Oblanski said. "And Butch's death as a suicide. The least you can do is stick around and help—"

Arn held up his hand. "I was hired to solve Butch's murder. I'm willing to go along with it if you decide to keep the Spangler secret buried. But"—he leaned closer to Oblanski—"I might be persuaded to come in as a consultant on those other cases."

"For a fee, no doubt."

Arn held up his hands. "So call me a mercenary. Renovating Mom's old house is costing me a mint, and I need the bucks."

Oblanski leaned back and tossed his chewed pencil in the trash can. "It's more than the money with you though, isn't it?"

Arn pulled his neckerchief away from his collar. His wound had scabbed up with the salve, but it still itched. "This is personal. It was personal when Johnny was murdered. And now that I know Gaylord and Steve's deaths weren't accidental, it's even more so.

"And the Five Point Killer?"

"Those cases are important because I'm convinced they'll lead us to Steve and Gaylord's murderer."

"There might be some problems getting the town council to release money for a consultant that failed to solve the Spangler murder." Oblanski looked to the ceiling fan for answers. "But right now—with the department in chaos over Johnny's murder—the council and mayor will probably give me whatever I ask. Let me make a call." He winced as he picked up the phone and talked with Gorilla Legs. He told her—no, asked her, as no one *tells* a two-hundred-pound Bohemian woman what to do—to set up a meeting with the mayor. "I need combat pay just talking with that woman," Oblanski said as he hung up the phone.

Laughter came from outside and Oblanski swiveled in his chair. He pulled back the window blinds. Two kids had piled on one sled and raced along a snow-packed alleyway pulled by a large yellow dog. "Now that you're in the consulting business, who would float to the top of the shit pile of suspects in Gaylord and Steve's deaths?"

"Frank. Maybe you were right about him all along."

Oblanski tapped his fingers on the desk. "No, I was wrong about him. I fingered him for Butch's murder. I never figured him to be involved—"

"In a couple accidental deaths?"

"All right, so we were wrong about Steve and Gaylord's deaths being natural. You proved they were homicides. But Frank had no reason to kill them. Butch went to the prosecutor and asked that Frank's burglary charge be dropped."

"About two weeks after they were both murdered. And only when Butch thought Frank would implicate Hannah." Arn scooted to the edge of his chair and leaned on Oblanski's desk. "Frank would still have a lot to lose with them alive."

"I *wanted* Frank to be Butch's killer." Oblanski paced in front of his desk. "As much as I *want* him to be involved in the other deaths, I'm not so sure. I've been wrong all these years. It's about time I rethink Frank."

"Consider this," Arn said. "Frank might have known Butch was close to solving the Five Point cases. And he would know Butch's partner and his supervisor would be privy to whatever information Butch had. So he killed them. One at a time when the opportunity arose. But when it came time to kill Butch, Butch did the job himself."

"You really think Frank could be the Five Point Killer?"

"He fits what little information we know about the killer," Arn answered. "Ana Maria found out that Frank got a severe leg injury when he was serving time in that Colorado prison. The suspect who picked up Joey Bent from the Leapfrog the night he was murdered had a limp. Frank knew Joey. They were both mechanics. Joey even tossed Frank work now and again."

"And how do you square Frank knowing Delbert Urban?"

Arn shrugged. "He could have found him on the Internet. Maybe it was just random, and Delbert was unlucky enough to be at the Hobby Shop when Frank broke in. He's a good enough home burglar, he would have all sorts of ways to gain entrance to homes and businesses."

"And maybe he was the one who got into your house that night and stole your slippers just to toy with you."

"Good possibility," Arn answered. "Frank hasn't broken into all those houses you suspect him of these last years without being able to do so quietly."

"I don't know." Oblanski pulled the curtains aside, but the kids and their dog were gone. "You forgetting about Johnny. Why would Frank want him dead?"

"Ana Maria's special brought Johnny to the forefront of reopening the investigations. Remember, Frank used to service the hospital vehicles. He probably still has a key to the maintenance door."

"And as long as he came and went in the hospital," Oblanski said, turning and dropping into his chair, fumbling for reports, "he'd know where the surveillance cameras are located and their area of coverage." Oblanski grabbed a one-paragraph report from the bottom of his stack and handed it to Arn. "Hospital security took a report that someone has been stealing things from the supply room. They didn't connect anything until…Johnny's murder."

Arn put on his glasses. "Booties, masks, and a gown. Just like Johnny's killer wore." He handed the sheet back to Oblanski. "Makes it less likely that Dr. Dawes killed Johnny that day. He wouldn't need to steal anything from the supply closet. He already has access to everything on that list."

"I thought of that." Oblanski hunted his desk drawer for a victim-pencil to chew on. "But we found that shoe print that exactly matched those found at Gaylord's—both when he was murdered and after the assault on you in the basement—and identical to the one on Delbert Urban's back, in Johnny's room. And it matched the shoes we recovered from Dr. Dawes' Caddy."

"Frank," Arn said. "If we're right about him, he damned sure would know enough to get into Jefferson's car and plant those shoes there. He may be a crappy mechanic, but even crappy mechanics can break into most cars. And place that anonymous call that led to your search warrant."

Oblanski slumped in his seat. "We're screwed."

Arn waited for an explanation.

"We brought Dawes in on suspicion of Johnny's death. And unless there's two killers—assuming your theory about Frank holds water—Dawes is pure as the driven snow."

"I guess you'd better grab your city attorney and visit Dawes this afternoon. Patch things over as best you can," Arn said. "And have Frank brought in for another interview."

Oblanski guffawed. "You expect Frank to break down and confess?"

"I don't expect him to say anything. But what a person doesn't say often sinks him. Tell him you're a hair's breath away from pinning Butch's murder on him."

"But we know now Butch wasn't murdered."

Arn smiled. "Frank doesn't know that."

Fifty-Six

ARN THOUGHT DORIS WAS reading the same *Good Housekeeping* as the first time he'd stopped by the television station. She looked up and dropped her magazine. "Thank goodness you're here. I told Ana Maria she should have called you."

"Tell me what's going on," Arn said.

Doris kneaded one hand in the other as she looked around the office. "Ana Maria didn't say?"

"Give me the headline version, and I'll talk with her."

"That same man called again."

"The one who called last week?"

Doris stood and walked back and forth behind her desk. "This time it was serious, Mr. Anderson. This time there's no denying he means to hurt her."

"Is she in her office?"

"She is," Doris said. "But she's a nervous wreck."

Arn laid his hand on Doris' shoulder. "I'll go talk with her."

He walked the hallway, empty at this time of the afternoon. Ana Maria's door was shut, which was unusual for her unless she had visitors. She always kept an open door for anyone to come in and pass the time. He knocked on the door but got no answer. He knocked a second time, and still no answer as a young man wearing a headset passed him. "I just saw her go inside," he said.

Arn rapped again. "Ana Maria. It's Arn."

She cracked the door. When she saw it was him, she flung it open and closed it just as quickly after he stepped inside. Arn slapped the door. "Little unusual for you, keeping fortressed-up like this."

She retreated back behind her desk, and Arn noticed the gun he'd let her use was sitting on top of her desk, the barrel pointed toward the door.

"Doris said you had a threatening call again."

"Busybody."

"I'd say she's looking out for you. Want to tell me what's going on?"

Ana Maria grabbed a bottle of mineral water and handed Arn one, but he waved it away. "I get enough healthy things at home with Danny doubling as Dr. Oz."

She didn't smile, placing a book over the gun as if Arn hadn't spotted it yet. "I received a call again this morning while I was out."

"And it wasn't Nick Damos again trying to scare you off? Weren't the childish notes he left around enough?"

"It wasn't Nick Damos." Ana Maria forced a smile. "He's recuperating at DeAngelo's condo outside Estes Park."

"Recuperating?"

She exaggerated a solemn nod. "Seems like when he went to Denver to follow up on that hot lead, the neighborhood banded together to repel an intruder, so to speak. Nick got busted up. Bad. DeAngelo sent him to recover at his condo. The way DeAngelo talks, Nick's jaw is going to be wired up for some time, so I'm sure Nick's not the one who called and told Doris."

"Told her what?"

"The man said he didn't want to talk with me. He knew I wasn't in the office, and he might just visit me this afternoon. He said to pass along that he really means it. Unless I drop the special, he will kill me. Slowly. Like he did to Laun McGuire."

"This sounds like a credible threat. I'll call Chief Oblanski—"

"The guy already covered that. He told Doris 'no police' right before he told her to tell me to check my desk."

"Check it for what?"

"This." Ana Maria opened her middle desk drawer and grabbed a single sheet of paper. Arn recognized the fetid odor, the blackened discoloration of blood that had recently been smeared across the paper. A single word, *Laun*, had been scribbled across in blood. "Whoever this guy is, I'm certain he followed me when I drove to the Flying J to verify Laun worked there."

"I'm afraid he followed me, too," Arn said. He told her about meeting with Laun at the truck stop, and about how he could feel someone tailing him last night. Someone besides Sergeant Dan Long.

"Whoever this guy is, he waltzed right past Doris."

"That wouldn't be hard."

"But make it this far, pick the lock on my door and then my desk, and stroll out without anyone seeing him?"

Arn spotted a paper bag on Ana Maria's top shelf and took pens and paper out of it. He used a tissue to grab the bloody paper and slip it inside the bag. "I think we should call Oblanski. Have a tighter security placed on you."

Ana Maria wrapped her arms around her chest and rocked back and forth in her chair. "This scares the hell out of me. But if I have an officer shadow me—not outside in his car, but right on my heels wherever I go while I'm working—DeAngelo will cancel the special. That scares me even more. Arn, don't tell Oblanski."

"I don't know. This is serious—"

"Promise me. Doris already has said she won't say anything to the police or DeAngelo."

"Are we in the negotiating mode?"

Ana Maria leaned back and stared at the ceiling. "Not that old negotiating crap again?"

When Ana Maria worked at the CBS affiliate in Denver, she would sleep with the scanner next to her bed. And when she'd respond to Arn's crime scenes and want some tidbit to go to air with, Arn would dicker with her: tit for tat. She'd air just enough information that people thought it inevitable the killer would be caught. And in return, he'd arrange through media relations to give her an exclusive.

"I'm game," she said. "What's the offer?"

"Trust me?"

She looked warily at him. "Sure. What you got?"

"We found Butch Spangler's killer. But I can't let you go to air with it just yet."

She snapped her chair down and grabbed her notebook and pen. "Who was it?"

"I haven't heard that you accepted the offer yet."

"How long do I have to sit on it?"

Arn thought. "This is Friday ... you can air it for your weekend special."

"Damn you drive a hard bargain," she said, her pen perched above the notebook. "But I agree to the terms. Who killed Butch?"

"Butch."

"No, I mean who killed him?"

"Butch," Arn repeated, just to see the frustration on her face. He explained to her the circumstances surrounding Georgia and Pieter's confessions. "But I don't want the public to know about it just yet. If ever. It might be moot."

"Moot? There are still two more officers' murders that were unsolved, along with the Five Point cases, and you say Butch is moot?" She let the pen drop on the desk. "Any updates on those, now that we know Butch was a suicide?"

"Oblanski and I think Frank Dull Knife might—and I emphasize *might*—be good for the other murders." Arn reached over and lifted the book off the gun. He sniffed it. It had been fired recently.

"Practice," she volunteered.

Arn slid the gun back under the book. "We don't want Frank knowing Butch's death was a suicide. Oblanski thinks he can convince Frank he has conclusive proof that he killed Butch. If Frank thinks Oblanski has planted evidence, he may make a mistake. He may go back and make certain his ass is covered with the other murders."

"He hasn't made a mistake all these years, if he's the killer."

"He hasn't been this close to getting nailed."

Ana Maria jotted notes in her book. "Or Frank may start working his way through the people who could put him away. Like us."

"I'm banking on that."

Ana Maria threw up her hands. "Just great. Now you're prodding the bear."

"Look," Arn said, "with Frank cornered, I'm hoping he comes after one of us. Namely me."

"And why do you think he'll hunt *you* down?"

"He failed at killing me in Gaylord's old house. I'm sure that infuriates him. And with you safe with more security—"

"I said DeAngelo will shut the project down."

"Then at least let me talk with Oblanski and make sure his best officer is still watching over you."

Ana Maria took the book off the gun. "All right, but until then, this thing's never away from my grasp."

Fifty-Seven

"**ARROGANT BASTARD.**" **OBLANSKI SLAMMED** the door hard enough that it rattled the windows overlooking the alley.

"What did Frank say to get you spun up?" Arn asked.

"He admitted to more than twenty residential burglaries. Years ago. Gave specifics on what he took. But he knows they're past the statute of limitations and we can't touch him."

"What did he say when you told him you were gathering proof that he killed Butch?"

Oblanski smiled. "That was sweet. He accused me of fabricating evidence, just like Butch fabricated evidence on him ten years ago. 'Bring it on, you Pollack son-of-a- bitch. You got nothing on me,' he yelled, 'and if we go to trial, I'll testify it was you dancing with Hannah the night Butch was murdered. And maybe you offed him.'"

"What did you say?"

"I said 'bring it on, you Sioux Indian son-of-a-bitch.' I came this close"—Oblanski held up his thumb and finger—"to dropping him like a bad habit, but he stomped out of the interview before I could. He's been through the system enough to know that if I had enough to charge him, his ass would be sitting in the pokey."

"As long as he actually feels like we'll soon have enough proof."

"Like we discussed, I indicated you have some loose ends you need to tie up before you present the prosecutor with all your evidence. And as soon as you tie it all in, you'll meet with me."

Arn's hand brushed the gun in his pocket. "Then I'd better start looking over my shoulder even more."

"If you'd let me assign an officer to you—"

"You don't have the manpower," Arn interrupted. "Besides, if he was sharp enough to tail me when I went to the truck stop to talk with Laun McGuire without me spotting him, he'll spot an officer tailing me."

Oblanski nodded. "I see your point."

"But since you're so benevolent with security … " Arn explained the latest threatening phone call that came into the TV station and the man getting into Ana Maria's desk. He reached into his man bag and handed Oblanski the paper bag containing the letter. "Not much chance there's any prints on it, but you could fast-track a DNA workup just to verity it's Laun McGuire's blood."

"I'll run it down to the lab myself," Oblanski said. He grabbed a chain of evidence form and Arn signed it.

"Ana Maria insists she doesn't want more security," Arn said, meeting Oblanski's eyes. "But if you'd assign your best officer to watch over her on the sly—"

"Understood. Someone who is an experienced street cop," Oblanski said. "I got just the man." He put on examination gloves and slid the paper in the evidence bag. "Kingston. From an old ranching family around the original Fort DA Russell area. He's been on Frank the moment he stormed out of my interview, but I have a number of officers capable of following Frank without him catching on. It'll free Kingston up to watch Ana Maria."

"Thanks."

Arn stood to leave when the phone rang. He heard Gorilla Legs yell into the phone from the next room, and Oblanski held the receiver away from his ear before hanging up. "Damn, you're bad luck, Anderson. Half the time you're in my office, I get a call that someone else died."

"Who is it this time?"

"Our good friend Dr. Jefferson Dawes. Let's take a ride."

———————

Oblanski and Arn pulled to the curb across from the Dawes' house and parked behind the coroner's van. Two attendants dragged a gurney from the back, a heavy black bag strapped to the cot waiting for Jefferson to fill it. They hummed the theme song from *The Sound of Music*, and any other time Arn would have stopped to listen; they were in such good harmony. At least they enjoyed their jobs, he thought. A real rarity these days.

Arn shielded his eyes from the revolving red and blue lights as he watched Sgt. Long skid down the driveway, arms flailing on the icy concrete as he fought to maintain his balance. Arn held out his arm and stopped Long before he sailed by and crashed.

"Thanks," the cop said, pulling the collar of his police jacket over his neck and stuffing his hands into his pockets. "Damned near fell."

"What we got, Dan?" Oblanski looked up the circular drive at a squad car parked close to the house with the driver's door still open.

"Queens is inside talking with the widow—"

"Just the quick and dirty, Dan."

Long took a long breath. "Adelle Dawes came home and found her husband on the living room couch. DRT."

Oblanski looked at Arn, who shrugged.

"DRT," Long repeated. "Dead Right There. Don't you guys ever go to movies? Anyway, he didn't twitch a muscle after he'd shot himself."

"Anyone else in the house?"

"The doctor was alone at the time."

"Wife been tested yet?"

"First thing," Long answered. "Negative for gun shot residue."

"Go on."

"Victim left a note. The gun's sitting there in his lap where it fell." Long cupped his hands and blew into them. "The crime scene techs are just finishing their still photos now."

"Then let's go visit with the ever-pleasant and petite Adelle Dawes," Oblanski said.

Long eyed Arn trailing behind them, but kept quiet as he held the front door for them. "This is the ingress we used." Long indicated a pathway to where Dr. Dawes sat slumped in his couch. The detective guarding the door glared at Arn, but jotted his name in a notebook along with Oblanski's and Long's before allowing them to continue into the crime scene.

Jefferson Dawes sat with his chin resting on his chest. Blood trickled down from a tiny hole in his temple, nearly camouflaged when the blood met the maroon leather of the couch. A small Walther semi-auto lay between his legs where it had fallen after the shot, and a piece of parchment paper lay across his lap as if he'd put the note there for all to see. Oblanski donned examination gloves and handed Arn a pair. "Photos done?" Oblanski asked.

A man wearing two cameras around his thin neck nodded. "He's all yours, Chief."

Oblanski picked up the paper and separated the note, laying it on the carpeting away from any blood. Unlike doctors who wrote as if

English was their second language—indecipherable enough that military intelligence would be envious—Jefferson's note had been impeccable, each letter like a miniature work of art.

"Guess we can scratch one suspect in Gaylord's murder," Oblanski said. "And in the Five Point cases." He showed the suicide note to Arn. Jefferson had confessed to being the Five Point Killer. He outlined how he'd picked up Joey Bent at the Leapfrog, and how he'd met Delbert Urban at the Hobby Shop. *Delbert was stronger than I thought,* the note explained. *I sedated him and thought he was out cold. But he came to, and he struggled. I had to jump on his back to strangle him.* "Just like you thought," Oblanski said.

"I'm not celebrating."

I had to kill Gaylord, the note continued. *The day I spoke with him about Adelle, he said he and Butch were close to catching the Five Point Killer, and he didn't have time to waste worrying about Adelle's infidelity. I killed Gaylord first, staging the hanging. I did the others later.*

"Here's what he says about Johnny." Oblanski carefully laid the note beside Arn. *No one paid any attention to me at the hospital. I turned away from their primitive surveillance when I had to, slipping by the policeman unnoticed. The shoe print I left on the other side of Johnny's bed was a nice touch, I thought.*

"I guess that was Jeff's way of mooning the cops after all these years," Oblanski said. "He must have thought we were close." He stood and slid the suicide note into an evidence bag. "Guess we have to rethink Frank now."

"I'm not sure." Arn squatted close to Jefferson's note and put his reading glasses on. "Did you ever see a doctor with hand writing this neat?"

Oblanski shook his head. "Doesn't mean that he *didn't* have nice penmanship."

"When I was in the hospital the other day, Dr. Dawes said his nurse called him. She couldn't read what orders he had written. This"—Arn pointed to the note—"wasn't written by Dawes."

"I've known some that wrote like hell in everyday correspondence, but wonderfully when corresponding with their mother."

"Was Dawes right or left handed?"

Oblanski jotted in his notebook. "Adelle's down at the PD now, waiting to be interviewed. I'll ask her. Why?"

Arn took out his pen and indicated several places on the suicide note. "The slant makes it look like a left-hander wrote this. But there's just something not right. Like the lean of the letters is exaggerated."

"We'll get our documents examiner on to do handwriting comparisons."

Arn knelt and looked closely at Dr. Dawes' shoes.

"Now what are you doing?" Oblanski asked.

"Consulting," Arn answered. "Have Dan Long check Jefferson's closet for running shoes."

"What's wrong with the ones he's wearing?"

"He's wearing Nikes," Arn said. "When I saw him at the hospital that day I stopped to see Johnny, then again at his house when he was stretching for a run, Jefferson was wearing Adidas. Runners don't often change brands. They find one that works for them and it's brand loyalty to the nth degree."

Oblanski motioned to Long. "Check Dr. Dawes' room in a minute for the shoes."

Arn turned back to the victim and sniffed the air around Dawes.

"You got some fetish about smelling dead bodies?" Oblanski asked.

Arn bent over and sniffed again before straightening up. "I smelled Old Spice the other day when I went up to talk with Adelle. Dr. Dawes passed me as he was going out jogging. I just assumed he was wearing it."

"Congratulations," Oblanski said, exaggerating a sniff of Arn's neck. "I smell Polo. Is this what I get for my consulting budget?"

"I smelled Old Spice on the guy who attacked me in the park, and again that night in Gaylord's basement."

"Who the hell uses Old Spice?" Oblanski laughed. "Except old farts. Which Jeff isn't."

"Well, I'm pretty sure he was wearing it the other day."

He turned to Long. "When you go to the doctor's room to look for those shoes, see if he had a bottle of Old Spice, too."

After Long left the room, Oblanski bent and looked closer at the small gun that had fallen between Jefferson's legs. "At least we know what happened to that gun that killed Johnny."

"How do you know that?" Arn asked.

Oblanski moved to look at it from a different angle. "After Gaylord's death, Adelle auctioned most of his things off. But she kept some things. My guess is that that's Gaylord's backup gun."

"It wouldn't be my guess," Arn said, standing, his knees popping as loudly as he imagined that tiny gun had. "I doubt that it's Gaylord's."

"Then just whose gun is it?"

"Am I on the consulting payroll?"

"You mercenary SOB. Let's hear your thoughts."

Arn looked up at Jefferson. Except for the tiny hole and trickle of blood down the side of his head, Dr. Dawes looked like he could jump up and start running a marathon. "Ask the state lab to run ballistics comparisons with the slugs recovered from Butch Spangler and the one floating around the doctor's skull. You guys still retain that evidence, I'm assuming?"

"Butch was listed as a homicide." Oblanski lowered his voice. "Initially. So we still have all the evidence in our evidence vault. But Butch's gun? I don't understand where you're coming from. "

"Georgia described Butch's backup gun. It sounded like a PPK or a PP, .32 or .380. Just like this one Jefferson … used." Arn stood and walked around, eying him from different angles. "Georgia said Bobby Madden gave it to the officer in charge of destroying the guns in the department buyback program to be crushed."

Oblanski said, "I was junior man then, and I handled the crappy guns to be destroyed. But Bobby never gave me a Walther. I'd have remembered that. All we ever got was junk. Mostly guns that wouldn't fire."

"You keep records of them?"

"Sure," Oblanski answered, staring at the pistol. "We checked all guns dropped off for that program through NCIC—just to make sure there were none stolen—before we relegated them to the mulch pile." He shook his head. "But just how would Jefferson have gotten ahold of it?"

"Adelle," Arn said immediately. "My guess is that Bobby Madden knew it was a quality piece and had second thoughts about destroying it. Especially since Butch and Gaylord were partners." He pointed to the fireplace mantle where the two badges sat. "When I talked with Adelle the other day, she pointed to Steve and Gaylord's badges as if they meant something to her. She wanted Butch's, but Georgia wouldn't give it to her. I'm thinking Bobby gave Adelle Butch's gun for sentimentality reasons. Especially since Georgia wanted nothing to do with it."

Oblanski flipped open his phone. "Just to be safe, I'll have Gorilla Legs pull up the records for the guns that year."

Dan Long returned from Jefferson's room empty-handed. "Nothing there except Adidas shoes. Eight pairs in boxes." He handed Oblanski a bottle of Old Spice. "But I found this on his dresser."

"You print it before you picked it up?"

Long dropped his head.

"I figured as much," Arn said. "What did Adelle Dawes tell you when you initially responded here?"

Long grabbed his pocket notebook and flipped pages. "Mrs. Dawes left the house at 12:40 this afternoon to go to the hospital where she does volunteer work twice a week. She returned home"—Long turned another page—"at 4:30 and found the doctor—"

"DRT?" Arn said.

Long smiled and nodded to Jefferson. "Dead Right There."

"Did she say anything about him initially?"

"Just 'good riddance,' and grinned. What do you suppose she meant by that?"

Arn looked down at the dead man. "Good riddance to her philandering husband and hello to his sizeable estate, I would imagine."

He turned his attention back to Jefferson and squatted in front of him. Unlike with Butch, Jefferson's hand was positioned properly for a suicidal shot. He'd slumped after firing the gun, and Arn closed his eyes. In his mind, he reconstructed the scene as it happened, as he often did. He suddenly opened his eyes. Something didn't quite seem right. As he stood, he realized why. Tiny light-colored specks all but lost in the beige carpeting caught his eyes. Arn dropped onto his knees and donned his reading glasses. "Hand me your flashlight."

Long handed Arn his Surefire, and he held it close to the carpet at an acute angle. The specks were clustered to one side of Jefferson. "Give me an evidence marker."

Long handed Arn a yellow plastic tent with a number on it. "What did you find?"

"Who did the GSR test on Adelle?"

"Queen did," Long answered. "Was there a problem with it?"

Arn set the plastic tent on the carpet beside Jefferson's feet. He stood and arched his back. "Tell your crime scene tech to collect those little specks. If I'm right, it's talcum powder. Or at least the type of powder that's inside examination gloves."

Oblanski came back into the room. "I heard what you said. Jeff was a doctor. Don't you think it'd be natural for him to have talc on his hands from exam gloves falling onto the floor?"

"It would be," Arn said. "But given the doctor's running shorts and sweaty top, I'd wager it's been a while since he's been at the hospital. But Adelle just returned from there. "

"Grab Queen and get to the office," Oblanski told Long. "Draft a search warrant for this place, and specifically mention any discarded examination gloves."

After Long left, Oblanski sat on a chair across from the dead man. The coroner's team stood at the doorway, still humming like half a barber shop quartet. "We got a problem," Oblanski said. "The officer tailing Frank lost him ten minutes ago over by the refinery."

"Things just get better and better," Arn said. "How'd it happen?"

"Frank went into his shop. The officer waited outside, watching with his spotting scope half a block away. When he didn't see any lights come on in Frank's shop after a while, he put the sneak on it. Frank's got a back door that opens out into that junkyard of his. The officer speculates Frank just walked away. Probably has a car stashed somewhere within walking distance."

"But if he didn't kill Butch, why'd he take off?"

Oblanski pushed his ball cap on the back of his head. "Maybe I pushed him too hard."

"Isn't that what we wanted?" Arn said.

"It was. But you watch your backside." Oblanski motioned for the coroner's assistants. "There's one thing that Frank kept saying over again in that interview: 'if I ever get the chance, I'll slit Anderson's throat for bringing heat down on me after all these years.'"

Fifty-Eight

ARN NEARLY JUMPED OUT of his skin when Ana Maria burst through the door. She ran through the house and found Arn sitting in the sewing room, studying the white wall. "You promised to give me some information on Jefferson Dawes' suicide."

"Did you hit the deadbolt and arm the system?"

Ana Maria stopped and eyed him suspiciously. "My guardian cop is right outside." She took her purse from her shoulder. "You're worried about something more than the usual."

Arn explained that Frank Dull Knife had made threats against him, and might now be desperate enough to carry them out. He told her that Oblanski had convinced Frank that he'd worked up enough evidence to charge him for Butch's murder. "And there's that bloody note you found in your desk."

"This policeman's a little more on the ball than the others. Now do you have something for me? I go to air in three hours."

Arn sat up. A massive headache had begun even before she came into the room. "As soon as I have something concrete—"

"Concrete? The meat wagon left Dawes' house two hours ago. Oblanski won't tell me squat. That leaves you."

"I've just got to get some things straight first."

"What about that agreement we had?"

"What's all the commotion down here?" Danny came into the room carrying a putty knife and a tub of spackling paste. "You guys make enough noise to give me a headache."

"Don't you and Erv have wire to pull?"

"I gave Erv the day off," Danny said.

"How can you give someone the day off who doesn't work?" Arn asked.

"I figured it'd help his self-esteem," Danny answered, "if he thought he had a regular job."

"And we're all about building self-esteem around here," Arn said.

Danny dropped into a chair beside him. "Now what were you two fighting about?"

"We weren't fighting," Ana Maria said. "We were ... discussing a gentlemen's agreement we had."

"Well, there's your problem: Only one of you is a gentleman."

"I appreciate that." Arn smiled.

"I wasn't talking about you," Danny said.

Arn leaned back and pinched his nose. His headache was getting worse, and it wouldn't subside until he got some things straight in his mind.

"I've seen that look before." Ana Maria sat on an empty drywall bucket and rested her arms on the door-turned-table. "Something's not right."

"I've read and reread Dr. Dawes' suicide note in my mind. Something doesn't fit."

When Arn was a small boy, his mother had bought him a jigsaw puzzle at a garage sale. "Something's not right, Mom," he said when he emptied the box out onto the floor to put it together. His mother hadn't believed him even as he began linking pieces. There were some pieces missing, he discovered after two days putting the puzzle together, and a couple pieces from another puzzle that had wound up in the branding scene. He'd take those pieces and turned them over, but they never quite matched up. That's how he felt putting the pieces of this jigsaw puzzle together that didn't quite fit, trying to match pieces that never were quite right.

"Dawes described each of the Five Point killings, and Gaylord and Steve's murders, with details only the killer would know."

"Then what's the hang up," Danny said. "You have a confession to all the murders. Go out and get a celebratory beer."

"I don't feel like I can celebrate anything," Arn said. "The note is … too neat. Dawes wrote piss poor. Like most doctors. Unless he had an alter ego who wrote neatly, or he took his time and penned that note so we could read it, someone else wrote it."

"Adelle," Ana Maria said immediately.

Arn nodded. "We thought of that, and Oblanski is getting a handwriting sample from her after he interviews her. But"—he slapped one fist into the other—"there's just one piece of this puzzle that's eluding me. And I won't get a decent night's sleep until I figure out what it is."

"You don't seem to have been doing too bad," Danny said, "as loud as your snoring's been."

"You ought to sleep in the next room from him," Ana Maria added.

Arn's cell phone rang and rescued him. But the feeling wasn't for long. "Did you forget the time?" Georgia asked.

"Oh crap." Arn looked at his watch.

"We can make this another night."

But Arn wasn't so sure there ever would be another night. When Georgia had suggested they meet on neutral ground—like two combatants meeting on the field of honor—to discuss how he had tricked her into revealing the truth about Butch's death, Arn had jumped at the opportunity for one more chance. Now he almost wished he hadn't. "Something came up," he told her. "I'm on my way over now."

He grabbed a sport coat and headed for the door. "Lock the door," he called to Danny and Ana Maria. "And arm the security system." And as he wiggled into the Clown Car to drive to Georgia's, he had to work to spot the unmarked police car half a block away in the shadow of a building. And felt certain Frank wouldn't spot it.

———

Arn started down Pioneer Avenue, keeping his eyes glued to the rearview mirror. Frank could be driving most anything, from his own beat-to-hell pickup to any number of customers' cars. Oblanski's men were hunting Frank hard—not to arrest him, since they had nothing to arrest him for—but because he was dangerous now that he thought Arn had worked up evidence linking him to Butch's death. "He might go back to the reservation," Arn had suggested.

"He won't leave Cheyenne." Oblanski had assigned two more officers to find Frank. "If you'd have been in that interview room, you'd know how Frank hates you. Hopefully, we'll find him before he finds you."

Arn had thought of how Frank had acted in Oblanski's interview. "Perhaps he's afraid of me for more reasons than Butch's murder."

"Gaylord and Steve's?"

"And the Five Point killings. Just like we thought."

Arn had never run from a fight. Never feared anyone would best him. Never felt as if his place as the Alpha male at the head of the pack was threatened. But Frank Dull Knife was different. He'd posed as just another drunk the two times Arn had confronted him at his shop. But the man had stayed out of jail the last fifteen years, since before Butch's death. His cunning had allowed him to conduct his burglaries with little chance of being caught. Frank would think through his attack. When it came.

Arn pulled to the curb in front of a truck a block from Pieter's house and doused his lights. He waited, his mind momentarily wandering back to his grandfather Will Anderson's tales of men dueling in the Western fashion. Men killed one another at a hundred yards with rifles in this part of town. And face-to-face disputes with Bowie knives were common. Would Frank and he meet in such a fashion? Arn thought it couldn't be any scarier than meeting Georgia tonight as he walked the steps to her front door.

Georgia opened the garage door and stood with her arms crossed. She wore tan slacks and a cowl-necked sweater, with no makeup. As she stood eying Arn, he couldn't figure out if she wanted romance or to chew him out.

She motioned through Pieter's garage, the yellow Karman Ghia sporting dirt and black specks on the rocker panels, tar remover and a rag on the garage floor beside it.

Arn followed her through the garage into the house. When they reached the living room, she motioned to the couch, and she sat across the room in an overstuffed chair.

"I'm waiting for some kind of explanation I can live with," she said. "Like, 'Georgia, I set you up because the truth had to come out.' Or, 'Georgia, Butch's death has gone unsolved long enough.' Some logical explanation." She shook her head. "Even some philosophical explanation."

Arn stood and paced in front of the fireplace mantle. He wanted to occupy his time straightening Georgia's high school cheerleading picture. Or dust off Pieter's basketball photo showing him with the team and their sponsor's shoes and soda they'd been awarded that year. He wanted to serve anything on a silver platter that would smooth things over between them. But he could only stand in front of her and think how he could explain himself so she would understand his good intentions. "I suspected Butch committed suicide—"

"I know. You already explained that," she said, defiant, and Arn was certain there would be no romance tonight.

"I knew you had to protect Pieter," he began. "You didn't want him to go through life with the stigma that his father, the legendary detective Butch Spangler, killed himself because he couldn't handle his wife's affairs."

Georgia nodded.

"But there were more reasons for Butch to feel enough anxiety to overdose on Xanax."

"Like what?"

Arn had been rehearsing his explanation since Georgia said she wanted to meet after her interview at the police department. "He couldn't live with himself after Steve was murdered. And later Gaylord—"

"But they weren't murdered. They died naturally. As naturally as a house fire and a suicidal hanging can be."

"There was nothing natural about their deaths. They were murdered."

Georgia waved the air to dismiss the notion. "Ana Maria's television special. Even though she claims they were connected, she's never gotten any new information. If they were homicides, she'd spill it all across the television screen."

"She didn't," Arn said, "because we agreed to keep the information under wraps. For now."

He sat back down, his thoughts coming to him easily now. "See, that's another thing that bothered me. It didn't take me too much digging to figure out Gaylord didn't die an autoerotic death as the official reports claimed, but was hung from the rafters by his killer. And Steve's house fire was no accident. If I could see it, surely an excellent investigator like Butch could."

"I talked with him at the time Steve and Gaylord died. He gave no indication they were homicides," Georgia said.

"And his reports never mentioned any suspicions of murder," Arn continued. He leaned forward and rested his elbows on his knees. "See, I think it weighed even heavier on Butch that his partner and supervisor were murdered than that Hannah was catting around. He knew they were murdered yet he couldn't square it in his mind. And he couldn't take it anymore."

Georgia's eyes welled up and she avoided Arn's look. "But what you did, implicating Pieter to trick me—"

"Was necessary," Arn said. "You didn't volunteer anything when I asked you. Like Butch's suicide note."

"What note?"

"Georgia." Arn stood and walked to the chair, looking down at her. "Butch was a very organized man. He would not have left something as open-ended as his death without leaving an explanation. He left a note for you, didn't he?"

"What makes you think I have any note?"

"That hour between when you arrived at his house and when you called 911, you were cleaning up. Getting rid of anything that indicated a suicide. Did Bobby ask for the note?"

Georgia looked up at Pieter's photo on the mantle and dabbed her eyes with the back of her sleeve. "I'd stuffed it in my purse by the time he arrived. I told him Butch didn't leave a note. He didn't believe me either."

"May I see it?"

"I don't have—"

"Please. This is the last thing between us." Arn laid his hand on her shoulder. "Then maybe we can start over."

Georgia nodded and stood slowly, almost painfully, and disappeared down a hallway. When she reappeared, she had an envelope in her hand. "It's one of the few things I kept that was my brother's. And don't you know, it's the damned suicide note."

Arn carefully unfolded the note and laid it out on the coffee table while he put his glasses on. *Of all the criminals I've pursued*, Butch said, *the Five Point Killer is the only natural predator I've hunted. He killed Gaylord and Steve, and has kept one step ahead of me. But I can smell him even in my sleep, he's so close. I may be next.*

"Butch sounded fearful that he would be killed next." Arn turned the paper over. "That had to have weighed heavily on him."

There was no apology to his son for finding him dead. Arn handed Georgia the note. "Even in death, he was abusive to Pieter."

Georgia held it to her chest. "Pieter won't admit it, but finding his father shot like that has stayed with him all these years." She tapped the note on her forearm. "This is the proof that Chief Oblanski would need in order to reopen Butch's homicide and get it ruled a suicide."

Arn thought a moment. "I'm not sure what Oblanski's going to do. But as far as I'm concerned, the Spanglers have suffered enough. Keep it and do whatever you want with it."

He buttoned his sport coat and grabbed his Stetson from the hat rack. As he started for the door, Georgia stopped him. "You're just going to walk out? Without that second chance you talked about?"

"I thought—"

"You think too much." She grabbed her jacket from the bent wood coat tree. "I worked up an appetite waiting for an explanation. By the way, what kept you tonight?"

Arn debated telling her about Jefferson Dawes' death, then decided it wouldn't be anything she wouldn't hear Ana Maria report in the morning anyway. When he finished, she asked, "And you think Adelle might have shot Dr. Dawes?"

"Reducing it to who would benefit the most from it, Adelle would stand to make millions from Jefferson's estate, even after taxes."

"But you don't think she really did it?"

Arn helped Georgia with her coat and she looked around the house a final time before leaving by the garage door. "She's capable, but everything is just too pat. The suicide note explaining things about the Five Point cases, and about Steve and Gaylord's murders, that only the killer would know. And written so neatly we are just about certain the doctor didn't write it. Just too pat."

"Well, don't look that gift horse—"

"Understood. But there's something else you may want to consider." Arn told her about the threats Frank had made about intending to kill Arn when he saw him next. "I'm not so sure you want to be seen with me."

Georgia punched in the security code to arm Pieter's system. "Look. I've been on an emotional roller coaster all day, worrying if the government will make Pieter repay the money. Not knowing if there's anything we could be charged with, or if the state will revoke his builder's license. The least of my worries is Frank Dull Knife."

"Then let's grab a bit to eat." Arn smiled.

He helped Georgia into the car before he went around and shoehorned himself behind the wheel. As soon as he flicked on the headlights, he noticed a small note stuck under his wiper blade. His hand went to the gun in his back pocket as he looked frantically around, ready to shove Georgia over in the seat. As if there was room to do so.

"What is it?"

"The dome light," Arn snapped. "Cover it with your hand."

Georgia covered the light long enough for Arn to open the door and grab the note. He slammed the door and tried scooting lower in the seat. "There's a flashlight in the glove box."

Georgia handed him a small light and he held it low to the floorboard to read the note. "What is it?" Her voice faltered, expecting something bad. "What's it say?"

"It's a warning. I think." The note, scribbled on the back of an IHOP menu, told Arn to drive to his house. That Danny and Ana Maria needed him. ASAP. He showed Georgia the note as he fumbled for the ignition key.

"What do they need? Who put this note here?"

"I need to get home ASAP, it says."

"Danny or Ana Maria need you?"

"If they wanted me, they would have called my cell," he said as he pulled out of Pieter's driveway. "As for who put it here, my best guess is the same person who wrote Dawes' suicide note, by the neatness of the writing."

Fifty-Nine

TAILING ANDERSON, I SEE why he's survived in his dangerous world as long as he has. Just when I thought I'd see him come out the front door, he surprised me by coming out of his house by the back way. He stood at the corner of his house and looked around. Checking, slowly accessing the safety of making it to that miniature car he drives. But I've lived in my own dangerous world too long to be spotted. Not like the cop watching the house. If I hadn't known they use those old Crown Vics for undercover work, I may not have spotted him parked in the shadows of that brick building down the block. I'll have to talk with the cop. Later. In my own special language.

For now, I'm having a hard time keeping distance from Anderson as he drives through town. He's already pulled to the curb twice to see if he was followed. He's pulled into someone's driveway once. All three times, I had to turn off and parallel him on another street. I thought I'd lost him when I realized he was driving with no lights, using the emergency brake to stop rather than illuminate his taillights.

Now that he went into the house, I have all the time in the world to put a love note under his windshield wiper. And then I'll drive to his house and visit with his people. And the cop.

I tremble thinking what it will be like talking with Anderson and his peeps in the Hobby Shop, where Delbert Urban and I danced one night ten years ago. And that almost gave the cops enough to catch me. Almost. Damn, that old feeling's back.

Sixty

ARN CUT HIS HEADLIGHTS a block from his house, once again using the emergency brake to stop. Twice he'd pulled to the curb, and twice Georgia had refused to climb out. Arn reluctantly agreed to let her stay in the car with her finger poised over "911" on her cell phone. "I think you ought to wait for Oblanski and his men," Georgia said.

"I'm not so sure Danny and Ana Maria have much time, if I'm reading between the lines on that note." On the way over, Arn had conjured up images of them. Terrible images. And he couldn't help but think of the throat-slashed victims of ten years ago, or of Gaylord hanging or Steve burning up. Which way would Danny and Ana Maria die if he didn't pull this off? "Cover the dome light until I get out."

"You're not even sure they're in any danger," Georgia said.

"I'm not sure they're safe, either. Place the call now."

While Georgia dialed Oblanski's personal cell number, Arn stripped off his sport coat and tossed it inside the open driver's window. He left his Stetson on the back seat and grabbed his pistol from his pocket. "Keep your ears open for any gunfire. If Oblanski gets here before I come out, tell him not to shoot me. If Frank's inside with them, there'll be shooting enough to go around."

"Just wait for help—"

"Sitting in that car over there"—Arn squinted in the darkness at an unmarked Crown Vic—"is a perfectly fine officer."

"If he's so sharp, why didn't he see anyone go into your house?" Georgia said, then answered, "Because there *is* no one in there holding Danny or Ana Maria hostage. This is ridiculous."

"I hope I'm wrong. But the one thing I am certain of is that the officer will go inside with me and check."

Arn picked his way from tree to abandoned house to a car up on cinder blocks, following shadows that concealed him, squatting low to prevent the street light from illuminating him. He hunkered down twenty yards in back of the squad car. This would be the most dangerous thing about his approach: the policeman might shoot him before Arn could explain what he wanted.

He took several deep, calming breaths before walking bent over toward the police car. He whistled, but the policeman remained with his head on his chest, and Arn could almost hear the snoring coming from inside the car. He kept his house in his peripheral vision as he stood upright and rapped on the side of the driver's window.

Silence.

He cupped his flashlight in his hand, shading the bulb, and flicked the light once at the officer. Then he jumped back, startled, and shined the light again. The policeman's head slumped on his chest, his lifeless eyes seeming to mock him. His throat had been slashed, and he appeared to have bled out. DRT. A piece of notepaper was jammed into the throat, bloody. Staged. Just like Steve and Gaylord's deaths. *You're wasting your time,* the note read, neatly, legibly. Like Dawes' suicide note. *Inside.*

Arn ran bent over toward his house, his footsteps crunching loud on the ice, the full moon illuminating him like a spotlight announcing his approach.

His front door stood ajar, the snow swirling around in the threshold. He caught a sound coming from in back of his house: the generator he'd bought to get them through until lights could be turned on hummed like distant high-line wires in the cold night air. It hadn't been run for days. It shouldn't be running now.

Light seeped through cracks in the plywood over the windows, and Arn paused at the porch. He bent and ran his hand over tracks leading to the house, but he couldn't age them with the stiff wind.

He stepped to the side of the stairs, knowing the center of the steps would creak and alert anyone inside that he'd arrived. He stopped to one side of the door, his breaths coming in great gasps, searing his lungs. He willed himself to take deep, calming breaths. He drew a final breath and buttonhooked through the door, leading with his revolver.

He flicked on a light in the entryway. No light, and he silently cursed Erv for another botched wiring job. Until he realized whoever held Danny and Ana Maria had tripped the main breaker, leaving only the generator to power the only light shining.

Arn dropped to his knees while his eyes adjusted to the darkness, the faint light he'd seen from outside coming from somewhere toward the living room.

Outside, the streetlight filtering through the evil-looking cottonwood tree cast shadows on the wall that looked every bit like a man's arm waving a warning to him. It had been twenty years since he'd had to search a room by himself, and he tried remembering what his old training officer had said. "Don't lead with your gun, dummy," Rolf

Vincent had told him. "The bad guy will see you coming even before you clear the corner of the wall. Pie the corner, cutting it so that not much of your head's exposed. Then you can enter. And most important kid," Rolf said repeatedly, "don't ever shit your pants. Don't let 'em smell you coming."

Arn was thankful he hadn't shit himself yet as he shuffled along the floor, careful not to trip on construction materials or knock over any tools lying about. The generator hummed louder as he approached the living room, the single bulb suspended from the ceiling in front of the white wall swaying with the wind from the open door, the light reflecting in the hallway. The white wall. In the next room. Where Danny and Ana Maria might be held.

Arn cut the pie, Rolf beside him telling him to calm himself, to take things slow, to move out from the wall an inch at a time. He had moved out far enough to see the bulb, naked and accusing, swinging suspended over a body slumped next to the Five Point victims' photos pinned to the drywall. A body slumped in a folding chair. Propped up from falling by plastic ties securing him to the chair. Arn scanned the room, but the body was the only one there. He entered the room and knelt by the corpse.

"Damn, Erv," Arn heard himself say. He didn't check for a pulse. He'd attended to enough dead men that he didn't need to waste his time. "I guess your hearing wasn't so good after all." He hastily searched the rest of the house, looking for Erv's killer, and was sweat-drenched when he finished. He kept his gun beside him as he returned to the living room. A note, pinned through a five-point star badge, had been nailed to Erv's forehead with an air nailer left in the corner. "Damn, Erv."

Arn relaxed his death grip on his gun and walked to the front of the chair. The nail had been shot right above Erv's nose. A tiny trickle of blood had oozed down his cheek and neck when he slumped over.

Erv had died instantly, Arn suspected, his heart having no chance to pump out more blood.

He resisted the urge to grab the note. The crime scene tech would need to document it. "To hell with the crime scene tech." Arn snatched the note off the nail. The note, printed neatly, every letter a miniature work of art—like Frank's invoice Arn had read that day in his shop—instructed him to come to the back door of the Hobby Shop: *Come alone. Ana Maria and Danny wish you to join our meeting before they die.* "Come alone" had been underlined; a grease spot showed where the corner had been torn off a Snap-on nudie calendar.

Arn ran out the door. As he shuffled to his car, he flipped his phone open and called police dispatch. He climbed in and started the car. "I need you to stay at my house," he told Georgia.

"For what?"

"Erv—Danny's friend that's been staying at the house—is inside. Dead. Someone drove a nail right into his head. And I need you to stay here." Arn explained that time mattered if he were to save Ana Maria and Danny. "I talked with police dispatch. They're sending two officers over. I need someone to be at the house when they arrive. Tell them what's inside."

"Let *them* go to the Hobby shop," Georgia argued. "That's what they get paid to do."

"I can't," Arn said, jamming his gun in his back pocket where he could reach it easier. "I can't risk officers busting in there. The note said come alone, and for Danny and Ana Maria's sakes I'd better."

"You're not leaving me alone with a dead man in a dark house."

"I turned the breaker back on. The lights and furnace just kicked in. You remember the white wall?"

Georgia shook. "Where those gruesome photos hang?"

Arn nodded. "That's where Erv is."

"I'm not—"

Arn reached over and unlatched the door. "This is non-negotiable. I go it alone."

Georgia nodded her understanding and started climbing out when she turned back. She drew Arn's face close and kissed him. "Watch yourself, Arn Anderson."

He waited until he saw Georgia enter the front door of his house before heading to the Hobby Shop.

Sixty-One

ARN DROVE PAST THE Hobby Shop. It had closed hours ago, and he expected it to be darked out, expected Frank to be waiting for him somewhere in the shadows. But it appeared as if every light in the business was burning.

He parked a block down the street. He walked the opposite side of Lincolnway, keeping the front of the shop in sight. Cars parked at the curb offered him concealment as he kept the Hobby Shop in his vision. A city maintenance truck idled beside an exposed manhole cover while two city workers passed tools between them. One looked askance at Arn as he walked by, the worker's breath frosting from his ski mask stuck inside his orange hard hat, snot frozen to the outside of the wool.

When Arn arrived parallel to the Hobby Shop, he leaned over the hood of a parked pickup and studied the storefront window overlooking the street. He detected no movement inside, nothing to indicate where Danny and Ana Maria were being held. *If* they were still held there. *If* they were still alive.

He recalled the back door from the crime scene sketches Butch had made when investigating Delbert Urban's murder. Butch noted that Delbert's killer had gained access to the building via the back door, but had left by the front door. At rush hour. With no one spotting him cloaked in blood. Arn had never been to a knifing where copious amounts of the victim's blood covered the suspect, and that part in particular had puzzled him. Until this moment.

"It was the damned mask and gloves." Arn startled himself with the words. That day at the hospital, waiting for word on Johnny's condition, the surgeon who'd tried saving an accident victim had been covered in blood. Moments later, the doctor strolled out of the room, clean. Bloodless. Delbert's murderer had done the same thing, he realized: murdered him wearing a gown and mask and booties. The killer must have stripped off his garb—probably stuffed them in a garbage bag he carried—and just waltzed out of the business. No wonder no one had reported a man walking downtown covered with blood.

Other things were coming together, those pieces of the puzzle he just couldn't quite fit but that now were becoming perfectly clear. Of course the killer used a mask. He had access to hospital supplies. Just like he had the day of Johnny's murder.

Arn squatted by a car and punched in Oblanski's number. When it went to voicemail, he outlined as quickly as time would allow what he had just now realized. And how everything fit together. Not with what Butch reported in his investigation. Just the opposite. And the real reason, Arn suspected, that Butch had committed suicide.

He took his pen knife from his front pocket and stuffed it into his back pocket beside his bandana. He slipped his gun out of his pocket and concealed it beside his leg as he crossed the street to the alley. Arn had had some of his most interesting police experiences in alleys like this one: lonely, dark, and dank, with an overriding atmosphere of foreboding. An alley where sometimes he'd stumble over a sleeping form. Or a dead one, which is what the man in front of him appeared to be, huddled under a blanket covered with a tattered blue tarp. The homeless man yelled and sat upright when Arn accidentally stepped on his leg. His hoodie was pulled tight around his face like a dirty condom, and what few teeth he had chattered in the frigid night air. "Hey pal, you could show some decorum—"

"Sorry, friend," Arn whispered. He kept his gun beside his leg and away from the man's eyes as he walked past him toward the Hobby Shop.

Arn arrived at the back door. He'd been here many times in his mind, studying the photos and sketches tacked to the white wall. Would he confront Delbert and Joey Bent's killer on the other side of the door? In his own twisted way, he hoped so. He was tired of being hunted. Now all he wanted was to find and destroy the man who had kept the city hostage a decade ago. Who had abducted Ana Maria and Danny and perhaps killed them. The son-of-a-bitch had crossed the line in taking them. Now it was personal.

Arn turned the knob, not surprised it was unlocked, and paused. His training officer, Rolf, screamed in his memory: "Don't ever make the hunt personal. That's the way you make mistakes, dummy." Arn took a moment to think about his entry into the building. The killer would have anticipated his coming in through the back door. He wanted him to come through the back door, and Arn knew he had no choice if he wanted to save Ana Maria and Danny.

He opened the door and slipped inside, keeping his gun tucked close to his body. "Don't lead with your gun, dummy." Rolf Vincent's words echoed in his mind, and he pulled his gun in tighter to his side.

He slowly made his way to the office area, careful not to brush against the wall and make noise, careful to avoid Hobby Shop inventory parked in the aisle. But he was certain the man he hunted would have known he'd arrived at the shop. He just might not know exactly where.

When he reached the waist-high windows overlooking the office area, Arn squatted and peeked over, careful that no one on the other side could see him. Ana Maria sat tied to a chair. Her head rested on her chest, and Arn strained to see her take a shallow breath. She was alive, but had been worked over. Her nose appeared to have been broken. Blood dripped onto her white sweatpants, and one eye had swollen shut.

Danny sat across from her. Duct tape had been plastered across his face, and he thrashed around trying to free himself from plastic ties that anchored him to a metal chair. One of his eyes was quickly closing and blackening, and the skin under that eye was split to the cheek bone.

Arn ducked back behind the safety of the wall. They were alone, in the next room, and he had heard no one. Yet he knew Erv's killer lurked close by, waiting for him to step into the trap. He had no choice. Ana Maria may not have long, by the sounds of her agonizing, labored breaths.

He chanced a last look over the office window and opened the door. Danny turned his head, and Arn flinched. Danny had taken more of a beating that Arn realized. His blood-crusted eyelid hung by a flap over his split cheek, and a red impression the size of a man's boot had crushed his nose. A wave of recognition overcame Danny along with something else: a warning, his eyes darting between Arn and the closet. Arn and the partially opened closet. Arn and...

Too late, Arn realized Danny's warning, and a strong hand came crashing down on his hand. His gun skidded across the floor, a moment before something hit him squarely in the back of the head. Arn's last thought before he lost consciousness was of his attacker, and how everything fit together at last.

Sixty-Two

ARN CAME TO, FIGHTING the plastic restraints holding him fast to a chair. He looked about the room, shaking his head to clear his vision. Blood, sticky and flowing too freely for his liking, dripped onto his hands in back of him.

Pieter leaned against a wall and pointed a small caliber handgun at Ana Maria's head, Arn's gun tucked into his waistband. "I'll bet you were expecting that buffoon Frank Dull Knife," Pieter laughed. "'Cause I plan to rig this little party so he gets credit for it."

"No," Arn sputtered, spitting a broken tooth onto the floor. "I knew it wasn't Frank."

"Bullshit. You had no idea—"

"Jefferson Dawes' note gave you away. Among other things."

"Oh?"

"Sure," Arn said. "Dawes didn't write that rambling suicide note, telling us all sorts of things only Gaylord and Steve and the Five Point Killer would know. You only made it appear to be his writing."

"I knew you'd check Dawes' handwriting and discover he usually wrote like he was scribbling with his toes," Pieter said, waving his gun around in a lose figure eight between Arn and Danny and Ana Maria. "I had to write neat enough that you knew it wasn't the good doctor. Aunt Georgia said you told her Frank Dull Knife was in your sights. And his writing's impeccable."

"How did you know that?"

Pieter leaned against one wall and smiled smugly. "I got into Frank's shop one night—he's not the only one who can get in and out without leaving a trace. When I went through notes and invoices on his desk, I noticed how neatly he wrote. Like my third grade teacher."

"I knew it wasn't Frank's writing."

"Then let's hear how you figured out this little piece of information?"

"Frank writes like an artist," Arn said. "But he's left-handed. When you wrote the note, you tried duplicating his angle. But a right-handed person can just never get it right. So Oblanski and I naturally thought of you."

"I gotta call bullshit on that, Mr. Anderson."

"You're a top architect," Arn said. "Your writing has to be neat. Like a work of art."

Pieter held up one hand. "Okay. So I confess. I have to write perfectly on my blueprints."

"And on notes like the one nailed to Erv's head."

"Was that his name?" Pieter said. "This is such an impersonal thing I sometimes don't know—"

"Your victims?"

Pieter turned red. "I considered them … an experiment in pleasure."

Arn wiggled his knife from his back pocket while he nodded to Ana Maria and Danny. "I'm here. So there's no reason to harm them any further. Release them."

"Ana Maria and that old guy?"

"He's homeless. He won't say anything. He'll hop the first freight out of the Union Pacific yards."

Danny glared at Arn like he didn't appreciate the homeless remark.

"I just can't let either one wander around knowing—"

"That you're the Five Point Killer?"

Pieter tilted his head back and laughed. Stalling, Arn recognized. He was wondering what Arn knew and who he might have told it to. "That's what Dad used to call a SWAG: a Scientific Wild Assed Guess," Pieter said.

"Is it? Chief Oblanski doesn't think so."

"Neither one of you know squat."

"We know enough that you'll be getting that forever juice at the State Pen once you're convicted. Or"—Arn forced a grin—"you'll love this: Wyoming may go to the firing squad to execute their killers."

"But you won't see it," Pieter said, his voice rising. "You won't see anything after tonight."

"And Chief Oblanski? You going to kill him, too? And the other detectives who know about you?"

"If they knew anything, they'd be hunting me up right now."

"They will. As soon as they finish with the search warrant on your office and home," Arn lied." And the evidence techs finish processing my home."

Pieter's smile waned. "And just what do you think you know?"

"Yeah, what *do* you know?" Georgia entered the office and shut the door behind her. Her eyes widened as she took in the scene. She stepped toward Pieter, and he swung the gun on Ana Maria.

"You can talk from there, Aunt Georgia. I wouldn't want to hurt Mr. Anderson's friend. Just yet."

Georgia sat on the couch where Delbert Urban had bled out. The cheap bastards hadn't even replaced the couch, Arn thought as he sawed slowly on the plastic ties with his pocket knife. "How'd you get here? I left you at my house—"

"You mean you left me stranded there," Georgia said. "I left a note for the detectives on where that dead guy was and called a cab. Now what evidence *do* you have against Pieter?"

"Enough!" Pieter put the barrel of the gun against Ana Maria's temple. "What do you know about me?" He glared at Arn.

"I know you're the Five Point Killer—"

Georgia slapped Arn across the face. It opened his cheek up more, blood dripping down anew. "That's nonsense. How could a fifteen-year-old boy overpower grown men? It's not like he shot them from afar."

"Tell your aunt how you first sedated them with your dad's Xanax," Arn said.

Pieter remained silent, and Arn talked directly to Georgia. "Dr. Delaney said Butch was taking too many pills. But not enough to account for being nearly out of his prescription. It was Pieter who was taking Butch's Xanax. Five or six pills in a drink and it was lights out for Pieter's victims. A little kid could have overpowered them. Except Delbert Urban"—he nodded to the couch—"who was too big and fat and he came out of the Xanax just in time to put up a hell of a fight." Arn turned to Pieter. "I got this right?"

Pieter smiled wide, as if he enjoyed telling about the murder. "I crushed up Dad's Xanax and slipped it into their drinks. They thought they were going to get lucky with some little gay boy. But the Xanax put them out like babies. Except Delbert came out of it just like you figured." He motioned like he was sitting a bronc. "That was one wild ride."

Georgia stepped toward Pieter, but he swung his gun toward Danny and she stopped. "But why did you kill those men?"

"It was exciting when Dad took me to homicides. Suicides." Pieter's eyes got a dreamy look to them, like the second eyelids lizards have. "Dad was God's gift to detectives, and I thought, what the hell, I can fool the old man. I know enough. And I did, for a while. Until he got suspicious. 'I'm so close I can smell him,' Dad used to say just about every night. He'd lay his investigation strategy out for me. He'd tell me what he intended doing. It was impossible for him to catch me."

"But why Steve DeBoer and Gaylord?" Georgia asked.

"Why else," Pieter said. "They knew what Dad knew. And Dad was getting close."

"I imagine Gaylord was the easiest," Arn said, using his body movement to mask how he was cutting away the plastic tie around his wrists. "All you had to do was stage it so it looked like an autoerotic death."

Pieter smiled. "A few Xanax in Gaylord's rum and coke ... slip a rope around his neck and toss the little bugger over the rafters. Drag that big old mirror down from upstairs. Scatter a few porn magazines around. Pretty smart, huh?"

"Except I figured it out."

"And if this old man hadn't saved your butt..." Pieter backhanded Danny with the gun. It knocked him to the floor. A fresh gouge opened over his eye and he kicked out at Pieter, who deftly stepped aside.

"Steve was a little more difficult, wasn't he?"

"He called one afternoon and wanted to share a beer and pizza," Pieter said. "Now and again I'd go to his place and he'd give me a beer. But just one so's nobody would know."

"But you were off on his address by one house when you called the pizza order in," Arn said. His knife cut through the plastic tie and he held the free ends so they wouldn't fall. "You put enough Xanax to choke a horse in his beer, I'd wager. But you couldn't stage the fire right then."

"How do you know that?"

"Dr. Rough, Assistant ME at the time, found larvae in Steve's body, indicating he died at least a day earlier than the fire. Maybe as much as thirty-six hours earlier."

"Tell Arn you didn't do that," Georgia said.

"You taught me well, Aunt Georgia: I can't tell a lie." Pieter laughed. "You said it's a sin to lie." He paced the floor in front of his captives like he was pacing in front of a jury. "I was always…thorough." He smiled and pointed the gun at each of them in turn. "I didn't have time to set the fire and stage the scene that day—I had to get to the ball game in Casper. So as soon as Steve went out, I smothered him and ran for the bus. We got snowed in overnight. When the roads opened the next day and we returned to Cheyenne, I went to his house. It wasn't easy dragging a dead man and his recliner close to the curtains. His ratty old curtains. They caught fire with the first cigarette."

"And poor old Laun McGuire could place you there the day before."

"When you and Ana Maria spoke with him, I couldn't chance that he'd remember seeing me at Steve's place."

"He knew nothing," Arn said.

"His loss," Pieter said.

"Oh Pieter, you *really* didn't kill Steve, too?" Georgia asked.

"He was as close as Dad was to knowing who their famous Five Point Killer was."

"Pieter, they have so little hard evidence." Georgia jabbed a finger at Arn. "It's all circumstantial. Tell him it's all circumstantial."

"It is," Arn agreed. "But an overwhelming amount. Simple things. Like when you gave me conflicting stories about hearing someone downstairs the night Butch died." He nodded to the couch. "Like Delbert's death. Were you planning to kill him all those times you stopped by the Hobby Shop? 'I bought a ton of glue' is how much your project took, according to you."

"You think you got things figured out," Pieter said. "Not that it'll do you any good."

"Like your teacher, Mr. Noggle? He knew you spent a lot of time at the Hobby Shop with Delbert. And when his death was reported in the news, Noggle suspected you. Did he threaten to expose you?"

Pieter looked at the tiny gun in his hand. "He hinted at it. He said after class one day that if I met him at his house, he'd tell me more of what he knew." Pieter shook his head. "He met me at his door that night wearing a Speedo and a wry smile. Needless to say, I wasn't interested in sex with him any more than the others."

"And Old Mr. Noggle didn't actually run off with Dawes' wife?" Arn asked.

Ana Maria groaned, and Pieter turned to her. He brought his gun under her chin, and Arn had to fight to keep from springing on him. But he kept hold of the cut ties and his pocket knife while Pieter let her head drop back to her chest. "Now that's the only coincidence in all this. I can tell you for certain Mr. Noggle did not run off with Dr. Dawes' wife. She is not where Noggle has been for a decade."

"Which is where?" Arn asked.

"I'd tell you," Pieter laughed, pointing his gun at Arn's head, "but then I'd have to kill you." He snapped his fingers. "But I'm going to anyway, so no one will know about those murders."

"Chief Oblanski knows. He knows you hung around Joey Bent when he worked on that fine old Karman Ghia in your garage. And by the way, when you tail someone, do a better of job in not getting caught."

Pieter's smile faded. "How's that?"

"The night I talked with Laun McGuire and with the policeman following me—seems like you were right in back of him. Remember the fresh tar along 5th Street? The tar that you couldn't get off your VW in your garage? So you know, Oblanski knows that, too."

"If this is all true," Georgia said, pleading and in tears now, "your home life—Hannah never home, Butch dragging you to those terrible crime scenes—will mitigate things. You don't have to kill anyone else, Pieter."

"You want me to spend the rest of my life in the looney bin in Evanston, playing dominoes with criminally insane people, Aunt Georgia? Not on your life."

"Did you kill Johnny White?" Georgia asked.

Danny tried sitting up, but Pieter kicked him in the back and he fell back down. Arn weighed jumping Pieter now, but he was halfway across the office. And Arn knew he wasn't nearly as quick as he once was.

"Johnny went on television, pleading for any new leads," Pieter said. "If I was to ever send a message to Ana Maria and Anderson here to call off the TV special, I had to kill Johnny."

"But you shot him with your dad's gun," Arn said.

"I told you Bobby Madden slipped Butch's gun in with the guns to be destroyed," Georgia said, trying to convince herself. "So Pieter couldn't have done it."

"Bobbie Madden never took Butch's gun that night from you," Arn said.

"Of course he did—"

"Ned Oblanski was in charge of the gun buyback program that year," Arn told Georgia. "He never remembered a quality Walther. You kept it." Arn worked his hands down to where he could rub circulation back into them without Pieter seeing. "You kept the gun, Georgia. And later gave it to Pieter."

"He didn't kill Johnny—"

"I did so, Aunt Georgia. When I approached Johnny in his driveway, he thought we were going to talk about the Broncos game. He never saw the gun in my coat sleeve. Dammed anemic little gun didn't kill him right off. So I had to sneak into his room."

"Wasn't much sneak to it," Arn said. "You still retained keys to the maintenance door from when you delivered for that freight company in high school."

"That's nonsense," Georgia said. She walked toward Pieter.

"Stay where you are."

Georgia stopped. "You were having lunch with Meander when Johnny was murdered."

"But he wasn't." Arn chin-pointed to Pieter. "When the hospital was locked down after they found Johnny, Pieter was trapped inside. He had to stay inside. I got to admit it was genius to concoct that lunch offer with Meander off the cuff."

Pieter smiled and exaggerated a bow. "I came through the only door without a camera. But Frank Dull Knife has a key, too. And he'll get all the credit for this night."

"Frank doesn't fit the video."

"How so?"

Arn nodded to Pieter's shoes. "You wore Nikes that morning. They hurt your feet. You've always been a New Balance man. Frank limps a little, but it's pronounced on one side only. The hospital video shows someone limping on both feet. Like the Nikes hurt when you walk."

"You *are* a detective." Pieter smiled. "I had to wear the same shoes I always did: Gaylord's house, Delbert's back. Johnny's room—"

"Outside my car at the Shady Rest."

Pieter nodded. "I put the same print every time so you yokels could find it. Not over obvious. Dad always said to discount evidence that looks too obvious."

"And planting those shoes in Dawes' car? And I'd bet you tossed some of that Old Spice around the doorway, knowing I'd eventually get around to interviewing Adelle."

Pieter shrugged. "It caused you to look at him as a suspect. And when you figured out it wasn't a suicide, to look closer at Frank." He turned to Georgia. "You're going to have to step into the alley now."

"You're going to kill them?" Georgia said.

"I could have killed them that night I sneaked into Mr. Anderson's house. As it was, I wanted to just send a little message that I could take them any time I wanted."

"Pretty clever making it look like Frank was the one who came into my house."

"Why, thank you."

"But we knew it wasn't Frank."

"Oh, this I gotta hear," Pieter said.

Ana Maria's head came up and she tried focusing through her good eye, recognition coming as a passing nod before her head dropped back onto her chest. "Frank has a biker wallet with a chain that dangles down and slaps against shit you can hear for a block. There was no way he could sneak into my house without Danny waking up."

Pieter chuckled. "As sound as you sleep, I could have driven a motorcycle up those steps and you'd still be cutting Zs. But"—he motioned to Georgia—"she was sweet on you and I thought I might be able to scare you and Ana Maria off the cases." He smiled. "I couldn't hardly kill you off if we were going to be family."

"And now we come to the real reason your dad killed himself."

"It was Butch's anxiety at work," Georgia said. "The pressure of the Five Point cases, Steve and Gaylord's deaths. And Hannah catting around with every guy that looked her way."

404

"Is that right, Pieter?" Arn said, spitting blood, still working circulation into his hands behind his back. "Or was it that Butch was sharper than you gave him credit for? Was it because he found out you killed those men?"

"That's bullshit—"

"Is it? He got on to you when he discovered his Xanax was coming up short. 'The Five Point Killer is so close, I can smell him.' And he could. That damned Old Spice you plastered over everything to fool me. Steer me in another direction. Butch found out you were the killer, and he couldn't take it."

"Butch loved Pieter," Georgia pled.

"Of course he did." Arn's voice softened for the moment. "He loved his son so much, he knew it was his duty to turn him in. But he couldn't. And so Butch took his only other option: he killed himself because he knew if he didn't, he'd eventually have to arrest Pieter."

"Is that true?" Georgia asked. She stepped toward him, but Pieter swung his gun at Arn. She ignored it and walked to him, putting her hand on his shoulder. "Did Butch kill himself because of you?"

Pieter backed away, and his gun lowered ever so slightly. Arn braced himself. "Dad found that old Army survival knife of his in my room one night. Bloody. I'd gotten careless and forgot to wash it off. I told him I was out hunting rabbits with some friends, and we'd skinned some. He still didn't put it together until he found that bag of plastic badges under my bed. The ones Dad and every other cop on the force gave out to little kids. He started connecting the dots to my whereabouts when the murders took place. He asked me about it. But of course I denied it."

"But a good interrogator like your father saw right through you," Arn said, gathering his legs to spring.

Pieter lowered the gun a little further. "I'm afraid so. He acted like he wanted to believe me. But he didn't." He pushed Georgia aside. "You really have to leave us alone now."

Georgia stepped between Ana Maria and Danny and Pieter. "You'll have to kill me along with them."

Pieter's gun hand began to shake. "You know I can't kill you."

"But I can." Frank Dull Knife had walked through the door as silently as he'd entered dozens of houses in his criminal career. He jammed a slab-sided .45 into Pieter's ribs. "You know the drill, pretty boy. Drop it and set your scrawny ass on that couch before I shoot it. Setting me up..."

Pieter let his gun drop to the floor and sat down on the couch. Frank bent and picked the gun up. "Little prick." He motioned to Georgia, and she sat beside Pieter. Frank was too far away to make a play, and he looked at Arn. "Because of you, Ned Oblanski's going to pin Butch's murder on me."

"You didn't do it," Arn said.

Frank backhanded Arn flush on the cheek, nearly knocking him onto the floor. Arn struggled to keep his chair upright and his pocket knife concealed in his hand. "How's that for starters, Mr. Metro detective?"

Arn tasted the sweetness of his blood as he concentrated on waiting for the right moment. "I'll bet you bought that gun from Jerry Shine."

"This?" Frank grinned. "Like the little prick said, felons can't possess firearms."

"And just where is Jerry?" Arn asked. "About fifty miles from your shop?"

"You're smarter than you look."

Pieter started to rise, and Frank swung the gun on him. "Sit down, pretty boy."

Pieter sat back down and wrapped his arm around Georgia.

"I should have turned your ass in for those Five Point murders years ago," Frank said. "You always thought you were better than anyone else. Did I mention your mom was a bum lay?"

Pieter sprang from the couch and Frank hit him hard on the face. Pieter fell to the floor, blood spurting onto the tile from a shattered nose. Georgia grabbed him by the waist and hauled him back beside her. She turned to shield him with her body as best she could.

"One afternoon, boys and girls," Frank began, "Hannah and me did the wild thing at her house when the old man was out working. She showed me her little boy's room, and Pieter's collection of those silly plastic badges cops give out to kids. She showed me some hospital gowns and masks that he swiped from that freight company he worked for after school." Frank leaned closer to Pieter, and Arn thought he was going to hit him again. "She showed me where someone in the household had been swiping the old man's Xanax, and it wasn't her." He kicked Pieter on the knee and he howled in pain.

"Leave him alone!" Georgia said, hugging Pieter.

Frank shrugged and backed away. He sat on a chair and pointed the gun at them. "I was going to place an anonymous call to the cops, but Hannah talked me out of it. It wasn't like I didn't do my share of stealing, so I thought, screw it. Let him steal the shit for all I care. Until one night…" Frank lowered his voice, and his hand began a slight tremble. "Hannah wanted some excitement. 'Let's do a house,' she said. 'You know any?' She didn't care about the money. Just the rush of getting caught. So I says, sure, we'll take a drive to this friend of mine who's a mechanic at Import Motors. I thought he was out of town. Well, you can fill in the blanks," Frank went on. "When we motored darked-out up to Joey Bent's house, there was a yellow Karman Ghia in the driveway. We thought WTF, Pieter's getting ass-packed, 'cause everyone knew Joey was queer. We was going to leave when pretty boy staggered out of the house and sped away. When we went inside, there was Joey laying there, head dammed near loped off, leaking all over his shag carpeting. And there was this plastic badge just laying at his feet. Joey hadn't been dead for a couple minutes. He was even spurting from his neck. Even I got sick. You remember that?" Frank kicked Pieter again and he drew back, just catching Frank's boot on his shin.

"After that, Hannah was afraid to be in the same house with you, and she started crashing at my place. Until your old man's murder. Then she stopped being so interesting." He turned his gun on Arn. "The murder you tried to pin on me."

Arn's circulation had returned to his hands and arms, and he was sitting only ten feet from Frank. "So where do we go from here?"

"Go?" Frank smiled. "I go back to the reservation, but you five go six feet under. When the store opens tomorrow morning, they'll find your sorry asses soaking up the carpeting."

"You're really going to kill us like you killed Hannah?" Arn asked.

Frank shrugged. "I have more ... options than I did with Hannah. When she said she was going to talk with Bobby Madden about the burglary at Joey's place and about her kid, I had no choice. You know when I said I fixed her alternator? I lied. I fixed her brakes. Real good. So they wouldn't work when she most needed them."

"You got that? " Arn called out.

Two shotgun slides racking back sounded as if they were in a very loud tunnel; the sound that criminals fear and police love. Right now, Arn loved it.

"We got it," Oblanski yelled back.

Two uniformed policemen entered the room pointing shotguns at Frank's head, while another covered Pieter with his Glock. Oblanski and Dan Long entered the room after them, handcuffs dangling from their belts. Frank dropped his gun and snarled at Oblanski.

"Don't shit yourself," Arn told Frank.

"What?"

"Just something my training officer used to tell me."

Long and the uniformed officers handcuffed Frank and Pieter. Arn brought his hands around and rubbed them. Oblanski pointed to the pocket knife in his hand. "

"Just in case you didn't make it in time," Arn said.

Oblanski untied Danny, and Arn cut the plastic ties on Ana Maria's wrists. Oblanski talked on a portable radio, and soon paramedics entered the room. They set their jump bags between Danny and Ana Maria and began working on them. One peeled off and asked Arn to sit on the couch.

"You knew they were out there?" Pieter asked.

"I did," Arn answered. "When I left my house, I put a piece of the puzzle together. The note on my windshield and the note nailed to Erv's forehead was neat. But it wasn't Frank's writing, so I knew someone was setting him up. And I was convinced someone—Frank—had been following me all night. He couldn't have killed Erv and abducted Danny and Ana Maria if he was following me."

"But that was me following you," Pieter said.

"So even *I* make a mistake now and again."

Frank, handcuffed, lunged at Arn and a burly officer planted a knee on his thigh. Frank went to the floor screaming in pain. "You got nothing on me! The statute of limitations is up on that old burglary charge—"

Oblanski brought Frank's contorted face around to look him in the eye. "First, I'm sure we could push an accessory after the fact on Joey Bent's murder that you and Hannah nearly walked in on. But if not, there's the attempted homicide of five people tonight." He fished his micro recorder out of his pocket and showed Frank. "And you'll be pleased to hear your confession to rigging Hannah's accident made it clear." He nodded to an officer who stood Frank on his feet. "And you'll have time to decide if you want to be the wife or if you want to be the girlfriend when you get down to Rawlins," Oblanski called after him as they led Frank screaming out the door ahead of Pieter.

The paramedics struggled with the duct tape on Danny's mouth, and Arn knew he'd refuse treatment if he could talk. "Better wait until you get to the ER to take that off," he suggested. "He's tape sensitive." They secured Danny to a gurney.

The paramedics loaded Ana Maria onto a backboard and then onto a gurney. A saline IV tube dripped into her arm, and she looked over at Arn. Another look of recognition crossed her face, a moment before she went under as they wheeled her out to the ambulance.

"I put it at eight, maybe ten stitches," the paramedic said to Arn.

"Didn't anyone tell you old cops aren't supposed to take chances like this?" Oblanski said when the medic had finished his assessment of Arn's injuries.

"I had to earn my consulting fees somehow."

Arn sat on the couch next to Georgia, but she moved away from him. She stared at the back door while they escorted Pieter to a waiting ambulance. "What will happen to him?"

"After the ER docs patch him up? He'll go for arraignment within forty-eight hours."

"I should have seen the signs," she sobbed. She looked up at Arn. "Why didn't I see the signs? They were there for me."

"We can talk about it tomorrow," Arn said. "Would you like me to see you home?"

"If you're driving that little rental car"—Georgia stood and smoothed her slacks—"not on your life. We can take a cab. I've had as much of your Clown Car as I can stand."

Arn rubbed the small of his back. "I can't take much more either."

Sixty-Three

ARN STOPPED IN THE doorway of Danny's room and leaned against the door jamb. "Looks like you took a few stitches, too," Danny said, focusing on Arn with the eye not covered by gauze.

"Ten stitches, to be exact." Arn carefully patted his head and touched the Steri-Strip closing the gap on his cheek. "This will leave a shallow scar."

"Guess both our pretty faces will look like hell when we mend up."

"They looked like hell before." Arn smiled, and winced in pain. He came into the room and pulled up a chair beside Danny's bed. "I just had to come visit my friend Daniel Lone Tree."

Danny set the issue of *People* magazine on the tray table beside his bed. "I guess this means Oblanski got my prints back?"

Arn pulled his chair around to the foot of the bed so Danny wouldn't have to turn his head to see him. "He got a lengthy history back on you." He took a notebook out of his man bag, which was slung over his shoulder, and Danny snickered. "Army tunnel rat working the Chu Chi

411

tunnels in IV Corps, Vietnam. Honorably discharged." Arn flipped a page. "Attended the University of Minnesota under the GI Bill. Accurate so far?"

"Just finish it."

"It says here you became a structural engineer."

"I earned the degree, anyways."

"And you put it to such good use"—Arn turned a page—"when you and two other American Indian Movement activists bombed a building in downtown Minneapolis in 1969."

"We thought we would disrupt transportation in the city."

Arn snickered. "You didn't make much of a criminal. The building was abandoned. Scheduled for demolition. I guess you did the city's work for them when you took it down."

Danny laughed and his hand shot to his head. "Pretty rank amateurs, we were."

"And . . ." Arn squinted, his own writing a little shaky when Oblanski had passed the information along. "Minnesota issued warrants for your arrest."

"And I've been on the run ever since," Danny said. "I guess Oblanski's doing a jig, nabbing an international criminal. I'll be surprised if Interpol doesn't give him an award."

Arn closed his notebook and stuffed it back in his bag. "What did you do from the time you blew up the building until you squatted in Mom's house?"

"I began using another name." Danny reached over and grabbed a bowl of runny Jell-O from the tray table. "I had this romanticized notion that the Sioux tribe might want some help getting on its feet. Help with their housing development. That maybe an engineer would be of some use. But all the young bucks wanted back then was to raise hell."

His face scrunched up with the first bite of Jell-O and he put the bowl back. "I opened my own business in Rapid City doing high-end home modifications." He frowned. "Under a different name, of course. I spent all my money sending my boy to college." His voice wavered, and Arn waited until he composed himself. "But he and some of his friends got tanked up one afternoon and hiked to the back of Mt. Rushmore. They were so drunk my boy did a double gainer off Washington's head." He closed his eyes and settled back on his pillow. "When's Minnesota coming for me? 'Cause I'm not going to fight extradition."

"Never."

Danny opened his eyes. "What's that?"

"I'd like to say I got your charges dropped in exchange for working on my house. But the fact is, Minnesota purged their old warrants five years after you three stooges pulled that little stunt. They figured it would cost more in the long run looking for you guys than you're worth."

"So I don't have to hide out anymore?"

"Not unless you want to."

Danny smiled for the briefest time before he became serious again. "This mean you're kicking me out into society?"

Arn shook his head. "Not on your life. We had an agreement: you were going to renovate Mom's house. All this means is that you'll be able to get a driver's license so I won't have to do the Driving Miss Daisy thing anymore." He handed Danny a Trac Phone. "I stored my number in there. Call when they release you—probably tomorrow—and I'll come get you."

"Not in that micro-hearse you've been driving?"

Arn grinned. "I got the Beast back."

Danny lay back in his bed and his mouth downturned in sadness.

"I thought you'd be happy you're a free man."

Danny shook his head. "Erv tried warning me that Pieter had come sneaking into the house. When he tripped the circuit box outside, it disabled the security system. Next I knew, Pieter stuck that gun under our noses and led us out to his car. When Erv didn't join us, I knew he was dead." Danny wiped his eye. "He didn't have any family to make arrangements?"

"He had us." Arn laid a hand on Danny's shoulder. "I've taken care of it. Erv's funeral is Friday."

Danny closed his eyes. "Thanks, Arn." He sat up straight in his bed. "I forgot to ask how Ana Maria's doing?"

"Good," Arn said. "At least the nurses tell me she is. I'm headed over to her room now."

"Tell her to grab a wheelchair and come keep me company."

Arn smiled. "I will."

He walked to Ana Maria's room at the other end of the hall and paused at the door. Her breathing told him she was sleeping, and he was turning to leave when she called after him in a faint voice, "You better be bringing flowers when you come calling."

He turned on his heels and entered the room. "I'm headed to the gift shop downstairs now." He took her hand, careful not to disturb the IV tube. "How you feeling, kiddo?"

"Let's see." She forced a smile. "I got a fractured cheek bone, a cracked jaw where Pieter shoved me into the car door. I'll have eleven stitches across my forehead. How the hell you think I'm doing?"

"I think you're recuperating."

"To what?" She wiggled around, and Arn propped pillows in back of her. "The scars left on my head will look like hell on camera—"

"It'll give you character. Besides, they can do wondrous things with makeup nowadays."

She forced a laugh. "That's the least of my worries. Did you catch the morning news today?"

"That proves my point," Arn said. "As busted up as Nick Damos got down in Denver, he looked pretty good on camera."

"He might have looked good, but he sounded like a second grader, stuttering when he was reading the news about Pieter and Frank." She sipped ice water from a straw. "That was my story that Nick botched. I put all my heart into uncovering the killer. Now what the hell did I get for it?"

Arn patted her shoulder. "I'm sure DeAngelo will have you back in prime time once you're back on your feet."

"That might be," Ana Maria said. "And maybe it'll be Nick who catches the eye of some national producer."

"Then look at the bright side. At least Nick will be gone from Cheyenne."

Ana Maria smiled and winced, her hand going to her split lip. "At least he'd be out of my hair."

Epilogue

TWO DAYS AFTER THE Hobby Shop takedown, Oblanski scooted his chair close to one side of the conference table. He nodded to papers scattered the length of the table in front of him. "It'll take me a year to sort through all those reports and statements. Thanks a bunch."

Arn held up his coffee cup in a mock toast. "My pleasure. Glad I could wrap up my consulting gig on a positive note."

"How about one consulting freebie for the city? Off the payroll?"

"Just one. Someone once told me I'm a mercenary bastard."

Oblanski smiled. "Okay. Here it is: maybe you can tell me why Pieter retained the best attorney out of Denver, then didn't take his advice and told me whatever I wanted to know in the interrogation?"

Arn sipped gingerly from his cup, thinking. "I believe Pieter wanted it out how his father was the best investigator the department ever had. And he wanted the public to know that the only reason Butch didn't solve the Five Point Killings was that his son knew just where the investigation was headed and was always a jump ahead of him. Maybe he really did love his father deep down."

"Or maybe he's as egotistical as Butch was." Oblanski began gathering papers into neat piles ready for transcription. "With all the newspaper and television coverage, Pieter will be infamous. At least until they execute him. The prosecutor's going to try him as a death penalty case."

"With all the delays and automatic appeal," Arn said, helping Oblanski with the paperwork, "I don't expect to see that in my lifetime." He stood and walked to the coffee pot and refilled his cup. Oblanski held up his mug, and Arn topped it off. The coffee was fresh, strong, and just right. All Oblanski had to do was build up the courage to ask Gorilla Legs in just the right tone to make it.

"The news mentioned you found Mr. Noggle, Pieter's high school science teacher."

"He was walled up in the family room in Gaylord's old house that Pieter bought." Oblanski settled back and held his mug with both hands. "He was just where Pieter put him sometime after he purchased the place. That's the one thing Pieter wouldn't tell me—where Noggle was, from the time he killed him until he bought Gaylord's house five years later."

Arn rested his elbows on the table. "The thing that's puzzled me the most was why did Pieter plant those plastic stars at the murder scenes?"

"It was as simple as an accident," Oblanski said. "He told me he'd gotten a badge at school that day when an officer came to talk to the class. When he was doing his thing with Joey Bent, the star fell out of his pocket. He was worried to death about losing it, until the news dubbed it the Five Point Killings."

"And he got the urge to drop one at every scene?" Arn stood and walked to the window. Fresh snow had blanketed Cheyenne during the early morning, and kids played outside on a sled pulled by a large mongrel. "As much as I despised the man, it's a shame Pieter killed Jefferson Dawes."

"I forgot to tell you." Oblanski laughed, outwardly pleased. "That's the best part. Remember we put out teletypes to Customs and the Marshals? Well, the first—and as it happened, the only—Mrs. Dawes was located in the Dominican Republic. She left Jeff over his womanizing. And Jeff and Adelle never actually married."

"And that's the best part?"

"No," Oblanski replied. "The best part is, she's coming home to settle Jefferson's estate. When I told Adelle that Jeff's wife was returning to take possession of everything Jeff had, I thought she'd cry herself to sleep right there on the floor of her former million-dollar home."

"Justice comes in all forms, my friend."

"That it does." Oblanski held his cup high and toasted. "To Adelle Fournier and the cheap whisky she'll be forced to drink from now on." He checked his watch. "Visiting at the county jail will be over in fifteen minutes."

"So?"

"When I was there with the stenographer taking Pieter's statement, he mentioned he was looking forward to Georgia's visit today. In case you're interested."

———

By the time Arn pulled into the parking garage across from the jail, visitors were shuffling out the door. Arn went inside and spotted Georgia standing in front of a locker, gathering things she had to stow before being allowed inside to visit Pieter. Meander stood beside her, frail-looking, with her shoulders slumped and bags under her eyes from crying. Probably all night. She looked around the lobby of the jail as if in a daze.

They had started out the door when Arn called Georgia's name. She looked around and saw him. She walked toward him as she put her coat on, her arms crossed in a hug, a sad look on her face from seeing the only son she'd ever know. "Wait for me in the car," she said to Meander. "I'll be out in a moment."

Meander looked through Arn with bloodshot eyes. She had no expression as she stumbled past him and out the double doors without speaking.

"How's Pieter doing?" Arn asked.

"Like you care!" Georgia blurted out. "I'm sorry for that." She motioned to a bench and they sat. "I'm just upset—"

"Understood."

She nodded in the direction of the cell blocks as if she could see Pieter through the thick walls. "To answer your question, Pieter's in solitary. He's a celebrity in there." She laughed nervously. "Petty druggies. Burglars, like Frank Dull Knife. People who'd rip off their grandmothers or do a stop-and-rob." She threw up her hands. "But in there, Pieter's special. He's a serial killer."

Her eyes watered and she looked away. "His attorney says Oblanski doesn't have a case. 'Leave this up to me,' he said. 'By the time I'm through with the city, they'll be owing me for Pieter staying in this rat hole.'"

"Do you believe him?"

Georgia shook her head. "Butch always said that lawyers will say whatever you want to hear as long as they're on the clock—a healthy retainer, in this instance, is what Pieter's already shelled out."

Georgia watched the last of the visitors leave the building. "You've been in law enforcement all your life. What are the chances that Pieter will walk on those murders?"

"After giving Oblanski an eight-hour confession, with verifiable corroboration? None."

"Maybe he'll be found incompetent to stand trial."

Arn looked at Georgia clutching for emotional straws, for any thread of hope that Pieter would go free. He wanted to wrap his arms around her and hold her close, tell her that he'd be there for her whatever Pieter's outcome. But they'd talked well into the morning yesterday after leaving the hospital, and something had passed between them. Georgia knew that it wasn't Arn's fault that Pieter had murdered. She knew that it wasn't Arn's doing that Pieter began killing once again after so many years of dormancy. But she also knew that if the TV station hadn't hired Arn and his investigative skills to work with Ana Maria, Pieter would never have been caught. He would have just gone on with his now-quiet life.

"It's obvious from listening to Pieter that he prepared for the day he would get caught," Arn said. "During the interrogation, he admitted to exhibiting textbook signs of a sociopath. And he's right. But that doesn't mean he's criminally insane."

"Will the state execute him?"

Arn nodded. "Not this year. Or the next. Perhaps not even this decade, as many automatic appeals as he'll have. But at some point the public will demand their pound of Pieter."

"I understand," Georgia said, standing and wrapping a scarf around her neck. "All too well."

She started for the doors when Arn called after her. She stopped and waited for him to catch up. "I have to know something that's giving me fits," he said.

She stood with her back to him, not turning around. "What is it?"

"All those years you took care of Pieter … all those times you were at your brother's house … in all those times, did you *ever* suspect Pieter killed those men?"

"How can you even ask me something like that?"

"Because Pieter told Oblanski that when Hannah died, you came to clean out his room so he could stay with you. He said you probably found his stash of plastic badges, and his masks and surgical gowns. Did you know—"

Georgia turned around, her hand sliding into her purse. She handed Arn a plastic five-point badge. "Goodbye, Arn Anderson."

"Goodbye, Georgia Spangler," he said as he watched her walk out of the building on the heels of the last visitors.

The End

Acknowledgments

I would like to thank my friends and mentors, Craig and Judy Johnson, for their advice and support; my literary agent Tiffany Schofield for her faith in my writing; editors Terri Bischoff and Sandy Sullivan for their wisdom and guidance; longtime-retired Cheyenne Police Officer Steve Brown, retired railroad engineer Howard Dykes, and Roy Bechtholdt for their intimate knowledge of the area; and my wife, Heather—who *never* tells me what to do.

About the Author

C. M. Wendelboe is the author of the Spirit Road Mysteries (Berkley/Penguin). During his thirty-eight-year career in law enforcement, he served successful stints as a sheriff's deputy, police chief, policy adviser, and supervisor for several agencies. He was a patrol supervisor when he retired to pursue his true vocation as a fiction writer. Find out more about his work at www.SpiritRoadMysteries.com.